Gary Powell is a former London detective who served with the British Transport Police, retiring after thirty-three years' service. He is a frequent public speaker on his favourite subject: Britain's criminal history. He is also a guide at St Paul's Cathedral. He now lives in North Norfolk with his wife Karen.

ALSO BY GARY POWELL

FICTION

The DI McNally and DS Frost Series
Book 1: Mind the Killer

In the first McNally and Frost book, the discovery of skeletal remains in a disused London Underground lift shaft and a series of apparent suicides spiral the two detectives towards a deadly climax.

NON-FICTION TITLES

Square London: A Social History of the Iconic London Square

Death in Disguise: The Amazing True Story of the Chelsea Murders

Death Diary: A Year of London Murder, Execution, Terrorism and Treason

Convicted: Landmark Cases in British Criminal History

POETRY

That Damned Fly: A Life in Verse

A reflection on the author's secure but challenging start in life, followed by a police career that took him all over the world, witnessing the aftermath of many significant events. These reflections are often in verse, ranging from crime and riot to the lighter side of life, featuring everyday issues that concern us all: the lack of high-street banks to the taxman, or the need for an English national anthem, to the magnificence of St Paul's Cathedral.

THE CUTTING ROOM

GARY POWELL

The manufacturer's authorised representative in the EU for
product safety is Authorised Rep Compliance Ltd,
71 Lower Baggot Street, Dublin D02 P593 Ireland (www.arccompliance.com)

This is a work of fiction. Names, characters, businesses, places, events
and incidents are either the products of the author's imagination
or used in a fictitious manner. Any resemblance to actual persons,
living or dead, or actual events is purely coincidental.

Troubador Publishing Ltd
Unit E2 Airfield Business Park,
Harrison Road, Market Harborough,
Leicestershire. LE16 7UL
Tel: 0116 2792299
Email: books@troubador.co.uk
Web: www.troubador.co.uk

ISBN 978 1836282 372

British Library Cataloguing in Publication Data.
A catalogue record for this book is available from the British Library.

Printed and bound by CPI Group (UK) Ltd, Croydon, CR0 4YY
Typeset in 11pt Minion Pro by Troubador Publishing Ltd, Leicester, UK

MIX
Paper | Supporting
responsible forestry
FSC
www.fsc.org   FSC® C013604

To those emergency service men and women
who have paid the ultimate price.

ACKNOWLEDGEMENTS

Thank you again to those who have helped me on my way. Anne Armitage, former English teacher and RAF education officer, who examined my grammar with such dedication. Karen and Jay Moore, for their time in reading the earlier version of the manuscript and their observations regarding the narrative, coupled with honest feedback.

Shona Groves, Supporter Liaison Officer at Millwall Football Club, for her help in shedding some light on the running of a professional football club; Detective Constable Graham Wright for making sure my police procedure was as up to date as it can be and, finally, Charlotte Baker, for her editing skills.

Thank you all.

Any mistakes are purely of my own making.
G. Powell 2024

ONE

TUESDAY MORNING

A single florescent tube flickered into life, brightly illuminating the three-metre square room with purple iridescent light. The occupant paused at the threshold leading from the hallway, listening momentarily to the rhythmic humming of a large chest freezer resting in one corner. Half of the remaining floor space was occupied by a sturdy table; its four legs pinning a thick plastic sheet securely in place to catch the inevitable leakage of body fluids. Two portable air conditioning units hissed cold air, maintaining the ambient room temperature at a chilly five degrees.

Satisfied instructions had been followed to the letter; the Butcher removed several stainless-steel tools from a worn leather holdall, using a gloved hand. The bow saw, boning knife and cleaver were placed uniformly onto the table surface; the cold steel reflected the bright light, casting eerie shadows onto glossed white walls as the Butcher manoeuvred around the room.

Satisfied that weeks of planning were about to come to fruition, the Butcher backed out of the room, switched the light off, closed the airtight door and stepped from the partially furnished flat out onto a balcony just in time to see the last of the bright orange

1

winter sun disappearing below the urban landscape. All that was needed now was the victim.

⋆

Having drunk the last of his coffee, Jed Jennings started up his van and drove the couple of miles to Hendon Cemetery. He felt ashamed that his visits were so irregular, but this was one day he would never miss.

It had been five years, to the day, since his life had been turned upside down. He remembered it vividly, as if it were yesterday. Firstly, a phone call from Sophie's head teacher, followed by a visit from a uniformed police officer, informing him and wife Carol their beautiful daughter had been knocked down outside her school and was fighting for her life in intensive care. They never even got to say goodbye.

Jed parked his van as near to the grave as he could. The air was freezing. He bent his six foot one frame into the vicious wind that fired tiny shards of ice, like darts, from a nearby tree into his face. This was the second year he'd visited the grave alone on the anniversary of his daughter's death. He and Carol had drifted apart, each blaming the other for the death of their only child when, in fact, it was neither of their faults. 'What ifs' were often a precursor to many of their arguments. 'What if' he'd picked her up from school instead of accepting an emergency plumbing job? 'What if' she had kept her off school that morning when Sophie had complained of a headache? They tried desperately for another child, but Carol believed they were cursed.

He opened the back of his van and removed a small bouquet of flowers. It was more of a symbolic gesture than anything else, a sign to let Carol know he'd been here, when she visited later, and hadn't forgotten – not that he ever would.

She would have been fourteen now, a young woman, her whole life in front of her. He wondered what they would have been

2

doing. She hated the cold, so something indoors – the cinema or maybe her favourite: bowling.

The blooms that adorned the grave with colour throughout the summer had shrivelled, almost to dust. He brushed away the dead flowers that disintegrated and disbursed in the wind and replaced them with the new offering, before taking a rag from his pocket and gently wiping the headstone that recorded his daughter's short life and violent death. He lowered his head in reverence and, although not a religious man, mumbled the words of the Lord's Prayer as best as he could remember them from Sunday school. He kissed the small portrait smiling back at him. He'd waited five years. His hatred for the man who took his daughter's life had not diminished; an unabated desire for revenge still burned inside. It was now time to act.

*

Eddie Lee was a professional thief operating on mainline trains out of Paddington and St Pancras, stealing from Royal Mail mailbags stored in the train's secure brakes. The risks were high – plain-clothes Transport Police officers and Post Office investigators regularly travelled the vulnerable trains and knew him well – but the rewards were worth it: cash, jewellery, traveller's cheques, passports and credit cards among a normal haul. He always worked alone; he would never trust another thief.

Lee ordinarily put his hands up – pleaded guilty – to anything he'd been nabbed for in the past. He was nearly always caught in the act, with stolen property, and by acknowledging his crimes, saving the courts time, it ultimately led to shorter prison sentences in cushier prisons. The authorities had tried to rehabilitate him, but Eddie Lee was a thief; stealing was all he knew, and he wasn't going to change.

His last conviction resulted in a ten-year prison term for theft and attempted wounding, the extended sentence resulting from a combination of a lengthy criminal record and a trumped-up charge of trying to stab the arresting officer. Yeah, sure, he was guilty of stealing from mailbags on the London to Sheffield train, and yes, he'd been armed with a knife but only in order to slash the mailbags open – the attempted stabbing was a total fabrication; 'gilding the lily' was an accusation hurled at the arresting officer, by his barrister, in his client's defence. But Eddie Lee was a realist – getting nicked and serving time was the downside of his job, so he settled down to serve two thirds of his time at HMP Nottingham.

He'd started to become suspicious of his wife Jasmine when her visits became less frequent. He accepted her excuses – at first – which were that her journey to Nottingham was both arduous and expensive, but when she did visit, he noticed a change in her. She'd lost a lot of weight, changed her hair colour and was wearing nice clothes – all for his benefit of course, she said – wanting to remind him of what he was missing. When asked where she was getting the money from for her new look, she lied about a job working in a local casino. He knew this for a fact. A couple of calls to some loyal friends had revealed she wasn't working for a living but was shacked up with a new man. Worst of all, he was a police officer. This discovery sent Eddie mentally over the edge. He became more aggressive with fellow inmates, often getting into fights, and got involved with the smuggling of drugs and mobiles into the prison. His behaviour resulted in additional time added to his minimum sentence.

With two weeks until his release date, and with revenge very much at the forefront of his mind, he was transferred to a prison closer to London – HMP Bedford.

The screw had come for him at 7.30am on the morning of his release. He'd washed and shaved and gathered his few belongings before being escorted down to a holding cell just off the prison reception area. The clothes he'd arrived in had vanished – lost in the system, he was informed by a smirking prison officer, although

4

he had lost so much weight during his incarceration, he doubted they would have fitted anyway.

He waited patiently for remand inmates to be transported to various courts, before his paperwork was processed, receiving the standard £42 in cash. He was escorted to the front gate and pushed out into the real world. He stood at the gate, tasting freedom for the first time in nearly a decade. What few possessions he had were in a carrier bag. He shivered as a fine rain permeated his prison-issue grey jumper and jogging bottoms, the only clothes he had to his name. Lee looked around on the off chance that he might spot a familiar face. He had nobody in his life apart from his elderly mother, who lived in Finsbury Park. Ducking his head and shoulders into the breeze, he headed for Bedford station and a rendezvous with an unsuspecting wife and lover.

TWO

TUESDAY AFTERNOON

'You are a liar, Mr McNally,' the barrister bellowed across the courtroom in the direction of the jury. 'You left the gentlemen's toilets in Da Luca's restaurant on the night in question; you saw Mr Roger Knight standing in the al fresco smoking area at the rear of the premises. You've already told the jury that, throughout the evening, you had formed a dislike for him. You took your opportunity to savagely beat him, leaving the victim with a broken nose, before nonchalantly returning to the group and leaving the restaurant with your wife. That is the case, isn't it, Mr McNally?'

Ryan McNally scanned the courtroom from the witness box at Southwark Crown Court. He'd appeared several times in this very court, as a police officer for the prosecution, since transferring down to London from his native Manchester, but *never* as the defendant undergoing cross-examination.

The public gallery was a sea of faces – some familiar, others not. His wife, Kate, looked pensive, attempting to project a confidence in the British judicial system she didn't truly feel. McNally was pleased to see Detective Sergeant Marcia Frost sneaking in the back row. She gave him the briefest of nods, which portrayed an impression that all would be well and buoyed his mood slightly. They'd formed a close, professional bond in the short time they'd worked together, before his suspension, and he owed her his life.

Detective Superintendent Nigel Plummer sat behind the prosecution barrister, flanking the Crown Prosecution Service representative on one side. DCI John Masters from Professional Standards sat on the other. Plummer was McNally's senior officer on the British Transport Police's Major Investigations Unit. Although forced to suspend his detective inspector from duty for the past five months, he'd generally been very supportive. Masters, on the other hand, was the type of copper who'd prosecute his own grandmother. He sneered at McNally, appearing to enjoy the tension that was building.

'Well, Mr McNally? The jury is waiting – as are we all, for your answer.'

'Sir,' the detective looked over at the panel of twelve, who would decide his fate, and made eye contact with the individuals he knew were on his side. It was a skill he'd developed many years before. Generally, those congenial members of the jury were happy to make eye contact with the prosecution witness or indeed, depending on which side of the fence they were sitting, the defendant. The jury were a fair representation of British society in gender and race. He was pleased to see that all the jurors were thirty-plus, which he thought an advantage. They all seemed engaged with the process being played out in front of them and concentrated on the evidence being presented. McNally believed that as long as they tried him on the evidence and not on his occupation, he would be cleared. Glancing towards the prosecution counsel, he continued.

'I'm still trying to figure out if your last lengthy oration was an allegation, a question, an observation or merely a personal view. Maybe you could clarify which it is before I commit to any answer?' A rumble of laughter drifted from the jury. The prosecution barrister's face reddened slightly – McNally had scored an important point, but he didn't want to push it any further and risk coming across as an arrogant smart-arse and alienate the jury.

'The defendant has a point, Mr Alder.' Her Honour Judge Penhaligon peered from her elevated position down into the well of the court. 'Perhaps you could clarify your line of cross-examination into sizeable chunks, which resemble pertinent questions that can be answered by the defendant, to further the prosecution case towards some sort of conclusion this side of next Christmas. You are not on a West End stage, Mr Alder, so please do not use my courtroom as if on one – carry on please.'

'Your Honour – of course.' Alder peered down to his notes and composed himself, after the double rebuke, before continuing. 'Mr McNally, is it correct that you formed a dislike for Mr Knight early on that evening?'

'Yes, sir, I did.'

'Is it also correct that when you left the gentlemen's toilet at the restaurant, you saw Mr Knight in the small al fresco area used by some diners as a smoking area?'

'No, sir, that is incorrect. I did visit the toilets, but as you can see from the layout of the restaurant on the map, produced by yourselves the prosecution,' McNally glanced at a copy of the map in front of him and waited for the jury and the judge to do the same before continuing, 'I would have had to in fact divert from a direct route back to the restaurant in order to see outside. When I left the toilet, I was anxious to get back to my wife, who'd been upset by Mr Knight's drunken behaviour, pay our bill and leave. I was unaware that he'd also left the table until I returned to the dining area. So, the answer to your question is, no. I didn't see Mr Knight at any stage after I had gone to the toilet.'

'We have seen CCTV footage from the restaurant's security camera, which, fortunately for you, covers only the inside dining area, the bar, till and the entrance/exit to the high street and not the rear of the building where this offence took place,' Alder sneered before continuing. 'You can clearly be seen returning from the toilet area. The close-up images appear to show you to be – shall we say – in a slightly antagonistic frame of mind. Would you agree with that impression?'

'Firstly, let me deal with your point about the camera positions. I would challenge your observation that the lack of CCTV coverage at the back of the restaurant was fortunate for me. In fact, it was very *unfortunate*, because if any such footage existed, it would clearly exonerate me. As for your second point, I'm not sure how you can interpret – slightly or otherwise – successfully, a state of mind from a CCTV image some ten metres away. But I will admit that I was annoyed with how the evening had turned out, as it'd been quite an important occasion for my wife.' McNally glanced over to the public gallery; Kate gave him a supportive smile. 'She has struggled to make friends since our move south a couple of years ago. I still feel guilty about dragging my family down to London to fulfil a professional ambition of my own. I'd had a very long day and didn't particularly want to go out that evening, but this was a chance to support her, and it was ruined by Mr Knight and his inability to control his drinking and his boorish opinions about my profession and anything else I introduced into the conversation.'

'No further questions, Your Honour.'

'Mr Stafford, any questions in re-examination?' Horace Stafford rose to his impressive height of six foot three slowly, for effect, and looked along the two rows of jurors. He made eye contact with each individual juror in turn, accompanied by a smile, before turning his head to the judge, to whom he delivered a barely perceptible but respectful nod of his head. He pulled his gown forward from his shoulders to his chest before directing his attention to the witness box.

'Detective Inspector McNally…' A five second silence allowed the tension in the courtroom to build; McNally was really pleased that his counsel was addressing him by his professional title rather than that of a civilian preferred by the prosecution. '…Is it fair to say that insults and some – let's say – provocative vocabulary, aimed at both you personally, and on occasions, your family members, even, at times, questioning your mother's integrity, are part and parcel of this wonderful society we have created for our children?'

'Mr Stafford, I will remind you – as I have the learned counsel for the prosecution – this is a British courtroom and not some American farce or chat show – please save the amateur dramatics for the day you retire.' Stafford replied with a deep bow from the waist in acknowledgement of his chastisement and hid a cheeky grin. 'Inspector,' Penhaligon continued without looking up from her notes, 'please answer the question – if I remember correctly, there was one uttered.'

'Your Honour, my front-line uniform colleagues are more prone to such language and personal abuse than I am nowadays, but I still get my fair share.'

'I have your personal records in front of me, as do the prosecution and Her Honour the judge.' Stafford waved a buff-coloured document folder at the jury to reiterate the fact. 'Let me see. You are approaching twenty-three years of police service, without a single blemish on your record, most impressive, I must say, in today's woke society, when one can't even voice an opinion on the most trivial of matters without being slated by the Metropolitan Elite or their tree-hugging friends.'

'Mr Stafford – your point?'

'It's coming, Your Honour,' Stafford grumbled under his breath, knowing he was reaching the limit of Her Honour's patience, before theatrically turning a page and waving his hand at the printed contents. 'Not even a reprimand for the most inconsequential of the multitude of petty disciplinary offences available to your senior officers, often unnecessarily hurled at our hard-working police officers of today.' Stafford looked, and smiled, at the jury and received several nods of agreement to his last statement. 'Certainly nothing referring to any incident involving violence. Is that correct, DI McNally?'

'Yes, sir, it is.'

'Since the subject of the CCTV footage – which I suggest has contributed little to the prosecution's case and in fact bolstered the case for the defence by showing Mr Knight's behaviour and its effect on those diners seated nearby – has been raised by my learned friend for the prosecution in cross-examination, I would like to revisit it. Members of the jury, if you look in your evidential packages in front of you and turn to exhibit twenty-seven, the CCTV image referred to in my client's cross-examination...'

Stafford waited until he was sure that every member of the jury, and the judge, had found the relevant image before he continued. 'DI McNally, have you the image to hand?'

'Yes, sir.'

'Would you describe to the court the suit you are wearing on the night in question?'

'Yes, it was a lightweight, grey, linen suit, white shirt, with a bright orange tie.'

'Yes, very striking if I may say. It certainly makes you stand out from the crowd, but not, in all honesty, my style.' Stafford waited for the undercurrent of laughter around the court to calm down before continuing. 'We've heard medical evidence from a doctor at Barnet General Hospital, who examined Mr Knight on his arrival at the accident and emergency department that evening. The doctor gave his evidence professionally and eloquently, as we would expect from a member of our National Health Service, describing details of the injury and the force, in his opinion, rendered to inflict such an injury on the complainant in this case. He commented, in answer to a prosecution question, that in his opinion, the blow would have been delivered by a punch or a headbutt resulting in an...' Stafford turned a page in his notebook, ' "instantaneous explosion of blood" – his words not mine. I would like you to carefully examine the image, DI McNally, alongside the members of the jury, and tell me if you can see any sign of blood on your light grey suit, white shirt or orange tie?'

'No, sir, I cannot.'

'When arrested, is it correct that you were escorted to your home address by DCI John Masters from your own service and two Metropolitan detectives from Finchley – a Detective Inspector… Colin Robertson and a DS Lewis?'

'Yes.'

'They searched your house, I believe. Did they seize any property?'

'Yes, they did: the suit, the shirt and orange tie that I wore on that evening. If I remember correctly, they found the receipt for the meal in one of the suit pockets.'

'Indeed, they did. Now, as the prosecution's case has been completed with no mention of even a miniscule trace of Mr Knight's blood on your suit, or anybody else's blood for that matter – not a spot, let alone a spontaneous "explosion" of the red stuff – I would presume that indeed *none* was present. Bearing in mind the severity of the blow you are accused of delivering, it is my submission, if you were in fact responsible for delivering such a violent blow, that traces of Mr Knight's blood would have been found on your suit. Would you agree?'

'Yes. I would.'

'Thank you, no further questions, Your Honour.'

'In that case the court will rise. I will commence my summing up first thing in the morning.'

THREE

WEDNESDAY MORNING

Frankie Meeres turned left out of Bermondsey Underground station, pulling the collar of his thick overcoat up to cover his neck from the bitterly cold January wind, and walked west along Jamaica Road. He slowed his pace and glanced into a shop window, monitoring those following in his wake – old habits die hard. Satisfied he wasn't of interest to anybody else, Meeres took out his mobile and read, once again, the anonymous text message displaying an address, and a photograph of a young woman, that he'd received much earlier that morning: *91 Chaplin House Bermondsey estate Abbey Street SE16*. He'd tried to ring the originating mobile number back, but it was, not surprisingly, unobtainable. Was somebody playing games with him, or was this genuine information? He'd travelled to Bermondsey to find out.

He turned left onto Abbey Street and walked past the first of many entrances to the Bermondsey estate, locating Chaplin House on a simple estate plan set behind a transparent plastic-covered noticeboard scrawled with undecipherable graffiti. Abbey Street was a busy thoroughfare, with a continuous trail of commuter traffic passing in both directions. Meeres crossed the road and plonked himself down on a hard plastic seat at a bus stop adjacent to the address he'd been directed to and sank deep inside his overcoat to keep warm. The digital information display informed him several buses regularly stopped here; he calculated he could comfortably spend half an hour or so waiting and watching before attracting any attention from the locals and formed a cover story should anybody – friend or foe – engage him in conversation.

He remembered visiting an adjacent block many years before. Meeres and his old partner, Brian Garvey, had arrested a South London villain called Lenny Cunningham, who handled stolen traveller's cheques. They were good times – their investigation had cleared up over two hundred crimes nationwide and earned a Chief Constable's commendation to boot.

He and Garvey worked together for years and were mainly left to their own devices because they got results.

Meeres wondered what happened to Brian Garvey. They had been so close you couldn't slip a sheet of paper between them, but when Garvey retired a few years ago, they lost touch. The last he'd heard his old mate had moved up to Norfolk somewhere.

Garvey had always been careful with his money, investing in stocks and shares, and would never need to earn the King's shilling again. Frankie hadn't been so astute; two marriages, four kids and the inability to keep it in his pants meant he would have to work until he dropped. He'd managed to purchase a one-bedroomed flat in Catford using money from the sale of the family home after his second divorce and the lump sum he got from his recent retirement. He was happy in his own way; he'd become a bit of a loner and enjoyed his own company – he rarely saw, or even spoke to, his kids anymore.

Catford was up and coming, to use a local estate agent's spin. He knew it well anyway; he'd been born and bred in Southeast London. Now, since retirement, he was his own boss and spent most of his time following adulterous spouses around and serving court summonses. Occasionally, a juicy investigation would come his way, which involved a bit of travel and the opportunity to sting a client for some good expenses; today would be a good earner: a missing person inquiry.

He brought the earlier text message up on his mobile screen again: a woman aged thirty-two, with dark brown hair. She wasn't unattractive and appeared to be very happy; maybe she just didn't want to be found. Who was he to decide? But it paid the bills and supplemented his police pension. The anonymous information, as to her current whereabouts, was of no great concern; that's how his world operated. He would give it another twenty minutes before traipsing up to the ninth floor and knocking on the door.

FOUR

WEDNESDAY MORNING

The door behind the judge's chair opened and Her Honour Judge Penhaligon bowed to the court, before taking her seat. McNally looked around the courtroom, pleased to see Kate in the same place she'd been for the past two days. Marcia Frost had been joined by a couple more of his team – DS Ray Blendell, his office manager, and DC Sam Hodge. Sitting at the far end of the public gallery was his accuser Roger Knight and his wife Melissa, neither of whom made any attempt at eye contact with him.

Another door opened to the right of the dock, in which McNally nervously sat. The jury filed in and took their places. They'd had overnight to consider the evidence put before them by the prosecution and in his defence. They had sat patiently through the judge's balanced summing up before being invited to retire to their room to consider his fate. He was suddenly aware of how sweaty his hands had become. This was it! A defining moment in his career – his life! His family's future. He could go to prison – lose his job. Would Kate and the kids move back to Manchester? Yeah, sure they would, and he wouldn't blame them; there would be nothing to keep them here.

McNally concentrated on the faces of each member of the jury as they settled down. He knew a few were on his side, but were there enough? Most of the jurors were happy to make eye contact with him, which was a good sign, but two fixed their gaze firmly at their feet and then the judge. This was going to be close.

'Members of the jury, will the foreman please stand.' One of his perceived allies stood in answer to the court clerk's instructions, another ray of hope.

'Do you find the accused, Ryan McNally, guilty or not guilty of causing Mr Roger Knight actual bodily harm?'

*

He was pretty sure his presence had been noticed. The odd parting of a net curtain, the same faces in and out of the Bermondsey estate, with the odd glance in his direction. Maybe he was getting a bit paranoid in his old age, but rarely did his gut feeling let him down that something was amiss – it had saved his skin several times in his long career.

Frankie Meeres looked at his watch. He'd been here nearly forty-five minutes, longer than he'd intended. The only way he was going to get to the bottom of this missing person case was to go and knock on the door. The earlier anonymous text message was putting a slight doubt into his mind – probably from a family member or friend of the missing woman, who knew of her whereabouts but wanted to remain anonymous, was one explanation he considered.

A local yob, who gave Frankie a wave, shouting, 'Morning, Officer', was the last straw. He had to decide whether to back off and return another day or go and knock on the door of no. 91 Chaplin House. The thought of a quick result and a couple of grand in his pocket made his mind up for him. He stood and stretched his aching back, waited for a gap in the traffic, crossed back over Abbey Street and headed for Chaplin House.

It had been a pretty good morning for Joey Dryden. He'd delivered a stash of drugs to an address in Southeast London and got paid with a £50 note –something he'd rarely possessed before the commencement of his new career. He'd been running drugs all over the Home Counties for six months now and was slowly climbing a hierarchical social ladder within an East London drugs empire.

He'd started local to where he lived in Forest Gate. But now he was trusted to go further afield, with larger consignments and collecting ever larger wads of money. He'd been tempted to skim a bit off the top on occasions but had witnessed, first-hand, the consequences of such a stupid action – he liked his legs the way they were, straight, unbroken and useable.

He was now earning more money than he could spend. He couldn't buy a flashy car – at sixteen he was still legally too young. But he'd learnt to drive in stolen vehicles round his estate and was counting the days until his seventeenth birthday.

He made his way back to the local station, aware that, being from an East London postcode, he was on enemy territory and needed to get back on safe ground, north of the river, as soon as possible. He looked at his mobile: 11.50am. The later he left it, the more chance the locals would be stirring from their beds. A car horn alerted him to a slow-moving Mercedes with tinted rear windows. A huge black hand emerged from the driver's window, beckoning him over. Quickly realising the driver wasn't after directions, Joey looked around at his options. He could run the fifty or so metres to the station entrance and relative safety, but he could easily be felled by a bullet between his shoulder blades. Or he could front it out with a confidence and bravado he didn't really feel. The huge hand, adorned in gold rings, again beckoned him over; this time the driver showed a little more of his face. A big grin revealed a row of gold upper teeth, dazzling in the sunlight, and a flattened nose, struggling to support an expensive pair of designer sunglasses. His black, crew cut hairstyle menacingly revealed several scars, as if somebody had used it as a wood block at some stage.

'Come 'ere. Nuffing to worry about. Just wanna quick word. There's money in it for yer.' Joey approached the vehicle tentatively, ready to run and take his chances that the driver was a bad shot.

'You ain't from round 'ere, are yer? Just seen you come out of that 'ouse. Been dealing a few drugs, 'ave we?'

'What, you the Feds?' Joey answered with a hint of a swagger, trying to hold on to a little self-respect, at the same time not wishing to reveal that he was about to shit himself.

'Do I look like the filth? My boss 'as got a little job for you. You interested?'

Joey looked at the tinted rear window and thought he saw movement. 'Yeah, sure I might be. How much you paying?'

'Straight to the point – I like that. Hundred quid.'

'What've I gotta do?'

'There's a large sports bag in the boot. We want you to take it to the left luggage at Liverpool Street station. Pay the fee for one day and then leave it. That's it. Got it?'

'Just take a bag to a left luggage place and leave it for £100? What's inside?'

'I'm a bit disappointed with that question. That's your first mistake – don't make another one. Where you from? Cause you ain't from round 'ere.'

Joey considered another lie, but this guy looked dangerous. 'Forest Gate.'

'Well, this side of the river we don't ask questions like that. You up for it or not? You got five seconds.'

'Yeah OK, I'll do it.'

The driver peered into the rear of the vehicle and had a short conversation before looking back to Joey. 'What's yer name?'

'Joey Smith.'

'Fair enough, Joey *Smith*. Two things I wanna make clear. If you don't deliver the bag, I'll find you. If you look in the bag, I'll find you.' The driver indicated, with a flick of his enormous head, to the rear of the vehicle. The boot opened silently. Joey removed the bag, surprised by its considerable weight, and returned to the driver's window. He was handed six crisp £20 notes, which he quickly placed inside his jeans pocket.

'The extra twenty is for the storage charge. You can keep the change. If they ask you what's in the bag, make up some bullshit answer – got it?'

Joey nodded and turned to walk away.

'Hey, Joey, one last thing,' Joey turned back and heard the camera click on a phone, 'just in case I need to find you.' The driver's window smoothly closed, and the powerful car accelerated away.

*

The Horniman pub, Hay's Galleria, was a stone's throw from Southwark Crown Court. In hotter weather, it offered terraced views of the River Thames, but on a cold January day, only desperate smokers ventured out onto its riverside terrace and the freezing London air. The river was grey and fast-moving with a hint of sea salt in the chilly breeze. The pleasure crafts, full of tourists, wouldn't appear again for a few months – the river belonged to working barges and the odd police or RNLI patrol vessel.

McNally sat with a double brandy in his hand, looking at the smiling faces that surrounded him, but he didn't feel like celebrating. The jury's unanimous decision of 'not guilty' was the end of a torturous five months for him, Kate and the kids, Ava and Max. All he really felt was a sense of relief. Kate sat next to him, gripping his hand so tightly he could feel her trembling. If they were alone, he knew she would burst into tears.

Marcia Frost, Sam Hodge and Ray Blendell tried to lighten the atmosphere with some soft banter, which invariably came back to another, not-so-popular detective on the team – Stuart Graves – and his latest antics.

McNally thought about a small speech, thanking them all for their support, but just raised his glass in the air, signalling his appreciation with a nod of his head, and threw the fiery liquid to the back of his throat.

A blast of cold air crept across the bar, snapping at their ankles as the entrance door opened. Detective Superintendent Nigel Plummer looked around, adjusting his eyes to the dim light until he saw the group. He met McNally's eye and summoned him over to the bar with a flick of his head. McNally prised his hand from Kate's and kissed her gently on the cheek.

'Good to see you, Ryan. I know congratulations aren't the appropriate response to this morning's verdict – there were very few winners in this whole affair – but I'm pleased for you and Kate that this awful business is over with. I know we haven't always seen eye to eye, but you are one of *my* officers, and I'm glad to have you back among us.'

'Thanks, boss, your support has been appreciated by me and my family.'

'I can't stay. It wouldn't be right for me to do so in the circumstances.'

McNally smiled.

'But take this and buy you and the team a drink on me. I'll see you at Camden tomorrow morning. By the way, you're the on-call DI from midnight tonight, so take it easy.'

FIVE

WEDNESDAY NIGHT

The left luggage office, located near platform ten at Liverpool Street station, was run efficiently by late turn supervisor Gayani Bandara. It was one of the busiest on the transport system. She had travelled to the United Kingdom, with her parents, from Sri Lanka, when only eight years old to escape civil war raging in their country of birth; she now called London home.

The late shift concluded at 11pm. Her husband, Pranith, was a London bus driver, which suited them both as they could often arrange for their shifts to coincide, allowing them a lot of free time together. The couple had three children: two boys, who were both at university, and one married daughter, who had her own family. Neither Gayani nor Pranith worked weekends, which they enjoyed with family and friends.

The left luggage facility was open twenty-four hours a day. At 10.30pm Gayani topped and tailed her paperwork to facilitate a smooth handover to the night supervisor. Paperwork complete, she left her office to make her final rounds; she was summoned, by a concerned member of staff, to one of the storage areas lined with wall-to-wall shelving accommodating a variety of suitcases, rucksacks and other luggage. Before the attendant could open his mouth, her nostrils filled with the smell of decay.

'Glad you can smell that as well, boss.'

'My God, where is that coming from, Sully?'

The attendant pointed to a large sports bag to the rear of the room located on one of the top shelves under a large air conditioning unit pumping out warm air. 'I think it's that one. It was left early afternoon, due to be picked up in the morning.'

Gayani instructed the young employee to lift the sports bag down and place it on the floor in front of her. Gayani watched as Sully struggled with the heavy contents; she feared the worst. The rancid odour aroused nightmares she still regularly experienced from back home. She recognised the smell; it was the smell of rotting flesh.

*

Marie Relish missed the buzz of the Major Investigations Unit. Following the conclusion of the London Underground serial killer case and the suspension of DI McNally, she had been posted as a civilian crime analyst to another fraud investigation. It was dragging on and she had considered transferring back to her former role of uniformed detention officer.

She still enjoyed working out of British Transport Police's headquarters on Camden Road. The area had a real buzz; she loved walking around Camden Market at lunchtime, experiencing the sights, sounds and smells of hundreds of different stalls and shops. But she found fraud investigations mundane and laborious, and she had little chance of expressing any of her personal initiative, an opportunity she'd enjoyed on McNally's team. The only light at the end of the tunnel was the arrest and charging of four suspects earlier in the day. She had volunteered to stay on until the interviews and charging was concluded; she was exhausted.

She boarded the No. 31 bus from Camden Town station and

sat on the upper deck. She was cold and could only distinguish the bright illuminations of shopfronts and traffic lights through the steamed-up windows. She shuddered, pulling her thick winter coat tightly round her for extra warmth. She smiled at the text from Marcia Frost about McNally's earlier acquittal and the promise to get her back on the team when the next big investigation broke. She had formed a good, solid base for a long-standing friendship with the detective on the previous investigation, and she hoped that Frost's promise wasn't just hot air – however welcome that would be at this precise moment.

The journey to Carlton Vale in Kilburn normally took half an hour or so, depending on London traffic. She looked over her shoulder at a sea of uninteresting faces – most people were travelling alone and cocooned in their own thoughts: listening to music, engaged in social media or simply sleeping and paying little attention to those around them. She had learnt, within weeks of moving up to London from her family home in Bristol, that being surrounded by people whilst feeling so alone was a London thing. A little paranoia was taking over, but she felt as though she was being watched, even followed. It had been over a year since her last meaningful relationship had finished. She had dated a detective inspector on B Division, who was a complete control freak. She had ended the affair, but he took it badly. It was one of the reasons she had applied for the analyst job at Camden – a fresh start, make new friends. She had been on edge for the last few weeks. Personal items on her desk had been moved; a silk scarf given to her by her mother last Christmas had disappeared. She wanted to talk to Marcia Frost, the only person she really trusted, about her suspicions, but their paths rarely crossed nowadays.

She jumped off the bus at Carlton Vale and walked the short distance to Hamilton House, a twenty-story tower block, in which she rented a small two-bedroomed flat on the fourteenth floor. She scanned the area before activating the outer door with a key fob. She pulled the door to and relaxed. She regulated her breathing whilst waiting for the lift, admonishing herself for being so paranoid.

On the far side of the road, a man stepped from behind a large London plane tree. He had been waiting for over an hour, but it'd been worth it. He extracted a silk scarf from his coat pocket and inhaled the pleasant scent. He pulled his collar up against the chill wind and waited five minutes before pressing the speed dial on his mobile and smiling.

SIX

WEDNESDAY NIGHT

McNally ducked under the blue police cordon tape and passed through the doors of the left luggage office on platform ten at London's Liverpool Street station. McNally met by a police inspector, who looked as if he had just been unwrapped from a presentation box – he was immaculate, from his smart flat cap down to his glass-polished shoes. His appearance augmented by the sack of shit, with chevrons, standing next to him. McNally introduced himself.

'Inspector Reece, the late turn duty officer, and this is Sergeant Gray.' McNally nodded – unimpressed – at the sergeant, who looked as if he'd slept in his uniform. He stood with hands tucked behind his ill-fitting stab-proof vest, looking totally disinterested, as if what they were about to investigate was an everyday occurrence. He found it difficult to comprehend how a police officer could run nowadays as he glanced at the sergeant's so-called utility belt, something he associated with *Batman and Robin*. It had everything, from first aid kit to radio, CS gas canister to water bottle; his athleticism wouldn't have been helped by the extra few stones in weight he was carrying around his midriff.

McNally knew that fitness tests were now compulsory; so far, he had escaped such a task. But looking at Sergeant Gray, he thought he didn't have too much to worry about.

Reece continued, 'Two of my officers were called just after half ten by the late turn supervisor. One of her staff reported a suspicious item of luggage emitting a noxious smell. She thought it may be a dead animal of some description. One of the officers unzipped the bag a few inches. The object inside is wrapped in clingfilm and he was unable to determine what it was. He sensibly left the bag in situ, told the staff to leave the premises and radioed for assistance. I decided to cordon the area off as a potential crime scene and call yourselves and the on-call CSI.'

'You mean the on-call SOCO? We're not in bloody America, Inspector.' This cracked a slight smile on the sergeant's face. McNally continued before the inspector could answer. 'Has the SOCO arrived yet?'

'Yes, sir,' answered Gray. 'Just gone to get her equipment from the van. She's a bit laid-back, calls everybody *dude*.'

*

Once the double lock and chain were secured, Marie Relish felt safer, and a glass of Pinot helped her relax a little more. She went into the bathroom and turned the hot water off, looking forward to a relaxing soak, followed by last weekend's *Dancing on Ice*. The shrill ringing of her landline made her jump, spilling half the glass of wine into the bath water. The landline rarely rang; everybody at work used her mobile, and in fact, she was thinking of having the dammed thing disconnected, saving her thirty-odd pounds a month. The only person it would likely be at this time of night would be her mother. She lifted the receiver on the fourth ring.

'Hello.' Just silence.

'Mum, is that you?' The line went dead. She tried to put a positive spin on it. It wasn't her mother complaining of illness or that she'd fallen down the stairs and was sitting in accident and emergency. It was probably a cold caller from India and her voice didn't fit the profile of a vulnerable victim. She tapped in 1471 to find the number – not surprisingly, blocked. She crossed the tiny living room and peeked out of the curtains, down fourteen floors to street level. A shiver travelled the length of her spine as a shadow moved from behind a tree into the darkness of the night.

*

The left luggage facilities' manager Gayani Bandara and her assistant had been taken to the British Transport Police Station nearby, awaiting interview. McNally had arranged for DS Marcia Frost and DC Sam Hodge to debrief the witnesses.

'Good to see you back, boss.' DC Stuart Graves held out a hand, which McNally shook. 'Hell of a few months I'd imagine?'

'Yeah, it was a bit of a rough ride, more for the family than me – I always knew I was innocent, but we both know jury verdicts can go either way. So, apart from a bag and a bad smell, what've we got?'

'Not sure yet, boss, waiting for Sally Cook to show up. She's here, just gone to get her gear out of the van. I poked my head into the storage area; there's a bit of a whiff, not sure if it's human or animal.' McNally and Graves stepped into protective suits and overshoes and double-gloved.

'Hey, dude! So, it's true, they let you out?'

'Hi, Sally, and I've missed you too!'

'Of course you have – who wouldn't? You're only human.' Both detectives waited for the SOCO to dress before all three ducked under the inner cordon tape.

The sports bag sat in the middle of the floor; the zip, as Inspector Reece had informed them, was open a couple of inches. Cook took a few preparatory pictures of the entrance to the storage area and the bag itself.

'Do we know if the person who deposited the bag would've had access to this area?' Cook asked.

'No, it's staff only back here, obviously,' replied Graves with a hint of sarcasm, which got Cook's back up. She'd forgotten what an arsehole Graves could be.

'I'll ask the questions. You supply the answers, Constable,' Cook snapped back.

'So, the only areas we have to concentrate on are the front desk, the bag and contents, method of payment and any paperwork the owner of the bag had to fill out or just sign,' McNally thought aloud.

He rang Frost. 'Marcia, are you with the witnesses yet?'

'Yes, sir, just waiting for Sam to turn up. Any update?'

'No not yet. Sally's just starting to examine the sports bag. I need a few answers quickly.' McNally could hear Frost opening a notebook.

'OK, fire away.'

'Do either of the staff remember the person who brought the bag in? If they do, how did they pay? If it was by cash, has the till been emptied? I also need a quick explanation of the procedure they adopt when accepting an item. I'll sort the CCTV out for here, if you can make sure our people secure CCTV for the station. Got all that?' McNally didn't wait for an answer. 'Get back to me ASAP.' Of course, it could turn out to be somebody's leg of lamb, but he was taking no chances. He returned his attention to Sally Cook.

'You'd better come and have a look at this, dude.' Cook was crouched down next to the bag; the smell was getting worse. She'd opened the zip halfway and shone her Maglite torch onto the contents. It took the detective a few moments for his brain to unscramble the image. A human arm and hand, wrapped in transparent cling film, nestled in between two blood-soaked towels, a gold wedding band on the ring finger of the hand reflected the torch light; the middle finger had been crudely hacked off.

SEVEN

WEDNESDAY NIGHT

Brian Garvey sat with his back to the wall facing the pub's only way in and out. He nursed a pint glass of Guinness, now half empty and warm to the touch. Glancing at the clock over the bar, he decided to give it another ten minutes and then he was off.

The Boot had been a favourite watering hole for him and Frankie Meeres back in the day when they worked out of British Transport Police headquarters CID, situated nearby in Tavistock Place, a building affectionately referred to as 'The Dairy' due to its previous occupants.

The pub was situated in Cromer Street, five minutes' walk from 'The Dairy' and close to King's Cross station. He grinned at the irony of its location; a pub where he'd spent many hours during his service years in a street with the title of his post-retirement home – a seaside town in North Norfolk. He'd travelled down earlier in the day and booked himself into a Travelodge on King's Cross Road. The phone call he'd received yesterday, from a former informant, had intrigued him; not much dragged him down to the 'Smoke' nowadays. He made a mental note to change his mobile number – he wasn't interested in visiting the past too often.

It'd been a friendly pub in his day, mainly patronised by local people, nothing flashy, just good beer and friendly staff and a carpet you wouldn't want to touch with bare skin. He'd been away for a couple of years now. The decor hadn't changed, and the same dated furniture was dotted around the floor space. The pub *had* changed hands though, and Brian wondered if the new landlord was as accommodating as the old when it came to closing time and a locked door.

The pub door opened, and a familiar face peered in, looking nervously at the occupants. When he spotted Brian in the corner, he tentatively made his way over. Charlie Wells looked like a London sewer rat. A pointed nose, which seemed to twitch autonomously from the rest of his face, underlined by a pencil-thin moustache; he had an annoying habit of continually licking his lips. His hair was greased back tightly against his scalp; darting eyes took in everything and everyone around him.

'You look a bit nervous, Charlie. You been talking to people you shouldn't have?'

'You know how dangerous my profession can be, Mr Garvey, and it don't help when I gotta meet you in here; this place has bad memories for me.'

'Well, grassing up a few major villains wouldn't have been my choice of career, I grant you that. You wanna drink?'

'Yeah, a large brandy, to calm my nerves, wouldn't go amiss.' Garvey walked to the bar and smiled at the barmaid, who he'd never seen before; she looked like she'd been hit in the face with a shovel and incapable of physically reciprocating any similar gesture. He had to keep reminding himself he wasn't in Norfolk now – friendly banter wasn't the norm – as she looked at him with suspicion and grunted that she'd understood his order. He returned to the table with a brandy for Charlie and a double Scotch for himself.

'Staff ain't as friendly as they used to be in here. Well, Charlie, what've you got for me? It'd better be good, dragging me all this way – 'ave you forgotten I'm not in the job anymore?'

Wells took a large gulp of brandy and coughed as the fiery liquid hit the back of his throat too fast.

'Hope you're not expecting a large wad of cash. I don't have access to the informants' fund anymore, and I'm fucked if I'm paying you out of my own pocket.'

'This is a favour for you, Mr Garvey, old times' sake an' all,' he croaked. Wells looked around before moving closer to Garvey, who smiled at the cloak-and-dagger tactics.

'Who d' ya think you are – some Russian spy?'

Wells ignored the slight. 'I hear you're not in London anymore, Mr Garvey – moved out somewhere on the coast. Maybe, after what I heard, Moscow might not be a bad option for you?'

Garvey looked a little more interested and waited. He had no intention of telling Charlie Wells anything about his domestic situation, as he knew it would be all over London before his head hit the pillow that night.

'Have you seen your old partner since he retired?'

Garvey took a gulp of his whisky whilst maintaining eye contact but didn't comment. He'd purposely lost contact with Frankie Meeres when he'd moved; they'd lived in each other's pockets for so many years, he'd just wanted a clean break. There was no retirement party; he just cleared his desk and left.

'Did you know that you and your old mucker, Frankie Meeres, have got a price on your heads? Whoever you've upset in the past has decided to come looking. Got any ideas?'

'I don't have a notebook long enough to list people Frankie and I pissed off. What else you heard?'

Charlie again paused and looked around the pub at the ever-diminishing number of drinkers. This time, Brian Garvey kept his comments to himself.

'Apparently, one of you was banging a mailbag thief's wife for a while. He's out of nick and not happy.'

Garvey offered no confirmation either way. He knew it hadn't been him, and that Frankie had a reputation for putting it about, so why a price on both their heads? Having bought another drink, he left Wells to finish and walked the familiar route towards King's Cross station. At that moment, spring and summer time in Norfolk looked more attractive than ever. The cold, damp streets of his old stomping ground were empty, the area's inhabitants tucked up safely behind closed, locked doors as Brian Garvey looked over his shoulder for the first time in his life.

*

The strong smell of train diesel and the faint metallic sound of public information announcements infiltrated the interview room. Neville Sullivan sat nervously biting non-existent fingernails, two of which were now bleeding. He almost jumped out of his chair when the door opened – he was a bag of nerves.

'Hi! Sorry to keep you. Sam Hodge, I'm a detective with the British Transport Police – how're you doing, mate?'

'I'm alright thanks. Am I in any trouble?'

'No, I don't think so. The last time I looked, doing your job wasn't a capital offence.' Sullivan looked puzzled. 'What's your name?'

'Neville Sullivan. Most people call me Sully. I hate Neville. It's a bit old-fashioned. Have you found out what's in that sports bag yet?'

'Colleagues of mine are just examining it now, as we speak. Did you open the bag?'

'No. It's not my place. I just take 'em, put 'em in the store and give 'em back when people return for them – that's all.'

'Hey, Sully, relax. It wasn't an accusation just a question. That's what my job is all about – asking people questions to find out what happened – you OK with that?'

Sully nodded his head and used his teeth to pull a loose piece of skin from the base of a thumbnail.

Hodge's mobile rang. He mouthed an apology and answered.

It was McNally. 'Yes, boss... OK... understood... speak later.' Hodge made a couple of notes and returned his attention to his witness, who was now looking more restless. 'Can you remember the person who deposited that bag with you?'

'Yeah, I can. I started at twelve noon – I'm working a long day as we're short staffed, so it was about one-thirty some bloke came in; he was a bit younger than me, seventeen – eighteen maybe – mixed race Asian English. He 'ad a baseball cap on pulled down over his eyes, dark hair, I could see that when he walked out. I get a feel for people in this job. He seemed a bit cagey, you know. He asked for the bag to be stored until tomorrow morning. I told him how much that would be; he had a wad of £20 notes but paid me with a £50 note. Most people pay by card nowadays; we don't get too much cash anymore – I think he was just trying to be a bit flash. We got one of these machines for checking notes – ultraviolet or infrared, you know what I mean.' Hodge nodded. 'I checked it under there – seemed pucker, not that I really know what to look for.'

'From your recollection, can you remember taking any other £50 notes today?'

'No, as I said, it's pretty rare, especially from a kid that age.' Hodge concealed a smile with a hand – Sully couldn't be much older himself.

'So that note will still be in the till?'

Sully thought about the question before answering. 'No, because the supervisor cashes the till up before the night duty comes in. She would leave a small float, so that bank note will probably be in the safe for banking in the morning.'

'Do you ever ask what's in the bags? You know, like they do when you post a parcel nowadays.'

'No, not really. We've got signs up on the wall – no drugs, explosives, offensive weapons etc. I usually bring the customer's attention to it. It's up to them if they read it or not...'

'What colour was the baseball cap?'

'Black. It had the white Nike tick on the front. Got one myself but in pale blue.'

'Anything else you can remember about this lad? Take yer time, Sully. Just relax, close your eyes for few seconds and run the whole incident through your mind.'

'He 'ad a London accent but didn't really say a lot, and I remember he was wearing gloves, which is no surprise as it was cold... oh and a blue puffer jacket... looked quite trendy and expensive. Other than that, I can't really help much more with description.'

*

The dark room lit up as the mobile buzzed on the bedside cabinet. Marie Relish looked at the time: 12.30am. She was loath to answer, the earlier call had really spooked her, until she remembered, through her sleepy haze, that that call had been on her landline. As her eyes adjusted to the light, she let out a sigh of relief at the caller's identity.

'Hey Marie, it's Marcia. Sorry to ring so late, you, OK?' Relish hesitated just long enough for Frost to latch on that all was not. 'What's up, mate? I know I've probably woken you up but us real cops work all hours, not nine to five like you analysts,' she joked.

'Yeah, I'm OK thanks, Marcia,' she lied. 'Bit of a weird time for a social call. Don't you *real cops* have homes to go to, husbands or wives to piss off?'

'That's what I like about you, your razor-sharp sense of humour. Listen, we've got a job on the go; McNally's asked for you to be on board and has cleared it with the Fraud Squad DI. We've got a briefing at 9am at Camden. You up for that? Only downer is Graves has survived another six months so will no doubt be drooling over your every move – I think he definitely fancies you.'

'Really...?'

'Hey, c'mon, Marie, I was joking. You know what a tosser he is, all gob and little between his legs – I would imagine, I should add. You sure you're alright, mate? Thought you'd jump at this chance.'

'Sure. I'm up for anything that'll get me off the fraud investigation; it's nearly finished anyway. See you in a few hours. Thanks for the call.' Relish put her phone back on the bedside cabinet and crossed her bedroom to the window. She again looked down at the empty street; sparkling ice had already covered vehicle windscreens; a car alarm sounded in the distance. Although standing next to a warm radiator, she shuddered as Stuart Graves' sneering face flashed through her mind.

EIGHT

THURSDAY MORNING

The black Mercedes ghosted onto the estate and parked across two parking bays. The huge figure of Maurice Stone unfolded from the driver's seat. The luxury vehicle stood incongruous with its nearby neighbours – a Ford Mondeo and a Nissan Micra – separated by the shell of a burnt-out Vauxhall Corsa. Maurice looked around as, even at this early hour, a few curtains twitched. He smiled to himself; his gold front teeth reflected the briefest flash of orange light from a nearby streetlamp.

He knew the car would be safe; everybody knew him in this part of London. He again checked the area before opening the offside rear door. His passenger got out. Maurice locked the car and followed the Butcher towards the cutting room; they had more work to do.

★

'Well, look who we have here. *Detective* Constable Jim Wakefield. Where did you get that suit, an army surplus store?' The rest of the team produced a ripple of laughter, just glad that Graves' venom was being spat at somebody else.

'Piss off, Stuart. At least I haven't worn my pyjamas to work; stripes don't suit you – looks like you've put a bit of weight on.' Wakefield's retort was met with genuine laughter this time. He knew Graves would come back at him soon enough, but now he'd equalised and then gone two-one up.

Sam Hodge was busy photocopying the statements he and Frost had taken in the early hours, stifling a yawn as he listened to the copies monotonously spew out.

'That's another tree wasted,' he mumbled to himself. Even though he was one of the youngest on the team, at the tender age of twenty-four, he struggled with very late nights followed by very early starts. He heard the banter in the briefing room, in particular Stuart Graves' opinionated view of the world, but for once he took no interest; he had other things on his mind.

A soft round of applause and a couple of wolf whistles greeted Ryan McNally's entrance into the room, quickly silenced when he was followed by Detective Superintendent Nigel Plummer. It was Plummer who spoke first.

'OK, another day and another inquiry. I would just like to officially welcome back to the fold Ryan McNally. As you will know, he was suspended following the successful investigation into the serial killer Michael Brewster, whose trial is set for three weeks' time at the Old Bailey, on a spurious allegation of assault, which I never doubted his innocence of.' A few glances around the room between colleagues questioned the last statement, but nobody was going to raise their heads above the parapet – not even Graves. 'Over to you, Detective Inspector.'

'Well, it's good to be back. I've missed most of you…' McNally let the rumble of laughter die down before continuing. '…But we've certainly hit the ground running. Firstly, my congratulations to Jim Wakefield on being made up to Detective Constable during my absence, and welcome to the newest member of the team, DS Linda Doyle, whom I've been trying to entice onto our team for a while now.'

'Of course you have, guv – *entice* – that's a new word for it.'

McNally ignored the anticipated remark from Graves; Linda Doyle wasn't as charitable, giving him a look that could kill.

'As you will all know by now, I and a couple of the team were called out to Liverpool Street station late last night. The initial call came in from uniformed officers, who suspected some human remains had been discovered in a sports bag deposited at the left luggage facility on platform ten. The area was sealed off. Stuart and I accompanied SOCO Sally Cook to examine the bag.' McNally looked over at Ray Blendell and nodded; an image flashed up on the screen. 'This is what we found. A human arm, severed just below the elbow, covered in blood, with the middle finger missing.' McNally nodded again. 'This gold-coloured band was found on the ring finger, the date the 16th of April 1992 inscribed on the inside. The bag and its contents were recovered from the scene by SOCO and transferred to a local mortuary for a post-mortem examination later this morning, which Stuart and I will attend. OK, Sam, Marcia.'

Frost looked at Hodge and indicated that he should go first. 'I interviewed a young lad called Neville Sullivan, a nice lad, liked to be called Sully...'

'Wouldn't you if your first name was Neville?' Graves added.

'DC Graves, my middle name is Neville.' Graves looked at Plummer, turning a light shade of red.

'Sorry, boss... you know what I mean... it's a bit of a...' Graves was unable to stop himself. '...You know... nerdish name, isn't it?'

'Will somebody pass DC Graves a shovel so that he can dig himself a little deeper,' Ray Blendell said.

'OK! Let's get on with this.' McNally was starting to get wound up with Graves already. 'Sam, carry on.'

'To be honest, he wasn't the sharpest tool in the box, and he was pretty shaken up. He remembers the customer coming into the facility and gives a limited description, but he did remember he paid with a £50 note. We managed to retrieve that note from the safe. It's with Sally for DNA and prints. He had gloves on, but that's not to say he hadn't previously handled the note without them. The CCTV doesn't tell us a great deal.' This time Marie Relish did the honours. The detectives watched a three-minute segment showing the suspect entering the left luggage, reading a prohibited items list, handing over the note and receiving change before turning and leaving.

'He always keeps his head down with the baseball cap pulled low over his eyes. Sully thought he had a London accent, but for some reason he thought I was Welsh, so not sure how reliable he is.'

Frost jumped in. 'The supervisor, a lady called Gayani Bandara, can't really add anything. She was called over to the bag by Sullivan, decided caution was the best option, told him to leave it where it was and called the police. She didn't see our suspect.'

'OK. You and Sam get back to Liverpool Street this morning. See if you can pick our man up on the station's CCTV. We should be able to discover how he entered the station, if he was with anybody and how he left.

'Jim, team up with Marie and liaise with the Missing Persons Bureau at Scotland Yard and start a dialogue with them.' Wakefield and Relish exchanged the briefest of smiles. 'We know our victim is white, male and married; he could be at least fifty years old if he was married in 1992. It's not a lot to go on. We should have more after the post-mortem, and I'll update you when I can. When you've done that, I want you to concentrate on our suspect. See if we can enhance any images Marcia and Sam retrieve, look for any tattoos, scars, piercings, anything that could give us a clue to identification.

'Linda, I want you to speak to Sally Cook. Get some images of the sports bag and start some enquiries re origin – who produces it and where it can be bought – and make sure the bag has been searched thoroughly. OK! Let's get our heads together again at five o'clock.'

The team dispersed into huddles as the volume grew. Graves brushed past Marie Relish, who theatrically brushed her sleeve in distaste.

'You should be so lucky. I'm a bit more choosey than that. You need to get yourself a man in your life.'

'How d' ya know I haven't, you been spying on me?' Relish asked with a bravado that disguised genuine fear.

'Well, come on, have a look in the mirror.' Graves laughed and walked away, feeling pleased with himself. Relish felt a hand on her shoulder, which startled her.

'Hey, Marie, you're a bit jumpy.' She looked up to see Ray Blendell, the office manager. 'Don't let that arsehole get under your skin. It's not just you. He makes it his ambition for the day to annoy as many people as possible. I know the boss is getting to the end of his patience with him. Any more problems, let me know, and I'll deal with him. OK?' Relish nodded. She cheered up as Jim Wakefield approached her with a steaming cup of coffee. She glanced over at Graves as he sat down at his desk; she shuddered as he held her stare.

*

Although the early morning frost had kept the outside temperature below freezing, the air conditioning units in the cutting room had maintained a steady five degrees centigrade. The naked corpse – minus its left arm below the elbow – lay on the table. The skin was now a pale colour as the remaining blood had sunk to its lowest point after the heart had ceased pumping it around miles of veins and blood vessels.

The Butcher waited patiently as Maurice Stone removed the straps that had secured the victim during his pointless struggle to survive, followed by the bloodied gag from his mouth; the jaw had locked wide open, reminding the Butcher of Edvard Munch's *The Scream*. Interestingly, the victim had managed to bite his own

41

tongue in two through the material. The Butcher was assisted into a protective gown and wriggled fingers into nylon gloves. Stone looked at his boss with anticipation and grinned as the Butcher pointed to the bow saw; he delicately placed the implement into the Butcher's hand.

NINE

THURSDAY MORNING

Home Office Pathologist, Doctor Felix Lowther, walked into the examination room at the City of London mortuary at exactly 11am, dressed smartly in a dark suit, white shirt and multicoloured bow tie.

'Good morning, gentlemen, I'll just get gowned up and we'll start. Have you found the rest of the body yet?'

'No, sir,' McNally answered through his face mask.

'I'm sure it will turn up sooner rather than later,' Lowther added before disappearing into a small changing area off the main examination room.

Graves whispered into McNally's ear, 'Does he remind you of anybody?'

'Can't say he does. Is it anybody we know?'

'Did'ya ever watch *The Sopranos* on TV, guv?'

'No, I don't watch any of that American bollocks.'

'Really? I do.'

'Why doesn't that surprise me?' McNally whispered to himself.

'Tony Soprano was the name of the character who led the New Jersey Mafia; I can't remember the actor's name, James Gando…

something or other, great actor – dead now though. Honestly, he's a ringer for Dr Lowther, although I could never imagine Tony Soprano wearing a gaudy bow tie like our man or, on the other hand, our man being involved in mass murder, extortion or drug-running.'

'OK, gentlemen,' Lowther glanced at the wall clock, 'this shouldn't take us too long.' The mortuary assistant wheeled in a trolley; the single limb, looking a little lonely, swayed from side to side with the motion of the trolley, as if waving a greeting to long-standing friends.

All the parties stood back as the photographer took images from every conceivable angle. Graves then stepped forward and opened a small wooden box containing some ink, a small roller and several small square-shaped pieces of card, onto which he transferred fingerprint impressions. He had the urge to shake the hand and introduce himself, but even he realised there was a time and place for everything. Lowther waited patiently, switched on a voice recorder and commenced his examination.

'I am examining the left lower arm of a yet unidentified Caucasian male. The middle finger has been neatly amputated.' Lowther bent over the limb, his nose almost making contact. 'The forearm has been, in my opinion, expertly disarticulated around the humeroulnar joint.'

'In plain English, please, sir,' McNally requested.

'The humeroulnar is simply the hinge pin that allows the lower arm to move independently of the upper arm. Whoever did this, Inspector, has, I would suggest, great knowledge of the anatomy of the human body and, without doubt, has carried out such surgery before. The implement used was probably a very sharp knife, proficiently employed, as there are no tool marks on the bone, which you would expect to see if such an implement as a saw or an axe had been used.'

'It may be a stupid question, sir, but would this amputation prove fatal?'

'On the contrary, Inspector, it would depend greatly on what happened after the amputation. But I would suspect the amputation would have occurred whilst the person was still alive, and possibly conscious, due to the amount of blood staining on the forearm and hand, as the heart would have still been pumping. So, I would suggest, what with the missing finger, this was some sort of punishment and, if I were you, I would start to look for the rest of the remains. As far as the perpetrator is concerned, I could give you a list, but I'm sure you could summon such an inventory yourself. I'll start you off: surgeon, vet or even a butcher, would be my guess.'

'What's interesting is no attempts have been made to hinder identification. The fingerprints have not been erased in any fashion, together with the wedding ring, recording the date of the marriage,' McNally commented. 'Why the middle finger? It must signify something.'

'Ah… Inspector, you're the detective, not me.'

*

DS Linda Doyle watched as Sally Cook slit the top of the property bag with a scalpel, carefully removed the sports bag and placed it on a worktop covered by a sterile sheet.

'You worked with McNally before, dude?'

'Yeah, I was seconded onto a major investigation he was running in the north-west a few years back, before he got his promotion down here. He was a DS then and I was a DC. We got on alright.'

Cook looked at Doyle and raised an inquisitive eyebrow.

'No, Sally, nothing like that. He's a married man.'

'Yeah right, as if that makes any difference. I've never known such a bunch of shaggers than the British Old Bill.'

'Well, between me and you, it's not that I didn't want to, but he's a real family man.'

'You mean boring.'

'Principled, shall we say. Anyway, this was years ago. Since then, I've been married, had a child and got divorced.'

'Boring.' Cook feigned a yawn.

'You like him though, don't you?' Doyle asked.

'Only worked with him once, before he got suspended. He makes a decision and sticks by it but also listens to his troops, which is a rarity nowadays; most bosses can't decide what hand they're going to wipe their arses with – yeah, a good egg.'

'You have a way with words.' Doyle smiled.

'I say as I find, dude. I might upset a few people, but hey-ho!' Cook refocused on the bag. 'There are a couple of inner pockets that appear to be empty.' She carefully turned the bag upside down and gave it a shake. 'The good news is this bag wasn't purchased for this particular reason; all this dirt means it was used before so improves our chances of finding something useful.' Cook took a pair of pincers and moved particles of dirt and dust around. 'There you go.' She raised the pincers towards the light. Doyle strained to see what Cook had discovered. 'Bingo!' Cook exclaimed.

TEN

THURSDAY AFTERNOON

Jasmine Lee was sure she had drawn the sitting room curtains before she'd left the house that morning. But she'd been late leaving for work and nearly missed her usual bus so probably forgot. She inserted the front door key and turned it clockwise. It was yesterday morning she'd drawn the curtains; she convinced herself; the days of the week seemed to merge into one. She threw her coat on the bannister and headed for the kitchen.

'Hello, Jas. Long time, no see.'

Jasmine jumped and screamed as she turned and saw her husband Eddie Lee sitting at the dining room table with his feet resting on a chair.

'What you doing 'ere, Eddie? When did you get out? You could've given me some warning.'

'Well, it's nice to see you as well, Jas.' Lee looked around. 'You've done so much with the place, must've cost you a few quid.'

'Just a few splashes of paint here and there, that's all. I weren't going to wait ten years for you to do it, was I?'

'Where'd ya get the money to do that?'

'I've been working.'

Lee launched himself from the chair and pinned his wife to the wall by the throat. 'You're a lying bitch! You've been shagging one of the coppers who put me away.'

'Honest, Eddie, I ain't. Look around the place – it's just me – nobody else. I got a secretarial job at a solicitors in Peckham.' She was gasping for air.

'Which one of them was it?' Lee tightened his grip until his wife's face turned tomato red, before releasing the pressure to allow her to answer. She took in lungfuls of air and blurted out a name. Lee let her fall to the floor, her head making a sickening thud as it made contact with the linoleum surface, before kicking her in the stomach and leaving the house for the last time.

*

Jed Jennings sat at his kitchen table and opened the cover of a scrapbook. Sophie's smile shone from the most recent school photograph, taken only months before her death. Jennings turned a few more pages; most were adorned with newspaper cuttings reporting the incident that had robbed him of his daughter, the subsequent trial and the acquittal of her killer. He looked at the face of the detective who'd taken his girl's life, smiling as he left the court building, looking as if he'd just visited the cinema to watch the latest blockbuster, not having stood trial for causing death by dangerous driving. Jennings hated the fact that this man would've resumed his life, his career, as if nothing had happened. He picked up a kitchen knife and thrust it through the image of the detective's face so hard it pierced the tabletop. The hate-filled trance was broken by the shrill ring of his mobile. Jennings grinned as he recognised the caller's number. 'Hello, Eddie, you out at last.'

*

Frost and Hodge sat side by side in the video-viewing room at Camden. They could hear the usual pre-briefing raucous building in the incident room just down the corridor; a mixture of information sharing coupled with banter and piss-taking.

'You OK, Sam? You've been quiet all day.'

'I'm fine, sarge, just a few problems outside of this place – you know – private stuff. My whole world doesn't revolve around work, you know,' he answered a little sharper than he'd intended, which he regretted instantly – Frost had become a reliable, likeable colleague as well as a good friend; she wasn't being nosey, just concerned.

'Sure, I get the hint – keep my nose out.' Frost looked at Hodge's reflection on the TV screen and gave him a few seconds' silence to see if he wanted to talk before continuing. 'Well, you know I'm here if you need to offload – OK?'

Hodge nodded and changed the subject. 'There he is – our man in the baseball cap.' Hodge slowed the tape and they both watched their suspect moving across the main concourse at Liverpool Street station. He stood out a mile, head down, walking fast like an arrow towards the entrance to the Metropolitan and Circle line platforms. Hodge uploaded the footage from the London Underground cameras.

'OK. It'd take him less than a minute to enter the platforms unless he diverts down onto the Central line; let's concentrate on the Met and Circle line platforms first,' said Frost.

'There he is walking eastwards along the eastbound platform. C'mon, look up and give us a smile,' Hodge urged, 'just a little glance. Go on, you know you want to.' They watched as their suspect sat down on a platform bench, both detectives frustrated they were not viewing live with the capability to zoom in and out on his facial features.

'It's definitely him,' offered Frost as she ran her gaze over the statement Hodge had taken from the witness Sully. ''bout the right age, blue puffer jacket and dark baseball cap with the white tick on the front.'

Marie Relish popped her head round the door. 'Briefing's starting in a couple of minutes, you two.'

'Thanks, Marie, won't be long. Tell the boss we've just found our suspect on the CCTV,' Frost replied.

'Any chance of a chat after the briefing, Marcia?'

Frost took her eyes away from the screen, sensing a little emotion in her friend's voice, but she'd gone back to the incident room.

'OK. A train's just about to come in. According to the destination board, it's going to Barking. Our man is on his feet; c'mon, have a little look up, mate. Yes, there; did you see him? He couldn't resist it.' Hodge took the footage back thirty seconds; his finger hovered over the pause button. He stopped the footage just as the suspect got to his feet, nudged forward frame by frame until he got the image he needed and pressed print.

'Got yer,' Frost whispered.

*

The black cab nudged slowly along Victoria Street towards Victoria station. Isaac Levy glanced in his rear-view mirror at his latest fare. The only thing about cabbing Isaac still enjoyed, after nearly forty-five years, was meeting and talking to people. He'd had the rich and famous in the back, some friendlier than others. It was the 'don't you know who I am' brigade that wound him up the most – pretentious bastards; all they do is learn a few lines, dress up as somebody else and perform – some better than others. It's not like they're out there saving lives like doctors, nurses and firemen – the true heroes in Isaac's eyes. Some of them are nice enough and manage to hold a conversation about a subject other than themselves for as long as five minutes – if you're lucky. The 'celebrities' – God he hated that word – rarely asked him about his life; they just weren't interested in a sixty-something cab driver, even though he had more life experience than most of them.

He glanced at his watch – it was pushing 5.30pm – and cursed himself for taking this last job. He was an early bird – up with the sparrows – he enjoyed London at that time of the morning, and he nearly always picked up a fare early on travelling into the City from Gants Hill, where he had lived, with his family, since he was a young child. How that area had changed over the years! Twenty years ago, you would have seen a black cab parked on the driveway of every other house. It was the largest community of black cab drivers in London, mainly because the area had an established Jewish community. Now it was all Asians, nice people but mostly professionals – dentists, lawyers, doctors and the like – and kept themselves to themselves. The elderly Jewish population had slowly moved further out into Essex, as Jewish-run businesses disappeared from the high street, to be replaced by halal butchers, grocers and restaurants, which offered food from every conceivable part of the world.

He'd been on his way home, heading east along Commercial Road, when he got flagged down. It'd been a slow day, and he was lucky if he had £100 in his pocket. He decided to stop rather than ignore the young man with his outstretched hand, a look of desperation on his face, carrying a heavy Sainsbury's carrier bag. He thought it was probably a local job – a tenner in his pocket and home by six. Any hope of a local job evaporated when asked by the young man for Victoria station. He couldn't turn down the fare as he'd stopped, turned on his meter and nodded his assent; he cursed himself under his breath as the male got into the back of his cab.

He'd tried to break the silence with the usual topics of conversation: weather, football, cost of living, even a joke about a ham sandwich going into a bar and ordering a drink, only to be told that they didn't serve food, but got no reaction other than a grunt or the occasional 'yes' or 'no'. He didn't seem interested in the chaos the current Mayor of London was causing with his anti-black cab – pro-cyclist – policies making main routes such as

Bank Junction inaccessible to his trade. Even the current price of diesel didn't evoke any response from his passenger, so Isaac gave up. He turned the intercom off, shut the adjoining window in protest – his mood was not improving – and mumbled to himself, 'Fuck you, you antisocial twat. God help us – with the future of this country in your hands, I might as well emigrate to Australia.'

Isaac pulled the cab into Victoria station at just after 6.30pm; it'd taken him the best part of twenty-five minutes to travel down Victoria Street, and it had started to rain heavily. He wasn't surprised to see the pickup rank virtually empty of cabs – many people stumped up for a cab when it was wet – cabbies prayed for rain. He was being waved over by a railway employee marshalling the long queue of people before he'd even set his passenger down. The clock read £21.50; he thought he might get £25 if he was lucky so was surprised to be given two crisp £20 notes, which he quickly ran his UV light over. He went to give change but saw the passenger divert away from his cab and the entrance to the station and jump on a bus that was just about to depart. Before he could get his head round such strange behaviour, and before he could turn his 'for hire' light off, he was hailed to the front of the waiting queue. He prayed for a fare east and smiled at a young couple.

'Tower Bridge Hotel, please.' Levy set his meter and was about to pull away into Buckingham Palace Road when an urgent tap on his window caused him to stop and turn the intercom on.

'Hey, cabbie! Somebody's left a bag in the back here – it's pretty heavy.'

ELEVEN

THURSDAY EVENING

Ryan McNally opened the briefing with a summary of the earlier post-mortem. 'The pathologist believes the arm was removed while our victim was still alive…'

'Is that the technical term, boss?' Graves smiled and, for once, the rest of the team shared his wit.

'OK, Professor Graves, maybe you could avail us all of your deep knowledge of the world of pathology,' replied McNally.

'Yeah, c'mon, Stuart, give us all the benefit of your wisdom,' said Ray Blendell, egged on by the rest of team, who were enjoying Graves' discomfort.

Graves raised both hands above his head in submission. 'I understand why you're using such simplistic language, guv.' He looked around at the sea of amused faces and indicated with his thumbs at those seated behind him. 'Obviously to give these numbskulls half a chance of understanding what you're talking about.' This was followed by playful jeers and several objects being thrown at the detective.

'Let's move on, shall we?' McNally used a tone that a teacher would employ when trying to retain control of a rowdy classroom. 'OK, any progress on identifying our victim, Marie, Jim?'

'We've been in contact with the UK Missing Persons Unit, but until we get more of a description than a white male and an approximate age, the list will be in the thousands,' said Marie Relish, 'and of course that also depends on our victim having been reported missing in the first place.'

'How about the date on the wedding ring, will that narrow it down?'

'Much the same, guv,' answered Wakefield. 'The number of men getting married on that particular day throughout the UK, presuming that's where he was married, is vast.'

'Sally, anything from the crime scene or the bag that the limb was found in?'

Sally Cook moved to the front of the room and passed a memory stick to Marie Relish, who inserted it into a laptop and displayed a series of slides on the main TV screen.

'I recovered the £50 note from the overnight safe, where it'd been placed by the duty manager, but it'll be difficult to develop anything useful from it in relation to fingerprints or DNA.'

'What about drugs?' asked Linda Doyle. 'I mean, we're all probably thinking this is some sort of revenge or punishment killing – if our man is dead, of course – a warning to somebody? If not, why hack a man's arm off while he's still alive? If that *is* the case, it's likely to involve drugs somewhere along the line, isn't it?' She looked round the rest of the room.

'The problem with doing a drugs test is, virtually every bank note in circulation in this country will come back as positive for class A drugs – in particular cocaine,' Cook replied. 'There was a study a few years back by some dude at the Forensic Science Service concluding that a new bank note is in circulation for about two weeks before it becomes contaminated with drugs, so it's not going to take the investigation any further. However, we may have struck lucky with the sports bag. Linda and I examined it. It's not new and has been used before. I found a couple of hairs under the hard base at the bottom of the bag. From the thickness of the hair, I would say it's probably animal rather than human, but the lab can give us a better idea.'

'CCTV, Marcia, Sam?'

'We've got our suspect on CCTV at Liverpool Street station crossing the concourse and heading down onto the underground.'

Frost handed out enlarged photocopies of the still Hodge had printed. 'It's early days yet. We've only just got this, but we *can* say he boarded an eastbound Metropolitan line train going towards Barking. I've requested downloads from all the stations between Liverpool Street and Barking to see if we can identify where he gets off. Also, for the on-board CCTV of the train he travelled on. I should get all that by tomorrow. Hopefully, he would've let his guard down during the rest of the journey, and we may get a better image than the one from the platform.'

'We've also identified the particular gate barrier he passed through at Liverpool Street,' said Hodge. 'He used some sort of pass; with a bit of luck, it was an Oyster card or a bank card. If it's registered to him, then we may get a name and address.'

'Have we got any CCTV of our suspect arriving at the left luggage office with the bag?'

'Not yet, sir. We've only viewed the coverage post-incident. That's next on our list.'

TWELVE

THURSDAY EVENING

McNally drove out of headquarters onto Camden Road and headed north up Kentish Town Road and onto Dartmouth Park.

'You sure this isn't taking you out of the way? I only live a five-minute walk from Archway station.'

'No, it's alright, Linda, I can get back onto the Archway Road and up to Finchley easy enough, but don't expect it every night.' McNally gave her a grin.

'Just haven't had time to get a car sorted out yet; the live-in nanny took priority over a set of wheels; the amount of money she's costing me doesn't leave a lot for a car. It's the next right – Magdala Avenue – where the pub is.'

'That looks a nice enough boozer. What's it like?'

'Not sure yet, I haven't tried it. By the time I get home every evening, spend some time with Alex and get him to bed, the last thing I feel like doing is going out for a drink when there's an open bottle of wine in the fridge. Dee, the nanny, goes in there with some mates of hers, so I think it's probably a younger generation pub rather than for an old fart like me – God, I'm forty at the end of this year.'

'So why did you make the move down here?'

'Well, I'm from London anyway, as you know, but south of the river – Tooting. I only moved up to Manchester when I met that tosser. What do they say? Never marry a copper. Of course, I didn't listen. The only good thing that came out of six years of hell was Alex. I needed a change – *we* needed a change – and much the same as you did, I followed the promotion. The money is better with the London weighting, but that soon gets swallowed up by the cost of living. I'm just up here on the left by the blue van.' McNally indicated and parked up outside a large townhouse split into flats.

'Has your son settled into a local school?'

'He seems settled. I've had a couple of problems – he's autistic; he can go into himself a bit at times and finds it hard to make friends.' Doyle glanced at her watch. 'How're your kids doing? They must be teenagers now.'

'Yeah, Ava was fifteen a couple of months ago and Max is seven in March. We had a few problems with Ava settling in – you know – she was at *that* age when we left Manchester. Had some friends she left behind. We found her at Euston one night trying to sneak on a train back to Manchester; another time she travelled up to the in-laws in North Norfolk.' McNally smiled but remembered what a trying time that'd been for the whole family, especially Kate. 'But she's a lot more settled now; in fact, I'm the coolest dad in her class.'

Linda glanced at him enquiringly. 'Go on.'

'If this ever gets out, your history.' McNally smiled. 'Her class were doing something on Victorian crime in London and my daughter talked me into going into the school dressed as Sherlock Holmes, with my warrant card and handcuffs, and investigating a crime scene the teacher had set up in the classroom – you know, a murder weapon and tomato ketchup on the floor etc… I arrested and handcuffed a few of her classmates, and now she's flavour of the month.'

'Oh, that's brilliant!' Doyle howled. 'Your secret is safe with me. Thanks for the lift, Sherlock. I gotta go. It's his bedtime in twenty minutes and I wanna see him for a bit. I'll see you tomorrow.' Doyle jumped out of the car and gave a half wave, still laughing, as she turned towards her door. McNally watched as she climbed several steps to the front door and gave him another wave before disappearing inside. He was about to pull away when his mobile rang out the familiar *Big Brother* theme tune programmed in by his daughter. Recognising the number, he turned the car back in the direction of Camden and answered.

*

Every time the door opened, Marie Relish glanced up nervously, expecting her worst enemy to walk in at any time.

'Marie, what is wrong with you? I've never seen you so edgy.' Frost took a gulp of white wine, sat back in her chair and waited for some response from her friend. She could see that she was juggling whether to tell all or just keep the problem deep inside; her drink remained untouched.

Frost liked the Lyttleton Arms; it was far enough away from Camden police headquarters to ensure they were unlikely to be disturbed and directly opposite Mornington Crescent tube station to allow quick access to the London Underground when it was home time.

Relish reached for her drink and turned the stem of the wine glass to and fro until a little spilled over onto her fingers, which she licked dry before looking at Frost.

'I'm being stalked, Marcia.' She blurted it out so fast she was unsure Frost had heard what she had said; she knew if Frost asked her to repeat it she would have discussed the weather instead. Relish steeled herself for her friend's reaction. If she laughed, she would stand up and walk out. Frost reached across the table and clasped her friend's hand tightly in her own.

Neither spoke for several seconds. It was Relish who broke the silence.

'I know you probably think I'm being paranoid, Marcia, but I'm sure I've been followed, and things have gone missing or been moved on my desk. I've also had a couple of phone calls during the night; the caller never speaks.'

'How long's this been happening?'

'A few weeks I suppose. It started when I was working for the Fraud Squad.'

'You got any idea who it might be? What about that control freak you used to go out with last year?' Relish was pleased that her friend immediately took her seriously – no hint of scepticism, just anger.

'We could both make a long list of the creeps we come across in this job, and they're just the coppers – both male and female. I just look at everyone with suspicion nowadays – I don't feel safe anymore. I've been thinking of moving on – you know – start again somewhere else.' She took a large gulp of wine that hit the back of her throat too quickly, making her cough.

'You're not going anywhere. We'll see this through together. Have you told anybody else?'

Relish shook her head.

'Look, why don't I get in touch with the criminal psychologist we used on the tube murders job – the profiler – Sara Hallam?'

'I don't know, Marcia. I know we both got on with her well, but that's another person who'll know.'

'I think we can trust her. She became more of a friend, didn't she? You know – girls stick together and all that. I had a conversation with her on the last job; it got round to stalking and how common it is – anybody can be a victim. It's mostly women, but also men, from all walks of life, and it's a crime nowadays. Anyhow, she can't be all bad – she hates Stuart Graves as much as we do – not that I'm saying it's Graves who is stalking you.'

Marie looked away as her eyes filled with tears.

'Marie, is it?'

Relish lifted her glass and sunk the remaining contents in one huge gulp.

Frost glanced with annoyance at her mobile screen that lit up the gloomy darkness of the pub's interior. She was about to reject the call but saw it was McNally. 'It's the boss, Marie, I'd better take it.'

*

Adrenalin rushed through McNally's veins as he reached speeds of sixty miles per hour in the bus lane travelling south on Finchley Road. Even with blue lights flashing through the front grill, headlights alternating at full beam and the siren blasting, you still got the idiots who never saw you, especially when he ducked back onto the main road to skirt around buses and taxis. Those that did see you were just as unpredictable in relation to their reactions – some just stopped dead, totally blocking your path; some tried to out-accelerate you; others just panicked.

He speed-dialled Frost and told her where to meet him. Even though he'd been in London only a few years, he knew his way around the capital well; he could see the route he needed to take in his mind's eye and went for it. If he was honest, this was the only part of being in uniform he missed – apart from the football violence.

He checked his watch; he would arrive at Victoria station within thirty-five minutes of receiving the call. As on-call senior detective for London, he had everything he needed for the initial stages of a criminal investigation in a bag in the boot of the car – a murder bag they called it – a bit dramatic and over the top, he thought; cops loved to tag everything with a name. The initial call from the information room at headquarters sounded like the second piece of the missing puzzle he and the team had been expecting.

Park Lane was clear; the traffic parted around Hyde Park Corner. He'd read somewhere that police vehicles were supposed to avoid activating sirens along Buckingham Palace Road in respect of the royal family, but didn't His Majesty reside at Balmoral or Sandringham at this time of year? McNally negotiated the Victoria one-way system and entered the front of Victoria station. A uniformed officer waved him towards a stationary black cab sealed off with blue crime scene tape. Buses and taxis continued moving through the busy area. McNally wasn't surprised; to shut off the whole of this area would cause chaos and have a knock-on effect throughout the capital for hours.

His arrival stirred interest from onlookers, who recorded his face on mobile devices; in a matter of minutes, his face would be beamed across the world on several social media channels. If he'd been watching this on the television, there would've been one of those warnings about flashing imagery. He briefly wondered what it must be like for those members of the film and TV world who are permanently under the spotlight.

One onlooker standing well back from the crime scene wasn't interested in recording the events; he just wanted visual confirmation that his instructions had been carried out to the letter. Satisfied, he smiled. The blue flashing lights of the emergency vehicles reflected off his gold teeth.

THIRTEEN

FRIDAY MORNING

t'd been a long night for half the team. McNally had supervised the removal of the body parts, found in the supermarket carrier bag in the rear of the taxi, to the City of London mortuary. He wanted the continuity of evidence that would be achieved by Dr Felix Lowther carrying out the post-mortem. The taxi, much to the annoyance of its driver, was seized and driven to Camden for a closer forensic examination by Sally Cook. McNally called in Frost, Hodge and Stuart Graves to assist in the initial enquiries and statement taking; he wanted the rest of the team fresh for the busy day ahead. He'd managed four hours' sleep stretched out on a makeshift bed in his office. Having showered and consumed something resembling a cooked breakfast, accompanied by a gallon of coffee, he was ready for the briefing.

'OK, let's quieten down.' McNally looked around the briefing room and, when assured he had everybody's attention, carried on. 'Sally, let's deal with last night's events.' The SOCO came to the front of the room.

'Hope you all enjoyed your breakfast; anybody a bit squeamish had better look away now. I can't stand the smell of vomit.' Having received a few expletives from the more experienced members of the team, Cook gave a cheeky grin and proceeded to load the first of several images onto the flat screen. 'This is a right foot and right arm of – subject to confirmation by Dr Lowther the Home Office pathologist – a male. These body parts were found inside an orange supermarket "bag for life" left on the back seat of a London black cab at Victoria station late last evening.' Cook let the information be absorbed through some of the early-morning brain fog displayed by several of the team.

'What's that on the upper arm – a tattoo?' Jim Wakefield asked between two gulps of coffee.

'Just coming to that, Jim, nice to see somebody's awake.' Cook moved onto the next slide, which displayed an enlarged image of the upper arm and shoulder. 'It's a tattoo of what looks like a rampant lion with the date the 22nd of May 2004 underneath.'

'Gotta be something to do with football,' Frost offered, 'what other numbskull would label themselves with something so crude?'

'You got any tattoos, Sarge?' Graves genuinely looked excited in anticipation of an answer. 'Well, at least any we could look at?'

Frost ignored the jibe; McNally looked furious.

'Chelsea Football Club has a lion featured on their club badge,' said Blendell, moving quickly on.

'No, it belongs to Millwall.' Everybody turned in surprise. 'Women do follow football as well you know, so don't give me that look,' Linda Doyle said. 'My dad's been a follower of Millwall Football Club for years and has the same tattoo and date as the one on the slide.' Doyle glanced briefly at Frost, who looked like she wanted the floor to open. 'Millwall got to the FA Cup final for the first time in their history on the 22nd of May 2004 at the Millennium Stadium, Cardiff,' Doyle continued. 'They were beaten three-nil by Manchester United, but it's still viewed by Millwall supporters, of that generation, as one of the greatest days in the club's history. The former ground was called "The Den", and when they moved, they renamed it the "New Den", you know after lions…' Doyle let her voice trail off as everybody in the room looked astonished. '…Our victim supported Millwall with a passion.'

'OK, Jim, you and Marie look at the football angle. From my experience, supporters of smaller, local clubs like Millwall tend to be local people, so let's concentrate on southeast London in relation to missing persons as well as the wedding ring and date. Stuart, have we got any results back from the dead man's fingerprints?'

'I chased it up this morning, guv. There's no hit on the fingerprint database; the DNA will take a bit longer, but I'm not hopeful. I've submitted DNA swabs from the arm and foot from last night to at least confirm either way that they match the DNA from the Liverpool Street scene.'

'Marcia, Sam, anything on CCTV or from our taxi driver?'

'Well, apart from being pretty pissed off that we took his cab, he was quite helpful,' Frost responded. 'I took a statement from him late last night. He was a little shaken – it's not every day you find an arm and a foot in the back of your cab—'

'No, they're more used to charging an arm and a leg,' Graves interrupted, initiating a wave of giggles around the room, which turned into a louder laugh when everybody realised McNally was joining in.

'He gives a pretty good description of the passenger,' Frost continued. 'I've made an appointment for him to compile an E-fit later this afternoon. He's got a dashcam, which shows the passenger hailing him down in East London, but it's not that clear. I've seized it and sent it over to the tech boys, hoping they may be able to enhance it.'

'Sam?'

'Yes, guv, we are sure, from the description given by the cabbie, that our man got on a route 390 bus – whether by design or the fact it was the nearest bus to the cab drop-off point. I've spoken to Transport for London. There were two 390s at the stand; one was late leaving, the other on time. Apparently, they both left together, so he could've been on either. I've got the CCTV downloads for both buses on their way to us – should have 'em by the end of this briefing.'

'Where does the bus go – do we know?' asked Wakefield.

Hodge looked at his mobile. 'Up Park Lane to Marble Arch, along Oxford Street, up Tottenham Court Road to Euston and King's Cross, then north to Camden and terminates at Archway. I think he just jumped on the first bus that would get him away; this bus wouldn't have taken him back east where he jumped in the cab, so he's probably jumped off midway.'

'OK, let's move on, anything else? Yes, Sam.'

'I've just got the information back from Transport for London about the gate the Liverpool Street suspect went through to get onto the tube after leaving the bag at the left luggage; he used an Oyster card. I'll liaise with Marie after this briefing and do some background checks – we should be able to identify the owner, as it was registered. I've also got the CCTV from the eastbound Metropolitan line train our suspect jumped on but haven't had time to view it yet.'

'Let's make tracing the owner of that Oyster card the number one priority. Do the checks, then Marcia and Sam take a couple of uniform and track this man down. That's all.'

*

Brian Garvey shivered as he sat on a hard, wooden, east-facing bench on Cromer Pier. His hands were warmed by a large Americano he'd purchased from the North Sea coffee shop on the promenade, one of very few open at that time of the morning. He watched the winter sun peeking over the horizon. The sea was as flat as a pancake and reflected the glistening sunlight. The blue sky was immense and cloudless. Seagulls – the size of small dogs – perched on the pier railings, closely watching him with cold, beady eyes, ready to swoop at the first sign of a tasty snack. Garvey had been unable to sleep and yawned loudly, bringing a smile and a friendly 'good morning' from a passing dog walker.

He'd travelled back from London the previous morning, troubled, following the meeting with Charlie Wells. Wells had always been reliable with his information in the past – one of the main reasons for the journey from Norfolk to London – he'd been intrigued by what information the little weasel had for him. He stretched the early morning stiffness out of his bones and concentrated on a small fishing boat cutting through the calm sea, probably heading back to shore laden with fish for local restaurants and cafes.

Garvey had been a regular visitor to the North Norfolk coast for several years and moved to the seaside town, with his wife June, after his retirement from the police service. They'd bought a small bungalow half a mile from the town centre. It was near enough to enjoy the sea but far enough from the thousands of holidaymakers who descended on the area during the summer months. Sadly, within six months, June had been diagnosed with pancreatic cancer; she passed away shortly after. Garvey had considered moving back to Essex, where his only daughter and two grandchildren lived, but the explosion in property prices in the south made this financially unworkable, and anyway, he'd made a new life for himself here – new friends and a relaxed routine, a million miles away from the hassle and stress of being a detective in Central London.

Garvey had retired from the police service nearly a year before his former partner. Meeres had rung him several times during that period, but Garvey, preoccupied with his wife's palliative care, ignored the calls. He didn't have the strength to explain what they were both going through, and when the end finally came, he struggled with the loss, the emptiness, until he came to a conscious decision to move forwards and try to make a life for himself in this beautiful county.

It'd been hard at first; he'd often break down when explaining to the grandchildren that Nanny wasn't there anymore. He chose his friends carefully and shied away from forming any relationships with the opposite sex; his friends tended to be couples, people he felt comfortable with. He'd decided when he retired that he'd shun any social media sites for retired police officers or any attempt to keep in contact with any former colleagues; he had just needed a complete break.

The late winter sun warmed his face as he closed his eyes and listened to the sound of gently undulating waves retreating through the shingle. His thoughts were disturbed by a high-pitched drilling coming from the roof of the nearby Hotel de Paris. He was never one for heights but watched with interest as workmen scaled the scaffolding laden with equipment. His thoughts returned to Charlie Wells and the possible price on his head – their heads! He stood up, discarded his coffee cup into a nearby bin and headed towards the exit from the pier.

He'd come to a decision late last night that he should attempt to contact Frank Meeres. He'd heard on the grapevine that his former partner had retired at the beginning of last year. He tried the phone number Meeres had contacted him on some time ago, during June's illness, but wasn't surprised to discover the number unobtainable as it'd been a job-issue mobile that Meeres would have handed back when retiring. He thought of people still in the job, who may know where Meeres was, but drew a blank. Why would he be a target for his former partner's sexual indiscretions? It was a question that ran through his mind time after time. He couldn't even pin down the thief Charlie Wells was referring to. Between them, they'd arrested scores of mailbag thieves. He narrowed it down to three or four who may've been released from prison in the last few weeks. He had to speak to somebody, but who could he contact? He had only one choice – he had to find Frankie Meeres, and fast.

As Garvey walked along the promenade, he took no notice of

two distant figures looking down at him from the car park of the old Victorian hotel.

*

The Ford Mondeo's satnav directed Marcia Frost around the busy Stratford one-way system onto The Grove, bearing right, passing Maryland station, and onto Forest Lane.

'You've hardly spoken a word for the past half an hour, Sam. You, OK?' Frost glanced sideways at her passenger, who mumbled an answer she couldn't understand. 'Bloody hell, Sam, either snap out of it or tell me what it's all about. You're starting to really piss me off.'

'It's personal…'

'We're all entitled to a personal life, Sam, as long as it doesn't affect your job and the team's morale. People have noticed you walking around with the long face; even McNally asked me what's wrong with you.' Hodge looked sharply at Frost, as if she'd smacked him round the face. The satnav instructed Frost to turn left onto Odessa Road in one hundred metres.

'D' ya remember Madalina…?' Hodge whispered, as if the whole world was listening into a secret he was about to reveal. '… You know, the girl we interviewed at St Paul's Cathedral last year during the Brewster investigation. She witnessed the murder at Mornington Crescent Underground station.'

'Yeah, of course I remember her, the pretty Romanian girl who made you blush every time you looked at her.' Frost turned left into Odessa Road and was then directed to turn right into Pevensey Road, where they arrived at their destination. She again glanced at Hodge. 'You didn't, did you…?'

'I've been seeing her for a while. Not since the conclusion of the investigation,' Hodge quickly added. 'I've been keeping her up to date with the progress in relation to trial dates etc. I know it's a bit unprofessional but…'

'Love knows no bounds, eh…?'

'Well, something like that.'

'So, what's with the long face? Have you told the girlfriend?'

'No, she couldn't deal with the long hours I was working so decided some nine-to-five tosser was a better future prospect than a worn-out detective she hardly ever saw so saved me the trouble of breaking it off by telling *me* to push off.'

'Oh, so Madalina was on the rebound – not a great basis for a loving relationship, Sam.'

'No, she wasn't. I think my girlfriend knew I'd lost interest in her and probably used the long hours thing to get out.'

'Blimey, Sam, that's a bit conceited. Maybe she genuinely found somebody more suited to her lifestyle than you.' Hodge just shrugged his shoulders, conceding the point. 'Just be careful, will you. You can't be seen using your position to get sexual favours from witnesses and victims of crime.'

'Bloody hell, Sarge, you know I'd never do anything like that. In fact, it was Madalina who asked me out. I'd never abuse my position in that way.'

'Yeah, I know, Sam. She isn't trying to use *you*?' Frost saw the look on her colleague's face and quickly retracted her comment. 'Sorry, Sam, but as your supervisor and as a friend I need to ask these questions – we've all been in love, you know, and rational thinking doesn't always come to the fore. All I'm saying is, just be careful – OK?'

Hodge nodded and looked out of the window.

Frost found a spot to park fifty yards from the address they were interested in. She could see the Transport Police marked vehicle further down the road and gave them a quick flash of her headlights. They would have travelled the short distance from their police station in West Ham so had probably been there for a good half an hour and the occupants, a male and female, looked suitably bored.

'So, what's the problem? You hardly look like you're in love.'

'From what I can gather – and to be truthful, she gets a bit emotional and evasive when the subject comes up – her visa to work in the UK is about to run out and, post-Brexit, she's worried she'll have to return to Romania.'

'OK, Sam, look, I've got a friend who works in the Home Office. When we get back later, I'll give her a ring and see what the score is, alright? I'm not saying she will do anything to help extend Madalina's visa – it's not worth her job – but she can at least give you both some advice in relation to the current policy.'

Hodge nodded and looked a little relieved that he'd shared the problem and maybe identified a possible solution.

'Let's concentrate on the job at hand. The local election voter's check on the registered owner of the Oyster card used at Liverpool Street comes back to a Tim Vickers, who lives in Pevensey Road.' Frost glanced over her shoulder to the house they had just passed. 'I'll go and have a word with the uniformed officers and ask 'em to just move up to the address as we knock on the door. If it's all OK, we can stand them down.' Hodge nodded.

The property was mid-terraced with no access to the back of the house. It was in a shabby state. The pointing between the bricks was crumbling and the red paint on the door was peeling, revealing its original colour of pale blue. The other houses in the terrace were well maintained; Vickers' – in comparison with its neighbours – had the appearance of a decaying front tooth.

One of the uniformed officers joined them and Hodge knocked on the front door. Frost looked at the image they'd lifted from the eastbound Metropolitan line at Liverpool Street and shared it with her uniformed colleague. Hodge knocked again with more authority.

'Police, open the door, Mr Vickers,' Hodge shouted through the letter box.

'I've just seen a curtain move in an upstairs room,' commented the second officer, who'd stayed back on the pavement.

Hodge took a step back from the door as he heard the creaking of stairs and a security chain sliding out of its metal casing. The door was answered by a white male, with short blond hair, in his forties. He was dressed in a thin woollen cardigan drawn across him tightly in a defensive mode, which covered a white T-shirt tucked into the bottom half of a pair of striped pyjama bottoms. His feet were bare and bony. It was obvious to Frost, Hodge and the uniformed officer that this wasn't the same man in the video still. All three glanced at the image to confirm the person standing in front of them was not their man.

'Can I help you, officers?'

'Are you Tim Vickers?' Hodge asked. Vickers, who was moving his weight from one foot to another as if preparing to run, nodded nervously. 'Can we come in and have a chat? We won't take up much of your time.'

Vickers looked behind him – not because anybody else was present in the house but more due to the state of the interior. 'Yeah, sure, but I haven't tidied up for a while,' he said tentatively, as if that may change their minds and send them on their way. 'I've not been that well recently.'

Frost thanked the uniformed officer, who told her they'd hang around for a couple of minutes just in case they were needed. Frost and Hodge followed Vickers into a front room, which was indeed untidy but relatively clean.

'At least there's no dog and cat shit,' Hodge whispered in Frost's ear, remembering the last time the two officers had been inside a house together. Frost smiled, happy that Hodge seemed to be returning to form after their little chat earlier. They cautiously sat down on a sofa Vickers directed them to but turned down the offer of tea or coffee. The interior of the room was relatively old-fashioned: ceramic ornaments – mostly of shire horses with leather reins – covered in dust stood in line on a dated marble-effect fireplace. Vickers noticed the officers taking in the contents of the room.

'Most of this stuff is my mother's. She died last year, and I haven't got round to clearing it all out. I was going to hire a big skip and dump the lot and then modernise the place, but I just haven't had the energy. I lost my job a few months ago and was diagnosed with diabetes shortly after that.' He rubbed his hands over his face to hide his embarrassment.

Frost got to the point. 'Mr Vickers, we are investigating a serious offence at Liverpool Street station on Wednesday of this week. Can you tell us where you were between, say, one and five o'clock?' Vickers moved uneasily in his chair and looked at his fingers, as if for an answer. He shook his head in a negative action before returning his gaze to the officers.

'I'm not sure... what do you mean a serious offence? I've never been in trouble with the police before... well, apart from a bit of weed, which I got a caution for when I was eighteen.'

'We're only talking about Wednesday – just two days ago, Mr Vickers. Have you no idea where you were or what you were doing?' Hodge asked.

'I only really go out for a bit of shopping and to get my medication, and that's normally in the morning, so I must've been here Wednesday afternoon. To be honest, one day blends into another. That's the problem when you haven't got any structure to your life – no job, no reason to get out of bed.'

Frost stood up and crossed the room and showed Vickers a copy of the video still. 'Do you know this man, Mr Vickers?' she asked.

Hodge looked closely at the man's reaction; he thought he picked up on some recognition whilst again shaking his head in a negative fashion.

Frost said, 'Have a closer look, because the man in the photograph was in possession of your Oyster card on that day at Liverpool Street railway station, having just deposited a bag containing human body parts at the left luggage facility. I'll ask you again if you know this man, and please think carefully before you answer.' Frost rejoined Hodge on the sofa and both detectives waited in silence as Vickers considered his options.

'Yeah, I recognise him, but I don't know his name. He lives in Forest Gate somewhere. He deals a few drugs in a local pub by Forest Gate railway station. I've got a bit of a habit, and I get my supply from him a couple of times a week. I contact him by mobile and normally meet him in the pub.'

'When did you last see him?' Hodge asked.

'I think it was last Monday or Tuesday evening; I can't remember, you know every day—'

'Blends into another,' Hodge finished the sentence. 'Why was he in possession of your Oyster card?'

'I met him to get my supply for the week and I was ten quid short; money has been tight for the last few weeks after losing my job. Mum left me a bit of cash, but it didn't last long. He wanted my gold signet ring as collateral; he said I'd get it back when I settled up next time, but you can never trust these people. I made out I couldn't get the ring off. He started to get impatient, and I was desperate for the drugs, so I offered him my Oyster card to make the payment up; I knew he travelled round by train delivering drugs, not sure he's even old enough to drive a car. I told him it had about thirty pounds' credit on it – I hadn't used it since I wasn't travelling into work. He took it and I got my drugs.'

'What's this guy's name and where do we find him?'

Vickers made eye contact with Frost for the first time. 'I don't know his name, but I've got the mobile number I used to get hold of him early this week, although he does change it every few weeks. The pub's called the Railway Tavern about a hundred yards from the station.'

FOURTEEN

FRIDAY AFTERNOON

The journey from London Bridge to South Bermondsey had taken Jim Wakefield less than five minutes. The walk from the station to Millwall Football Club's ground would – according to the map on his mobile – take no more than six or seven minutes. He'd considered just calling the club with his enquiry, but he had always found face-to-face contact the best way of getting information, and it would have been difficult to explain what he wanted over the phone. He had little to go on: a white male with an approximate age in relation to the marriage date on the ring; that he was probably a Millwall supporter, according to Linda Doyle; and… well, that was it.

The young detective wasn't a great football fan. In fact, this would be only the second time he'd visited a football ground in his life; he had vague memories of being dragged along to Leyton Orient's Brisbane Road ground by his father when aged about ten. All he could really remember about the day was a tasty hamburger and Dad having the hump on the way home because the O's had lost; probably why he never took him again. Wakefield was more of a rugby man – that's Rugby Union not League, which he had little knowledge of. He'd recently moved to a smart two-bedroomed flat in Holloway, to be nearer to work at Camden, which allowed him to take the thirty-minute drive to Barnet and watch Saracens.

He pulled the collar of his raincoat up and dipped his head into the strong wind, wishing now he had utilised one of the squad cars, and headed for the ground. He turned left into Zampa Road and the ground appeared in front of him. It was much bigger than he'd expected and quite resplendent in its blue and white colours against the grey drabness of the surrounding area. He located the ticket office and saw, from information displayed, that the first team were at home the following day. A few supporters were milling around the small window purchasing tickets.

Wakefield waited patiently in the queue before producing his warrant card at the only window open. The young girl examined his identification and couldn't hide her excitement that her mundane day may turn more interesting. The rain was getting heavier, and the wind whipped round the stadium, carrying with it the unpleasant aroma of a nearby recycling centre.

'Is there anybody that could help me with an urgent enquiry please?' It was quite difficult to hear what the member of staff was saying through the thick glass with the wind whistling its tune, but he understood from her body language that she was going to summon her supervisor. The queue behind him was getting longer and ever-more impatient; there were a few grunts of disapproval when they saw the young girl leave her seat, so he was quite relieved when a door opened, and he was waved inside. He was met by a smart-looking male, in his early forties, dressed in a white shirt and a Millwall club tie whose knot had slipped half an inch from the collar, possibly in protest at having to be worn in the first place. He was directed into an office and offered a seat. He could see his host's beaming face in a framed photograph on the desk, flanked by several men in football shirts in front of a large stand that Wakefield assumed to be within the ground.

'I'm Alan Jeong.' The man took a seat on the opposite side of the desk. 'I'm the ticketing supervisor for the club. Sorry, can I just have another look at your warrant card again? It's not a Met Police one, is it?' Wakefield passed his warrant card across the desk, impressed that Jeong took the time to look at the picture and compare it to the face that sat opposite him before nodding his satisfaction. 'Thank you, officer – you can't be too careful these days, can you. So, you are from British Transport Police?'

'Yes.' Wakefield nodded. 'I presume you have dealings with my colleagues on match days?'

'Not me personally, unless they're after a few complimentary tickets for a Christmas raffle, but the club's police liaison officers certainly do. But you're a detective, so I'm assuming your reason for a visit is a little more serious than crowd control?' Wakefield still hadn't got used to be being called 'detective', and a slight lack of self-confidence still stirred self-doubt as to his qualifications for being so. He knew McNally had stood in his corner, even when he was suspended, presenting a strong case to Detective Superintendent Plummer as to why he wanted him on his team. Wakefield was determined that he wouldn't let his DI down.

'Your surname – is it Asian?' Wakefield wondered if the Christian name of Alan was a substitute adopted for easier use.

'It's Korean. My father was from South Korea and my mother from Battersea…' Jeong left the sentence unfinished, as if the information he'd offered would answer, in his mind, the unnecessary query concerning the young detective. Wakefield picked up on Jeong's slight annoyance at the futility of his question, nodded and quickly moved on. He opened his leather document folder – a present from *his* parents when appointed a detective – and pulled out an action in relation to the club, the few details of their victim and a notepad.

'I'm trying to identify a male we believe is fifty to sixty years of age and a follower of your club.' Wakefield looked at Jeong embarrassingly, realising how ridiculous his last statement sounded, and grimaced as Jeong raised his arms in the air in exasperation.

'And…'

'That's it, I'm afraid – we don't have anything else apart from a tattoo with the date the 22nd of May 2004, which I believe is a significant date in your club's history – something to do with a Cup final?'

'Well… yes, that was the day we played in the FA Cup final at the Millennium Stadium in Cardiff – unfortunately we lost, but it's the nearest we've come to winning it.'

Wakefield withdrew a photocopy of the tattoo from his folder and passed it across the desk, glad to have something of substance to produce. 'Above the date is a lion – can you confirm that's part of your club's identity?'

'Again, yes.' Jeong opened a desk drawer and passed a match-day programme to the detective. 'As you can see that same rampant lion forms part of our club badge and appears frequently on club merchandise.'

'Look, Mr Jeang…'

'It's Jeong, but please just call me Alan.'

Wakefield nodded, turning a slight colour of tomato. 'I know we don't have a lot to go on here, but this is one of very few leads we have at the moment, and I'd appreciate it if you bore with me on this.'

'Sure, I'll do whatever I can to help.'

'Our thinking is a local club like Millwall will be followed, in the main, by local people…'

Jeong sat back in his chair and glanced out of his office window, which overlooked the lush green playing surface before answering. 'In theory, you're probably right. I mean, we don't have the pull of Manchester United or some of the bigger Premier League London clubs. Our fan base is from this part of London and spreading out into Kent – so geographically still a large area.'

'What is your average crowd for a home game?'

'It's about twelve thousand, depending on the visitors and how many fans they bring with them. If it's a Cup game, say with premiership opposition, it would be a full house – just over twenty-one thousand; a cold night with lower league opponents – less than ten thousand.'

Wakefield took notes, mumbling the figures under his breath as he recorded them. 'How many season ticket holders do you have?'

'About eight thousand or so – give or take. We sold out this year; we have a very loyal following.'

'Would your season ticket holders have been guaranteed a Cup final ticket in 2004?' Jeong placed his elbows on his desk, entwined his fingers and placed them under his chin.

'I wasn't employed by the club in 2004, but if we were to reach a Cup final this year, then yes, season ticket holders would have first claim on the available ticket allocation.'

Wakefield chewed the end of his pen. 'OK, sir. Please stay with me on this. Let's assume our victim is of a mature age and a life-long Millwall supporter, together with the tattoo, which *could* indicate he attended the final in 2004, would you think it likely that he would still be a season ticket holder?'

'Well… I suppose so – there are a lot of ifs and buts there, detective, it's twenty years or so ago – he could be dead.'

'Oh, if it's our man, he's dead, sir. I know I'm grabbing at straws…' Wakefield paused, thinking through his next question carefully so as not to sound like a complete idiot, '…but I believe you've a home game tomorrow and next Tuesday – is that correct?'

Jeong nodded, wondering where this was going.

'Would you be in a position to provide a list of any of those eight thousand season ticket holders who do not attend either game'

'That would be a bit of a task, to be honest,' he considered the question carefully, 'but both games are high profile. We are pushing towards the play-off places and are playing teams around us in this league so both games are going to be well attended, with most season ticket holders present, I would expect. Of course, I would need a data protection form from you before I would even consider your request. Don't you think a lot of pieces of the jigsaw need to come together for you to get a result out of this, Officer? I mean, we are assuming that your victim is a Millwall supporter – although I admit the tattoo and date you provided on that photograph would indicate so, but that he's also a current season ticket holder at the club.'

'That, Mr Jeong,' Wakefield stated confidently as he placed his papers back in his folder, 'is what detective work is all about.'

*

Jake Knox walked into Leman Street police station at 4.30pm. He'd been instructed by the civilian member of police staff on the front desk to take a seat. He waited nervously, chewing on almost non-existent fingernails. The reports on the lunchtime news had shocked him into action. He was a sensible lad and knew that the best course of action would be to volunteer information to the police rather than wait for his picture to appear all over social media and on the front of newspapers. When he'd been approached to deliver a bag to Victoria railway station, and been paid £100 for doing so, he'd asked no questions, even though the instructions on how to carry out the task caused him to suspect the contents of the bag were not going to be legal, probably drugs.

An officer, in plain clothes, ushered him into a dimly lit room that smelt of stale human. He presumed the officer to be a detective, and this was confirmed when he introduced himself. Jake explained why he'd attended the police station; he was offered a cup of tea and told to stay where he was.

The news reports had been vague, and he was still unsure what he'd carried in the bag and left in the black cab. A couple of different officers appeared at the room's window and peered in. He felt like a goldfish swimming round in a glass bowl at a local funfair. The second one informed him that detectives from British Transport Police were on their way to the police station to interview him. He started to doubt the wisdom of carrying out the task in the first place and then, secondly, to place his head above the parapet by turning himself in. He swallowed the remnants of his tea and waited.

*

The North Norfolk sky turned a deep red as the sun disappeared below the western horizon. Brian Garvey peered from behind his drawn living room curtains. He was looking for anything different – a car that didn't fit; a person he didn't recognise. Very few vehicles passed his house at the busiest time of the day, let alone now. A distinctive brown UPS delivery van stopped outside his door, but the driver scuttled off to his next-door neighbour before roaring away to the next delivery point.

He took a sip from a steaming cup of tea and kept watch. Only two other vehicles passed in the next twenty minutes. A black cab – probably a London cabbie on a winter break with his family– and a plumber's van, which Brian assumed had slowed down looking for the address of his next customer. A good plumber was like gold dust up here but, annoyingly, he didn't have a piece of paper handy to take down the number. He watched the van disappear, turning right at the bottom of his road. Two uniformed police officers on foot – a male and female – wandered past who, Brian thought, must have been lost or bored. *This is bloody ridiculous*; he thought to himself. *I'm getting paranoid; nobody knows I'm here.* He looked at the phone and decided. Within a few minutes, he'd packed enough clothes for a couple of days and was in his car driving south to Essex.

As Brian Garvey joined the southbound A140 two miles from his house, two men pulled up outside his home, having given the two police officers plenty of time to clear the area. They were frustrated to see the address in complete darkness and the occupier's vehicle gone. The passenger replaced the plastic cord ties and the hunting knife back under the seat. They'd come back later that night.

*

It had taken McNally and Doyle the best part of an hour to travel from Camden to Leman Street. Doyle suggested it would have been quicker to travel across North London via Highbury and Islington, down New North Road to the Old Street roundabout, through Moorgate and into the City, but McNally had decided to go through Central London. McNally ignored the 'I told you so' look he picked up behind half a smile creeping across Doyle's face as they walked through the front doors of the police station. McNally introduced them both and they were shown up to the CID office, where they were met by a smartly dressed detective who introduced himself as DS John Collingwood. They were offered tea and coffee and settled down on two chairs next to the detective's desk.

'I hope I'm not wasting your time on this, guv,' Collingwood said, addressing McNally. He turned several pages in an A4 hardback notebook on his desk. 'I'd literally only just booked on duty when I got a call from the front desk that a male had walked in confessing to murder. I went downstairs and the civilian on the front desk had got a bit overexcited; in fact, the young man had information regarding your investigation into an incident that happened at Victoria station last night. I contacted your headquarters, and they directed me to you. I haven't arrested him but asked him to wait in an interview room just off the custody suite. His name is Jake Knox. He lives about a mile from here. I've done a criminal records check on him. He's been cautioned for possession of cannabis the middle of last year but nothing before or since. He's a student at London Met University. That's about as far as I've got.'

'I appreciate you giving us a call,' McNally replied. 'We're investigating two incidents involving the discovery of body parts we believe are the same person. An arm and a foot were found on the back seat of a black cab last night. The cab driver picked up the fare on Commercial Road and took the man to Victoria station. What's the guy downstairs look like?'

Collingwood turned a page in his notes. 'He was born 2004 so twenty years of age, five feet nine tall, slim build and mousey brown hair.'

McNally and Doyle nodded simultaneously. 'That matches the description of the suspect in the black cab,' Doyle commented to McNally, who agreed.

'OK! What d' ya intend to do with him?' Collingwood asked.

'I'm not going to mess around with him,' McNally answered. 'I'll ask him a couple of cursory questions and, depending on his answers, arrest him on suspicion of murder and transfer him to our custody centre and take it from there.'

Collingwood nodded his approval, relieved that the problem was disappearing from his caseload.

'Linda, can you ring for transport to convey him to the custody suite, and then we'll go and have a quick chat. As soon as he admits to being the man in the black cab, we'll arrest him and get him transferred.' Doyle nodded. 'Then ring Ray Blendell and get the team in for a briefing at, say…' McNally looked at his wristwatch and made a few rough calculations, 'let's say six o'clock.'

Collingwood escorted the two detectives down to an interview room off the custody area. McNally asked his questions and arrested Jake Knox on suspicion of the murder of a person unknown. McNally and Doyle glanced at each other, knowing that, in all probability, this young man was not capable of knocking the skin off a rice pudding.

*

Terence Nunn waited patiently for his cellmate to give him the all-clear. On receiving a nod, he dialled the only number saved in the mobile's contacts list and waited. He thought back to the very first occasion he'd done time in the late '70s. Communication with the outside world was through an odd phone call or a letter, both vetted, and a whispered conversation during a visit, but he'd always managed to run the family business from whatever institution he'd found himself incarcerated in. Now it was much easier. Money bought as much influence inside as it did outside the walls of Pentonville Prison. Drugs, cigarettes, porn or mobiles were two a penny if you knew the right people and could pay the right price. The phone continued to ring as he was losing patience.

'Hello, is that you, darling?'

'Who else you expecting? Is everything going to plan?'

'You not been watching the news?'

'Yeah, of course, but I don't want this coming back on me; I'm out of here in less than twelve months; I don't want any loose ends – you understand, Haze?'

'Look. We've both waited a long time for this, and I've been careful the Old Bill will not trace anything back to us, so relax – I'll see you next week on visiting day.'

Nunn dropped the mobile to the cell floor and crushed it with his foot. He handed the pieces to his lookout and instructed him to get rid of it.

FIFTEEN

FRIDAY EVENING

The incident room buzzed like a beehive. The workers had returned with information, intelligence and evidence to push the enquiry forward. Marie Relish was adding the information gleaned from completed actions, submitted by detectives, onto the HOLMES 2 major enquiry system, and then on to several whiteboards dotted round the room. Sam Hodge whispered conspiratorially into a mobile in a quieter corner of the room. Marcia Frost attempted to stay awake as Stuart Graves regaled, to those of his colleagues who would listen, one of his many war stories. Jim Wakefield tried to explain the rules of Rugby Union scrummaging to Linda Doyle, who retorted with her interpretation of football's offside rule. Scene-of-Crime Officer Sally Cook discussed the investigation's forensic strategy with Office Manager Ray Blendell. They all felt the pressure building; they needed a breakthrough in the case before the expectations of the press, the public and senior officers progressed to yet another level. This tight-knit group rarely received pats on the back; it was a result-based business, involving long hours and dedication, often to the detriment of family and social lives, which most of the nation took for granted. Being a detective was not a nine-to-five job; rarely could the pressures it brought be left at work for the evening or the weekend – it was a dominating part of their life.

The start of the briefing had been delayed as McNally had returned from the custody suite in Central London to the Camden headquarters and was briefing Detective Superintendent Nigel Plummer. When McNally finally entered the incident room, he looked a little flushed and mumbled an apology for being delayed and something about petty politics. He was in no mood for any further delays and demanded the room's attention immediately.

'We have a male in custody, who Linda Doyle and I are confident is the suspect who left the carrier bag in the rear of the taxi at Victoria station and not some timewaster. He certainly fits the description from the cab driver and the CCTV images we have. He gave himself up at Leman Street Met Police station earlier today. I'll come back to where we are in relation to him at the end of the briefing, but first let's go round the room. Marcia, Sam, how did you get on with our suspect with the Oyster card?'

'After a little persuasion, Tim Vickers identified the man in the photo as a local drug dealer, whom he paid partly with the Oyster card for his last batch of drugs due to a lack of cash. Vickers has got one previous caution for possession of cannabis four years ago but nothing since.' Frost passed a picture of Vickers round to the rest of the team. 'As you can see, he certainly isn't our suspect at Liverpool Street. He doesn't know the dealer's name but says he's normally found in a pub adjacent to Forest Gate railway station, which he tends to use as his "office". Vickers supplied us with a mobile number. We've put through for an urgent subscribers check, but it's unlikely to be traceable apparently, he changes it frequently. Sam…'

'We dropped into Forest Gate nick and showed the CCTV images of our suspect round to a couple of local beat officers, and we got lucky.' Hodge handed another photograph round the room. 'This is Joey Dryden, last known address half a mile from

Forest Gate station – it's a good likeness to our man from Liverpool Street, and he's got previous for dealing drugs – even served time in a young offender's institute. We showed the photograph to Vickers, who confirmed it was his dealer and the man he paid in part with his Oyster card. We had a drive past the address – it's a bit of a shithole, possibly a former squat. The voters' register doesn't give us any clues, probably well out of date.'

'OK, Marcia, you, Sam and Stuart pay a visit early tomorrow morning. Take a couple of uniform.'

'Shall we get a warrant, guv?' Graves asked.

'No don't bother. If he's there, nick him and bring him to the custody suite after searching the place – if he's not, circulate him on PNC and inform the local nick we want him, and ask them to detain him on sight for conspiracy to murder. OK, who's next – Jim?'

'Yes, guv, I've been following up on the tattoo on the arm of our unidentified male. DS Doyle was a hundred per cent right – it's Millwall Football Club's emblem, and the date also ties in with the FA Cup final of 2004. Although the club was willing to help, it's a bit of a needle in a haystack. Even if we're certain that, say, he was a season ticket holder, without more info it would be impossible to identify him. I've asked that a list be compiled of any season ticket holder who doesn't attend the next two home games and supplied to us, to hopefully narrow down the names and compare to any other information we might get in – it's a shot in the dark but worth a try, I thought.' A few members of the team nodded in agreement. 'They weren't too keen to do that with GDPR rules, so we'd have to serve the relevant production order. But otherwise, it's a bit of a dead end at the moment.'

'Thanks, Jim, good work.' Wakefield looked pleased with himself; Graves just sneered. 'Any update on the forensics, Sally?'

'Quite a bit actually, dude. The hair found in the sports bag from Liverpool Street left luggage is animal, not human. Their best guess now is domestic pet – dog, cat…'

'...Guinea pig, hamster, rat, mouse – squeak, squeak pass the cheese...' added Graves.

Several others joined in. '...Alpaca, horse, donkey, Shetland pony...'

Back to Graves. '...Monkey, parrot – who the fuck knows?'

'A parrot, you twat, has feathers,' offered Ray Blendell. When the laughing subsided, Sally Cook carried on.

'I know it's not much, but they're doing other tests and of course we can't be sure the pet hair came from the owner of the bag or the owner of the arm and hand. More importantly, it looks like the left arm and hand from Liverpool Street and the right upper arm and right foot from Victoria are from the same body as we all – I'm sure – thought was obvious. The blood grouping is AB negative, which is a result as that group is the rarest in the UK. I'm still awaiting DNA confirmation. Dr Lowther stated that the same level of skill had been used to dismember these body parts from the main torso as with the first case. Regarding the foot, I've taken foot impressions from the sole and—'

'Can you really do that? Hodge interrupted.

'Of course you can, dude. It's called plantar evidence. Forensic science has advanced a bit, you know, fingerprints or tool marks left at a crime scene are a bit old hat now – still useful of course. There is a lot of research throughout the forensic world into the science of plantar evidence – the anatomy of the sole of the foot, for you dimwits. There were a couple of cases back in the 1950s and '60s of footprints securing convictions...'

'You making this up, Sally? It's not April Fool's Day for another few months – I mean, shoeprints, of course, but foot impressions – you're having a laugh.' Graves looked round the room for some support and he was pleased to see a few heads nodding.

'Where did you do your CID course, Stuart – Enid Blyton's Noddy Land Detective School with PC Plod as Chief Instructor?' Cook fired back. 'The first case was a break-in at a bakery in Scotland, where the intruder left a toeprint in flour and the jury accepted the evidence and he was found guilty of breaking and entering, as it was in those days. The following year, in a different case, another break-in at a different warehouse led to a second conviction. The offender had broken into the same warehouse on two previous occasions – the first time he got convicted on fingerprints. So, the second time he wore gloves but got convicted because of shoeprints, so the third time he wore gloves and took his shoes off but, unbeknown to him, he had a bloody great big hole in his sock and the police were able to match the partial footprint to the suspect on his arrest.'

'What a thick bastard,' shouted Jim Wakefield through the hesitant round of laughter – some unsure if he was referring to the offender or Graves.

'Lucky most criminals are idiots, or what chance would you lot have of catching them? Anyway, it's another way of putting our man at a crime scene in the future and aiding possible identification. We'll need to engage a forensic podiatrist – that's somebody who deals with feet, Stuart – if the occasion arises.'

'They might be able to extract that size ten permanently in Stuart's mouth,' offered Frost.

'In the meantime, the pathologist estimates that the victim has a shoe size of eight to nine,' Cook continued. 'Unfortunately, foot size doesn't always equate to a specific height. Somebody relatively short can have quite large feet and vice-versa…'

'You know what they say about people with big feet, Stuart? What size are yours – tens, maybe twelves?' Frost waggled her little finger at Graves. Graves reddened and mumbled something nasty under his breath. Frost was enjoying herself.

'But Dr Lowry has come up with a possible height for our man,' Cook continued. 'He has used human body ratios. For most people, their arm span is about equal to their height. Let me demonstrate. Marie – if you wouldn't mind.' Cook beckoned her over. 'Spread your arms out fully for me.' Relish did as she was asked and ignored Graves as he blew her a kiss. Cook measured her arm span, recorded the measurement on a piece of paper and nodded that she was satisfied before asking Relish to sit back down. 'OK, Marie, how tall *are* you?'

'Five feet seven,' she replied.

'OK – good. I measured your arm span at sixty-eight inches – five feet eight – so pretty accurate. On this basis, Dr Lowry measured the length of the victim's left lower arm and the right upper arm and calculated that our victim is approximately five feet ten inches tall. It gives us something more to work on.'

McNally got to his feet. 'So, what've we got on the victim so far?' The DI looked round the room. 'Ray, can you list this on a whiteboard please. Let me start it off – he is male, white.'

'Approximately five feet ten tall with a shoe size of about eight or nine,' Hodge added.

'Married in 1992, is a Millwall supporter so probably has links to the south-east area of London,' from Linda Doyle. She added, 'So we know he must have been at least sixteen in 1992 to get wed so must be at least forty-six years of age now, but let's assume that not many men get married at such an early age so probably age between fifty and sixty.'

McNally nodded. 'It's all conjecture, but it's the best we've got now and gives us something to work on. I don't think we're going to make progress until we ID our victim, so all efforts on doing so please. Linda and I will interview Jake Knox later this evening, but he is shit-scared so only time will tell if he'll be of any use. Let's have a one o'clock get-together tomorrow and see where we stand after we've spoken to him and any result we get from the drug dealer in Forest Gate.'

*

Marcia and Marie walked arm in arm down Camden High Street towards Mornington Crescent. The night air was freezing. They hugged closer for warmth.

'Did you see the way he looked at me, Marcia, when I was standing writing on the whiteboard during the meeting? He's just a misogynistic pig.'

Frost squeezed her friend's arm tighter as they entered the Lyttleton Arms and guided her to a table on which a distinguished redhead sat with her back to them. 'Look who's here,' she said with mock surprise.

'Hi, you two – long-time no see.'

A broad smile crossed Relish's face as she recognised Sara Hallam; they shared a hug before turning back to Frost – this was no accidental meeting, but she didn't care – it was great to see Hallam again.

Hallam thought it a good idea to get the drinks in while Frost explained. She'd enjoyed working with the two girls in her role as a forensic psychologist during the Michael Brewster murder inquiry last year and hoped the reason for the pre-planned meeting, following an earlier call from Frost, wouldn't sour the friendship she and Relish had formed during that investigation. Hallam returned to the table with the drinks and saw that Relish had been crying. She placed the drinks on the table and signalled for Relish to stand up before wrapping her arms round her and whispering in her ear, 'Everything is going to be OK, Marie. We'll get this bastard.'

Hallam listened carefully as Relish worked her way through the events of the last few weeks, with encouragement from Marcia Frost when she looked as if she may break down, occasionally interrupting to ask a question.

Hallam went into professional mode and summarised. 'So, you first noticed items were being moved around on your desk and some personal items – like the scarf – going missing. Then the feeling that you were being followed and, a couple of nights ago, a phone call.'

'It doesn't sound like a lot, does it, when you sum it up like that?' Relish smiled nervously, took a large gulp of wine and composed herself again. 'Also, I thought I saw a shadow outside in the street, but I'm fourteen floors up so I'm not sure; it could have been a cat or just my imagination.'

'Have you any ideas who it might be?'

'I'm not sure if it's *anybody*. Maybe I'm just being stupid and paranoid.'

'Marie, listen to me.' Hallam took her friend by the shoulders; her voice changed from one of friendship back to her professional role. 'Take any of the incidents you've mentioned on their own and perhaps we could write them off, but things being moved, missing personal property, phone calls late at night and your gut feeling cannot be ignored.' Hallam's voice softened. 'I'm not here to judge you. We're friends. I'm here to help in any way I can.' She ran her hands down the length of Relish's arms and squeezed her hands tightly. 'So, think, who are the likely suspects?'

'Well, Stuart Graves hates me for some reason.'

'That creep, you know he asked me out after the last case. I think he'd have run a mile if I'd said yes.' That at least made Relish smile. 'Anybody else?'

'There was a detective on the Fraud Squad a couple of years ago. We had a thing for a while, but it ended badly. I haven't seen him for ages, but he'd have been noticed by others in the incident room if he'd been poking round my desk.'

'Look, Marie. There is such a thing as the Stalking Risk Profile. It's not my area of expertise, but I've had dealings with various professionals in this field over the years. The SRP guides professionals in relation to categorising offenders/stalkers into several groups. The most common is the rejected stalker who is maybe seeking revenge on a former partner or, in some weird way, attempting to reconcile themselves with an ex-partner, so that could be your Fraud Squad detective or any other past boyfriend. You've also got the incompetent stalker, trying to lure an acquaintance or a stranger into some sort of short-term relationship, be it a simple date or a sexual liaison.' Hallam broke off as a couple walked past them and settled down at a table a few feet away. She continued but lowered her voice. 'The intimacy-seeking stalker believes they're already in a delusional, intense relationship with their victim, and then you have the resentful stalker, who believes they've been humiliated in some way by their victim and wants to settle the score by making the victim's life a living hell. The last group is the rarest, a predatory stalker. These are men who covertly collate information about their victim; they get off on watching their victim, following them, enjoying the sense of anticipation as to what they may discover and how they can use it in the future to frighten and intimidate. Perpetrators are usually male with a female victim, in whom they have developed a sexual interest, and their actions can ultimately be in preparation for a sexual assault. I'm afraid there is no easy answer to this. You and Marcia have just got to be observant and look for the signs. I would suggest it's highly unlikely to be somebody like Graves; if he's being openly hostile, like you say, although unpleasant, it's not typical behaviour in relation to a stalker; it's more likely to be somebody in the background, not necessarily on your team but, I would guess, probably somebody in the building, as they clearly have access to your desk.'

'Oh great, that could be any of maybe two hundred people, give or take.' Relish looked frightened and despondent.

Frost glanced worryingly at Hallam and then Relish, thinking maybe too much information had been imparted. 'Come on, Marie, you've got both of us on your side.' Frost attempted to console her friend and engender some sort of confidence. 'Look, why don't you come and stay with me for a few nights; it'll be a laugh. I've got a plentiful supply of wine, although my cooking leaves a lot to be desired. Bring a couple of changes of clothes and your toothbrush in with you tomorrow; you can sleep on my couch.'

Relish nodded and her face brightened up. The sense of relief that she didn't have to face this alone was palpable.

The trio finished their drinks and left together. Frost said her goodbyes and headed for Mornington Crescent tube station to catch a southbound Northern line to Stockwell. Hallam suggested that she and Relish share a black cab, as Kilburn was on her route home to Queen's Park. Hallam hailed a passing cab, and they climbed in; both started to giggle, falling back into the seat as the cab pulled away. Relish relaxed for the first time in a few days.

*

The man rubbed his hands together to get his circulation moving. He'd been surprised to see Relish and Frost meet up with Sara Hallam. He watched the black cab pass by from the darkness of an entrance to a disused furniture shop; he broke his cover and walked in the opposite direction towards Camden Town.

*

Frost entered the booking hall of Mornington Crescent station, glad to be out of the icy wind blowing from the north. She passed through the automatic gate and was about to enter the lift when her mobile rang. She hesitated and obstructed the lift doors, as she considered whether she should answer or wait half an hour until she arrived at Stockwell when she could reply to any message.

'When you're ready, lady,' one of two men shouted. 'I got a home to go to.' Frost stood back, allowing the lift doors to shut. She removed her mobile from her coat pocket and saw the caller was her mother. She was concerned at the lateness of the hour and answered immediately.

'Hi, Mum. What's up? It's a bit late.' She could tell straight away that there was a problem.

'Hi, darling, sorry to bother you, but it's your brother.'

'What? Has he been in an accident? Is he OK?' There was a pause on the line. 'Mum, what's wrong? Tell me.'

'Your father is fuming. He didn't want me to ring you.' Frost could hear her father in the background remonstrating with her mother.

'Mum, just tell me.'

'We got a knock on the door about an hour ago – it was your brother's best friend Benny. He's been arrested, Marcia. Your brother has been arrested for supplying drugs. He's being held at Brixton police station.'

SIXTEEN

FRIDAY NIGHT

He parked the car facing the block of residential flats in Glenfarg Road, Catford and killed the headlights. Brian Garvey remembered last visiting this address a few months after Frankie Meeres had been thrown out of the marital home in Bromley by a very pissed-off wife. Frankie had moved into the one-bedroomed flat on the second floor and Brian had helped him move some of the few belongings he possessed. Garvey had been saddened that his friend had so little – after years of marriage – that he could call his own, although he knew that Meeres' wandering eye had been to blame.

Garvey had driven from Norfolk to Essex to stay with his daughter, son-in-law and grandchildren for a few days. The journey had taken a bit longer than usual as he took the most indirect route he could think of and used his experience to employ anti-surveillance tactics to check if he was being followed. This included driving into service stations and then straight back out, circumnavigating roundabouts several times, stopping the car suddenly and changing direction until he was satisfied, he was in the clear. He'd dropped his bag off at his daughter's house, played with the grandchildren until their bedtime, driven round the M25, crossing the Queen Elizabeth Bridge, and then a convoluted route to Catford, arriving just after 11pm.

The second-floor flat was in darkness. The surrounding streets were quite busy as several local pubs started to spill out. Brian had to decide his next move– he was starting to attract attention from passers-by; it was that sort of area. He got out of the car, locked his door and crossed the road. The flats had a communal entrance – half glass, half PVC. He peered through into the hallway – the door opened under the slightest of pressure. An automatic light lit the hallway. Although the air was stale, the hall itself was neat and tidy, with an expensive-looking carpet, on which sat an oak table adorned with a vase of plastic daffodils. On the wall above the table were four key-operated letter boxes with the relevant flat number scribbled on with a permanent marker pen, each in a different handwriting. Brian wasn't sure of the flat number he was interested in but worked out that numbers one and two were on the ground floor, so the likely number of Meeres' flat was either three or four. He looked along the hallway and listened. Some reggae music thumped out from flat one and a television, with its volume turned up quite high – presumably to drown out the sound of Bob Marley – could be heard in flat two. He climbed a single flight of stairs. He remembered that Meeres' flat was to the left – number three. He was faced with a white PVC front door with a bronze knocker, no bell. He took a deep breath and knocked twice.

The reggae music was vibrating through the floor – he knocked again but this time a little more loudly; again, there was no answer. He returned to the ground floor and looked out onto the street. When satisfied nobody was about to walk past, he inserted the blade of a small penknife adjacent to the flimsy lock of flat three's letter box – it gave way easily. Several letters tumbled onto the floor. Garvey put on his driving gloves. He looked at each letter in turn: nothing extraordinary, just a couple of utility bills postmarked from the beginning of the week and some begging letters from local charities. Garvey smiled; his former colleague wasn't noted for his charitable work, and he knew these would be binned unopened. He removed a pen from his inside jacket pocket and scribbled on one of the utility bill envelopes. 'Frank, give me a ring when you can. Need to speak urgently, Brian', adding his mobile number. Garvey returned to the first floor and slipped the envelope under the door of flat three. He secured the letter box on the way out, eager to return to his car before it got vandalised.

★

McNally and DS Linda Doyle sat facing a tired and dishevelled Jake Knox, both familiar with the aroma that stuck to anybody who spent any length of time in a police cell. A duty solicitor completed the foursome. Doyle had contacted her son's nanny Dee, letting her know she probably wouldn't be home until the early hours. It was the first test for Doyle to see if her job/home balance was ever going to work. McNally introduced himself and waited patiently for the others to do so for the benefit of the audio and visual recording.

McNally looked at his watch. 'Jake, I'm aware that the time is approaching 11pm and you have been in police custody for about six hours now and you're entitled to eight hours' sleep, but I wanted to give you the opportunity to explain the circumstances that led you to walk into Leman Street police station earlier today.'

'I would like to remind you that my client, Mr Knox, gave himself up voluntarily, Detective Inspector, and yet finds himself arrested and incarcerated in a police station in Central London without really knowing why, and add to that the fact we have received little disclosure on your grounds for continuing his detention.'

McNally addressed the remarks by the duty solicitor, whilst looking at the frightened young man who sat opposite them. 'Jake, as you and your solicitor know, you've been arrested on suspicion of conspiracy to murder a male person, who is yet to be identified. You admitted to me and DS Doyle earlier that it was you who left the partial remains of this person in the back of a black cab at Victoria station last night. I have some urgent questions that I want answers to about your role and the possible identification of this person. Are you happy for the interview to continue?'

Knox nodded and finally said, 'yes' as Doyle pointed to the microphone. 'I'm just really scared about what's going to happen to me if I talk to you.'

'Did you know what the contents of the bag were?' Doyle asked.

'No, honestly, I didn't. In fact, I still don't. I was told by the man who gave me the bag not to look inside, so I didn't. It was only after seeing the news on the television I realised they were talking about me. I thought it was drugs or something. I'm a student. I needed the money, and it beats working for a pittance in a bar or restaurant to make ends meet.'

'OK, Jake. Tell us who approached you and where,' requested McNally.

'I was at a bus stop on Commercial Road waiting for a bus. I'm a student at London Met doing a degree in digital marketing. I live in digs just off Arbour Square. I'd had a bad day, you know, doubting I was doing the right course. I'd just handed some work in that wasn't up to scratch and just wanted to go home. My parents aren't rich; my grant just about covers the cost of living in one of the most expensive cities in the world. I was feeling very low. Some guy came and stood next to me – I've no idea where he appeared from, but he didn't look like someone who needed to catch a bus. We got talking. He asked a lot of questions – I guess I'm pretty easy to read, I suppose. The next thing he asks me is if I want to earn a bit of cash for an hour's work. He pulled out a bundle of notes and told me what I had to do.'

'Which was?' Doyle asked.

'Take a bag, hail a cab to Victoria station, leave the bag in the back and scarper. That was it. He then gave me a couple of extra twenties and told me they were for the cab fare. He warned me not to look in the bag. Before he got up, he grabbed my student ID from round my neck – it's in a plastic wallet attached to a lanyard that breaks under pressure to stop it strangling you if it gets caught on anything – he looked at it and just grinned and said, "Don't let me down. I'll be watching." '

'And you thought it was…' Doyle let the question hang in the air.

'Drugs or stolen property… I don't really know. At one point I thought it was a prank or one of these reality TV shows, where they set people up to do stupid things and then ask them why they'd been so fucking stupid in the first place.' Knox raised his voice, clenched his fists and banged them on the table in front of him, more annoyed at his own stupidity than the questions being asked of him.

'Didn't you think it strange you were asked to leave it in the back of a black cab? If it were drugs or stolen property, surely it would've had to be delivered to somebody?'

Knox just sat, head in his hands, and started to sway from side to side, not answering the question.

The duty solicitor intervened. 'I think my client has had enough for one day. Maybe we can continue this interview in the morning once he's had a chance for some rest.'

McNally nodded. 'One final question I want to ask, Jake. Can you describe this man to me?'

Knox put his fist in his mouth to stop himself screaming. His eyes filled with tears. Eventually, he pulled himself together, sat up straight and with some purpose. 'If I tell you that, he *will* find me and he *will* kill me.'

McNally nodded and ended the interview. He watched as Doyle escorted him from the interview room and looked down at the wet patch on the plastic seat.

'That is one frightened young man,' McNally mumbled to himself as he collected his papers together. The duty solicitor merely nodded his agreement. 'I'll see you in the morning, sir, say ten o'clock?' McNally escorted the solicitor from the police station. He stood for a moment and took a huge gulp of cold January night air before heading back inside.

*

The last time Marcia Frost entered Brixton police station, she'd been escorting a male arrested for indecent assault on a fourteen-year-old girl at Clapham Common London Underground station a few years back, when divisional CID. She remembered walking into the custody office and the custody sergeant asking the prisoner what he'd arrested Marcia for. Her anger was suppressed only by the look of humiliation on the custody officer's face when he realised that the black woman was the police officer. It was a reaction she didn't ordinarily expect nowadays but was never shocked when it happened.

Her brother, Anton, had never accepted her joining the police service. They rarely talked and only saw each other if their paths crossed at their parents' house. It made her and their parents very sad that he could be so narrow-minded and not respect his sister's career choice. She was aware of a few skirmishes he'd had with the police when he was a lot younger; he was now twenty-one – but had never been convicted of any offence, so this was a complete shock. Of course he could be innocent of any wrongdoing; to be arrested is not to be convicted. She approached the police station's front reception, just as a sleety snow hit the pavements, attempting to keep an open mind. But her personal feelings for her brother were fighting her professional instincts as a police officer.

She was undecided how to play it. Did she blag her way into the custody area on the pretence that she was dealing with another prisoner and try and get a quiet word with her brother? Or did she go up to the CID office and be upfront about her predicament? She knew that every inch of the custody area and cells would be covered by CCTV, so she opted for the latter.

Frost looked around for the late turn CID officer. She wasn't even sure her brother was being dealt with by them. If her mum was right, and he'd been arrested for dealing, he was possibly being processed by a drugs squad officer – although a street dealer was probably too insignificant to draw their attention. So, it may well be the local plain-clothes crime squad. Frost saw a young female detective tapping away at a computer terminal; she looked stressed. The caseload of CID officers was ridiculous. How they were ever supposed to investigate crimes thoroughly was beyond her. Frost was glad she'd left all that behind her. It didn't matter what force you served in nowadays; the problems were the same, not enough investigators and too much crime. At least where she was now, they were dealing with only one crime at a time – as serious as it was, they could concentrate and do a proper investigation.

'Hi. Can I help you?' the young detective asked without looking up from the keyboard she was physically assaulting with two fingers.

'Yes, hi, I'm DS Marcia Frost from the BTP Major Investigations Unit at Camden.' She immediately regretted saying where she was based; she could have just got away with her name and rank. 'You've got a prisoner in downstairs for drug dealing.' The detective looked up with a 'you're having a laugh' look on her face. Frost realised they probably had several drug dealers in their custody at any one time. 'Sorry. That was a bit dumb.'

The detective got up and smiled. 'Don't worry. If you're major crimes you've probably forgotten what a Friday night on division is like.' She held her hand out. 'I'm Eve Muirfield, Temporary Detective Constable and general dogsbody round here.'

'That's Scottish, isn't it?'

'Yeah, Mum was from Edinburgh, but Dad is East London born and bred – hence the accent; mind you, south of the river is a different kettle of fish altogether – even I can't understand what they're bloody talking about.'

'Hey, you, I'm South London…' Frost had a phoney shocked look on her face.

'Yeah, I know. Only taking the piss, but you're quite posh – for a South Londoner.' They both laughed. 'DS Fouracres is the late turn CID officer. He went to the canteen for some scoff about twenty minutes ago, but I'll help if I can. D' ya wanna cup of tea?'

'I'd love a coffee.' Frost remembered she'd had a few glasses of wine earlier and could do with the caffeine boost before the alcohol really kicked in at the end of a very long day. 'Is that Neil Fouracres?' Frost asked, thinking she just might get a break here.

'Yeah, that's him. Can't be too many coppers with a handle like that in the Met, can there? You want milk and sugar, Marcia?'

'No, I'll have it black please, or d' ya have to say without milk round here?'

Eve looked around with a concerned expression; her face broke into a smile when she saw Frost had been joking. She handed the cup to her and pointed Frost to a seat near the one she'd been sitting in earlier. 'You joke, but that's where it's going nowadays,' the young detective said. 'You never know what to say: black, coloured, people of colour, do you call him her or her him; drives me potty. I feel sorry for people like us – you know – who just don't give a shit about any of this bollocks, who just want to get on with life. To me you're a copper; we're both on the same side – us against the bad guys – right?'

Frost started to take a shine to Eve Muirfield, even though she was digging a bit of a hole for herself, but she was to the point and said what she felt – not always the best policy in this politically correct world, and she probably wouldn't make commissioner, but the police service needed people like them both. Today's police force should mirror society; when are senior officers and politicians going to learn that criminals don't play by the rules? 'What do you think of him – DS Fouracres?' This time Eve looked a little more circumspect and chose her words carefully; Frost was pleased to see that Eve wasn't about to slag off or sing the praises of her DS in front of somebody she'd only just met. 'Don't worry, Eve. I met Neil on my CID course a few years ago. We got on well; he's a decent bloke. I didn't realise he was here at Brixton; last time I heard he was at West End Central.'

'He's been here about three months. At first, I thought he was going to be a right posh tosser with a name like Fouracres, and as for his first name, what parent names their kid Neil? It's worse than Nigel or Adrian. I suppose it must've been popular in the '80s and '90s, way before I was born. My nephew's got a tortoise called Neil, who just eats, shits and sleeps twenty-four seven. I can't look at the tortoise in the same light anymore. But since he got here, he's been good; really looks after me.' She started to giggle. 'Not like that.' She'd noticed the grin on Frost's face. 'I mean professionally.'

Frost took a sip of her coffee. 'Do you know who's dealing with a prisoner in custody called Anton Frost? Eve glanced up at a whiteboard that had several names listed – presumably prisoners awaiting the late-turn cID's attention, be it for interview, bailing or charging. Frost looked briefly down the list but thankfully couldn't see her brother's name. Next to each of the names was a date of birth and an offence they were suspected of. Her relief was soon shattered when she noticed her brother's date of birth next to a name she didn't recognise.

'Marcia Frost. Well, I never.' Frost looked round and recognised Neil Fouracres as he entered the room holding two large custard tarts. He'd lost weight but seemed taller than she remembered him; his dark hair was shorter and a little greyer; she smiled, stood and put out her hand. He gave the tarts to Muirfield and grabbed Frost's hand, which he shook vigorously.

'Hi, Neil, it's great to see you. Where've the last five years gone?'

'Eve, meet the finest detective outside the Met,' Fouracres said to Muirfield. 'You two know each other?'

'No. We've just met,' replied Muirfield. 'Marcia has just been telling me about what a swot you were at detective training school, sarge.'

'Yeah, right, I just scraped through, mainly due to this one and a lot of late nights reciting definitions of acts and sections I'm very unlikely ever to use in this part of the world. So, what brings you here, Marcia? Are you still living at home with Mum, Dad and your brother?'

'No. I moved out ages ago, got a one-bedroomed flat in Stockwell. It's not bad for work, straight up the Northern line for Camden Town. Can I have a private word, Neil...?' She nodded in a direction away from Muirfield.

'Don't mind me, you two. I've got to get down to custody and charge a burglar before his twenty-four hours are up and they kick him out. Nice meeting you, Marcia, may see you later.'

'Thanks for the coffee, Eve, and if you ever fancy joining a less politically motivated force, give me a ring.'

Muirfield waved. 'Nah, I get train sick. See ya!'

'She seems a good find.' Frost swivelled her chair back to Fouracres.

'Yes, she's a quick learner and I think she'll go far. Now, what's troubling you at this ungodly hour? Last time I saw you with a face like that, it was your turn to buy the drinks.'

'It's my brother...'

'Is he still giving you grief for putting that smart brain of yours to good use?'

'It's a bit more serious than that. I think he's sitting in one of your cells.'

'Oh... right.' Fouracres did exactly what Muirfield had done and consulted the list on the far wall. 'I can't see his name up there. You sure somebody, maybe him, isn't taking the piss? It wouldn't be the first time somebody's been sent to a police station believing their next of kin's been arrested for some crime or other.'

'No, I'm fairly sure. You see the second one down?'

'Carl Jackson?'

'Yes. The date of birth is the same as Anton's. He has a best friend called Carl Jackman. Not exactly imaginative, is he?'

'Well, I suppose there's only one way to find out.' Fouracres paused for thought before continuing. 'Say it is your brother, there's not a lot I can do, Marcia. If the evidence against him is good, his case will have to go to the Crown Prosecution Service for a decision like anybody else. You know that just as well as I do.'

Frost nodded. 'Yeah, I know, Neil, but if the evidence is a bit thin, and he has no previous convictions I know about, maybe you could have a word with the duty inspector and suggest a caution. I know I'm asking a lot but nothing illegal.'

'Look. There's no point playing the guessing game. Let's go and have a look to see if it's him. Of course, giving a false name, and probably address, isn't going to help his case.'

Frost followed Fouracres down to the custody area. 'I'll get him into an interview room but will have to book him out on the custody record – you just stay in the background until I call you in.' Frost nodded. She normally felt at home in a custody suite but suddenly she felt as if she didn't fit in. Other officers were looking at her as if she were some sort of alien and should be in a cell, until they saw her identification.

The interview room, to which Fouracres took 'Carl Jackson', was out of her view. It seemed a lifetime before he waved to her to join him. She followed him into the room and saw her brother sitting with his head in his hands. He looked up; his expression was a mixture of shock and contempt. Frost had already decided that if he gave her any crap she'd walk out of here and leave him to his fate.

'Hi, Anton, surprised to see your big sister?' She pulled a seat out on the opposite side of the table and glanced at Neil Fouracres. 'Would you give us a couple of minutes please, Neil?'

'You got two minutes, Marcia. I'm sticking my neck out here.'

Frost nodded her appreciation. 'I'll be quick, I promise.' Fouracres turned and left the room, leaving the door half open.

'Who's he, your white pig boyfriend?' Anton asked with a sneer.

'No. Actually, he's a man who could well decide your immediate future. That being: do you stay in custody here for the night in some stinking cell and appear in court in the morning charged with a criminal offence? Or maybe even better: does he take you and your fucking attitude back home to *our* Mum and Dad and turn *their* house upside down to search for any more drugs you may have? Or does he try and help *this* black police bitch and her prick of a brother by looking at the possibility that this is your first offence and trying to convince other white pigs to give you a fucking break and a caution? Which one would you prefer?' Frost stood up and kicked the wall with such force she thought the vibration might set the safety alarm off. She turned and faced Anton, who could see utter belligerence on his sister's face and, for the first time since he was arrested, he was genuinely frightened. 'This is no game, Anton. With a conviction for drug dealing, you can forget travelling abroad to places like America; forget any job where you may need vetting or a DBS check, because they're all going to come back with a *big fat fucking no*! Do you understand?' He wiped his sister's spittle from his face and nodded. 'Finally, I'm getting through to you. What were you thinking?'

'I wasn't dealing. I was just picking some stuff up for some of the boys on a local estate – honest.'

'Why did you give a false name?'

'I don't know. It was stupid. I just gave the first name that came into my head.'

'Your best friend's you mean?'

'Well similar, I know. Look I'm sorry, sis, I know Mum and Dad are going to be mad, but I've been an idiot, and I'd appreciate it if you could get me out of this mess somehow. I know I've been a twat about you joining the police. I dunno, I suppose it's a bit of jealousy; Mum and Dad were so proud of you.'

'Look, stay there. I'll go and have a word with Neil, but to be honest with you, if I've got a choice between asking him to put his job on the line or you getting charged… well, I think you know the answer to that one.'

SEVENTEEN

SATURDAY MORNING

Frost had read somewhere that former Prime Minister Margaret Thatcher could run the country on four hours' sleep a night; she needed six to seven at least. She stifled a yawn and downed a large gulp of black coffee. She'd eventually left Brixton police station at 1am. Neil Fouracres and Eve Muirfield had interviewed Anton. She was sure they'd downplayed his role and criminal intent as the result was a caution for possession of a class B drug for personal use. Anton had been an extremely lucky boy. It was still a mark against his character and may come back and haunt him in the future, but he seemed to realise how fortunate he'd been. Frost had dropped him off home, spent half an hour explaining to her parents what had happened, before climbing into her bed just before 2am, only for her mobile alarm to wake her at 4.45am.

She'd driven through the Rotherhithe Tunnel and got to the BTP police station at West Ham just before 6am. Luckily, Hodge and Graves were early and had briefed the two uniformed officers, who were to accompany them to Joey Dryden's address.

Frost, Graves and Hodge were in an unmarked car with two different uniformed officers from twenty-four hours earlier in a marked carrier a couple of hundred metres behind. Frost had asked them to stay back until they had driven past the address. Graves drove along Tower Hamlets Road towards West Ham Cemetery. Dryden's address was on the offside and seemed to be in darkness, as they would expect; drug dealers tend not to be early risers. The rear entrance wasn't accessible from the main road, so one of the uniformed officers would be dropped off on Wellington Road, which ran parallel with Tower Hamlets Road, just in case he leapfrogged a couple of garden fences. The second officer joined them at the front door with a large metal ram, just in case they got no response. For once, Frost was happy for Graves to lead the way. At six foot two, he was an intimidating sight. Frost briefly thought of how upset Marie Relish had been last night but put affording any blame to the back of her mind and returned her concentration to the job at hand. Graves tested the door with one enormous shoulder to see if it would give way to a decent kick; he nodded his head at Frost and Hodge before taking two steps back and landing the sole of his shoe just below the keyhole; the door splintered and gave way. He looked back at his three colleagues and hunched his shoulders as if it was something he did every day.

Frost hesitantly called out, 'Police, anybody here?' The interior was in darkness until Graves turned on the hallway light. The uniformed officer remained outside, communicating with his colleague that entry had been gained and to keep his eyes open and focused. Graves, Frost and Hodge moved tentatively forwards into the premises. They stood still and listened – a faint smell of decay and a low buzzing sound resembling a fridge freezer grew louder as they approached a closed door leading to the front room. Graves extended his baton and used it to push open the living room door; as he did so, he was hit with a swarm of flies around his head. The smell was a lot stronger, a smell he was familiar with. He felt around for a switch and flooded the room with dull yellow light. It took all three of them seconds for their eyes to adjust and be able to see a figure of a male sat in a chair who, at first, appeared to be moving, before they realised the movement was a mass of flies and maggots. They presumed the male to be Dryden, but it was hard to tell, even with a recent photograph of him to hand, as his face was bloated and coloured with an awful purple tinge; flies were moving in and out of several orifices. A piece of cord bit into his neck; dried blood, which had emanated from his nose, formed a black, crusty moustache on his upper lip and chin.

'I don't think he's going to take our inquiry much further, do you?' asked Graves.

Frost turned to the uniformed officer who'd joined them; the blood had drained from his face, and he looked like he was about to bring up an early breakfast but at the same time unable to tear his eyes away from the macabre scene in front of him. Frost grabbed his arm, pushed him towards the front door and instructed him to call the local police.

*

'OK, Marcia, let me know any updates. I'll probably be interviewing Knox and have my phone on silent but text me with anything you think I might need to put to him.' McNally ended the call just as Doyle drove into the police station. 'That was Marcia; they found Joey Dryden with a cord round his neck – probably been dead a couple of days.'

'What, suicide?'

'No, he's been murdered.'

'May be a drug deal gone wrong?' Doyle asked.

'How are most disputes between drug gangs settled nowadays?' McNally asked, the late night and early hour making him a little tetchy. 'You should know, having just come from Manchester; it's no different here in London.'

'Well, by shooting or stabbing, normally in a public place… yeah, I see what you mean. So, his death is more likely to relate to our inquiry than a drugs war.'

'Exactly, if the people responsible for cutting up our victim are going round clearing up any loose ends, our man Jake could be next on that list, and I think it's only fair we inform him and his solicitor of that fact.'

*

Jed Jennings and Eddie Lee were opposites. Any punter in the White Horse pub would never associate these two men with each other. Jennings had worked all his life, had received a good comprehensive school education and, before tragedy had hit, been a happily married family man who'd never even received so much as a parking ticket. He was clean-cut and respectful of his surroundings and other people. The man on the other side of the pool table was the complete opposite. Eddie Lee was a thief. He cared little for anybody else in his life – a high percentage of which had been spent behind bars. He had no real friends. He was married but in name only, having discovered that his wife had had an affair with a police officer during his latest incarceration. A few days earlier, he ended the marriage in the only way he knew – violence. His sunken cheeks and dark-rimmed eyes portrayed a lack of good nutrition and sunshine; personal hygiene was not top of his daily to-do list. Jennings doubted if Lee even owned a toothbrush or had ever heard of deodorant – let alone used it.

Jed Jennings was fuelled by hate for the man who'd killed his daughter five years ago. His hatred had consumed his life – his marriage had broken up; his business was suffering; but he was no criminal. He had often asked himself the question – could he kill another man in cold blood? Even the man who'd taken away the life of his only child and acted in such a callous manner after his acquittal; it was a question that kept him awake every single night – until he'd received a phone call from HMP Nottingham six months ago.

111

Jennings had been on the brink of hanging up the phone – just another crazy phone call. Until the caller mentioned a name – a name that instantly had Jennings' full attention: former Detective Sergeant Brian Garvey. These two men were out for revenge.

*

Jake Knox's solicitor indicated, with a nod of his head, that he and his client were ready. Linda Doyle activated the audio and visual recording equipment. McNally made the opening gambit.

'Mr Knox, I'll remind you that you are still under caution.'

'I understand,' Knox replied with a barely noticeable nod of the head.

'We interviewed you late yesterday evening, and you made us aware of a set of circumstances that led to your arrest yesterday afternoon after you voluntarily attended Leman Street police station. DS Doyle and I were aware of the lateness of the hour and the need to provide you with an opportunity to rest. Are you happy to continue with this interview this morning?'

Knox again nodded.

'For the tape please, Jake.'

'Yes, sir.'

'We established that you were approached by a male person near to London Metropolitan University on Commercial Road where you are currently a student studying digital marketing. All correct so far?'

Knox looked at his solicitor and back at McNally and replied, 'Yes, sir.'

'Can you remind us of what happened from then onwards?' McNally sat back in his chair; he didn't want to appear aggressive. 'Take your time, Jake.'

'Well, as I told you last night, this guy approached me and sat down next to me at the bus stop. I was a bit wary at first; he was very smartly dressed and looked out of place for the area. We got talking.'

'Who initiated the conversation?' Doyle asked.

'He did. I'm not that self-confident, you know. I would never start a conversation with a stranger. He asked me where I was studying and then looked down at my student ID, which I still had on. He asked if I wanted to earn some money and told me what I'd have to do as I told you last night.'

'Did he make any threats, Jake?' asked McNally.

'No, not really; he didn't have to. He was menacing. He just told me what to do and not to look in the bag. Just as he got up, he grabbed my ID, and the lanyard broke as it's designed to do. He looked at it and smiled at me – I remember now – as he handed the bag over, he said my name – I suppose to let me know he knew who I was and where he could find me. Then he walked away.'

'Which direction did he go in?'

Knox looked at Doyle, rubbed his hands over his face and thought for a moment. 'He walked round the back of the bus stop – I didn't see him again.'

'Can you remember if he was wearing gloves?' McNally asked.

'No, I don't think so. No, definitely not because I could see he had several gold rings on.'

'What did you do with your student ID after he gave it back to you, Jake?'

'Because the lanyard was broken, I just put it in my pocket to fix later.'

'Where is it now?'

'It's still in my coat pocket.' Knox went to retrieve it from his coat hanging on the back of his chair.

Doyle stopped him. 'Jake, don't touch it; leave it where it is.' She got up, looked at McNally and left the interview room.

McNally, for the record, informed the tape that Doyle had left before continuing. 'I asked you to describe this man last night, Jake, but, understandably, you were too scared to do so. We'll find this man, but we may be able to do so quicker with your help. So can you describe him for me – firstly, can you tell me his ethnicity?'

Knox looked down at his hands, avoiding any eye contact. McNally maintained the silence, hoping the frightened young man would feel the pressure and break. Annoyingly, the solicitor interrupted. 'I think it's time for a break, Inspector.'

McNally reluctantly nodded and suspended the interview. Doyle returned with an evidence bag and a pair of gloves. She removed the student ID from Jake's coat pocket, sealed it in the bag, which she got him to sign; she countersigned underneath his signature and both detectives left the room.

*

Brian Garvey had spent a restless night at his daughter's house. He'd awoken at 3am – something had bothered him so much it had disturbed his sleep but, annoyingly, he couldn't put his finger on it, and now he'd forgotten. A weak winter sun was penetrating the bedroom curtains. Garvey glanced at his watch: 7.30am. He lay in the spare room, listening to the whispers of the grandchildren on the landing outside, discussing if they should jump on Grandad and wake him up. He considered the benefits of returning to Meeres' flat but decided against the idea; he'd left his contact number and was sure Frankie would call him when he returned home. He sat up in bed and awaited the onslaught.

*

Frost and Hodge went to Forest Gate Met Police station and liaised with DCI John Franklin, the appointed senior investigating officer, into the murder of drug dealer Joey Dryden; Frost instructed Graves to remain at the scene and liaise with the SOCO for continuity purposes as he'd been the one to first discover the body.

'Thanks for coming over, DS Frost. I suppose without you going into the address this morning, our victim could have lain undiscovered for a few more days. From initial enquiries, he seems to have been a loner. We don't believe he dealt his drugs from his home address.'

'No, sir, our information suggests he used the pub near the station to deal. We did the usual checks with your Intel Bureau regarding the address but were assured there was nothing untoward. We also informed your early turn duty officer that we were on your ground and the reason why.'

'Don't be so defensive. You did me a big favour and, let's be honest, between the three of us, he's no bloody loss to the community, is he?'

'Have we got anything from the door-to-door enquiries yet, sir?' she asked. Frost wasn't overly impressed with the DCI's comments, but people like him were dinosaurs in her opinion. She looked sternly as Hodge smiled and seemed to agree with him.

'It's a bit early yet; I've got a couple of the early turn CID making a few enquiries with the neighbours. It's a bit difficult now as the pathologist won't give us a definitive time of death until he gets the body back to the mortuary. It looked like he'd been there at least two or three nights – what with the flies and maggots. It always amazes me how the little buggers get in. The central heating, being on full blast, hasn't helped matters. The pathologist was fairly sure Dryden was killed where you found him; his fingers were gripping the chair handles and blood lividity indicates he hadn't been moved. There is no forced entry, so he must've known his killer. Run me through your interest again, will you?'

'Late last Wednesday some body parts were found at Liverpool Street left luggage office. From CCTV footage and the use of an Oyster card, we identified Joey Dryden as the person who deposited the sports bag, in which these body parts were discovered.'

'Good work. To be honest, I think he's more likely to have been killed in relation to your inquiry than a drugs dispute; a street shooting or stabbing would've been more likely in that scenario. Do you think he's a murderer?'

'Probably not, sir, we think he was just a paid courier. We had a similar incident at Victoria station a couple of nights ago. Similar MO – young lad given a bag to deliver, but this time he was told to get a taxi. We've got him in custody now, but he's too scared to give a description of the man who gave him the package.'

Franklin's mobile rang – the theme of some cop show Frost couldn't readily identify. What was it with senior officers and mobile ringtones? She thought of McNally's *Big Brother* ringtone – although he always blamed his kids for that. 'Franklin... yeah. OK, that's good work. Try the rest of the street. Somebody else might've seen him or the car – I'll get the house-to-house enquiries up and running as soon as I can... yep, keep me informed.' Franklin slipped his mobile back in his jacket pocket. 'A woman two doors down from Dryden's was putting her bin out for the next morning's collection and saw a black male leave the house and jump into a large, dark car. She doesn't drive but remembers the last three digits of the car's plate as they were the same as her initials: WDP – Wendy Dianne Patterson.'

'Did she get any description of the driver, guv?' Hodge asked, trying to keep the excitement out of his voice.

'Not great. It was about 9pm and bloody dark. But she's pretty sure he was black, big, and the weirdest thing was, his teeth reflected the streetlight.'

*

'OK, Marcia. Linda and I will get back on it. See you back at Camden later.' McNally turned to Doyle. 'I think we were right – this killing is because of our inquiry rather than drug related. Seems our killer, or killers, are tidying up any loose ends. This gives us a bit of a lever with Jake Knox. Let's go in and give him the full facts that he's probably next.'

EIGHTEEN

SATURDAY AFTERNOON

By 1pm, Jennings and Lee had drunk four pints of strong lager and were still going. They had returned to Garvey's address several times and were frustrated that he hadn't returned. Neither man was used to drinking. Jennings was a social drinker, but since his marriage break-up, alcohol rarely passed his lips; he knew if he started drinking, he'd probably never stop. Lee, on the other hand, loved a drink, but the past ten years had been dry. Drugs, mobiles and cigarettes in prison could be ordered on demand, but alcohol was more difficult to smuggle in, to conceal in a prison cell and its use much more obvious to prison officers. So, by their fifth pint, they were well oiled and attracting a lot of unwanted attention from locals, many of whom had dropped in for a drink before making their way to Norwich City's home game, kicking off at 3pm.

'Where're you boys from then? Not these parts I'm betting for sure,' said one in a deep local brogue; he had a yellow and green scarf loosely draped round his wide shoulders and his huge hand wrapped round a pint glass of lager. The enquiry was more inquisitive than aggressive. Jennings realised this and started to explain they were in Cromer visiting a mate. Lee was not so polite.

'I suppose this is as exciting as it gets up here, a pint and watching a shit football team?' The pub went very quiet, but Lee didn't take the hint. He just carried on potting the next ball. Jennings whispered in his ear, 'We're here for a purpose, and not to get into a fight with the locals.'

Lee just grinned. 'Can you smell pig shit in here?' Luckily only Jennings heard his comment.

'So, what football team d' ya support, mate?' The local directed his question at Lee. 'Chelsea or Spurs, or are you one of these wankers that supports Manchester United, even though you've probably never been anywhere near the north-west?' Several more locals were joining in the verbal tennis match, and the exchanges were becoming more heated.

'The mighty Crystal Palace, you thick carrot cruncher. Come on, you Eagles,' Lee shouted. The locals let out a roar of laughter and started to flap their arms up and down, a few attempting to mimic the squawk of a bird of prey.

The main man taunted Lee: 'What 'ave you won in the last fifty years? I'll answer it for yer – fuck all,' he shouted, accompanied by the jeers of virtually everybody else in the pub. 'In fact, even Norwich won the League Cup twice at Wembley, fucking Crystal Palace, the Eagles. You're having a laugh. Why don't you fly back to London?'

Jennings quickly sobered up and realised they were in deep trouble. He fleetingly questioned what the hell he was doing there. The contents of several pints were launched in their direction, accompanied by the shouts, 'out, out, out.' Jennings made a grab for Lee but couldn't prevent him raising his pool cue, bringing it crashing down on the local's head. All hell broke loose – objects flew over their heads, including glasses and bar stools, breaking several of the pub's windows. Jennings somehow managed to pull Lee out of the pub's rear exit, whilst fighting off pursuing Norwich fans with his feet and fists, and drag him into the car park, manhandling him towards his van parked nearby. He forced

Lee, who wanted to stay and fight, into the passenger seat, fired up the engine and reversed – at speed – onto the main road – nearly colliding with a huge tractor hauling sugar beet. Several beer glasses smashed into the side of his van. Jennings accelerated onto Cromer's one-way system. He glanced in his rear-view mirror and saw Lee's main antagonist standing in the middle of the road, his fist in the air, his yellow and green scarf slowly turning bright red.

*

The bleep of the tape machine seemed to make Jake Knox jump. He'd been in custody approaching twenty hours and his anxiety levels were multiplying every time McNally and Doyle entered the room. The detectives were genuinely worried about his mental state and McNally made a decision that the softly-softly approach was not the way to go and a little more pressure was needed. The duty solicitor sensed this when he and McNally exchanged glances and gave him a slight nod before looking at his client, whose eyes were fixed on a point between his feet.

'Jake, we've been here for some considerable time now. I want to reiterate the seriousness of the situation. We're talking about the taking of a man's life in the most violent of ways. Do you understand that?'

Knox looked up. 'Yes, sir,' he replied, nodding his head, before returning his gaze to the floor.

'That's good, because I believe everything you have told us so far. My colleague DS Doyle and I accept that you are, apart from being a little naïve, an innocent party in this dreadful affair. But I must tell you that we believe your life is in danger until we catch this man.'

Knox's head snapped up; he looked a little disorientated and likely to throw up.

'Take a few deep breaths, Jake,' Doyle suggested. 'We can help you, keep you safe, but you must help us find this man before he finds you.'

Knox looked at Doyle and McNally in turn and then to his solicitor, who gave him an encouraging nod. 'OK. I'll help, but what's going to happen to me?'

'You told us outside this room that you have close relatives in Manchester.' Knox nodded again. 'You'll be bailed from here for several weeks while we continue to investigate, but I'm satisfied with your explanation so far, and I'm quite happy to say that in front of you and your solicitor. So, I want you to go home. I will contact police officers in Manchester to keep you updated and make sure you're safe. But I need you to describe to us the man who gave you that bag.'

Knox took a sip of water and then inhaled deeply and nodded. 'He was a black guy – you know, really dark. I'm five feet eleven; he was at least three or four inches taller than me, heavy build, wearing a thick, expensive overcoat. He had a London accent – I don't know what part of London – he sounded a bit like a character off *Eastenders*. It sounded a bit put on, if you know what I mean. Like he is some sort of gangster; maybe he is, I don't know.'

McNally nodded. 'Anything distinguishing about him – anything that stood out?'

'Yeah, he had gold teeth, three or four – I think – on the top row, in the middle, and several scars on his shaven head. He frightened the hell out of me. He was pretty strong; the way he held that bag and handed it to me, it was as if it contained a pillow. At first, I could hardly pick it up. I hailed a passing taxi that was travelling east; the driver didn't seem too impressed when I asked for Victoria. I hoped that he'd take me. I must have looked desperate. I felt as if the guy was still there, you know – watching me. I just sat in the rear of the cab, put the bag on the far side of the back seat and looked out of the window, trying to decide what I was going to do when I got to Victoria. I don't think I looked at it again before I jumped out. The cabbie wanted to talk all the time but gave up in the end. When I got out of the cab, I threw a couple of twenties at the driver, and I jumped on the nearest bus; I hadn't a clue where it was going. I just prayed that it was leaving straight away. It left after about two minutes. I looked round from the top of the bus and thought I saw him again – the black guy – but I can't be sure.'

*

McNally made several phone calls while Doyle dealt with Jake Knox's bail and release. The first was to BTP Euston to arrange a travel warrant for Knox's journey to Manchester Piccadilly, followed by a call to BTP Manchester to arrange secure transport at their end on his arrival. Although Knox was technically still a suspect, and therefore being released for further investigation, McNally knew he was more likely to become an important witness when a suspect was arrested and charged. Knox was worth the investment of their time and energy.

The next call was to Jim Wakefield in the incident room, instructing him to widen the search and seize any CCTV coverage of the bus terminal at Victoria station. If their suspect had been checking Knox had followed his instructions, he shouldn't be too difficult to find on good-quality tape. Sally Cook was next on his list to arrange for the collection of the student pass they knew their main suspect had handled and the set of elimination fingerprints Doyle was in the process of taking from Knox. Their number one suspect had been either confident that he couldn't be identified from his prints or very stupid – McNally hoped for the latter; they needed a break.

*

Doyle met McNally in a small coffee shop in Goodge Street, a few hundred metres from the police station; neither had eaten all morning, and it was now approaching 2pm. Both detectives took the opportunity to ring home. McNally explained to Kate that it would be another late finish – he could hear his seven-year-old son

Max in the background bemoaning his father and another broken promise to play football later that afternoon.

'Where's Ava?' he asked.

'Out with some school friends. She hardly talks about Manchester anymore; she's even developing a North London drawl – just part of trying to fit in, I suppose. Anyway, don't worry about us – I've had you home for so long I was getting sick of the sight of you to be honest.' She laughed.

'Oh, thanks very much, I love you too. Say sorry to Max – I'll make it up to him. Remind him I've got those tickets for the Arsenal v West Ham game in a few weeks. I'll see you later.'

Linda Doyle was in conversation with her son and gave McNally the thumbs up. He was in the process of draining his cup when his mobile rang.

'Hi, Ryan, it's Shirley Tresidder – BTP Press Officer. Can you speak?'

'Yeah, of course, Shirley, how're you – long time no speak.'

'I'm good – glad to have you back after your little enforced holiday; nice to see you've hit the ground running.'

'Yeah, no peace for the wicked. I've been meaning to ring you. Just wanted to say thanks for keeping the press off my back as much as you could during my suspension; it really helped me and the family out. I owe you a large drink.'

'I might have to hold you to that, Detective Inspector. The reason I called is the press interest is really picking up on your investigation, and somehow, they've connected the murder of the drug dealer in Forest Gate to your inquiry, so we need to get on the front foot and use it to our advantage.'

'OK. What've you got lined up?'

'Well, how about a press conference at headquarters at four-thirty – for starters?'

'What… this afternoon?'

'Yeah, of course, can't leave it till Monday – it will be yesterday's news.'

'OK, Shirley. I've just finished up at the nick. I'll be back at HQ in about half an hour. We can get our heads together before our friends arrive.' McNally terminated the call and looked at Doyle. 'Did you get all that?'

Doyle nodded and gulped down the rest of her coffee. 'Let's go.'

*

Brian Garvey constantly checked his mobile, hoping Frankie Meeres had tried to ring, or at least left him a message. Although it was a January afternoon and the air was bitterly cold, the sun was out, and he'd been running round the garden with his two grandsons. He slumped in a garden chair to get his breath back, fending off the boys as they tried to drag him back into action. His daughter brought him a cup of steaming hot tea, which he warmed his hands on.

'They never get tired, Dad,' his daughter remarked telling the boys to leave Grandad alone for a few minutes. 'I just gotta go and call a bloody plumber. The downstairs toilet isn't flushing. God knows what they've been putting down it; last time it was a tennis ball – keep an eye on them please, Dad, I won't be a minute.'

'You want me to 'ave a look at the toilet, love?'

'No. It's OK. Jim's best mate is a plumber; I'll give 'im a ring at work. No good asking Jimmy unless it's got anything to do with computers.' Garvey smiled. He knew his son-in-law wasn't the handiest of people when it came to the home.

Garvey nodded and got up for round two before stopping dead in his tracks. 'Plumber,' he mumbled to himself. The plumber's van that'd passed his house before he'd left late afternoon yesterday; he knew there was something that had registered subconsciously in his mind – gut instinct or copper's nose, whatever you want to call it; he hadn't lost it. He put his hands to his head to claw the information from the darkest depths into the here and now.

What was it? He remembered a mobile number and the dark blue lettering on the side of the van as it passed his window fleetingly.

His concentration was disturbed by a loud scream as one of the boys fell over and crashed into the garden fence. Garvey ran over to the far side of the garden. His daughter shouted from the kitchen window, '*Josh*, what've you done now?' Garvey picked his grandson up, who just laughed the slight mishap off and wriggled out of his grasp before chasing after his sibling. That was it! It'd been at least five years since the accident and the trial that nearly finished his career. The lettering on the van: 'J.J Plumbing Services'. Jed Jennings, the father of the little girl he'd knocked over. It was him. He'd come to even the score up. That little weasel Charlie Wells had been right all along. He ran up to the spare room and packed his overnight bag.

*

Jed Jennings brushed off fragments of beer glass from his hair and clothes as he sped round Cromer's one-way system following road signs for the A140 and Norwich.

'Where the fuck are we going?' Eddie Lee shouted above the screaming van engine as Jennings clumsily tried to engage third gear. 'We got unfinished business, JJ. Think of your little girl; think of that wanker in bed with my wife.' Jennings nearly pulled the van over to rip Lee's head off – he didn't need some piss-head scumbag to tell him to think of his daughter; he thought of her one hundred times a day.

'We can't – thanks to you – hang around here any longer. Somebody is bound to have clocked the van's number and reported it to the local police.'

'Are you 'aving a laugh? How many coppers 'ave we seen since we been here?'

'What, apart from the two walking down Garvey's street last night – remember? Having a good old look at us, weren't they?

Place like this, everybody knows everybody else. A van like mine – it would've stood out to them. We need to get out of here. If you hadn't kicked off in that pub, we would've been OK. They were a good-natured bunch until you started to wind them up.'

'You ain't got it, have ya?'

'Got what?' Jennings replied, concentrating on obeying the rules of the road; the last thing they needed was a speeding ticket or, worse, being stopped.

'The bottle! You ain't got the bottle to do what we came up 'ere for. I saw your face when you saw the knife I was holding. What d' ya think we were going to do, kiss him to death?' Jennings tried to block Lee's insults out – if he was honest, after the incident in the pub, he was a little scared of him. This whole thing had gone too far; he was way out of his depth. Could he really kill a man or be party to it? Maybe Lee was right. He didn't have the stomach for it.

Jennings guided his van round two small roundabouts as they drove through a small village called Roughton. He spotted a marked police van sitting on the forecourt of a petrol station and realised that it was a speed trap. He instinctively looked down at his speedometer and relaxed as the needle rested on thirty miles per hour. They crept up a hill towards a forty miles per hour restriction, Jennings looking in his rear-view mirror, and then onto the A140 proper.

NINETEEN

SATURDAY AFTERNOON

McNally and Detective Superintendent Nigel Plummer stood just outside the press room at British Transport Police headquarters in Camden. McNally quickly scanned, for probably the third time in the last five minutes, a briefing note compiled by Office Manager Ray Blendell of all the relevant leads they had so far. The ones highlighted in yellow, they'd all agreed, were to be disclosed to the press. Those in red, including the fact that the suspect had several gold teeth, were to be withheld.

Plummer gave McNally a reassuring nod. Press Officer Shirley Tresidder gave the two officers the run-down as to how this would work. She'd introduce both detectives and ask Plummer to give an overview of the case so far, and then he would hand over to McNally to highlight the areas of the investigation where he needed assistance from the public. Tresidder told them to be guided by her and answer questions only from people she had pointed to. All three could hear the buzz from the room next door. Tresidder gave them the thumbs up, and the two detectives followed her in.

*

Jed Jennings was sure that his passenger had taken something. Yes, they'd both had a skinful, but Eddie Lee was agitated and couldn't sit still. Jennings recalled standing at the pool table in the White Horse waiting for his return from the toilet. When Lee finally reappeared, he was accompanied by a local man, who left the pub immediately. Had Lee scored in the toilet? Maybe that explained the erratic behaviour and the violence thirty minutes later. Jennings put his foot down – the sooner they were out of Norfolk the better; then he saw the marked police patrol car parked in a layby, partly concealed by a mobile food van. He stamped on the brakes but, on reflection, that was the worst thing he could have done. His senses dulled by alcohol, he momentarily lost control and dangerously veered towards the middle of the carriageway. He glanced nervously in his rear-view mirror as the patrol car's blue lights burst into life and the vehicle accelerated onto the carriageway behind them. Jennings gripped the steering wheel and pressed the gas pedal to the floor.

*

It took McNally a few seconds to adjust his eyes to the glaring camera lights at the back of the room; the air conditioning was struggling to dissipate the rising temperature fuelled by the human scrum. Many of the press sensed this could be one of the biggest crime stories of the year. McNally noticed that winter overcoats had been discarded and were strewn over the backs of seats and piled on top of some tables next to the tea and coffee urns. He wanted to loosen his own tie but resisted. Plummer had briefly introduced himself and McNally and welcomed the members of the media, before passing the hot potato over to his detective inspector. At this point the reporters were respectfully attentive and waited for McNally to speak.

'Thank you all again for coming; I will endeavour to give you as full a briefing as I can without compromising our investigation, which is still in its early stages.' McNally cleared his throat and took a sip of some ice-cold water from a glass that he held so firmly, to camouflage the fact that he was so nervous, he was afraid it might shatter.

'Last Wednesday evening, British Transport Police uniformed officers were called to the left luggage facility at Liverpool Street station at about ten forty-five. They were directed to a sports holdall by staff who believed it to be suspicious. On examination by a scene-of-crime officer, it was found to contain body parts of a white male, whose identity is still unknown to us. This was followed by a similar incident on Thursday evening, when further body parts were left in the back of a London black cab at Victoria station.'

'Are the two incidents connected, Inspector?'

Due to the bright lights, McNally couldn't see who the question came from but quelled his irritation at being interrupted whilst in full flow and answered, 'Yes. We've now linked the body parts by way of DNA – they *are* from the same victim.'

Shirley Tresidder jumped in, 'DI McNally will be very happy to answer your questions at the end of his briefing if you could wait until then please.' She looked back at McNally and gave a comforting smile. McNally refocused and continued.

'We are currently following several leads, but our main focus is to identify the victim, which will hopefully give us a clearer picture as to why he was killed.' McNally nodded at Tresidder, who used a remote control to operate a large television screen to the left of him. 'The bag at Liverpool Street contained a severed left arm and hand. The limb had been expertly dismembered below the elbow of the victim. The middle finger of the hand was missing. However, on the wedding finger was a gold wedding band with the date the 16th of April 1992.' Everybody's attention turned to the screen as an image of the ring appeared, together with an enhanced image of the date inscribed on it.

'So, we know our victim is male, white and at least fifty years of age if he was married in 1992 at the earliest legal age of sixteen; of course, this could be way out, so we are estimating him to be between fifty and sixty-five years of age.' The next image was of the football club tattoo. 'The body parts found wrapped in a supermarket "Bag for Life" in the black cab on Thursday night were an upper arm and right foot. On the upper arm was this tattoo – a rampant lion with the date the 22nd of May 2004 underneath. Our enquiries have established that this is the club emblem of Millwall Football Club, and the date corresponds to an FA Cup final appearance by the club at the Millennium Stadium, Cardiff against Manchester United that they eventually lost. We've made enquiries with the club – who've been very helpful – but a white male between the ages I have referred to covers probably sixty to seventy per cent of their core attendance at any home game. Images of the tattoo, the wedding ring and inscribed date are included in your press packages being handed out to you now.

'I would make an appeal to anybody watching this briefing, who recognises the tattoo or the wedding ring and the significance of the date and believes they know the identity of the victim to come forward to us by contacting the incident room here at Camden or by speaking in confidence to Crimestoppers. All calls will be treated with respect and with the utmost confidentiality and thoroughly investigated. It is our number one priority at this point of the investigation to identify the victim of this abhorrent crime. In our opinion, this man would have last been seen alive sometime last Tuesday. If you have a member of your family or a close friend that you see frequently but have noticed his absence in the last few days, please contact us.'

Shirley Tresidder pointed at a short, stubby woman seated in the front row.

'Detective Inspector, Ann Crabtree from the *London Record*. Do you have any suspects at the moment?'

'Our enquiries are at an early stage, but we have identified a man of interest to us who we believe handed over the bag at a bus stop on Commercial Road on Thursday evening to a young student whom we have traced. He described the man as: black, very tall in relation to the witness's height – we estimate about six feet three. He had a London accent and was very smartly dressed. I was handed, just before we came into this briefing, a rather grainy CCTV image of a man matching the description seen in the vicinity of Victoria station thirty minutes after the discovery on Thursday night. If anybody recognises this person or believes they saw somebody resembling this man at either the Commercial Road bus stop near the London Met University or in the bus terminal at Victoria station on Thursday evening, then please come forward and tell us. This will allow us, at the very least, to eliminate him from the investigation. We are keeping an open mind at this time but believe that it may be the same man described by the witness and somebody we urgently need to trace.'

McNally had earlier decided, after a phone conversation with his Metropolitan Police counterpart leading the hunt for the killer of Joey Dryden in East London, not to mention the description of a similarly described male leaving that murder scene and details of the car and part-registration given by a witness. Both senior detectives believed it would cloud the issues, as they were still uncertain that Dryden's murder was connected to McNally's investigation.

Tresidder pointed to the back of the room. 'Inspector, you've mentioned several body parts belonging to one man, confirmed by DNA – are you expecting more finds in the near future?'

'At the moment we've substantiated no motive for the killing of this man and the reason for the sick distribution of his body parts around the capital, but I believe it is inevitable that more discoveries will be made. I strongly believe that if we can identify the victim, then we can expedite the investigation; it is so important for members of the public to come forward if they have any idea who this victim or suspect are.'

'Why railway stations – do you think this crime is connected with the transport system in any way?' the same reporter asked.

'It would be pure speculation on my part if I attempted to answer that question at this time; again, I believe this will be evident when he is identified.' Tresidder pointed to another reporter at the back, the same one who'd interrupted him earlier.

'This is a question for Detective Superintendent Plummer – if I may. Superintendent, may I ask if you have full confidence in DI McNally to lead such a serious investigation, bearing in mind he has only just returned from suspension, having been on trial for a criminal matter at Southwark Crown Court earlier this week?'

McNally bit his tongue and, for a second, he thought that Plummer was going to hang him out to dry.

'DI McNally has been cleared of any wrongdoing, unanimously by a jury in a case that – in my opinion – should never have even been brought to the attention of a judge and jury. I have every confidence in his ability as a detective and as an SIO. He also has the full backing of his team, who have worked successfully under his leadership, and of the chief constable. To be quite honest, questions like that deflect from what we are here to achieve today, and I would urge you all to consider not only the victim in this matter but also the friends and family who are yet to face the anguish of learning this man's identity. Thank you all for coming. We hope to hold a similar update when we've significant leads to report to you.' As McNally and Plummer got up, a barrage of questions were batted off by Tresidder. As the two detectives returned to the incident room, McNally turned, knowing the boss had stuck his neck out to defend him, nodded to Plummer and said, 'Thanks, boss.'

*

'Victor Kilo five-five in pursuit of a white Ford Transit van driving erratically, speed seventy-five miles per hour on the A140 heading towards Aylsham, registration, partly obscured, is Delta... Papa... six-three... X-ray... can't read the last two numbers. Has blue lettering on the back doors, Juliet Juliet Plumbing. There are two occupants; driver has no intention of stopping – request further units to assist, over.'

'Victor Kilo to five-five this vehicle is connected to two suspects wanted for questioning regarding an earlier affray and assault at the White Horse pub in Cromer. Proceed to follow with caution and maintain commentary; we'll endeavour to get units in front of you to disrupt, over.'

Jed Jennings could see the patrol car shadowing him some fifty meters behind. He was continually flashing his headlights for him to pull over. Lee was having none of it; he pulled the knife out from the glove compartment and waved it in Jennings' face. 'You ain't stopping – I ain't going back to prison for another ten. Put your foot down and lose 'im, or I'll cut you up and then the pig.'

'For fuck's sake! Are you having a laugh? I'm driving a van with one hundred thousand-plus miles on it, and you want me to outrun a top-of-the-range police vehicle. Are you nuts?' Jennings accelerated towards a mini roundabout bathed in the green light of a BP petrol garage. A tractor, orange lights flashing, slowly emerged from the right and entered the roundabout.

'Don't stop,' shouted Lee, 'go for it. This will fuck that wanker right up.' Jennings squeezed at speed just ahead of the tractor and accelerated round the tight roundabout and back onto the A140 towards Norwich. This delayed their pursuer for a short while, but within ten seconds, he'd closed the gap.

'Victor Kilo five-five we have traffic unit Victor Kilo four-three half a mile from your location. They can deploy a stinger – you have talk through. Keep your distance but continue with your commentary – over.'

'Victor Kilo five-five to four-three, vehicle is travelling erratically, speed eighty miles per hour, approximately half a mile from your location, over.'

'Four-three to five-five, I have him in sight – stinger deployed, hold back, over.'

'Five-five – yes, yes.'

'From four-three, vehicle fifty metres from stinger – he isn't slowing down: twenty-five metres until contact. Contact with stinger – tyres blown out – vehicle is continuing towards the Aylsham roundabout. Driver is slowing and struggling to maintain control. He is approaching the roundabout, brake lights showing; he can't stop in time. He's hit another vehicle and continued onto roundabout – the vehicle has turned over. Smoke coming from the transit, second vehicle badly damaged. I'll need urgent backup, ambulance and fire brigade attendance.'

TWENTY

SATURDAY EVENING

Marcia Frost opened a chilled bottle of Chardonnay and filled two glasses, handing one to Marie Relish. After her early start in Forest Gate and her late finish the previous night at Brixton, she was done in. McNally had told her to go home, and suggested Relish did the same. Hodge and Jim Wakefield had volunteered to stay in the incident room with McNally and Blendell to sift through any calls that came into the inquiry generated by the earlier press conference. Detective Superintendent Plummer had arranged several uniformed officers and some civilian staff from the force's Intelligence Bureau to come in and man the phones and social media. Graves remained at the murder scene in Forest Gate working with the Met SOCO; he'd been instructed to go home from there.

Frost kicked her shoes off and lay on the bed while Relish sank into the only armchair.

'Cosy, Marcia – I'll give you that.'

'Yeah, I know, you couldn't swing a skinny hamster in here, let alone a cat. What's your place like?'

'It's OK, on the fourteenth floor of a high-rise. But it's got two bedrooms and probably a lot cheaper than here. Anyway, I would've thought you must be on a good whack being a DS. Can't you afford something a bit bigger?'

'I suppose so, but I like it round here, you know, not far from Stockwell tube, never any problem getting home after finishing late and I'm from round here. Mum and Dad aren't far. Where's your family?'

Relish took a gulp of wine. 'Dad's dead – died when I was twelve.'

'Oh, I'm sorry. I shouldn't have asked – can't leave the detective in me at work.'

'No. It's alright. He'd left me and Mum in the lurch a few years earlier. Cleared off with some barmaid ten years younger; probably what killed him.' They both burst into laughter. 'Randy old bastard. Mum lives in Wembley behind the old town hall. She's got quite a nice place, but she's never driven and suffers from osteoarthritis so doesn't get out much. I go and see her as often as I can and ring her most days. She'll be on the phone tomorrow asking why I haven't been round. She doesn't realise that people work outside office hours.'

'She can't be that old. What're you, forty?'

Relish picked up the only cushion in the flat and lobbed it at Frost. 'You cheeky cow, I'm only twenty-nine. What time we got to be back in for tomorrow?'

'Boss wants a meeting for nine o'clock – means I can't go to church and confess.' Relish looked at Frost with a bemused expression before receiving the cushion back with twice the force. 'I'm joking. Could you imagine me telling some priest all my sins? I'd be in there for days.'

'Oh yeah, like what? You got a thing for Nigel Plummer? You fantasise about running your hands through his thick brown hair?'

Frost stuck her fingers down her throat and made retching sounds. 'Oh please, Marie. You could've at least said Ryan.'

'You two on first name terms now?'

'No, of course not...'

Relish's mobile rang and she looked at the display. The number was withheld. Frost told her to put it on loudspeaker. 'Hello,' Relish answered tentatively. The only sound was some background traffic noise and the distinctive sound of an emergency vehicle. Both looked out of the window onto Stockwell Road and saw an ambulance speeding past.

Frost grabbed the phone. 'Now listen here, you fucking pervert. If you don't…' The phone went dead.

'My God, Marcia, he followed us here – the ambulance, you could hear it in the background on the phone. The bastard followed me here. I'm not safe anywhere.'

Frost sat on the armchair and held her friend tightly. She could feel and hear her muffled cries. 'Come on, Marie. There are hundreds of ambulances and other emergency vehicles zooming round the streets of London on a Saturday night – you know that. It's just a coincidence.' Frost held Relish even tighter and glanced nervously out of her window.

*

Brian Garvey arrived back in Cromer just after 11pm. He'd driven round the surrounding streets for half an hour – now confident of what and who he was looking for. There was no sign of the transit van with the distinctive lettering on the side of it. He considered contacting the local police, but what would he tell them? That he thought the father of a young girl he'd accidently run over several years before had travelled up with the purpose of hunting him down, seeking retribution. He'd be laughed out of the nick. No – he decided to sit tight, lock the doors and wait and see what developed. He started to doubt what he'd seen; maybe it was his mind playing tricks. He had already researched the internet for plumbers in Cromer and North Norfolk – he hadn't found any that resembled the 'JJ Plumbing' he was sure he'd seen on the side of the van. He wished he'd never gone down to London to meet that rat-faced bastard Charlie Wells.

He lay back on his sofa and turned the television on. He knew he wouldn't sleep. He caught the last five minutes of the national news; the local news followed. He was about to turn the TV off, as a big news day in Norfolk would be no more serious than the serial theft of farming equipment, which is what he loved about the place. In London, nowadays, the killing of young people on the streets hardly got a mention. But what Brian Garvey saw on the screen put a broad smile on his face. If only he'd turned on the TV twenty minutes earlier and watched the national news, he could've blown a murder inquiry apart.

*

McNally sat in his office in company with Nigel Plummer. It had been a long night, and the boss hadn't come alone – a bottle of Jameson Irish whiskey sat on the desk between them. McNally was not usually a spirit man, but for the second time in a week – the last being a brandy half an hour after his acquittal at Southwark Crown Court, which seemed like a year ago – he sank the drink and enjoyed it. They'd received forty or fifty calls following the press conference transmitted on national and local London news programmes, as well as a wide spectrum of radio channels – the phones continued to ring. They also had officers scanning social media sites; most of the information was about the identity of the victim. A lot of the names could be ruled out quickly by a simple phone conversation with the caller. Often the time scan in relation to the length of time the person had been missing or even, on a few occasions, the sex of the missing person, saved any more wasted time. But McNally and Plummer were happy with the response and sat back and savoured the smooth taste of the whiskey.

'How's Kate and the kids since you've been back at work?'

'I spoke to her earlier. She seemed glad to get me out from under her feet; the last six months haven't exactly been a barrel of laughs. We tried to keep as much about the trial from the kids, but they're both old enough to know something was wrong, so in the end we were upfront with them and that seemed to work. They were very supportive. But I obviously haven't seen much of them since Tuesday. You got any kids, boss?' McNally realised that he'd been working with Plummer for nearly two years now, although six months of that had been on suspension, and knew very little about him. He assumed he was married – often the only item on his desk was a picture of a stunning younger-looking woman, but he'd never had the bottle to ask; it could have been his daughter for all he knew.

'No, I've got a couple of young nephews on my sister's side but Abigail – my wife – and I have always been career orientated. She's a senior lecturer at the London School of Economics. I don't ever think I've missed out on anything; you know. I remember the stress you and Kate went through last year when your daughter went missing – I know she turned up, but it must've been hell.'

McNally nodded. He didn't really want to go there and quickly changed the subject. 'So, how's the BTP shaping up to the Met? How long were you with them before you crossed over?'

'Done my thirty years; I joined very young. To be honest, Ryan, there's good and bad things in both forces, you know. The Met is a huge organisation – you're just a number – and they have their wankers, as do the BTP, but it's easier to hide them amongst twenty-odd thousand than it is among three thousand. God knows how many detective supers there are in the Met – maybe thirty or forty, I don't know. In the BTP, there's me, so I can make a difference, but at the same time, if I cock up, there's nowhere to hide. The powers that be can't brush me into a broom cupboard somewhere and bring in a new one, and I quite like that.'

'Talking of wankers, you noticed any strain between any of the team lately?' asked McNally.

'Well…' Plummer gave it some thought, 'I don't really see them that much,' he replied with an inquisitive look. 'Why – have you?'

'Something's going on between Marie Relish and Graves. I know Graves can be a pain in the arse, and he pushes me to the limits sometimes, but he's a good copper, can act on his own initiative and has a lot of experience. I don't really want to lose him; he is by far the most experienced on the team. I don't know if they rub each other up the wrong way. DS Frost knows something, and I think she's dealing with it, but I'll keep a handle on it.'

'Well, let me know if it escalates. To be quite honest with you, I wouldn't be too sad to see Graves out on his ear if he crosses the line once more.'

Plummer sank the remnants of his whiskey and was pushing his chair back when an excited Sam Hodge stuck his head round the corner, waving a piece of paper in his hand, before stalling slightly when he saw the detective superintendent, who asked, 'Well, Hodge. What've you got? You look like you're going to piss yourself with excitement.'

McNally waved him into the office.

'One of the civilians just took a message from a woman who would only give her first name – Holly. She thinks she may know who our victim is. She sounded really frightened. In the end, she agreed to meet one of the team tomorrow.

*

Maurice Stone walked into the flat, ducking his head under the door frame. Bending slightly at the knees, he looked into a wall mirror to check his appearance. He could hear the Butcher at work in the cutting room. This would be the last of the victim's body parts to be disposed of tonight, and he was to deliver. He smiled, his gold teeth reflecting the dim energy-saving light bulb. He'd been tasked to pick the specific drop-off point, and having called in a favour, he was ready to go. He sat back in a deep armchair, stretched his long legs out in front of him and picked up the local newspaper; he had no urge to watch the Butcher's work. He wouldn't have too long to wait.

*

The high-speed East Midlands train from Sheffield to London St Pancras was on time. Wesley Brown the driver had been with the company for ten years and been on this route for the last three. The hours suited him. He lived in North London and did two trips per shift – St Pancras to Sheffield and the return journey, arriving in the capital just before midnight. He would be home in bed before 1am and rest day tomorrow. The train cruised through Mill Hill Broadway station around eighty miles per hour and, although allowing his concentration to drift slightly as he thought about how he would spend the next day with his wife and two boys, he remained alert; the few passengers waiting on the platforms for the last local trains were a blur at that speed.

Brown slowly decreased the train's speed as it prepared for the approach to its final destination. An inviting row of green signals could be seen for at least half a mile in front of him. He saw the object on the track ahead quite late – maybe two hundred feet away. Travelling at the speed he was, he had little time to react, let alone stop, and within seconds, he'd hit whatever it was. He'd applied the emergency brakes and reported the incident via radio but knew by the time he had stopped he would be up to a mile from the contact point so was sensibly instructed to carry on to St Pancras. He thought it looked like a grey Post Office mailbag, probably thrown onto the track by local yobs, and reported such. He was just glad it hadn't been a lump of concrete or a piece of wood.

TWENTY-ONE

SUNDAY MORNING

Due to engineering works north of Stockwell on both the Victoria and Northern lines, Marcia Frost decided to drive into Camden – she couldn't face a replacement bus service. It was Sunday. The roads should be quiet, and she could park at force headquarters with no problems, as most of the building's occupants would still be at home in bed. Marie Relish was quiet for most of the journey, ignoring Frost's small talk and just looking out of the window as they crossed the Thames via Waterloo Bridge and headed north round the Aldwych, up Kingsway, Southampton Row, Euston and, eventually, Camden. Frost stopped outside a Costa Coffee.

'You want one, Marie? The canteen won't be open today and the coffee in the office tastes like gravy.' Relish nodded, deep in her own thoughts. Before she knew it, Frost was back in the car with her drink. Relish took small sips through the plastic cover, wincing as the hot liquid burnt her lips; she was in two minds whether to jump out of the car, tell Marcia that she was sick, go home and lock the door and stay there until this was all over. Frost pulled up at traffic lights and took hold of Relish's hand – as if she knew what she was thinking – and squeezed it tightly. Relish relaxed a little until her mobile started ringing.

*

The press conference and subsequent media coverage had given the investigation new momentum and rallied McNally's tired team. DS Linda Doyle had been sent to Archway to meet the woman who'd rung in the previous night, believing she knew the identity of the victim. McNally awaited the arrival of Frost and Relish to start the morning briefing. Frost walked in holding a cup of coffee and an almond croissant.

'You OK there, sarge? Where's our coffee? Buns all round, is it?' Graves joked.

'You all got money in your pockets, haven't you?' Frost replied. She was followed in by Marie Relish, who was saved from the same abuse by the fact that she was on the phone to her mother. McNally had come to realise that the banter was part of his team's DNA – a ritual that took place before they got down to business, and he was happy for it to continue. It was a therapy present in all emergency services but often discouraged by the senior ranks as inappropriate. He'd asked a lot of them in the last few days and would ask even more soon. The team also recognised when it was time to turn the banter off and concentrate on the job at hand.

'We got quite a few useful calls last night resulting from the press coverage,' McNally said. 'Linda Doyle is interviewing one of the most promising – a caller who said she might know our victim. Ray Blendell's been sifting through other calls and issuing actions for you all to follow up on today. From reading some of them, I think many can be bottomed out by a phone call, but it'll be up to you to take it further if you think it's necessary. Stuart, bring us up to date with the Forest Gate inquiry.'

*

The cafe was situated a few hundred metres from Archway tube station on Holloway Road. Linda Doyle walked the short distance from her home and arrived at the premises, chosen by the caller, ten minutes early. Doyle wasn't sure the reason for the cloak-and-dagger liaison but was of course aware of the reluctance of some members of society to talk to the police or, more importantly, be seen talking to the police.

The name of the witness was Holly – that was all Doyle knew; it could be an alias, she didn't know; she had refused to give details of her address or date of birth over the phone. Doyle was thinking this could be a complete waste of time. Some sad, lonely person had seen the press conference, decided to call the police to waste their time. In fact, she could be in the local vicinity, watching from a distance with a group of her mates, laughing and giving herself a good pat on the back. Doyle furtively looked up and down Holloway Road at locations people would legitimately congregate – bus stops, some public benches outside a library – but she could see nobody paying her any attention.

The cafe was what her dad would describe as a 'greasy spoon'. He frequently moaned at her about the lack of such establishments in London nowadays. 'Too many of these poncy coffee shops selling drinks I can't even pronounce,' he'd whine on endlessly. 'You want a decent bacon sandwich and a proper cuppa where you can't see the bottom of the cup and it don't smell like an 'erb garden, you haf'ter search high and wide. It's all down to those bloody wops bringing their fancy drinks over 'ere – cappa this and mokka that, and what the fuck is a babychino?'

Doyle peered into the cafe, still smiling to herself; it would be a place where her dear old dad would feel at home. Every time the door opened, a waft of fatty, bacon-scented air rushed out; her preference would be a nice latte and an almond croissant. The windows were starting to steam up and she stamped her feet on the ground and rubbed her hands together to maintain blood circulation to her fingertips and toes. She glanced at her mobile, hoping for a message from the incident room telling her that it was all some sort of joke and to get her arse back there – in the warm. She was going to give it another ten minutes before putting it down to a timewaster. The tap on her shoulder temporarily startled her.

'Hi. I'm Holly Harrison. Are you the police lady?'

'Hi, Holly, yes, I'm Detective Sergeant Linda Doyle.' Doyle rummaged round in her handbag with numb fingers until she found her warrant card holder and showed the young girl her identification. 'Shall we go inside, Holly? Don't know about you, but I'm freezing and could do with a cup of coffee.'

*

The St Pancras mainline had been shut for most of the night, causing early trains between London and Sheffield, Nottingham and Derby to be cancelled or seriously delayed. The police search teams had covered an area of one and a half miles between Mill Hill Broadway station in the direction of St Pancras. This distance was calculated on the approximate braking distance a train travelling at eighty miles per hour would have covered before coming to a halt. The search was co-ordinated by Police Search Advisor Inspector Neil Williams.

So far, the team had recovered several body parts cut up into small chunks of flesh by the wheels of the train and scattered over many hundreds of metres. Williams' team had to act quickly as the flesh was beginning to attract rats and scavenging carnivorous birds looking for breakfast. The train itself had been taken to a nearby depot for other members of Williams' search team to examine; in these situations, human remains can often be wedged in the train's undercarriage. Williams made sure each body part, described as accurately as humanly possible, was carefully bagged and labelled with details of who found it and where it was found, before they were transferred to a local mortuary. Williams knew this was no

144

suicide. The train driver had been interviewed in the early hours of the morning at his home address; he'd been understandably in shock after being informed of what they had found. Eventually, after a lot of patient questioning by the officers, driver Wesley Brown described the events leading up to the incident, including a description of what he maintained to be a grey Royal Mail mailbag.

Inspector Neil Williams was not a man to make rash decisions – he collated all the physical evidence his team had collected, together with the statement taken from driver Wesley Brown, before scrolling down his contacts' page and speed-dialling a familiar number.

*

Holly Harrison looked nervously round the cafe for anybody she knew or who looked familiar, her dark brown eyes darting towards the door every time anybody entered. She was a skinny girl, probably weighing no more than seven or eight stone, but fashionably dressed and had a likeable, friendly manner. Linda Doyle quickly picked up on the fact that she was nervous and tried to get her to relax by talking about anything but the point she really wanted to get to – the identity of their victim.

'Do you live far, Holly?'

Harrison sipped her tea with a slurping noise. 'Yeah, I had to get two buses to get here. That's why I was a little late – sorry.'

'No need to apologise, love. You look a little nervous. It's unlikely you'll know anybody in here – isn't it?'

'I used to live round 'ere a while ago. I was married to a bastard who loved to use his fists on me. He got put away for five years, so I moved, but I don't want anybody seeing me talking to you lot where I live now. This was the only place I knew would be safe, but thinking about it, my ex has probably still got friends round 'ere that's why I'm a bit wary. Mind you, since those days, I've lost a lot of weight and changed my hair colour and things.' She smiled at Doyle, but her heavily mascaraed eyes revealed real hurt.

Doyle looked at her watch – it was nearly 9.30am and she knew McNally was going to be chasing her up sooner rather than later – she needed to get to the point. 'Holly, you rang the incident room last night. Presumably you had watched the news and saw my boss appealing for information about the identity of a man who was murdered. Do you know who the guy is? If you do, it's so important that you tell me. Your name or any other details won't be disclosed to anybody else – I promise.'

Harrison stirred her spoon round in a half-empty cup and seemed momentarily in a world of her own; Doyle noticed that she was trembling. She didn't push her. 'It was a couple of summers ago…' She started her account hesitantly, with a whisper so quiet Doyle moved her chair closer and leant forward. 'I was still living round 'ere and still married to that prick. It was really hot, and everybody was in T-shirts. I'd been down a pub in Holloway Road with my husband and his mates. They were all really pissed. It was always worse when he'd been drinking, especially when he was with the others; he treated me like shit.'

'Can you remember what pub it was?'

'No, not now, but it was quite big inside – I think it was an old cinema or theatre, quite near Holloway Road tube station. It was about eight o'clock – he and his mates 'ad been drinking since two. It was a Saturday, I think. They'd been watching football on the television. He didn't allow me to drink – I was just there to provide a waitress service any time he or his mates wanted another round. We left the pub and started walking home – we got into an argument. I think it was about one of his mates touching me up. He was blaming me, telling me that I'd led him on.' Harrison's eyes filled with tears and Doyle handed her a napkin from a dirty, greasy glass that hadn't been washed in years.

'Take your time, Holly. Tell me what happened next, love.' Doyle didn't really know where this was leading but realised it was the young girl's chance to get this all off her chest.

Harrison blew her nose noisily, which attracted the attention of a man about to take a bite from a huge sausage roll dripping in fat. 'He started to push me around,' she continued, 'which is normally a precursor to being punched or kicked, but we were in public. Fucking coward only really hit me in private and in places where bruises can't be seen. I lost my footing and crashed into a shop front – you know where they 'ave all the fruit and veg outside. The storekeeper came out and started yelling at me. My husband looked at me with disgust and shouted at me to clear the mess up and come home when I'd finished, and he walked off.' They both remained quiet whilst a waitress cleared a table next to them and wiped it down.

Doyle displayed a patient smile, encouraging her to continue. This was not the time to push her too hard. 'I started picking up some things on the floor. I was crying now, knowing that I was going to get a good kickin' when I got home; he would've started on the gin by then. A guy, a stranger who I'd never seen before, came up to me and started picking up some of the spilled fruit and smiled at me and asked if I was OK. I was a bit wary. I weren't used to people being nice to me – 'specially men. He pointed to a burger bar across the road and asked if I wanted a cup of tea. He seemed nice, and what alternative did I 'ave?'

'Did he give you a name?'

'He did, but Linda, I can't remember it,' she got annoyed with herself, 'the only man who's ever been nice to me and I can't remember his bloody name.'

Doyle's heart sank, but she tried to keep the disappointment off her face. 'So, what did you talk about?'

'Funnily enough – football; he was a Millwall fan. That's why I remembered him when I saw the news last night. I'm sure the officer mentioned the person you were trying to find was a Millwall fan. I remember the guy showed me a tattoo on 'is upper right arm – it looked the same as the one in the picture you showed.'

Doyle rummaged in her bag for the second time since meeting Holly, but this time her hands were nice and warm. She pulled out a thin, brown cardboard document holder and took out a photograph, which she laid on the table in front of Holly. 'Did it look like this?'

Harrison looked carefully at the image and nodded. 'Yeah, I think that was it. He didn't say anything about the date, but I remembered it was the 22nd of May because that's my mum's birthday, but I can't remember if it was the same year – sorry.'

The waitress came back over and stopped at their table. Doyle quickly slid the photograph back into the folder. 'D' ya want anyfing else?' she asked with an attitude that meant she didn't give a toss if the answer was yes, or no. Doyle shook her head and waited for her to move away.

'What else did you talk about?'

'He was really kind; he showed me some identification – I think to reassure me. I was pretty sure he saw that pig shouting at me. We got talking about life really – he 'ad a nice manner about him. He asked me questions a little like you're doing now. He was really interested in me as a person – you know. I told him about my husband and the beatings, and he seemed genuinely concerned for my safety.'

'Did he say any more about himself, Holly?'

'Yeah sure, he said he'd been married twice before; he was wearing a ring like the one you showed on TV, but it was quite plain – just a gold band, I think. He told me he could help me and that I shouldn't go home tonight. At first, I thought he was going to suggest that I come and stay with him and thought – here we go again. But he didn't – he made a few phone calls and he got me into a hostel for battered women in Dalston. They convinced me to report my husband to the police and my life changed from that moment. I only ever saw that pig once more when he got sent down at Wood Green Crown Court after I'd given evidence against him.'

'If in the future I were to show you a photograph of this man who helped you, would you recognise him again, Holly?'

'Of course I would; he changed my life.' She looked down

at the table at her empty cup and picked at a chip on the cup's handle with her fingernail. 'He's dead, ain't he?'

Doyle looked at her and nodded. 'We can't be sure if the man you're describing is the same as the victim we are trying to identify, but if it is then yes – he's dead. You mentioned that he showed you some identification – can you remember what it was? Was it a driving licence, a work pass?'

'No.' Holly smiled. 'It was exactly the same as yours – he was a policeman.'

*

Graves brought the team up to date with the Forest Gate end of the inquiry. McNally told the team that he'd decided – in conjunction with the Met DCI – that the Met would continue with the investigation for now as BTP simply didn't have the resources. They would follow up on the description, and particularly the part-registration of the car seen leaving the scene. Graves would be the point of contact between the two investigations and McNally made a note in his decision log to visit Forest Gate within the next two days.

DC Jim Wakefield raised his hand. 'Guv, just before the meeting, Millwall FC got back to me. They had a near full house for their local derby yesterday, and they've supplied me with a list of names of those season ticket holders that didn't show for yesterday's game. They'll do the same for Tuesday's game as well. They won't give other details like addresses etc until they're served the appropriate data protection forms. I've printed the list off – there are 107 names. Twenty-one are women, so that leaves eighty-six men. Of course, this is a big shot in the dark, but if our man was a season ticket holder at the club, he'll obviously be on this list as we suspect he's been dead since at least last Tuesday.'

'OK, Jim. Good work.' McNally turned to Ray Blendell. 'Ray, get those data protection forms done and served ASAP. We need addresses for the remaining eighty-six so we can narrow it down further.'

Blendell nodded but added it would probably be tomorrow before they could get them served on the club.

'OK. I want it done tomorrow and, Jim, put some more pressure on the club. It's a good line of enquiry to follow. In the meantime, Marie, start researching the names we have on that list, cross-reference them with missing persons, look for any presence on social media, messages posted since last Tuesday to eliminate as many as we can as quick as we can. We might get lucky. I don't want to throw any more people at this for now; it might just be a wild goose chase. When we get the additional information, let's narrow it down – if they had the tattoo done in 2004, they would've had to be at least eighteen years of age – right?' Everybody nodded. 'So that would make them at least thirty-six or thirty-seven years old now. Does everybody agree?' Again, a sea of nods. 'So, Marie, let's dismiss anybody obviously below the age of thirty. Hopefully that will bring it down to a manageable number. OK. You've all got something to be getting on with – I know you're all tired, but keep it going, and unless anything develops, let's call it a day by five o'clock.'

McNally picked up his papers and indicated to Frost that he wanted a word with her in his office. As Frost followed him in and closed the door, McNally's mobile rang.

'McNally.'

'Hi, Ryan, it's Inspector Neil Williams. I think I might have something of interest for you.'

TWENTY-TWO

SUNDAY AFTERNOON

Search Advisor Inspector Neil Williams had set up a local RVP in a small church hall just off Mill Hill Broadway. McNally brought most of his team with him and told Linda Doyle to meet him there. Williams had sourced several ordnance survey maps and local street maps for the area, which he'd laid out on wooden tables. The hall was full of tired-looking uniformed search officers, some sleeping, others drinking tea and coffee and tucking into bacon rolls supplied by a local cafe.

'The driver gave us a pretty good location of where he first saw the mailbag,' Williams explained to McNally and Marcia Frost as he pointed to a local map. 'He was right; we found this containing some human remains,' Williams picked up a large police property bag, through which could be seen a Post Office mailbag, 'about a quarter of a mile from where the driver saw it, so carried by the train for some distance. There were human remains spread over a further half mile or so; the nearest access point to the railway, where the driver had seen the bag, that I could pinpoint, is a scrap metal dealership in a location called Bunns Lane, which is only separated from the mainline by a wire fence. I got the key-holder out of bed earlier and went and inspected the fence; it's full of holes. There is only one entrance to the yard, and therefore to the railway, and that is from Bunns Lane itself and, lo and behold, when I met the owner at the yard, the chain, fastened by a padlock, on the main gate, had been cut through.'

'OK, Neil. Thanks for calling us in. We won't know if these are the remains of our victim until blood and DNA testing comes through, but the circumstances tend to be taking us in that direction.'

'Where are the body parts?' Frost asked.

'At a local mortuary. I spoke to Ray Blendell in the incident room when you were travelling up here and he has asked for them to be transferred to the City mortuary, where Dr Felix…' Williams looked at his notebook, blinking several times; he looked very tired.

'Lowther?' Frost helped him out and he nodded.

'I got one of your SOCOs to take 'em over – Sally Cook. Was she the one on the Underground killings we helped you out on last year? Calls everybody *dude*?'

'Yep, that's the one; apparently she only calls people she likes *dude*,' Frost informed him.

'Oh, right, she called me sir.'

'Don't take it personally, Neil.' McNally smiled but the point was lost. 'Did you find anything resembling a head?'

'To be honest, Ryan, the remains were a mess. Could the head be mashed up amongst them? Yes possibly, but I don't know. I'm sure your pathologist will come back with an answer to that one. Look, my boys and girls are knackered, so we need to get back, get our gear and vehicles washed and get some sleep. Control of the mainline has been handed back to the railways and they're starting to run trains in about an hour after a track inspection by their people.'

'Thanks, Neil. We always seem to meet across a body of some kind. I'll buy you a drink when this is all sorted.'

'OK, Ryan. Good to see you back in the fold. I wasn't particularly looking forward to visiting you in prison.' Williams turned and rallied his troops for the journey back into town and to some well-earned sleep.

*

The City mortuary was extremely busy, not with the living but the dead. Each of the dozen fridges were fully occupied. Most of the incidents, leading to the full house, had been non-suspicious, among them: two teenagers killed in a road traffic accident; a drugs overdose, found in the toilets of a small shopping centre nearby with a syringe protruding from their groin; and a suicide from a five-storey building. All these cadavers were safely stored away awaiting post-mortems on Monday morning.

Pathologist Dr Felix Lowther was –in general – a good-humoured human being. Some questioned how he could afford to be so in his occupation; others took the opposite view – how could he not? But Sundays were sacrosanct. He enjoyed a visit to the pub, a game of darts followed by a good Sunday roast and just being plain boring. All his fellow Sunday drinkers thought he was an insurance broker. But one person who didn't give a toss about his mood was SOCO Sally Cook, a Kiwi by birth and somebody who generally didn't give a shit. Both had a respectful measure of each other and reached an unspoken compromise in order to get the job done as thoroughly and expeditiously as possible.

Having completed his preliminary examination and taken samples of blood and DNA for grouping and comparison with the previous body parts, he started to try and arrange – as best he could – what he had in front of him.

He spoke aloud both for the benefit of the recording device above his head and Sally Cook. 'The human remains are made up mostly of the torso of a white male who was overweight. The examination of the vital organs shows that he'd been a

153

heavy smoker and drinker for most of his life; I would estimate his age to be somewhere between fifty and seventy. I cannot – yet – confirm if these body parts are from the same victim that I examined earlier this week, but I would suspect this to be the case. I can also identify the presence of a right hand and a left foot. The left foot was contained inside the stomach of the torso. I cannot determine if this was as a result of the severe trauma that these remains suffered by being struck by a fast-moving train, or if it had been placed there prior to this by the killer. What I can say, is the remains have been frozen at some point. The inner lining of the stomach, for example, is still somewhat frozen, as are other internal areas. I would say the remains were in a freezer for maybe an hour, or at the most two, before being deposited on the railway line. The cold overnight temperature has maintained this condition to a degree. Most of the body parts have, to an extent, thawed. But it's like a piece of frozen chicken, the last part to thaw is the centre. That's why so many people get food poisoning,' he added, chuckling to himself. 'The only body part I can definitely state is *not* present here today, or in the two previous finds, is the head of the victim, which is still unaccounted for.' Lowther lowered his face mask, pulled off his protective gloves and overalls with a practised efficiency and threw them in a nearby bin. 'Job done, Miss Cook. All this talk of food is reminding me of how hungry I am; I'm going home to tuck into a large portion of beef with all the trimmings. I would be obliged if you could inform DI McNally that he'll have my final report, via your good self, no later than 4pm tomorrow afternoon – happy?'

'Cool, dude.'

*

Light rain had started to fall, turning a little sleety as the temperature in North London dropped. McNally had identified an area around Bunns Lane and Woodland Way for the house-

154

to-house teams to canvas. The properties on the latter overlooked the railway and the M1 motorway, which ran almost parallel with the mainline for some distance. McNally tasked Linda Doyle to lead the house-to-house enquiries, using several territorial support officers from Euston and King's Cross. He tasked Sam Hodge and Jim Wakefield to look at the M1 motorway and liaise with the Met Police traffic department and National Highways to see if they had any cameras, other than ANPR, along the stretch of motorway south of Mill Hill Broadway station. The DI jumped in his car with Frost and headed to the scrapyard described earlier by Inspector Williams. The owner had been told to stay at the yard until McNally arrived.

'Sounds like Linda Doyle's interview reaped some good info, guv.'

McNally nodded. 'Yeah, it's something we need to look at seriously once we've finished up here. Linda said this witness, Holly Harrison, was adamant he was a copper. The tattoo was right as well. What bothers me is how many Millwall fans had the same tattoo – Linda said her father had had something similar. It sounds promising – at least it's a solid lead we can work on. I've got Marie working on that as well, but she won't get far today – a Sunday.' McNally waited at a red traffic signal before moving on.

'Is Marie OK, Marcia? She seems a little distracted. I mean, she was a right live wire when she worked with us last year, full of ideas; she's wasted as a civilian. We could do with more cops like her – an intuitive thinker. But she seems a little preoccupied. I know you two are close, and I don't want to pry, but if it's affecting the way she does her job, then it is my concern.'

'She's got a few personal issues that she needs to sort out. I'm just a shoulder to cry on at the moment. I'll let you know if it becomes a real problem.' McNally nodded and seemed satisfied with Frost's answer.

'I got asked a question yesterday in the press conference about why these body parts are turning up at railway stations and now, if this is connected, on a railway line. Obviously, I and probably everyone else on the team have been thinking the same. To be honest, it's kept me awake for the last few nights. Maybe I'm being too tunnel-visioned about identifying our victim. We need to think about motive. Why is the killer following this course? Why not dump the body as one in the same place? It's got to be a message to us – a challenge, a reason why the victim was killed in the first place. What's that saying about woods and trees? It could be smacking us in the face, and we can't see it. What was that woman's name we used last year – the criminal psychologist? Doctor Sara somebody…'

'Sara Hallam, guv.'

'Give her a call, Marcia – see if she can come in tomorrow for a chat. I'd like her opinion on a few things. Just keep Romeo Graves away from her. I remember him chancing his arm with her just before I got nicked last year.'

'Oh, no worries on that score, she can look after herself, guv – no doubt about that.'

Frost directed McNally along Bunns Lane and under a low expansive bridge, which both the St Pancras mainline and the M1 motorway travelled over. By now, the winter night had drawn in and the grey skies had turned to black and looked heavy with snow.

'Bloody hell, this must be a traffic accident hotspot,' commented McNally as he drove round a couple of blind bends. They emerged from under the bridge and saw the scrapyard immediately on the left. The gates were partially opened. McNally nudged the gates a little further apart with the front bumper of the car, edged into the small yard and headed towards a Portakabin.

Scrapyard owner Tommy Roddy was sitting in a faux leather office chair, which had seen better days, with his muddy boots resting on a desk covered in papers, unimpressed that he'd been called in to open his yard in the middle of the night and that he was still there late afternoon on a Sunday. McNally introduced himself and Frost.

'Transport Police! Yer the feckers responsible for all this paperwork – are you not?' Roddy fanned his hands out across his desk to make the point. 'I've never dealt in a stolen piece of copper cable – on my life – even on my *mother's* life. Now I can't deal in cash and got to record every fecker's name and address and bank details that come through that door. How the feck is an honest man supposed to make a living in this game now, eh? You answer me that, Mr Detective Inspector.' Roddy was a big man with huge hands. McNally estimated him to be in his late forties; he had a deep southern Irish accent that was surprisingly rather soft in relation to the man's rough-and-ready look.

McNally and Frost tried unsuccessfully to keep straight faces but both broke into smiles. 'We're not here to discuss this governments, or any previous government's, policies on scrap metal dealers or in any way question your honesty and integrity, Mr Roddy. We believe your yard was broken into last night for the sole reason of gaining access to the mainline, situated just the other side of your boundary fence, to deposit the remains of a murder victim. On your arrival with police earlier this morning, the padlock on your gate was broken. Is that correct?'

'Well, you know the feck it was and if I catch the little bastard, I'll… well, you'd better hope I don't. Whoever it was, they were lucky I took the dogs home with me last night or you'd have more bodies to deal with.' Frost looked nervously around. 'Don't worry yourself, Sergeant, they're in the back of my truck – mind you, they do like a bit of black, don't we all?' Roddy sneered.

'You keep talking like that, Mr Roddy, this bit of black will be kicking your arse into the nearest police cell.'

McNally smiled at Roddy and nodded. 'Shall we keep this a bit civilised, because she's not kidding, and I'd be delighted to add my boot to the equation.' Frost got up and walked over to a photograph mounted on the far wall, more to control her temper than anything else. It showed a group of a dozen or so boxers, arms crossed, and hands gloved, posing in the centre of a boxing ring. Frost and McNally sensed a little unease and a change in attitude from Roddy.

'OK, officers, just a bit of light banter between professional people, nothing wrong with that, is there? What can I do for youse?'

'Do you have any CCTV on the premises? I see the signs but no cameras,' McNally said.

'No. The signs are for show. I used to have a couple on the front gate and on the Portakabin, but they got vandalised; youse lot were fecking useless, so I didn't bother replacing them, but I keep them for show; keeps the insurance company happy. The dogs do a better job – to be honest.'

'That'll be the first time today,' muttered Frost as she returned to her seat. 'Have you seen anybody hanging around the yard in the last few days? Paying particular attention to the railway lines?'

'Not that I can remember. We get all sorts in here. People looking for parts for various models of cars – you know. If they buy something, I record it. If they don't and waste my time, I forget them quick. I suppose you want to have a look around like that nosey uniformed fecker earlier – started talking about the condition of my fence – can you believe that?' Roddy looked genuinely indignant. He moved his heavy legs from the desk, picked up an impressive handheld flashlight and nodded towards the door. 'After you, Princess,' he said sarcastically to Frost. 'Don't want to lose you in the dark, do we?'

'Where was the picture taken, Mr Roddy?'

'What picture is that, Princess?'

Frost looked sarcastically around the office and hunched her shoulders. 'I can only see one at the moment.'

'Oh! That picture. It was taken at York Hall in Bethnal Green years ago when I used to do a bit of amateur boxing. Gave it up a long time ago – my knees didn't want to co-ordinate anymore with my hands.' To reiterate, Roddy clenched his huge hands into fists that resembled wrecking balls. 'Shall we go?'

He had memorised the number. If he was caught with a scribbled version by either his fellow inmates, or even the screws, he'd be a dead man. Daniel Corbell waited in line for the phone situated in the recreational area of his wing in Pentonville Prison. He tried to look relaxed, as if he were about to ring his mum or sister, but he was struggling; a bead of sweat trickled down his back towards the elasticated banding of his prison-issue training bottoms. He pulled at the waist to allow it to continue its journey towards the crack of his arse. He wasn't renowned for his personal hygiene. He ran the number through his mind again and stepped forwards when the phone became vacant. He looked nervously over his shoulder as he pushed each digit, moving his body position so the next in line couldn't read the digital display. He waited and was about to give up before a breathless female voice answered.

'Incident room – can I help you?'

*

Roddy scanned the darkness of the scrapyard with his powerful torch. The shadows cast by towers of metal gave Frost the creeps; she could hear the metal screaming in the light wind. She looked nervously around her, expecting Roddy's dogs to come bounding out of the darkness and savage her.

'Mind where you step, officers, there is scrap all over the place. Wouldn't want you hurting yourselves and suing me for damages now, would I?' He chuckled; he seemed to be enjoying himself. This was his turf, and he knew it.

As the party approached the boundary fence, McNally and Frost could see lights coming from the direction of the railway and the sound of vehicles screaming down the M1 – London-bound at excessive speeds.

'Hey, what're you doing?' A shout came from the direction of the railway line.

'We're police officers investigating the earlier incident – and you are?'

'Track inspection team making sure the line is undamaged before we open up.' Both parties acknowledged each other; the light beams slowly danced and disappeared into the darkness in the direction of London. McNally inspected the boundary fence and asked if this was the condition of the fence before last night.

'I expect so,' Roddy replied. 'I haven't been in this part of the yard in months. It looks like old damage to me, probably these fecking graffiti artists who paint walls and bridges, fecking nuisance! Should be strung up – little bastards.'

'I think some of it is quite artistic; it's a shame they can't find somewhere else to do it,' Frost commented.

'Yeah well, your sort would.'

Frost was just reaching her tolerance level with this dinosaur's racism.

McNally noticed and said, 'No need for you to stay out here and freeze, Mr Roddy. Thanks for all your help. We just want to have a look around and we'll meet you back in that nice warm Portakabin in a short while.'

Following a silent standoff, which lasted several seconds, between the owner and the senior detective, Roddy nodded and moved away before stopping and turning. 'Don't you start nosing around, will you – you need a warrant for that – I know my rights. And don't be too long. The dogs need a piss.' Roddy waved his hand in the air and headed back to the warmth of his hideaway.

The detectives waited for Roddy to move out of earshot and turned back to the hole in the fence. McNally took out a much smaller torch and examined the boundary. 'Looks as good a place as any – don't you think?'

Frost nodded, before realising McNally couldn't see her so said, 'Yes, guv.'

'If my calculations are right, we are only a few metres from where the mailbag was first seen by the driver.' He looked over to the motorway and saw several cameras on top of tall poles. 'I think they're just ANPR cameras so won't be much good to us.'

'Hang on, guv.' Frost tugged on McNally's coat sleeve. 'Shine your torch down there – that's a recent footprint.'

McNally did as he was asked and nodded. 'Good spot, Marcia. He placed his foot adjacent to the print. 'I've got size ten feet. That is bigger than mine. Go find something to cover it up, will you, before this rain gets any heavier – bit of plastic sheeting – your mate Roddy will find you something. And give Sally Cook a call – I want this footprint cast ASAP.' Frost nodded and turned back. 'Oh, and Marcia…' Frost stopped and turned, 'mind those dogs, won't you.'

'Sir, with respect – fuck off!'

*

Two hours later, McNally and Frost were in the car heading back to Camden.

'That was Linda on the phone,' Frost said. 'They've got nothing from the door to door. No sightings of any suspicious vehicles or of any six foot three black men with a mailbag.'

'He must have arrived by car. The place is in the middle of nowhere. Somebody must've seen something.' McNally's mobile rang. He pressed the hands-free into action. 'McNally.'

'Hi, guv, it's Ray in the office. Is Marcia with you?'

Frost spoke up, 'Yeah go ahead, Ray. We're just on our way back. What you got? Good news hopefully. We could do with some.'

'Well, yes and no. Marie Relish just took a call on the incident room information number given out yesterday. The good news: it was a whispered call from a prisoner in Pentonville, who says he recognises our suspect from the photograph shown on the news and is willing to speak to us.'

'You sure he's not another one throwing a name in the ring, Ray?' asked McNally.

'I don't think so, guv. When Marie pushed him for a little more information for us to take him seriously, he was reticent to speak over the phone; she could hear other people in the background – he was obviously on a payphone – but described the male as having three upper gold teeth – a fact you purposely held back yesterday.'

'OK, Ray. So, what's the bad news?' said Frost.

'His name is Daniel Corbell. He's got several conditions before he talks, one of which is – he'll only speak to you, Marcia.'

TWENTY-THREE

MONDAY MORNING

It was only 8am, but most of the team had been in the incident room for at least an hour, buoyed by the news that several leads were progressing fast. There was a cacophony of sound: phones rang; keyboards clattered; fierce banter ricocheted around the room. Jim Wakefield took the brunt, having made the bad decision to wear a sheepskin overcoat.

'Bloody hell, it's Jack Regan,' somebody said. The whole team started humming *The Sweeney* theme tune.

'No. He looks more like Del Boy,' Linda Doyle offered. It all went straight over Wakefield's head as he was far too young to remember the '70s cop show or the more recent sitcom, even though both were classics and often repeated on TV. Graves, helpful as ever, searched for a scene on his mobile as he glanced round the room. 'Where's *our* dynamic duo this morning?'

'Who's that, Regan and Carter or Del Boy and Rodney?' Blendell chipped in.

'No, you know, the boss and DS Frost.' Everybody laughed until Marcia Frost walked in with her usual coffee and was met with a muffled silence.

'Someone died?' she asked as *The Sweeney* tune started slowly and quietly circulating round the room before reaching a Boleric crescendo.

'Piss off, you lot.' She smiled. 'Boss said he'll be a couple of minutes. Get all your stuff together so we can rattle through and get on – OK?'

'OK, George,' somebody shouted out. Frost looked confused – Relish whispered that she'd explain later. McNally joined them, chewing a mouthful of bacon roll and sipping a cup of coffee.

'It's alright. We can relax. The boss *has* 'ad his breakfast.'

'You're on a *roll* now, Stuart,' Sam Hodge said, resulting in a collective groan from the others.

'Alright calm down, calm down, you lot,' McNally said light-heartedly in his best Scouse accent. 'Anybody would think we're on a day out at the seaside and not in the middle of a murder inquiry. I'm sure you're all aware that more body parts were found on the mainline between Mill Hill Broadway station and St Pancras Saturday night, Sunday morning. From the preliminary report from Dr Felix Lowther and DNA comparison, we can connect this incident with our other two last week at Liverpool Street and Victoria—'

'Watch out, everybody! The shrink has arrived,' Graves said, interrupting McNally mid-flow.

A familiar elegant figure slipped into the back of the room and caught McNally's eye. 'Just before we go on, I've asked Doctor Sara Hallam, a forensic psychologist, to join us this morning; many of you will know Sara from the Brewster investigation last year and remember her excellent contribution to the resolution of that inquiry.'

Hallam gave a short wave to everybody. 'Hi, everyone, nice to see you're on top form, DC Graves. I've missed your great wit, and particularly the great sex.' The room exploded in laughter and Graves went a crimson colour.

'You never learn, do you, Stuart?' Frost said.

'I'll get Marcia to bring you up to speed, Sara, but please chip in whenever. Thanks for coming. Getting back to yesterday, I'm confident that we've discovered the point of entry to the mainline – through a fence from a local scrap metal dealer. Sally, did we recover a decent cast of the footprint?'

'Yes, dude. I've printed copies of the photograph taken of the actual footprint and of the cast, which I've left with Ray Blendell. The shoe size is an eleven or twelve and looks something like a walking boot or a heavy working-type boot, certainly not a training shoe or leisure shoe. The impression has several identifying characteristics, which will be easily comparable with the actual footwear if recovered.'

'Linda, anything come in overnight from the house-to-house enquiries?'

'Got a phone call early this morning on my mobile from a woman who'd been away for the weekend and saw the leaflet we left at those houses we got no reply from. Her name is Judith Payne. She's a solicitor working for a firm in Hendon. She has one of those security video doorbells that record the front of her house and road; apparently, it's a bit of a burglary hotspot around there, a lot of professional people and money. She sent me some images via an email of a car parked across the road from her house. She lives a two- or three-minute walk from the scrap dealer. I forwarded the images on to Marie ten minutes ago – hopefully...'

Marie Relish tapped a few keys, and the images appeared on the big TV screen at the front of the room.

Doyle took up from where she left off. 'The time and date is accurate – I asked her to check it before she sent me the images. It corrects itself when the clocks go forwards and backwards; if you run it on, Marie, to half eleven... that's it. Stop there.' The room was silent as everybody watched a large black motor vehicle pull up adjacent to the house. The headlights are extinguished, and a dark figure emerges and goes to the rear of the car and pulls something out of the boot – it's obviously heavy. 'As you can see, it's difficult to get a look at his face before he moves out of shot, the street lighting isn't great, but he's definitely a black guy. OK, Marie, move it on to five past midnight. Yes. Stop there. Here he comes back to the vehicle – he doesn't go to the boot but jumps straight into the car and off. Got to be our man I'd say, guv.'

'That's the second sighting of a large black saloon car driven by a black male we've had, guv,' Frost said. 'The car seen by the neighbour outside Joey Dryden's address with a partial reg ending in WDP and now a similar vehicle and a similar suspect a couple of hundred yards from the scrapyard; add that to the description from Jake Knox of the man who approached him and gave him the bag and the CCTV impression of the male at Victoria station later the same night.'

'Why did he park so far from the yard? That bag must have weighed a tonne,' Wakefield commented.

'The scrapyard has CCTV cameras and signs, but they don't work, probably something our man was unaware of,' Frost answered.

'OK. Have the Met made any progress on that vehicle registration from Forest Gate, Stuart?'

'Well, guv. Let me start with our suspect – they're sure he doesn't live or operate on their ground. I told the SIO that we believe our victim may well be from Southeast London – tattoo etc. So, they're going to concentrate on ANPR cameras situated on the most popular vehicle river crossings from Southeast London into East London – for example the Rotherhithe Tunnel and the Dartford Crossing. ANPR has now moved on leaps and bounds, mainly due to AI. That's Artificial Intelligence, you thick lot. There are about eleven thousand Automatic Number Plate Recognition readers operating in this country at the last count. But now operators can refine searches down to a make and colour of a vehicle without any index number, but of course, we have the advantage of a partial number.'

'So how does that work in layman's terms for us thickos?' asked Hodge.

'Well, the way it was explained to me was, if a crime has been committed in a certain area, for example in our case Forest Gate with the murder of Joey Dryden or even – according to that piece of security footage we've just watched in Mill Hill – when one witness says it was a BMW vehicle but can't remember the colour and another says they can't recall the make of the car but remembered it was black, ANPR can be refined to search for Black BMWs that passed to or from the crime scene during a time parameter. Obviously, the narrower the time parameter, the more likely you'll pick up the vehicle. So, you may end up with six black BMWs in or around your crime scene, together with their registration numbers. They'll keep us updated. To be honest, I think they just want to link it to our inquiry and sling it over to us as quickly as possible.'

'Linda, can you give the team an update on the girl who phoned the incident room?' McNally glanced down at his notes. 'Holly Harrison.'

'Yes, guv, I met Holly yesterday. She lives out towards West London but wanted to meet away from her home. She'd been in a violent relationship with a guy who's been put away for a few years. She was very nervous about speaking to me and was constantly looking around for people who knew her or her ex. She relaxed after a while and told me about an incident that happened last year when her former husband assaulted her in Holloway Road after he'd been drinking all day with some of his mates. He left her on the floor outside a grocery shop, telling her to clear up the mess she'd made and get home after.'

'How old is she, Linda?' Marie Relish asked.

'She was born in 1999, so coming up to her twenty-fifth birthday. As she was cleaning up, she was approached by a male who helped her. She said he seemed kind, but she was, and still is, very wary of men for obvious reasons. The guy offered to buy her a coffee and said he thought he could help her. Again, she thought, "here we go again", but he made no move on her. Instead, he made a couple of phone calls and managed to get her into a hostel for women who suffer from domestic violence. She says the guy changed her life. When she saw the tattoo on the television the other night, she was sure it belonged to him as they talked about football, and he said he was a season ticket holder at Millwall. She gave me a description: white, five feet ten, a bit overweight, dark hair – which was thinning on top – probably in his early fifties. So, it falls into the rough description we've come up with in the last few days.'

'Did this guy give a name?' from Hodge.

'He did, but she can't remember; she was still pretty shaken up from the earlier incident. But he did show her some ID when she seemed to be getting a bit nervy. I asked what the ID was, and she said…' Doyle checked her pocketbook, '… "It was the same as yours. He was a policeman." She remembered his wedding ring – he still wore it even though he was divorced. I'm not saying this is our victim, I've no idea how many Millwall fans had the same or a similar tattoo, but he's got to be worth looking into.'

Sara Hallam raised her hand. 'Hi, Linda. Sorry to interrupt; we haven't met before.'

Doyle gave a friendly smile and said, 'Good to have you on board, Sara. Heard a lot about you – all good.'

'Have you been talking to Stuart as well?' A few jeers went round the room. Graves wasn't enjoying this, much to everybody's delight. 'Just an observation, Linda, I presume when you first met her, you showed her your warrant card?' Doyle nodded, wondering where this was leading. 'OK, bear with me. Could you just repeat what Miss Harrison said to you again about the identification presented by this man, please?'

'Yeah, sure, "It was the same as yours – he was a policeman." '

'Do you think she meant generically – as in just a policeman – or more specifically, did she mean a transport policeman?'

'To be honest, I just assumed a police officer – I'll ring her back after this briefing.'

'If it were a transport police officer, it could somehow explain the locations the body parts have been found in,' Hallam pointed out in a way that was not condescending.

'Good point, Sara.' McNally looked at Relish. 'Marie, get onto our force's HR and also the pension's office and cross-reference the names on the list from Millwall FC. We could be looking at a serving or retired police officer.'

Relish nodded. 'OK, sir. I'm hoping for further details from the club later this afternoon – the data production order was served first thing this morning, followed by a phone call. They anticipated the order and have been extremely helpful and are compiling the data now.'

'So, things are moving on our victim. What about the suspect? Have we shown the Victoria bus station CCTV image to Jake Knox up in Manchester yet?'

Linda Doyle jumped in. 'Spoke to a DS in Manchester, guv. He went round to his family's house and he's as sure as he can be that it's the same guy we are looking for.'

McNally was relieved – he would've looked a bit of a fool if Knox had said no after releasing the image to the press. 'Good. Marcia, bring us up to date with the phone call late last night.'

Frost produced an enlarged mugshot of a white male, which she fixed to one of the whiteboards. 'This is Daniel Corbell.'

'That's the thief we interviewed last year, whom we initially suspected of that murder at Mornington Crescent tube station, isn't it?' Graves said.

Frost nodded and looked over at Sam Hodge. 'Sam and I interviewed him, and he was eventually cleared of involvement in our investigation. He was a thief in the wrong place at the wrong time. He was handed over to the Pickpocket Squad, who charged him with several offences, and he got three years a couple of months ago.'

'Right gobby piece of crap.' Hodge chirped in. 'A racist arsehole; don't know how you didn't lump him one, sarge, the way he talked to you.'

'Well, it looks like we'll be meeting him again, Sam – later this afternoon in Pentonville. He says he can identify the suspect in the CCTV footage from Victoria, but of course he has conditions and will only speak with me.'

'Probably just trying it on, sarge, looking for some perks or a reduction in his time served,' said Wakefield.

'That's the first thing that crossed my mind – he is a conniving piece of work, that's for sure – until Ray told me that he mentioned the gold teeth. As you know, that's a detail the boss deliberately held back for this exact reason – to weed out the chancers. I don't know what these conditions are yet, but we are due at Pentonville at three o'clock, when I'm sure we'll find out.'

*

The loud knock on the door woke Jasmine Lee; she'd fallen asleep on the sofa. She gingerly got to her feet, wincing as pain shot though her abdomen before instinctively touching the bruising round her left eye. She hadn't left the house since Eddie had paid her a visit last week. She was trembling as she approached the door and peeped through the spyhole. Thankfully, it wasn't Eddie coming back for round two but two uniformed police officers. She knew whatever it was they wanted; it would be about her husband. Hopefully, he'd been arrested again and would be out of her life for another ten years.

'Mrs Lee?' the female officer asked.

'Yeah, that's me – what's 'e done now?'

'Can we come in please, Mrs Lee? We just need a quiet word, and the doorstep isn't really the right place.'

'You can't come in 'ere and start searching without a warrant; 'e ain't 'ere. I haven't seen him for a while. 'E's still in the nick – you lot should know that.' How ironic, she thought, the bastard had beaten her up just a few days ago and she was still protecting him.

'It's you we would like to talk to, Mrs Lee, and it's a little sensitive. Are you on your own?'

'Yes. I am.' She stood back from the door and indicated to them to turn left into the sitting room. 'What's this about? I ain't done nuffing wrong.' Jasmine indicated that they should sit in a two-seater leather sofa while she sat in an armchair by the small bay window.

The female officer took the lead whilst her male colleague looked uncomfortable. 'Mrs Lee, can I call you Jasmine?' Jasmine nodded. 'We believe that you are Eddie Lee's next of kin, is that right?'

'It's a bit of a stupid question seeing as I'm 'is wife.'

'You OK, Jasmine? You look in some discomfort, and I couldn't help noticing the bruising round your eye. Do you need medical attention?'

'Nah, I'm fine. Just get on wiv it, will ya. Where is he? Don't tell me 'e's pulled a knife on another copper?' She wanted to believe that scenario, bearing in mind what the bastard had done to her a few days ago, and that he'd been arrested and was back inside.

'Jasmine, Eddie was released from HMP Bedford early last week. But I think you already knew that didn't you?'

Jasmine nodded, unconsciously touching her bruised face again.

'This morning, we received a message from Norfolk Police, requesting that we make a personal visit to you to inform you Eddie was killed in a road traffic accident Saturday afternoon. He was a passenger in a transit van travelling at speed down the A140 between Cromer and Aylsham, being pursued by a police car, when the driver lost control at a roundabout – hitting another vehicle. The driver survived with serious injuries, but Eddie was killed instantly. They were able to identify him through fingerprints. We are very sorry to bring you such sad news.'

'Norfolk! What the fuck was 'e doing in Norfolk, for God's sake?'

'The other driver's name was Jed Jennings, a plumber by trade, it was his vehicle. Have you ever heard the name before?'

'No, never – what were they doing there?'

'We don't know the full story. Of course there will be an inquest, but as far as we can gather, they'd been involved in a fight in a pub in Cromer. They left the scene in a hurry in Jennings' vehicle and were spotted driving erratically and pursued by the police. Can I call somebody for you – a relative or a neighbour?'

'No – thanks – would you just leave, please? I need some time alone.'

'The Norfolk Police will be in touch in the next few days about the release of the body and the opening of the coroner's inquest – I'll leave my details if you need more information.'

TWENTY-FOUR

MONDAY AFTERNOON

A bitterly cold wind roared off the sea. Brian Garvey stood at the north end of Cromer Pier, wind full in his face; it was like having a cold shower and an ice bath at the same time, but it was invigorating. He truly felt alive. The lifeboat station stood quiet, proud and defiant against the wild, grey, North Sea. Garvey thought of those men and women going about their everyday lives; normal people with normal jobs, until that pager goes off and they turn into superheroes. He found their bravery and dedication humbling.

This was his thinking place, a place where, even when surrounded by hundreds of families in the summer, he could block the world out and think. On a cold January day like today – apart from a few diehard fishermen – he was alone in his thoughts; he had a lot to consider.

He took sanctuary from the wind on a row of benches protected by the end-of-pier theatre and studied the headline on the front page of the *Eastern Daily Press*: 'One Man Dies in Fatal Aylsham Car Crash'. Garvey had read the headline several times and the continuation of the story further on. There were –

reportedly – two men involved. Garvey took his reading glasses out and studied the black-and-white picture of the transit van involved for the umpteenth time. He could just make out the initials 'JJ' across the rear doors. He didn't know whether to laugh or cry. He had so many questions and nobody really to answer them. Who was killed? Was it Jed Jennings? Why were they being chased by the police? Who was the other man involved? What were their intentions regarding him? Did they mean to kill him, kidnap him? Was he now safe?

He looked out to sea and dragged memories from the back of his mind, memories he'd successfully boxed in his subconscious for the past five years. It was an accident. Yes, he'd been driving at an excessive speed in an unmarked police car on the day, but the little girl, Jennings' daughter, had run out in front of him, and he couldn't stop. Boy, how he'd tried. He thought of his own grandsons and the grief Mr and Mrs Jennings must have suffered. He was tried at the Old Bailey, of all places, and rightly acquitted by a jury of causing death by dangerous driving. The fact that he'd had his covert sirens and blue lights operating saved him, but not the girl. He remembered the feeling of complete emptiness after the trial. Colleagues had come to support him – including Frankie Meeres – he was embarrassed by their congratulations and pats on the back in front of Jed Jennings and his wife. He'd wanted to go and speak to them – explain what had happened again personally, face to face, not from a distant witness box. They were whisked away by a family liaison officer before he got the chance and, as time went by, it became harder and harder to summon the courage to meet them.

He dug his hands deep into his coat pockets, wrapped his scarf a little tighter round his neck and headed back along the pier to head home. He needed to speak to somebody. He alone knew why they were here. He decided to warm himself up and popped into The Rocket Cafe on the seafront.

'Morning, Gemma, large hot chocolate please, love – bitter cold out there.'

'Morning, Brian – it is January, you know. At least it's nice and quiet. Sit down – I'll bring it over. You been away? Haven't seen you for a couple of days.'

'Just seeing the grandkids – I came home for a rest.'

He relaxed in one of the big leather sofas and browsed through a discarded national newspaper. He started to lose interest when it was obvious such a local story was unlikely to reach the national press, until a story featured on page ten hit him like a sledgehammer – there in black and white. Everything was starting to fall into place. He jumped up and asked for the coffee to go and headed home as fast as he could.

*

The detectives decided to catch the tube to Caledonian Road and walk the short distance to Pentonville Prison. Trying to get your car booked into the prison car park was a nightmare and parking restrictions were enforced rigorously in the local area – they could've got away with charges for parking by putting the police logbook in the window but would be lucky to return to an undamaged vehicle or one not covered in dog mess or spit.

Following a thorough search and passing through several locked doors, Frost and Hodge sat patiently in an interview room waiting for the arrival of Daniel Corbell. Both officers had been offered a cup of tea. Hodge had accepted until Frost kicked him under the table and he changed his mind.

'What was that for?' Hodge complained, rubbing his shin.

'Who makes the tea in this place do you think – the prison officers?' Hodge looked puzzled. 'The prisoners do – you know, the ones who are trusted to work without much supervision – they make the tea – and what do you think we're likely to get in our tea to accompany the milk and sugar?' Hodge screwed his face up. 'Exactly, you got a lot to learn Sam – luckily, Aunty Marcia is here to look after you – anyway, stop being such a baby – I hardly touched you.'

'You're a bit nervy about this, aren't you? He rattled your cage last time we interviewed him, didn't he?' Frost got out a notebook and put a date and time on a fresh new page before looking at Hodge.

'Sam, we're here to do a job like we did last time – thanks to us, he got three years. Firstly, remember he called us so wants something in return for any information he's got and, secondly, we get to walk out of this Victorian dump – he doesn't – so he can try and wind me up as much as he wants, but don't forget we always hold the upper hand – got it?' Hodge nodded.

Frost was sure she could smell him before he entered the room. Corbell was escorted in by two prison officers – one of whom stayed. Corbell objected and Frost kindly asked if he would wait outside. Reluctantly, he agreed.

'As far as they know, you want to interview me for other offences.' Frost inwardly smiled at Corbell's naivety. The prison staff would know exactly why he was here. For somebody who'd spent as much time incarcerated in places like this as he had, she thought he'd know better.

Frost looked at Corbell, who returned her stare – each trying to gain the upper hand before a word had been spoken. Frost won. 'So, Daniel, how you been?'

'I'm OK thanks! See you brought your bag-carrier with you. Is he stuck to you or something, or can't you two bear to be apart?' Corbell grinned – pleased with himself for getting some of the initiative back. Frost felt a little sick as he revealed his yellow, crooked teeth before sticking his hand down the front of his prison-issue training bottoms and having a rummage, a disgusting habit he hadn't ditched since the last time they'd met.

'Let's get to the point, Daniel. I'm sure the less time you're in here talking to the police the better it will be for you. So, what've you got for us?'

'Well, let me tell you what I want out of this little chat first, shall I?'

Frost was tempted to be more forceful and inform him he was in no position to demand anything, but she let it go. She knew she could take control back at any time by just getting up and walking. She nodded for him to continue.

'I want to be moved from here to an open prison. I've only got a few months to go before I'm released, and I know I qualify, and secondly, I want some cash for when I get out. I mean, you still 'ave funds for informants, don't you? Or whatever you lot call them these days.'

'CHIS – Covert Human Intelligence Source,' Hodge replied.

Frost looked slightly annoyed. They were there to ask the questions not answer Corbell's.

'Fuck me, boy wonder. You lot gotta name for everything, ain't yer.' Corbell turned his venom into a verbal rant at Frost. 'I hear they call you lot LBTQ or something like that now?'

Frost smiled at his ignorance and didn't bother to get involved in a slanging match with somebody she knew, from previous experience, to be a racist, homophobic, misogynistic pig. She took a deep breath and asked again, 'I'll decide what we can do for you when you tell me what you have on this guy...' Frost showed him the CCTV image of the black male at Victoria station. '... circulated on TV in relation to an investigation we are running.'

'You recording this?'

'No. I'm not. We've nothing with us,' she waved her hands towards the empty desk in front of them, 'and handed our mobiles in to the reception staff.'

Corbell placed his other hand inside his tracksuit bottoms and looked up at the skylight, as if requesting guidance from a greater power.

'Are you praying, Daniel? That's a funny place to put your hands together.'

Corbell removed his hands and rubbed his face. Frost nearly threw up as she got a waft of sweaty groin.

'Look, the geezer on the TV the other night, him in the

photo. He's South London, used to live round Bermondsey, but he moved out a few years ago. I know his name and I know who he works for.'

'OK. Are you going to give us that information or not?' Frost asked, more nonchalantly than she really felt, and waited, trying not to let on how much they needed this break. It was important he spoke next, and she looked at Hodge to discourage him from any utterances.

'Look, I'll give you something today, but you'll get the rest when I get my move and the money in a bank account I've got on the outside.'

'This isn't some drugs deal, Daniel. You forget where you are and who we are. How do I know you know the identity of this man? It might be bullshit. Let's pull no punches here. You're hardly known for telling the truth, are you?'

'I'm not pissing about. I told your officer I spoke to on the blower that this bloke had gold teeth. I know you fuckers don't reveal all when doing these TV appeals in order to weed the crap out, but I heard the slightest hesitation when I mentioned the teeth. Anyhow, I knew I was right when everybody I was sitting with watching the appeal who're from South London went silent and started to look around, daring each other to say anything, including me to be honest. Now *that* is the truth.'

'OK. What're you going to give me?'

'A first name, that's all for now. You'll get the surname and who he works for when you come back here in person, Detective, and show me – in writing – what I want. His first name is Maurice. Oh, and you won't find him in any criminal records or on any computer because he's never been nicked or convicted of anything; he's a bloody ghost.'

'We'll be in touch.'

'Better make it fast, lady – I ain't got much patience.' Corbell stood up and stretched before offering his hand to Frost. 'Shall we seal the deal, Officer?'

Frost looked at his filthy hand. 'My word will have to do, Daniel – I know where that's been.'

'Shame that. I wasn't going to wash it and then 'ave a wank, by proxy, later.'

*

It had been a long day looking at lists and a computer screen for Marie Relish; she'd been rescued by Jim Wakefield and dragged out of the building to a little Turkish coffee shop on Camden Road, Wakefield was one of very few men she felt safe with at the moment. Mind you, saying that he was only a boy really. She thought he couldn't be more than early twenties. He'd really done well to get a job on a team like this so early in his career. She hoped he hadn't peaked too early and that the next thirty-odd years wouldn't be a huge disappointment.

'You OK, Marie? Seem a bit quiet.'

Relish thought that Jim had a soft spot for her, but she didn't need a relationship now, although she rather fancied the idea of having a toy boy, even though she was only a few years older than him. 'Just a lot on, Jim, think we're all tired, aren't we?'

'Yeah, I suppose so – it's not Graves, is it?'

'It's not Graves, *what*, Jim?' She went on the defensive. Did he know or suspect something?

'You know – bothering you. He can be a right mouthy bastard when he wants to. I should know, I've been the brunt of his tongue often enough.'

'No – nothing to do with him,' she lied, although not convincingly. The truth was she didn't have a clue who was stalking her. There – she had admitted it to herself after the chat with Sara Hallam the other night. She was being stalked; she was the victim in all this. She quickly changed the subject. 'You moved house since the last time we worked together? Going up in the world, first a detective, now a homeowner. Next it will be a wife and kids.'

'No not me, Marie. I like my freedom too much. Go where I want, do what I want, when I want.'

Relish looked down into her half-empty cup, a little bit disappointed.

*

He watched Relish and Wakefield leave the building and go into the coffee shop. He knew he had at least half an hour. The incident room was empty apart from a couple of civilians still manning the phones in case of any new information from the TV appeal or the subsequent coverage in the daily papers. He looked out of the window, where he could just see the entrance to the coffee shop, and felt confident he had plenty of time. He walked over to Relish's desk and smiled when he saw her keys resting on the desktop. He took them and went to the gents' toilets. Returning five minutes later, he replaced the keys where he'd found them.

TWENTY-FIVE

MONDAY AFTERNOON

The call from Frost was disappointing. McNally was hoping for a big breakthrough; instead, they had a first name of a suspect unlikely to be on any of their databases; however it was just the word of a con, so they would check. McNally walked into the incident room and bumped into Det Supt Nigel Plummer, who looked a little flushed.

'Everything alright, guv? You look like you're in a rush.'

'Yes, yes. The ACC for Crime wants an update. He's getting pressure from the chief, especially after the weekend. The train operating company is up in arms about the time it took us to search and return the mainline to them – just politics, Ryan, a bit of sabre rattling. Take my advice, don't go for promotion. You spend most of your working day bending over backwards to play one off against the other. Anyway, I'd better go upstairs before he starts shouting. You got *anything* to keep him off my back for a while?' McNally told him about the call from DS Frost – it seemed to cheer him up a little.

Ray Blendell, Stuart Graves and Linda Doyle were deep in conversation but relaxed when Plummer left the room.

'He's a bit uptight, guv.' Graves pointed out the obvious. 'Got a right strop on. Anything back from Pentonville yet?'

'Yeah, we got a first name, but Corbell is playing silly buggers. Where is Marie? I want her to start looking at some databases. The name we got is Maurice.'

'She's just popped out with Jim for some fresh air. Back in a minute,' Doyle answered.

'Corbell reckons this Maurice has never been nicked and he works for somebody south of the river. Linda, if you and Stuart can start speaking to any contacts in the Met in South London, see if we can come up with a surname. The description is pretty good. Email them the photo we've got from Victoria, if that helps. Anything else?'

'Just got a call from a DS at Forest Gate nick; they didn't get anything more from the house to house in Joey Dryden's road, but they've got a result of sorts from the ANPR on the black car our man was seen getting into.' Graves referred to a printed message. 'ANPR has identified twenty cars matching the WDP part-registration, travelling along Forest Road and through the Blackwell and Rotherhithe tunnels. They've eliminated six of them down to colour alone – you know, reds, greys and yellows – but have kept in black, dark brown, dark green etc just in case the witness got it wrong as it was late at night. So that left fourteen, of which five were registered to women; they haven't written them off but are concentrating on the remainder registered to men. Of course this won't be a definitive list. The car we're looking for could've come a different route not covered by the ANPR cameras, or may have false plates, or the car isn't legitimately registered. There are a lot of variables, so I wouldn't get our hopes up too high yet.'

'Let them have the name Maurice as soon as you can, Stuart. Corbell said something about this Maurice working for somebody, presumably for a criminal gang, so he could just be a driver and odd-job man, so the car wouldn't be registered to him.'

McNally headed back towards his office and was greeted by the landline ringing on his desk. He looked at his watch; his stomach began to grumble. He hadn't eaten for hours. He sighed, sat down and lifted the receiver – it was one of the officers manning the inquiry lines.

'Guv, sorry to bother you, but I've got a retired BTP officer on the phone. Says he needs to speak to the officer in charge. His name is Brian Garvey, a retired detective sergeant.'

*

The detectives dropped into a cafe opposite the prison entrance, imaginatively named The Breakout.

'Great name for a cafe; someone's got a sense of humour,' Frost said as they sat down by a window, looking back at Pentonville Prison. 'Apparently they used to hang people in there in the old days.' Frost glanced around. 'How d' ya know about this place?'

'Been here a couple of times when I was stationed down the road, rated one of the best cafes in London.' Hodge looked at the menu. 'If you're eating, you'd better hurry up – I think they close pretty soon.' They ordered and paid at the bar. Hodge went and sat back at the table. Frost rejoined him after visiting the ladies' and scrubbing her hands until they were red raw; she knew she wouldn't feel clean for days. Each considered the last half an hour or so, what had been said and how it would progress the case.

Frost looked at the cafe's clientele and decided it consisted of three main groups: prison officers, police officers and people who'd just come from, or were about to visit, their loved ones behind bars; it was a belligerent atmosphere as respect between the groups was distinctly lacking, everybody eyeballing each other. If this had been a pub, it probably would have kicked off by now, but the food was great.

'What d' ya think about Corbell?'

'He's an arsehole. You know what I think,' Hodge replied,

taking a huge bite from a burger that he had smothered with ketchup.

'I mean about the info, the name he gave us. Do you think he's serious or just playing us?'

There were several seconds of silence as Hodge forced a mouthful of half-chewed burger down his throat, followed by a large gulp of tea. 'I think it's legit. Why would he lie? He was taking a big chance talking to us in the first place – he'll probably be explaining to everybody on his wing why he was talking to the cops as we speak.'

'Yeah, I know, but I don't think McNally was too impressed, especially as it's him who's got to convince Plummer to try and get this sorted. We might not need that creep. I mean, how many black men are there in South London with a first name of Maurice who go around murdering people and disposing of body parts?'

Hodge burped so loudly several people turned round. He raised his hand apologetically. 'Sorry, Sarge, I'm starving, and you know what they say in this job – eat while you can.'

'I bet you don't eat like a pig when you're out with Madalina.' Frost's smile hinted a little sarcasm, or maybe some jealousy, bearing in mind her lack of any relationship with the opposite sex. Hodge tried to reply but only succeeded in spraying Frost with burger.

*

'DI McNally, how can I help?'

'Hi, there! Thanks for taking my call. My name is Brian Garvey. I was in the BTP CID for many years and retired some time ago now. I used to be based at the former headquarters in Tavistock Place. I need to talk to you about the case that you're investigating. I've got some information that I hope will be of great interest to you.'

'OK, Brian. My name's Ryan. Just give me a moment to get a pen and then you can fire away.'

'I can't do that, Ryan. I'll need to speak to you in person. Can we meet tonight?'

'Yeah, of course, whereabouts? I'm based in Camden.'

'Look, I live in Cromer in Norfolk, retired up here; I had to get away from London. I can be on a train by four o'clock and at Liverpool Street for about seven. Do you know the area that well? I can hear a trace of northern in your voice.'

'I'm originally from Manchester, moved down here on promotion a couple of years ago. You got anywhere in particular in mind?'

'There's a pub round the back of Bishopsgate nick in New Street, right opposite the entrance to the station. It's called the Magpie. Full of cops and bankers normally, but by seven it would've cleared a bit. I'll meet you in there just after seven. I'm sure we're both experienced enough to recognise each other.'

'Can you give me an inkling what info you have, Brian? Maybe I could get a head start on it while you're travelling down?'

'I'm not happy talking about this on the phone. Just call me old-fashioned and suspicious. I'd like to meet you face to face because, if I'm right, and I have put all the pieces together in the right order, this will blow your investigation apart.'

McNally replaced the receiver and shouted through his open office door for Linda Doyle and Ray Blendell to join him. He summarised what he'd just been told and requested they do some digging into the former detective sergeant, in particular the circumstances he left the job under – did he just retire as he said, or did he leave under a cloud? He wanted the information before seven so ushered them out and then called Marcia Frost.

*

Carol Jennings sat at her ex-husband's bedside at the Norfolk and Norwich University Hospital on the outskirts of the city. She still used Jennings as her surname – more out of respect for their lost daughter and convenience than anything else; she just couldn't face the hassle of changing bank accounts and credit cards and it seemed, to her, that she was disrespecting the memory of their daughter by doing so. She'd been here for several hours and was fighting sleep; the slow, repetitive bleeping of Jed's heart monitor was reassuring and calming, like an old clock ticking away in the hallway. She'd received the phone call late Sunday afternoon. She was still listed on his mobile under ICE – in case of emergency. The hospital had kindly found her a bed to catch a few hours' sleep. She still loved him, but their daughter's death, five years ago, had driven a huge wedge between them rather than uniting them, something she always regretted. She was all he had. Jed's father had died when Jed was twelve and his mother ten years after that. She studied the lines in his face as he lay in an induced coma. The doctors were unsure how long it would be before he regained consciousness but were confident it would be soon and that he'd make a full recovery. He was only thirty-one years old, but the loss of Sophie had aged them both.

Carol had the facts of the accident explained to her by a police officer but could offer no explanation as to why her former husband had been in Norfolk and had no idea who Eddie Lee was. She looked through Jed's wallet; a tear escaped from one eye and traversed across her cheek as she kissed the photograph of her daughter. There was a little cash and a few receipts for plumbing supplies and a return rail ticket to Bedford, which she found a little strange; she was unaware of anybody he knew in that town – maybe a business contact. She rested her head on her forearm and drifted off to sleep.

TWENTY-SIX

MONDAY EVENING

The Magpie was still relatively busy for a Monday night, McNally thought. It was a pub he had never been in before – traditional with proper beer pumps, offering a wide selection of real ale, ranging from light to dark, modern to traditional. He ordered a pint of Guinness and took up his usual position: a seat with his back to the wall, facing the entrance. He imagined many of the remaining customers were city workers dropping in for a couple of pints before jumping on a train home. McNally loved to people-watch. He thought it was an essential skill to possess in order to be a competent police officer. He wouldn't define himself as what the police service now described as a 'Super Recogniser': police officers who had the ability to retain hundreds of faces to memory and were often used to identify offenders from CCTV images for example. But he was good with faces. He couldn't always remember names but faces stuck in his mind.

It wasn't hard to pick out Brian Garvey as he walked into the bar, and to be fair, he looked straight at McNally. They exchanged an accustomed look that takes place when one police officer recognises the profession of the other, having never met before. Garvey raised his hand and shook it slightly, as if holding an invisible glass; McNally shook his head, pointing to the nearly full glass in front of him.

According to the information emailed over to him from Ray Blendell fifteen minutes earlier, Brian Garvey was approaching sixty; he'd retired four years earlier and now lived – as he knew – in North Norfolk. He had an exemplary police record having never been disciplined; awarded his police long service medal after twenty-two and a half years' service; and received thirteen commendations, ranging from judicial to chief constable's – three for bravery and the rest for excellent detective work. He'd finished his career as a detective sergeant – the forerunner of his own team – investigating major crime nationally. All in all, he seemed pretty sound.

McNally looked back to the entrance and watched Marcia Frost enter the bar. She paid McNally no attention and ordered a drink as Garvey walked over to him. She looked a little nervous and it was obvious she'd never received any sort of surveillance training and felt a little out of place in this white, male-dominated arena. McNally had asked her to back him up as he'd had a slightly weird feeling about the whole set-up. It looked like he needn't have worried.

Garvey offered his hand, which McNally accepted, and both took a slug from their glasses to fill in that often difficult silence that occurs when two people meet for the first time.

'Is this a regular of yours?' McNally enquired to break the ice, looking round at the decor again, as if he were the one who'd just walked in.

'It used to be. I'd often drop in for a pint on the way home – I used to live in Essex before I retired, and the wife and I moved up to Norfolk.'

'Yes, lovely place, the North Norfolk coast. My in-laws live in Sheringham. Are you and your wife happy there?'

'Sadly, she passed away a couple of years ago, cancer, fucking disease; gets one out of two of us eventually.'

McNally cursed Ray Blendell under his breath. He could've done with knowing that. He knew Garvey would have expected him to do some digging about his past before the meeting, so a major fact that his wife had died, a fact of which he was unaware, was slightly embarrassing, but to his credit, Garvey didn't show any animosity.

'This pub used to be a good RVP, if you were meeting a city police contact. They all get in here. Did you know, a few years ago, you had to be at least six foot tall to join the City of London Police? I remember the first time I went into Bishopsgate nick the coat racks were fixed to the walls about a foot higher than anywhere else, bit embarrassing if you were only five foot eight tall. Now, since they got rid of the height restriction, you can join at five foot nothing, hence why you get midgets in helmets wandering around the streets.' Garvey took another gulp of his drink.

'I'd imagine a lot of info has passed between cops in this bar over the years,' Garvey continued. 'It's also a handy place just to sit and listen. These city tossers can't keep their gobs shut and you pick up some good tips about stocks and shares. I mean, have a look at that group over there,' Garvey indicated, with a nod of his head, a gathering of six men evidently well into a serious drinking session. 'You go and prop the bar up next to them for an hour and you would hear some interesting info.' Garvey winked at him.

'Puts a new slant on insider trading.' McNally laughed. 'You dabble in all that? I could never get my head round anything as complicated; my limit is a few premium bonds.'

'It was an interest of mine a few years ago, but I can't be bothered anymore. The world's too unstable. I mean, you look at the price of petrol or the instability of oil and gas or the retail giants that have gone out of business; I got bitten when Woolworths crashed. Mug's game now. I'd advise you to leave it alone if you were thinking of it. You're better off sticking with premium bonds, a lot safer and less chance of developing an ulcer.' Garvey glanced over towards the bar and studied it for a second or two.

'You can ask your colleague to join us if you want.' Garvey indicated with his head towards Frost. 'I don't mind.'

McNally smiled and waved Frost over.

'She stands out a bit in here, doesn't she? A pretty girl on her own; if it's any consolation, I would've done the same. A little bit of backup.'

McNally was starting to like this guy. He introduced Frost to Garvey, and they all settled down after the posturing was over.

*

She stepped off the bus and headed towards her tower block. Marie Relish looked all around her; it was dark and misty – speckles of ice glinted as they passed through the dull glow cast by street lights, on their way to earth. She had spent the last two nights at Marcia Frost's flat but now needed to replenish her clean clothes. She'd been grateful to have had company, but this was her home.

Happy that she wasn't being followed, she took the lift to the fourteenth floor and searched around in her handbag for her keys. She felt safe now as she opened the door to her flat, quickly shutting it and leaving the outside world behind her, locking the door securely. She turned the heating and hot water on and kicked off her shoes; her plan: something to eat, a hot bath and an early night, in that order. She took the phone off the hook and turned her mobile to silent. She entered her bedroom and stopped suddenly a few feet from her bed. She felt unsteady and collapsed back into an armchair, her eyes focused, her brain trying to make sense of the image that confronted her. On the bed was her mother's scarf – neatly folded. She placed her head in her hands and cried.

*

Brian Garvey looked at the detectives and, for the first time since he had met them, appeared to be a little on edge – as nice as they seemed, he knew it was show time. He took in a gulp of air, before glancing around him in a conspiratorial manner. Satisfied nobody else was in earshot, he started to relay his story.

'About five years ago, I was on a surveillance team – we were behind a well-known mailbag thief. It was a fact-finding operation: lifestyle, associates, banks he used and places frequented. Anyway, halfway through the operation, we got redirected to assist counterterrorism police and security services in surveying several targets believed to be about to carry out an attack somewhere in Central London. Surveillance teams were being summoned and utilised from all over the UK, even the bloody Isle of Wight – what the fuck they follow over there I've no idea. It was a massive operation. We were instructed to get to a location in North London for a briefing before deployment. To be honest, I'd been on duty since five in the morning and was knackered, but that's the way it is in this job, as you both know, I'm sure. I put the covert sirens and blue lights on and started to make ground to the RVP for the briefing. I was doing probably fifty in a thirty and a little girl ran out from behind a parked car straight in front of me, and I couldn't avoid her.' He stopped a moment, as if he were vividly reliving the incident again. McNally and Frost didn't interrupt; they could see that it was still very raw, and Garvey seemed genuinely upset. Garvey took a gulp from his glass, composed himself before he carried on.

'She... she didn't move, and it seemed to take ages for an ambulance to arrive. She was taken to hospital, but she didn't make it. For an hour or so, I thought she would be OK, but I got a call from my DI to say she'd passed away without regaining consciousness. I got investigated and charged with causing death by dangerous driving, even though I was driving by the book. I got tried at the Old Bailey, of all places, because the *alleged* offence happened within the boundaries of the City of London; the parents were there throughout the trial – the worst part was the pathologist giving details of her injuries, but I was acquitted by a jury after only twenty minutes' deliberation. I was released from the dock; that's when her father – Jed Jennings – shouted death threats at me in open court. He was lucky – I suppose – not to get arrested himself, but obviously the threats weren't taken seriously and were put down to the stress of the situation. I never saw him again. I went back to work, and life resumed some sort of normality. To be honest, I never truly got over it. My wife convinced me that I should retire on thirty years, which I did.'

McNally and Frost – although sympathetic – were at a loss as to where this was leading in relation to their inquiry but remained patient. McNally got up and brought another round of drinks. He returned to a happier Brian Garvey, who looked to have shed some of the burden from his shoulders and was discussing with Frost how the service had changed in the short time he'd been gone. Garvey seemed impressed with the young DS and back to the relaxed, laid-back man of fifteen minutes ago. McNally wondered if they were the first people he'd ever really told what had happened, outside a police interview room or a court of law. He felt a bond with this guy, having just had a similar experience himself less than a week ago – although of course his case didn't involve the death of a young child. They settled back down again, and Garvey continued.

'A week or so ago, I got a call from an informant that I used to run, a reliable bloke who has given me some good info over the years. He said he wanted to see me. I knew it would be important even though I told him I was no longer in the job. He told me it had nothing to do with the police, but it was a personal favour to me, so we met up in town. He told me there was a contract out on the lives of me and my old partner Frankie Meeres. Now, I hadn't seen Frankie since I retired. We worked closely together for many years and were good mates, but after I retired, we lost touch. I went back home a little concerned, even though I know it sounds a bit Al Capone-ish – contracts to kill and all that – more for the TV than real life. Anyway, I thought I owed it to Frankie to give him the heads-up and tried to contact him, but I learnt that he'd also retired and had changed his mobile number.'

Frost's mobile rang and she saw the call was from Marie Relish; she diverted the call onto voicemail and turned her phone to silent, apologising for the interruption.

Garvey continued, 'I wasn't overly worried but became a little more aware of who was who in Cromer. This time of year, it's just the locals in places like that – I mean, it's bloody freezing. Last Thursday or Friday I was looking out of my window and saw a van go past. I saw it was a plumber's van, and something bothered me about it – I just put it down to paranoia. But I decided I needed to find Frankie so packed a bag and drove down to Essex to stay with my daughter and grandkids and took the opportunity to drive to Catford and visit the last address I had for him. He wasn't there. I left a message for him to ring me, poked it under his door, but he never got back to me. My grandson's called Josh, and it suddenly dawned on me what had bothered me about the van. It had the initials "JJ" on the side – Jed Jennings. I drove home on the Saturday night and caught the end of the local news reporting an accident on the A140, and there it was – the same bloody van.'

'Do we know what happened to him?' Frost asked.

'According to the television reports, he survived the accident and is in the Norfolk 'n' Norwich Hospital – in a coma. The other guy in the van was killed.'

'Who was he?' It was McNally's turn for the question.

'That I don't know.'

McNally looked at Frost quizzically and then turned back to Garvey, but it was the former detective who beat them to the obvious question.

'You're going to ask what this has to do with your investigation.' McNally and Frost nodded in unison. 'I was looking through the national papers this morning to see if there was any more information about Jennings and the other man who died, but it wasn't a big enough story for them to carry. But what I did see was your public appeal for help and a picture of a tattoo and a ring with a date on it.'

McNally and Frost stiffened, as if being ordered to stand to attention.

'Your victim is Detective Sergeant Frankie Meeres, my ex-partner. I recognise the tattoo. He was a big Millwall fan and went to that game in Cardiff. I remember him coming into the office a few days before the final and showing it off to anybody he could find.'

Frost jumped in. 'Brian, we believe quite a few Millwall fans had the same or similar tattoos done – the father of a police officer on our team has one. So how can you be so sure it is DS Meeres?'

Garvey held audience for a few seconds before draining his glass. 'Because the date on the ring is the date he got married. I should know; I was his best man.'

*

McNally and Frost shook Garvey's hand and thanked him as he dashed across the road to get his last train back to Norfolk. The detectives stood under the canopy of a fast-food outlet to keep out of the rain, which had turned quite heavy. Both looked at each other with a sense of shock. Each had a hundred and one questions to ask but decided to sleep on it as neither wanted to travel back to Camden at this hour.

'I'll get in early, guv, complete a briefing note and show it to you before you brief the troops.'

McNally nodded. 'Put a group message out, Marcia. I want everybody in by seven. We've got a busy day ahead – I'll see you in the morning.' McNally didn't wait for a reply and crossed the road towards the London Underground. Frost suspected he just wanted to be on his own to figure out the importance of what they'd just been told, in relation to their investigation. Frost suddenly remembered the call from Relish. She dialled the number and listened to her friend sobbing down the phone.

'Marie, calm down. I'll arrange for a twenty-four-hour locksmith to come and change the locks – I know one in Kilburn. He'll be there quick time when I tell him the circumstances. Just keep the door locked. I'll get him to ring you when he arrives outside your block. I'm coming over as well – I'll stay the night. We've got an early start tomorrow. Hope you've got some spare knickers.' That got a small snigger out of Relish. 'I should be with you in about forty-five minutes.'

TWENTY-SEVEN

TUESDAY MORNING

'What's the matter with you, sweetheart – cat got your tongue?'
'Why don't you piss off, Stuart, and go try your charm on somebody who gives a fuck about you.' Relish was in no mood for Graves. In fact, she only just stopped short of accusing him of breaking into her flat and stalking her. She had no proof.

Graves raised his hands in the air as a sign of surrender and backed off. 'OK, I *know* it's the wrong time of the month.'

Relish could have quite happily stuck a knife into that bastard at this point in time when he said he *knew*. How did he know? God, maybe it really was him. There had been no forced entry into her flat; somebody had a key. She knew she'd been stupid enough to leave her keys on her desk; her flat door key was only a simple Yale and easy enough to get a copy, but could it be him? It could be anybody with access to this room, and that was literally dozens of people.

Marcia Frost came over, looking a little dishevelled. She'd luckily had an overnight bag with some clean clothes under her desk, as most of the team were required to do. In this job, you never knew where you'd wake up the next morning. 'Marie, don't let him get to you; if he smells fear, he'll go for the throat. He's just a nasty piece of work. You're safe now. The locks have been changed, so keep those keys on you until we sort this out.'

Sara Hallam walked into the incident room and gave Frost and Relish a wave. The rest of the team were as busy as beavers. McNally followed Hallam in, reading Frost's briefing note of the meeting with Brian Garvey the previous evening, for a second time. The room went quiet.

McNally waved the briefing note in front of the team. 'Yesterday evening DS Frost and I had a meeting with a former detective sergeant, Brian Garvey.'

'I used to work with him years ago, nice bloke,' Graves added. 'He likes a drink.'

'He retired four years ago. The information he gave us has the potential to move our investigation forward significantly. Have you all had a chance to read this briefing note before we started?' Everybody seemed to nod; a couple of copies had been circulated as people arrived well before the 7am briefing. 'Good, so I don't need to waste time going over what was said. This is going to be a busy day. I want to discuss the lines of enquiry we're going to follow up on, and Ray will issue actions ASAP.' McNally turned several pages over in his decision log. He'd already discussed the way forward with Det Supt Plummer, who joined them in the incident room.

'Firstly, I want whatever we've got on former DS Brian Garvey. Early indications suggest that he was a good officer with an excellent service history – Ray, I'll leave that with you to continue. Marcia and Sam, I want you to follow up on the Norfolk connection; liaise with the Norfolk Police, go up there if you have to – might be worth looking at what was recovered from the van. I want to know the identity of the second male in the vehicle. I believe that we've probably established why they were there, but were they there for the sole purpose of avenging Jed Jennings' daughter, or did our mystery man have a motive as well?

There must be a connection between this incident and Garvey's partner, another former detective sergeant, Frankie Meeres, who I now believe is our victim.'

Wakefield respectfully raised his hand. 'Guv, I've had a look at that list of season ticket holders from Millwall; Meeres has been a season ticket holder since 1994 and one of those who didn't turn up for last Saturday's game.'

McNally took a large gulp of lukewarm coffee. 'Good, that's enough for me. I'm going to proceed on the basis that our victim *is* Frankie Meeres. Hopefully DNA will confirm. Stuart, Jim, I want you to get over to Meeres' last known address in Catford, provided by Garvey. It's in the briefing note. Take Sally with you and search it. Treat it as a possible crime scene initially – so a full forensic search. Sally, I want DNA taken from the flat and matched to the DNA profile we have for the victim – fast track it. I know it'll cost, but just do it.' McNally looked over at Plummer for confirmation and received a nod of the head. 'I want to know what Meeres has been doing since he retired a couple of years ago. Garvey told us that he would've still been working, as he was paying maintenance from a previous marriage. Look for anything in his flat that can fill in the picture of who this man was: phone records, tax returns, invoices for work he was doing etc. Marie, I want you to do some work on social media. Does he have some sort of website? Is he on Google? Does he use social media platforms privately or professionally? Also check to see if he has a driver's licence. Has he got any points? Contact BTP pensions and see if they've a different address for him. I want bank account details they pay the pension into.' Relish nodded enthusiastically; glad she had something else to concentrate on.

'Linda, we need a photo of Meeres, so liaise with Stuart and Jim. Hopefully there may be one at his home address. If not, his police records must have a warrant card photo of him. When you get one, go and show it to Holly Harrison. See if it's the same guy who helped her out. Ray, I want you to also have a look at any arrests made by Meeres and Garvey together over, say, the last ten years. The threat of a contract killing was made against both of them. The motive for all of this must be tied up with their work. Right! Has anybody got any questions? No? OK. Let's get on with it; we'll have another meeting tonight at six. By then, I want a definite identification on our victim.'

*

Frost and Hodge were racing up the A11 by 9.30am. They had tracked down the Norfolk traffic officer who was dealing with the traffic incident and a CID officer, who was in charge of an affray and serious assault in a pub in Cromer, in which Jennings and the unknown fatality were believed to be involved. The traffic officer had arranged for the detectives to view the vehicle and its contents, which, he said, would be of some importance to their investigation, but he wouldn't discuss it over the phone. They were also going to meet the detective, visit the mortuary to view the body of the unknown fatality and the hospital, where, thankfully, Jed Jennings was showing signs of coming out of his coma. They had a busy day.

'Are you hungry, Sarge?' Hodge asked. 'There's a service station coming up on the A14. We need some petrol anyway – I'll get us a sandwich.'

Frost nodded. 'Yeah, please, Sam. Who knows when we'll get to eat next?' Hodge pulled off the A14 and into a BP garage. He filled the car up and headed off to the shop. Frost's phone rang.

'Good morning,' an official-sounding voice spoke. 'DS Frost?'

'Yes, that's me – you are?'

'Peter Knowles, Deputy Governor at HMP Pentonville. I believe you visited one of our serving prisoners yesterday afternoon?'

'Yes, Daniel Corbell.'

'Right…' An uncomfortable silence followed.

'Is there any problem, sir?' Frost asked. 'We had the proper authorities in place.'

'Well, the reason I'm contacting you is we've had a serious incident at the prison sometime during breakfast this morning. Daniel Corbell was found hanged in his cell.'

*

By the time they arrived in Catford, Meeres' address had been sealed off by local BTP officers – no attempt to enter had been made until the arrival of Graves, Wakefield and SOCO Sally Cook. A locksmith gained entry to the flat and stood back as the forensically suited detectives and SOCO entered. The first thing they were thankful for was the absence of flies; it was unlikely he'd been killed here and they were confident they were not about to be faced with the missing head.

The detectives made a cursory search round the living spaces, impressed by how clean and tidy it was; everything seemed to have its place. Graves took the living room and Wakefield the main bedroom, while Cook took the smaller box room, which had been converted into an office. The walls of the office were adorned with framed commendations for outstanding police work and several course photographs with the names listed below – Cook spotted a couple of the pictures that featured Brian Garvey as well. She called in a photographer to record the position of items in situ, before she started to bag up a desktop computer, printer and an old-fashioned fax machine. She found several invoices addressed to various individuals and companies on headed paper, adorned with the title 'Meeres Investigation Services'. She bagged all these in police property bags. She shouted through to Graves and Wakefield to leave the bathroom to her as she wanted to secure personal items like a toothbrush or hairbrush for DNA comparisons.

'Anybody found a diary yet?' she asked the other two.

'In here,' Graves answered. Cook walked into the living

room. Graves was flicking through the diary to the beginning of the previous week. 'Which day were the first remains found at Liverpool Street?' he asked nobody in particular.

Wakefield joined them. 'Last Wednesday, wasn't it? A week ago, tomorrow. Got anything?'

Graves flicked through to the relevant page. 'This looks interesting – "Surveillance Bermondsey – missing person – early".' Looks like he just used this as a reminder as he's left it here. Probably uses the diary facility on his mobile or possibly a laptop or tablet. There are a few more entries for later in the week – looks like he was quite a busy man.' Graves got the photographer to take pictures of entries for the day in question and the preceding week, before he bagged and recorded it in the exhibits book. Sally Cook was satisfied that this wasn't *the* crime scene, but they carried on as if it was. The search continued meticulously; any relevant documentation was recorded and bagged.

Wakefield found a set of car keys under some magazines. 'Does this flat have a garage?' he asked one of the local officers standing outside in the hallway. He looked blank and said he'd make a few enquiries via the local neighbourhood policing team.

'I've got a logbook for a vehicle, guys.' Cook waved the document in the air before examining it. 'A red Audi A4. Blimey, he was doing well.'

'No garages with these properties, mate,' the uniformed officer informed Wakefield.

'We're nearly finished here,' he answered. 'Would you and your colleague have a quick look round the area? See if you can spot a red Audi.' Wakefield showed the uniformed officers the registration number on the logbook.

*

The visiting area at Pentonville was full, mainly women, many with young children, waiting for their husbands, boyfriends or sons to be shown in. Hazel Nunn looked as cool as a cucumber; completely unfazed and dressed immaculately; these places were like a second home to her. Since she and Terence had been married, he'd been arrested numerous times and spent half their marriage in places like this. He was an armed robber by trade but now the era of people getting paid in cash was a distant memory, resulting in fewer and fewer opportunities to turn over security vans, well, for any decent money anyway. He'd turned to drugs. To be honest, Hazel thought, he wasn't that great at that either, hence the prison terms. But she'd led a good life and wanted for nothing. They made a great team: he still ran the business from inside; she did the dirty work outside.

She crinkled her nose up at the smell wafting from two children running round her in some bizarre game of cops and robbers. The children were aged between three and four years but still wearing nappies, which, frankly, needed a change. The mother was tearing her hair out trying to control them. Hazel Nunn was glad they'd decided not to have children; she preferred pets. She was so focused on making sure the smelly little bastards didn't come anywhere near her; she hadn't noticed Terence sit down.

'You OK, Haze? You look a bit flustered.'

'Bloody kids,' she raised her voice for the benefit of the mother. 'Should keep 'em under control. If you can't – then don't fucking 'ave 'em.' The kids sensed her unease but were determined to continue with their game and made towards her again but scarpered when Terence raised his huge hand and swiped one of the kids round the back of the head. The mother was about to remonstrate until she noticed the look in his eyes and backed off.

'So, how're you doing?' Hazel asked.

'So-so, you know. One day is like any other in this dump; everything going OK outside?'

She nodded. 'Maurice 'as got himself noticed a couple of times, sorting out the loose ends, so I've told him to keep 'is head down for a bit. Nobody will grass him up – well, not in South

London anyway. You OK? Look like you've got a lot on your mind.'

Nunn looked round to where the prison guards were situated. 'It's not as tight as you think – got word yesterday that somebody in here was talking to the filth about the very person you just mentioned. Apparently, according to my source, he was looking for a deal to get out of here with a bit of cash.'

'And?' Hazel asked.

'And nothing, it ain't a problem anymore. Have you heard anything from that useless nephew of mine recently?'

'No, nothing, although I was told he got out the other day.'

'Well, find him, Haze, I want to see him. Got some work I can put his way.'

She nodded.

⋆

Norwich Police Station is a huge building located in the city centre, attached to the impressive City Hall. Frost and Hodge parked their car among dozens of marked police cars and rang the mobile number of the traffic officer they had contacted.

'No jokes about traffic cops prosecuting their own mothers, Sam, and don't mention black rats.'

Hodge smiled at the half-hearted warning. 'As long as he doesn't mention anything about trains and ticket collectors, we should be fine.' The officer spotted the two detectives standing by their car and introduced himself.

'Hi, Cameron Parks.' He shook hands with the visitors and showed them towards the main building. Frost didn't notice any adverse reaction to her being black. She didn't think there would be too many officers of ethnic origin in the Norfolk Police. She found the six foot one Parks rather attractive. 'You must be parched – fancy a cuppa?' Both nodded enthusiastically and followed the smartly turned-out traffic cop to the canteen.

As they sat down, they were joined by a man in his thirties dressed in a smart navy-blue suit and red tie, carrying an expensive-looking document carrier suspended on a strap from his shoulder. He seemed a little out of breath.

'Sorry, Cam, had to attend a bail application at the magistrates' court.' He looked at Frost and Hodge and introduced himself. 'I'm Detective Sergeant Ron Abbs – Norwich CID. You must be DS—'

'No. I'm DC Sam Hodge. This is DS Marcia Frost.' Abbs went a slight shade of pink, making out he was hot from the run. He loosened his tie and sat down.

'Great to meet you both! Have a good trip up?'

'Not bad,' Frost replied. 'The A11 was a bit of a pain.'

Abbs took a swig of water from a bottle. 'You said on the phone that you've got an interest in the fatal road traffic accident on Saturday.'

Frost explained to both officers, 'We're investigating the murder of a man we now believe to be a former detective in our own force. The man who was badly injured in the RTA on Saturday was – we believe – in Norfolk to avenge the death of his daughter in a car accident five years ago.'

'Jed Jennings?' Parks asked.

Frost nodded. 'The man who was behind the wheel of the car, the day Sophie Jennings was hit, is a former colleague of our victim – his name is Brian Garvey – who now lives in Cromer. Garvey had received information from a former informant of his that both he and our victim – Frankie Meeres – were on a hit list, basically. We've no idea who the order has come from or why; we're trawling through previous offences they jointly investigated over the last ten years. We do have a suspect – a black male from Southeast London – called Maurice, whose picture's been widely circulated. We've no surname for him. We're anxious to speak to Jed Jennings – if possible. You suggested earlier that he may have come out of his coma.'

Abbs looked at his mobile. 'Got a text from a uniformed officer about ten minutes ago who is sitting by Jennings' hospital bed – he is conscious. His former wife is with him. He's in police custody in relation to a fight in the White Horse pub in Cromer, where a Norwich City fan was hit over the head with a snooker cue, although we believe it was the man who died who's responsible for the attack and that Jennings played peacekeeper.'

'We're trying to establish the link, if any, between Jed Jennings, why he was up here and the murder of Frankie Meeres. Have you managed to identify the man who died yet?' Hodge asked.

'Yes. He didn't have any ID on him, but he has come back on fingerprints as Eddie Lee, aged thirty-six. Got previous for mailbag thefts on your ground, just been released from HMP Bedford about a week ago, having served ten years for theft of Royal Mail and attempted wounding of a police officer. We advised the Met yesterday. They sent two officers' round to his wife's house with the death message—'

Frost interrupted, 'Sorry, Ron. Sam, give Marie Relish a ring. She's looking at any previous jobs Garvey and Meeres shared. See if they dealt with this Eddie Lee if he's just come out and get her to go back ten years. Get her to check with the Criminal Records Office at New Scotland Yard, see if they can tell her who the arresting officer was.' Hodge got up and speed-dialled the number of the incident room on his mobile. 'Sorry, Ron, have we got details of calls made on both Jennings' and Lee's phones yet?'

Parks answered, 'We passed the phones on to our tech department for interrogation. I'll give them a ring in a minute; see what they've come up with. But before you go over to the hospital, I want to show you a couple of items recovered from the vehicle's passenger glove compartment.

TWENTY-EIGHT

TUESDAY AFTERNOON

A sharp-eyed uniform officer spotted the red Audi A4 parked three streets away from Meeres' building. Graves contacted McNally.

'I've searched the car, guv, nothing of interest. It's been there for a while, covered in leaves and bird shit. I'll get the car brought in – we might get an idea from the satnav history of where he'd been a few days prior. There is an entry in his diary for last Wednesday: "Surveillance Bermondsey – missing person – early". Jim is liaising with BTP at Victoria to get the footage downloaded covering both Catford and Catford Bridge stations as, presumably, he didn't drive – we haven't found any evidence at the flat that he owns another vehicle. We had a quick think about a possible route if he used the train to Bermondsey last Wednesday. He would probably have used Catford Bridge direct into London Bridge; it only takes eleven or twelve minutes. He could then change onto the Jubilee line, one stop to Bermondsey. So, we've asked for the footage from London Bridge and Bermondsey from TFL.'

'Is there anything of interest at the address?' McNally asked.

'Lot of paperwork – mainly invoices; he'd set up his own investigations company: MIS Meeres Investigation Services. Sally is sure this wasn't where he was murdered. No sign of a struggle; the place is very clean and tidy. There is also post in the letter box dated from last week. We're nearly finished here. Sally has got a comb and toothbrush for DNA samples as well as a number of fingerprints. I've sent Linda Doyle a recent photograph of Meeres from a passport issued only eighteen months ago. I'll secure the place and see you back at Camden in a couple of hours.'

'Just a thought, Stuart – Meeres would've been issued one of those Freedom Passes when he turned sixty last year – wouldn't he?'

'Guess so, guv. Want me to look into that?'

'No – ask Jim to do it when you get back here; he seems to have all the contacts with TFL – if I remember rightly, movements are logged on a database so, again, may help us confirm where he went on that Wednesday. OK, good work! I'll see you when you get back later.'

*

PC Cameron Parks led Frost and Hodge down into the traffic garage where a row of gleaming marked police cars stood.

'Got some vehicles here, haven't you?'

Parks just smiled and led them to the far end of the underground space. 'What were you expecting, tractors and combine harvesters?' All three laughed. They smelt it before they saw the vehicle – a strong aroma of petrol and smoke.

'Not sure how Jennings got out of here alive; it rolled over a couple of times and then burst into flames – from what witnesses saw, he was thrown out of the vehicle as it rolled over, probably not wearing a seat belt which, in this case, ultimately *saved* his life.'

Frost and Hodge could clearly see the initials JJ described by Brian Garvey on the side and back doors of the Transit. Parks went over to a locked cupboard and retrieved a sealed property bag and a long cylindrical plastic tube and handed them to Frost.

'These items were found in the passenger glove compartment.'

Frost held the tube up to the light. 'Now that's what you call a knife.' She handed the tube to Hodge and examined the sealed property bag. 'What are they, pull ties?'

'Yes, not official police-issue ones but a cheaper version – I dare say Jennings would've used them in the plumbing game.'

'Well, it gives us a clearer picture of what they intended to do with Brian Garvey.'

'I'll take you up to the CID office. Ron Abbs has got the CCTV from the pub in Cromer all set up to show you.'

*

Jim Wakefield's eyes were starting to water; since returning to Camden, he had been glued to a screen in the CCTV viewing room. He glanced at his watch – it read 5.25pm. He still had some time to come up with a result; McNally had delayed the office meeting until 7pm to allow Frost and Hodge to get back from Norwich via the hospital where Jennings was still under observation.

He'd started with the footage from Catford Bridge, the obvious station Meeres would have travelled from, if he'd used the train. It was twelve minutes direct into London Bridge, whereas Catford was a much longer journey with a change. He had a blow-up of the passport photograph, seized this morning, sellotaped to his monitor and continually glanced at it. He'd chosen a time parameter between 6am and 8am from Catford Bridge, which could be widened either way if he got no results. Marie Relish brought him a cup of coffee.

'How's it going, Detective?' she asked with a cheeky smile.

'It's taking a while to get used to being called that. No luck so far, but I'm only up to six forty-five – it's taking time – can't afford to miss him.'

'Do you want me to ask the boss if he can spare anybody else to help?'

'No, I'm OK, Marie. Everybody is working their socks off. How're you getting on?'

'I've found a couple of cases that could be significant investigations both Garvey and Meeres worked on, including the investigation into our dead man in Norwich, but they were a pretty active duo, nicking people all over the place; they had some really good results, ranging from armed robbers, mailbag thieves, traveller's cheques and a lot more; they were bound to have made some enemies along the way. Look, I'll leave you to it. Don't forget the meeting at seven o'clock.'

'Yeah sure, thanks for the coffee. Fancy a drink later?' Relish stopped, half turned and gave it some thought. To be honest, she could do with sharing some company with somebody she trusted, and it delayed going home.

'I'll think about it,' she teased.

'Oh, by the way, Marie, what the hell are traveller's cheques?'

*

DS Linda Doyle knocked on the door, stood back and waited. The woman who answered was slightly older than she'd anticipated; a bruise on her face was an ugly green-yellow colour; she peered through a small gap secured by a security chain. Doyle produced her warrant card.

'I've spoken to you lot already yesterday – they told me 'bout Eddie – what do you want? To gloat, I suppose.'

'Jasmine, can I come in for a moment? I don't want to discuss this in the earshot of your neighbours, and I've already seen a few curtains twitching.' She closed the door and Doyle could hear the security chain being released and the door opened fully this time. 'I'm very sorry for your loss,' Doyle said with some genuine sympathy.

'Don't be. I'm not.' She showed Doyle into the front living room and pointed to the same sofa the uniformed officers had sat on when delivering the previous day's death message; Doyle sat down.

'Was he responsible for that bruise on your face?'

Jasmine just nodded her head. She obviously didn't want to talk about it as she changed the subject quickly. 'What d' ya want? That was a transport police badge you showed me, weren't it?'

'Yes, it is. As you know, it was BTP who arrested Eddie a few years ago.'

'He hated your lot; said you fitted him up with an attempted stabbing. Normally he always pleaded guilty any time he got caught bang to rights. He would've for the theft, but you lot took the piss by making up the rest. Were you there?' she asked suspiciously.

'No,' Doyle sensed a building hostility and needed to calm it all down, 'this was way before I even joined the police. Anyway, the reason I came to see you is we now believe we know the reason why Eddie and a man called Jed Jennings were in Norfolk. Have you ever met Jennings before?'

Jasmine shook her head without any hesitation. 'I told the other lot that I'd never heard of 'im yesterday.'

'We believe the reason was a revenge attack on a former police officer, who'd accidently killed Jennings' daughter. We're not sure why Eddie was with him or how he even knew him. Jennings has never been in trouble with the police before, so that rules out them meeting in prison. They lived in totally different parts of London, so meeting at school is also out. I was hoping you could shed some light on how they might have met and what their relationship was like?' Jasmine shook her head again. 'But if you say you didn't even know him then I've intruded long enough at, what must be, a very difficult time for you.' Doyle got up and handed Jasmine a business card. 'If you think of anything or you've got any questions, please give me a ring. I'll leave you in peace.' Doyle opened the front door and half turned. 'Do you live alone?'

'Yeah, 'ave done for a while now. I gotta new job and I was just starting to build a life for myself when 'e came 'ome. I won't be shedding any tears.'

Doyle placed her hand on Jasmine's shoulder and gave her a reassuring smile. 'Anything – OK?'

'Wait,' Jasmine looked at the card, 'Linda, is it?' Doyle nodded. 'Sorry. I 'ated the bastard, especially after he came around 'ere the day he got released and kicked the shit out of me, but it's been a shock – we were together since we were at school – you know? I try to act the 'ard bitch, but I ain't really. Can I get you a cup of tea or coffee?' She stepped aside and invited Doyle back into the living room.

Doyle shook her head as she removed her coat and placed it on the bannister. 'No, I'm fine thanks. What's on your mind? Whatever it is, it's not going to hurt Eddie now, is it?'

Jasmine sat down and started to pick at some skin at the base of her beautifully manicured fingernails. 'After Eddie got sent down last time, I got lonely. We were going to 'ave kids, but he was never 'ere – always inside. We always had plenty of money, always wads of cash about the house, from the thieving I suppose. I never asked any questions, just helped myself when I needed it, but he never worked a day in his life, well, not a proper job anyway. He came from a family of villains; his dad got killed in a dispute over drugs years ago. His uncle is doing time for robbery and drugs importation. All he had left was his mother, who lives up in Finsbury Park somewhere. I ain't seen her in years. I'd always stuck with him – always waited. But this time he got *ten years*,' she exclaimed, 'looking at a minimum of five.'

She sighed, got up and poured a measure of gin, adding a splash of tonic. 'You want one of these? You look like you could do with it.'

Doyle shook her head. 'I've got to drive. Still have a few more hours to do.'

Jasmine continued, 'Anyway, I went up to see 'im a few times in Nottingham, bloody journey and a half that was. He came out with the usual bullshit: how much he loved me, how sorry 'e was and was only doing it for me. I'd 'eard it all before. A couple of months after he went down, I got a knock on the door – it was one of your lot, one of the coppers who gave evidence against Eddie. I said to him straight, "What the fuck do you want?" He held up a property bag in front of my face, told me 'e had a few of Eddie's bits and pieces that they took off of him on the night of his arrest. There was some cash in a wallet. That was a surprise, thought it would've gone into one of your lot's pockets. He came in and sat right where you are and we got talking about things, mainly how life had dealt us a shitty deal in relation to partners; he had a few drinks, and he left. Couple of days later he rang me and asked if I fancied going out for a bite to eat. I thought, why not, if it was uptown somewhere. It wouldn't 'ave been good for my 'ealth if we'd popped down to the local Indian, and I ain't talking about dodgy food – everybody can smell you lot from a mile away round 'ere. We got on alright and eventually we sort of got it together for a while, until a neighbour grassed me up – must've seen him coming and going – and Eddie found out and went mad in prison. He usually just kept 'is 'ead down and did his time, but 'e lost it, got into all sorts of things and ended up doing the full ten years – probably lucky not to get more.' She took a large, noisy slurp of her gin and tonic, wiped her chin with her sleeve and licked her lips.

'Eddie must have come straight 'ere on being released. He didn't really 'ave anywhere else to go apart from 'is mums, and she sort of disowned him years ago; fed up with your lot keep turning 'er place over, looking for 'im every five minutes. I knew it weren't going to go well. I'd been expecting 'im for some time. He gave me a few punches, mainly to the stomach, and kicked me while I was on the floor, and then he took some cash out of my purse, 'bout 'undred quid. He wanted to know who I'd been living wiv after 'e'd got put away. I told 'im no one, which weren't a complete lie as the guy never ever lived here – just popped in a couple of times a week to – you know… he had me by the neck and was throttling me, demanding a name – I couldn't breathe, so I gave 'im what he wanted – sort of.'

'Whose name did you give, Jasmine?'

'The guy I was seeing for a while was a man called Frankie Meeres – I really liked 'im, treated me proper. I knew what Eddie would do when he found 'im, so I told him a lie – I gave Eddie the name of his partner – Brian Garvey. It was Garvey who searched the place after Eddie got nicked last time – bit of a dry fucker; I didn't like him at all. That's why Eddie was in Norfolk – to kill Brian Garvey.'

TWENTY-NINE

TUESDAY EVENING

The office meeting didn't start until just before 8pm – everybody was knackered and McNally wanted to get it done as quickly as possible, so his team – and he – could grab a few hours at home with family before going at it again tomorrow, but they had a hell of a lot to get through. Ray Blendell had started to compile a timeline of events from the beginning of last week – it always helped to see things in a simple chronological order, McNally thought; he was all for technology, but seeing stages of an investigation in black and white on a board helped clarify the most significant events in his mind. One whiteboard recorded what they knew about their victim, Frankie Meeres; another featured Brian Garvey; another their main suspect, Maurice; and finally, the recently added Jed Jennings and Eddie Lee.

'OK, so we've established a link between Lee, Garvey and Meeres. It would appear, from what Jasmine Lee is telling us, Eddie Lee – her husband – was accompanying Jed Jennings to Cromer to either kidnap or kill Brian Garvey. Lee's previous convictions leave us in no doubt he had a propensity for violence – even though in this situation, he would be barking up the completely wrong tree. So obviously the connection with our victim is his affair with Eddie Lee's wife. We need to find out how Lee and Jennings contacted each other.'

Sara Hallam came up with the obvious answer. 'It has to be the prison system,' she pointed out. 'Jennings' daughter was killed five years ago. Lee was halfway through serving his ten years; by this time, he was aware of his wife's infidelity and would have suspected either Garvey or Meeres.'

'Ray, raise an action for Stuart to contact Nottingham and Bedford prisons for any visits Lee got during that time, in particular if he was visited by Jennings. Thanks, Sara.'

'Well done, Sara. At least you've earned your fee. What you on, a grand a day?' Graves said.

'If I earned that much, DC Graves, I would gladly take you to the nearest Salvation Army shop and buy you a new suit, one that fits and is slightly more modern than the one you are attempting to wear today, and transform you from the bag of shit you look like at the moment into some sort of half-decent human being.'

Cheers went up from round the room. Even Graves nodded in surrender, followed by a polite bow, acknowledging the presence of a greater wit.

'Well, seeing as you're in such great voice, Stuart, let's deal with the search of Meeres' flat.'

'Not much to add, boss – the diary has a lot of appointments for the future and for the past, but he didn't record client names or contact numbers in there. He must've had some other way of doing so, maybe on his mobile or a tablet that we haven't recovered yet. The car was pretty clean inside and looked like it hadn't been used for a few weeks. There was a petrol receipt from three weeks ago in the passenger footwell for fifty-odd quid; the car's tank is full to the brim; looks like he used public transport or maybe cabs for most of his work.

'As we were leaving, a neighbour came and spoke to us. She lives in the flat opposite and remembers bumping into Meeres about ten to seven on the Wednesday morning. She'd been out for an early morning jog; it was her day off – that's why she recalls it – and spoke briefly about the weather as they passed at the entrance door. She remembers he was wearing a blue raincoat but was fairly sure he wasn't carrying anything.'

'Sally, any update on confirming the identification of our victim?'

'I got a bit of a break there, dude. The articles we seized this morning – toothbrush and hairbrush – have been submitted for comparison to the DNA profile of our victim. I've asked for that on the hurry-up but may take a day or two. I also lifted several fingerprints from the flat and the car. On the off chance, I researched our records to see if Meeres had ever provided elimination prints for crime scenes he'd attended in the past, and bingo! He had, and they were kept on file, with other forensic evidence, for a job where a suspect was charged but absconded on bail and has never come to trial. I got the fingerprint bureau to compare the elimination prints provided by DS Meeres in that case with those in the flat and car and with the dead set that was taken from the hand left at Liverpool Street station – they all match; our victim is Frankie Meeres.'

'Nice work, Sally – I think we were all happy who he was, but it's good to know for definite, and it's something we can report to the coroner so they can open an inquest. Great work.' A constrained ripple of applause reverberated round the room.

'Marcia, Sam, I hope you had a nice trip up to sunny Norfolk while we've all been working our bollocks off here.'

'You ain't got much of a suntan, Sam.' Graves was back in his stride after the recent put-down – he looked at Frost, who gave him a 'you fucking dare' look and decided against including her in the joke.

When the jeering had quietened down, Frost opened her notebook.

'Let's start with our informant in Pentonville who gave us the name Maurice yesterday,' McNally suggested.

'Daniel Corbell was found hanged in his cell this morning. I've spoken to the deputy governor and to local police from Islington, who're dealing with the investigation. It apparently happened when the prisoners were out of their cells for breakfast this morning, including Corbell's cellmate. Of course there are no witnesses.' Frost glanced over to Hodge. 'I think Sam and I agree that he was obviously got at. This was no suicide. He certainly wasn't suicidal when we met him yesterday. In fact, he was his usual cocky, arrogant self with high hopes that the info he gave us was going to get him his move and some money for when he got out. A coroner's inquest will open tomorrow. His cell was searched but nothing of interest was found in relation to what he partly gave us yesterday, so that really is a *dead* end.' Everybody groaned – it seemed to go over Frost's head. She continued.

'The trip to Norwich was well worth it. Eddie Lee has been positively identified as the fatality,' she pointed at the whiteboard on which his picture was affixed, 'well known to this force over the years as a prolific mailbag thief and certainly well known to DS Meeres and DS Garvey – in fact, it was those two officers who were instrumental in getting him locked up. There can be little doubt, from what was found in the vehicle, and info gleaned by Linda Doyle this afternoon from Lee's wife Jasmine, that they were there – in Norfolk – to do Brian Garvey some serious harm.

'Sam and I went to the hospital in Norwich but Jennings – although conscious – was heavily sedated, so asking him questions was not an option. He's not going anywhere; he'll be immediately taken into custody when he's fit to be discharged, and Norfolk CID will be dealing with the incident in the Cromer pub and possible conspiracy to kidnap in relation to Garvey. I've compiled a briefing note regarding Norwich, which will be available to you all before we finish tonight.'

'Good. Sam, you got anything else to add to that?' McNally asked.

'Just the fact that Norfolk Police have asked if DS Doyle could be a liaison with Mrs Lee as they'll need her to officially ID her husband and give evidence at the subsequent inquest.'

'Are you happy with that, Linda? Or would you prefer me to allocate a family liaison officer?'

'Yes, guv, I'm fine with that; I've got her trust.'

'Have we got any further in identifying Maurice – anybody?' McNally's question was met by silence. 'Well, let's renew our efforts on that tomorrow.' McNally looked at his watch – nearly 9pm. 'Jim, CCTV. For those of you not up to date, and further to what Stuart was saying earlier, we decided to assume that Meeres must have travelled by train that morning to get up to Bermondsey as noted in his diary. Jim?'

'Got some good news on that, guv.' Blendell operated the control for the big screen, which revealed the entrance to Catford Bridge station. 'This is Wednesday morning at five to seven,' Wakefield continued. 'We know that Meeres' neighbour saw and spoke to him as he left the building about ten to seven. I started the search of the CCTV at six-thirty to allow a little discrepancy in the time given by her. If you could fast-forward to two minutes past seven, please, sarge.' The room went silent as Blendell edged the recording forward. 'OK. Hold it there and just forward it frame by frame please. There he is – blue raincoat, very good likeness to the passport picture, which is fairly current. I tried to pick him up again at London Bridge, but we're talking about twenty past seven in the morning, and it would be like finding a needle in a haystack. Give me some time, and it will be possible.

'I went straight on to Bermondsey station, which is one stop from London Bridge on the Jubilee line. Most people at that time of day are entering the station, so the camera on the exit gate easily picked him up leaving the station at seven thirty-three. He appears to turn left from the station onto Jamaica Road, heading towards Abbey Street I've arranged for a couple of late turn CID from

West Ham to have a trawl along Jamaica Road to see if they can identify other CCTV opportunities.'

'What about coming back, Jim?' Hodge asked.

'I've fast-tracked through CCTV footage of the entrance to the station for about two hours after he'd arrived – as I said, it was busy going into the station – but haven't picked him up on the return. Of course, he could've gone anywhere from then on.'

'Or nowhere,' added Frost.

'Have we got anywhere with his Freedom Pass?'

'Had a look at it, guv,' answered Ray Blendell. 'He was issued one, and TFL are attempting to trace a record of movement on it. We should hear something tomorrow.'

'Right, we've had a good day – let's reconvene in the morning—'

'Wait a minute, guv,' Frost chipped in. 'Ray, can you go back to the Catford Bridge footage and freeze it with Meeres in the shot please?' Blendell did as asked. 'OK,' Frost got up from her seat and moved closer to the screen, 'right, Ray, slowly, frame by frame, please... there – *stop!*' She looked over at McNally, who looked back quizzingly. 'Ray, now the Bermondsey footage – same thing – freeze on Meeres... there. Now slowly, frame by frame – *stop!* Bloody hell, it is him, I'm sure,' Frost mumbled to herself rather than to anyone else. 'Guv, come and have a closer look – there.' She pointed to a figure several seconds behind Meeres.

'Well, I'll be damned,' McNally exclaimed.

THIRTY

WEDNESDAY MORNING

McNally was woken by the vibration of his phone. It felt like he'd only just rested his head on the pillow. He slipped from underneath the duvet, trying to avoid waking Kate. He closed the door of the en-suite and answered.

'Sorry to wake you, guv, DS Laura Quinn – surveillance team leader; you said you wanted notifying of any significant movements. The CROP officer has identified two males in the property; the first is Subject One, who arrived at the premises just gone midnight. He was joined about an hour later by a black male – at least six foot two, big build, driving a black Mercedes car. They've been in the premises ever since. We've managed to get a footman close. They seem to be drinking and in good spirits.'

'OK. Laura. We're briefing at a nearby police station at five-thirty and looking to go in at six-thirty. Would appreciate if you could keep your CROP officer in position until—'

'Hang on, sir,' Quinn interrupted. 'There is some movement – our CROP officer is reporting the black male is out and towards his car – what d' ya want us to do, guv, stay with Subject One or go with the black male?'

'Can they see the registration of the car?'

'I'll ask.' It seemed ages before Quinn got back. 'He can't get it all but starts with a G for Golf and ends Whisky, Delta, Papa. It's moving, guv.'

'Get your team to go with the car and keep the CROP officer in place – give him my mobile number.' McNally could hear Quinn passing on his instructions to her surveillance team. He sent a text to Frost and Graves, bringing the briefing forward half an hour.

*

Maurice Stone was looking forward to his break. He headed west on the North Circular to pick up the M4 at the Chiswick roundabout and then Heathrow Airport. He glanced at the dashboard – 5.10am. He would get to Terminal Five well within time for his 6am check-in and 10am flight to New York. He stopped at a red light at the junction with Uxbridge Road and checked the passport he'd collected. It was a new blue British passport with a forged US visa stamp and driving licence in the name of Neville Beckford. He got a toot and a flash of headlights from a vehicle behind as the signal went green. Normally, a look out of the driver's window to the car behind would deter any further such behaviour, but Maurice just smiled and moved slowly forward, observing speed limits. He knew this was a quiet time for the police and, being a black man, in a top-of-the-range Mercedes, made him an easy stop before clocking off time.

The car behind turned left into Uxbridge Road, leaving the road behind clear apart from a motorbike that seemed to be going at an unusually low speed and hanging back. He approached the Chiswick roundabout and relaxed as the motorbike left the roundabout onto Chiswick High Road. He continued, taking the fourth exit onto the elevated section of the M4 and picking up signs for Terminal Five.

*

McNally, Frost and Graves were in one car; a police uniform carrier sat fifty metres away, filled with heavy-duty-looking men and women, itching to move. McNally had liaised with the surveillance team leader Laura Quinn at the earlier briefing. She had decided to remain in Mill Hill as a backup to her officer out in the field and joined the three detectives in their car. Quinn had two covert radios, the first tuned into the frequency of the mobile surveillance team following the black Mercedes and the second to listen and communicate with the CROP officer, who had the target premises and Subject One under observation. It'd been agreed that, if the occupant of the black Mercedes, now designated for the purposes of the operation and the surveillance log as Subject Two, entered premises resembling a home address, the surveillance team would hold back and continue with surveillance. When commentary came through confirming Subject Two was heading towards Heathrow Airport, McNally decided that he should be arrested on suspicion of the murder of Frankie Meeres and Joey Dryden – if and when he entered the airport's departure lounge.

The uniform carrier was beginning to steam up as its occupants became more restless.

'You might have to release them soon, guv,' Quinn remarked to McNally, 'before they start beating *themselves* up.'

'Not long now.' He looked at his watch; he was waiting for confirmation from the CROP officer of further movement from inside the target premises. It would appear the occupant had bedded down for a rest after Subject Two had left.

'Stand by, stand by,' a hushed voice came over the radio. 'Light has come on in the premises, Subject One seen at the window. I can confirm I've seen no sign of any dogs.'

McNally picked up the vehicle's radio transmitter, which was on a back-to-back channel with the uniformed carrier. 'Stand by, go, go, go.' He watched as the headlights of the carrier illuminated the dark street and raced off in the direction of the railway bridge, leaving a blue cloud of diesel fumes in its wake. McNally followed.

The carrier smashed through the partially opened gates of the scrapyard and screeched to a halt outside the Portakabin. Its occupants spilled out; the first officer kicked the flimsy door open. McNally got confirmation that Subject One had been secured and that they could now enter.

Before McNally even entered the Portakabin, he could hear the angry occupant yelling a stream of obscenities towards the uniformed officers. McNally had already briefed Frost; this was her arrest. As she entered the brightly lit room, she smiled sweetly and informed Tommy Roddy, 'Your little black princess has returned and you are under arrest on suspicion of conspiracy to murder former Detective Sergeant Frankie Meeres,' she cautioned him.

'That piece of shit deserved everything he got, and you,' Roddy bawled with a venomous tone and pure hate in his eyes, 'you, you fecking bitch, may well be next.' Frost took a step to one side to avoid the spittle aimed at her and smiled sweetly.

Roddy was taken out of the Portakabin and placed in the carrier for transportation to the nearest custody facility.

'Well done, Marcia. You handled that well.' Even Graves nodded his approval. Frost went over to the far wall and looked at the picture of Roddy and his fellow boxers in the ring at York Hall. The big Irishman was easy to pick out at the back of the group.

'Guv, come and have a look at this.' She waited to be joined by McNally and Graves. She pointed to a face in the front row. 'You know who that is, don't you?' McNally took a closer look and shook his head. 'That's Eddie Lee.'

Then it was Graves' turn to point. 'And I bet that's Maurice.'

*

Maurice Stone headed towards the long-stay car park at Terminal Five, Heathrow. The M4 had been quite busy up to the T5 junction, with a slight tailback onto the motorway. It was at this point he saw the motorbike again. He didn't recognise it from make or model, or colour, but the style in which it was being ridden. If you were on a motorbike, why hang back in a queue of traffic that you could easily ride through? He was now sure it was the same motorbike he'd seen on the North Circular half an hour earlier. Stone had lived on his wits for many years. He suddenly felt very trapped and paid particular attention to the cars behind and in front of him. The car behind had a female driver, on her own. She was dressed in a beige overcoat with a black T-shirt; she looked very tired. Maurice stared at her in his rear-view mirror. The whites of his eyes stood out starkly against the dark blackness of his skin. He saw the woman making eye contact with him for a split second before looking away. He could see her lips moving – she wasn't singing along to the radio as her hands remained tightly gripped to the steering wheel. She could've been having a conversation with a friend or work colleague on her hands-free but highly unlikely at that time in the morning. The traffic came to a standstill. Maurice jumped out of his car and looked at the woman. He opened his boot on the pretence of searching for something. She looked away and started to fiddle with the dashboard – Maurice was now sure; he was being followed.

*

The reason for the tailback was broadcast on a local radio news channel – roadworks on the roundabout at the end of the slip road. People around Maurice Stone started to get agitated, afraid they were going to miss the latest check-in times for their flights – a few horns started to sound – as if that was going to help! He looked in his rear-view again. The lady driver looked a little more at ease – probably gave her the fright of her life when he got out of the car – but he was still convinced she was a police officer following him. He leant over and opened the glove compartment.

The self-loading Beretta pistol and ammunition reassured him that there'd be only one winner. He decided he would have to revert to plan B. If he entered the airport terminal, he would be trapped. The police would have the advantage with access to numerous resources, mostly armed. Stone was betting that his followers were unarmed. The traffic moved slowly to the roundabout. He again weighed up his options; he calculated that two or three of the vehicles following would be in the queue of traffic; one may have gone ahead on the M4, one covering the reciprocal route back into Central London and, of course, the bike, which would be much more mobile. He decided what to do. He slipped the gun out of the glove compartment and laid it on the passenger seat, checking that it was loaded, and then just bided his time.

*

The handcuffs were removed from the Irishman's strong wrists. Roddy looked round the custody suite as he rubbed vigorously to get the blood flowing. He had told the arresting officers they were too tight. They didn't give a toss. The prisoner had failed the attitude test and therefore was unlikely to gain any sympathy. He was searched and informed of his rights whilst at the police station. He'd listened carefully to what the DS had said and decided the best course of action now was to say fuck all.

*

He eased the powerful Mercedes ever closer to the traffic lights controlling the roundabout. Stone watched the last two changes very carefully, timing each at exactly twelve seconds before they changed to red. He noted that the next traffic movement was from the right – presumably traffic coming off the M4 from the west; they would all be in the same position as him and the queue coming from London – on tenterhooks about missing their flights

– he had to time this perfectly. He took a few deep breaths and waited for the amber light – he was four cars from the lights so would have to hold back a little to make sure the lights changed to allow traffic from the right to go and then move, leaving the car behind him stuck. The light sequence changed as amber joined red and then to green; the three cars in front accelerated through; this left Stone having to stall for five seconds, accompanied by a cacophony of car horns screaming at him from behind to move, before the lights changed back to red. He counted to two and then accelerated through the red light onto the roundabout, just missing the cars coming from his right. He glanced in his rear-view mirror and smiled at the frustration on the surveillance officer's face. He navigated his way round the roundabout and exited back onto the westbound M4.

*

Roddy pushed away the detention officer's hand as he was shown down to a cell. He'd been stripped of all his clothes, except his underwear, and given a white forensic suit to wear. He looked tentatively into the accompanying cells, expecting to see Maurice Stone glaring back at him. He asked to make a phone call but was denied; it was explained to him the investigating officers thought it likely he'd contact other suspects in the case and compromise the ongoing investigation. *Fecking right I would*, he thought.

*

The speedometer registered 110mph. He looked up ahead for any vehicles parked on the hard shoulder but thought it more likely any surveillance vehicle covering the westbound M4 would hold at the next junction, aware by now of his direction of travel. The traffic was light as daybreak cut through the dark night to reveal a grey, damp morning. The Mercedes was now cruising at 120mph.

Three cars joined the M4 as he passed the next junction – two saloon cars that were politely indicating and a blue BMW that cut straight across all lanes; it disappeared from Stone's rear-view mirror as the Mercedes increased to 125mph. Stone's plan B was an associate's house in Reading, where he could lay low for as long as he needed, which was the next turn-off – junction eleven. Stone eased off the gas pedal and brought his speed down to just below a hundred miles per hour and watched.

*

'Bravo One: we have contact, contact, contact, Subject Two just north of junction ten M4 going west, backup?'

'Zulu One is your backup. I'm half a mile behind you making ground.' Bravo One looked in his mirror to try to spot the motorbike but knew at the speed he was travelling the backup must be doing up to 130mph to catch them.

'Bravo One: subject vehicle is now middle lane, M4 – 110mph just passing mile marker board for junction eleven – Reading.'

'Zulu One: just approaching mile marker about four hundred metres behind you – keep commentary going.'

'Bravo One: half mile marker board. Subject Two nearside lane. Speed a hundred miles per hour. Visibility poor. Three hundred metre marker, nearside lane, speed ninety miles per hour. Two hundred metre marker – speed eighty miles per hour. Zulu One, are you in position to take over?'

'Zulu One: yes. yes. I have eyeball.'

'Bravo One: one hundred metre marker subject approaching junction – speed seventy miles per hour – is passing junction. No wait. Subject Two is left, left, left junction eleven – Reading. We had to overshoot. Over to you, Zulu One.'

'Zulu One: has the eyeball. Subject Two is heading towards Reading city centre A33, speed sixty miles per hour. Subject Two now pulling over into layby. Subject Two out of the vehicle. He is armed – shots fired. I'm down – bike's tyre has blown. Subject Two walking towards me, aiming his gun...'

★

Sam Hodge and Jim Wakefield were standing in Jamaica Road on the junction with Abbey Street with several uniformed colleagues, handing out leaflets adorned with the passport photograph of Frankie Meeres, hastily put together by the press bureau. It had been one week exactly since their victim was last seen leaving Bermondsey station, turning left towards their position.

Hodge knew that the idea behind such an operation was a sound one; seven days after a serious incident – be it a murder, terrorist attack or even a serious road traffic accident – they hoped to catch local people who may have been in the area a week earlier but also those people who visit the area on one particular day each week, maybe to visit a relative or attend a regular business meeting.

Hodge and Wakefield were a little frustrated with being here – they would have preferred to be on the arrest up in North London, but somebody had to do it and they, being the newest members of the team, got the job.

'God, I'm bloody freezing,' Wakefield said as he rubbed his hands together and stamped his feet on the hard pavement to try and improve blood circulation.

'You're lucky you're not the CROP officer they've got out on the Mill Hill scrapyard. They can't get up and have a stroll around and go and get something hot to eat. Sod that! I wouldn't have the patience or the dedication. I mean, why would anybody volunteer for a job like that?'

'I don't even know what one of them is,' Wakefield admitted with an air of embarrassment.

'Covert Rural Observation Point. They basically dig a hole or find a bush and stay there, for days sometimes. We use them when a conventional observation point like a house or other premises isn't available or practical to watch from – you know, somewhere warm with a toilet.'

'What happens when they do need a piss or, you know…?'

'They have to do it where they are – in a bottle or a bag or something.' Wakefield gave his colleague a suspicious glance, wondering if Hodge was winding him up. He didn't want to embarrass himself any further by asking any more questions and was glad when the press officer came to his rescue.

Shirley Tresidder had arranged for local and national television crews and press reporters to cover the appeal, so they were hopeful of somebody coming forward to supply information about where their victim went and if he met anybody.

The presence of police officers in such numbers was starting to create interest and a little anxiety within the local community. Many people diverted to the other side of the pavement or even crossed the road to avoid being approached by somebody in uniform.

'This is going well!' Hodge sarcastically said to Wakefield. 'Just had a message from Marcia; they nicked Roddy and are starting to interview him. We'll give it another half an hour and call it a day. They were just about to go their separate ways to liaise with uniform colleagues, when a bus stopped near the junction with Old Jamaica Road and the doors opened.

'Hey, Officers, you looking for that guy on TV the other night? This him, is it?' The driver held up an appeal notice.

'Yes, can you help?'

'You'll have to jump aboard; I can't stop here – it'll cause chaos.' Hodge said he'd deal with it and left Wakefield on the cold pavement.

Hodge stood by the driver's position. 'Have you seen this man before, Mr…?'

'McDermott – Harry. You gotta name, Officer?'

'It's Sam, Mr McDermott. How can you help? I see you've got one of our notices there.'

'Yeah, one of my passengers gave it to me earlier on. This is my return trip. Call me Harry by the way.'

'OK, Harry, what you got?' Hodge had to stand back momentarily as a number of passengers boarded, most using their passes. Harry closed the doors and manoeuvred back into the traffic.

'It was last week some time, early, Tuesday or Wednesday. I stopped at the bus stop in Abbey Street. I saw the guy in the picture. Had a nice-looking dark raincoat on, looked a little like a flasher – you know, likes to get his—'

'Yeah, Harry. I know what a flasher is.'

'Anyways, I asked him if he wanted this bus, but he shook his head – not very communicative, seeing as I was only being polite – you know. I didn't think anything more about it. Get used to rude buggers in this job. I completed my trip, had a cuppa and a bacon roll – or it might've been sausage, can't remember now, Tuesday's normally sausage, Wednesday's bacon. Anyways, does the return trip and I see him again – at the same bus stop – hadn't moved in over forty-five minutes. Obviously, this time I'm on the other side of the road. He looked at me and gave a nervous wave, as if to say, like, bugger off, will you, I don't wanna talk. That was it.'

'Are you sure it's the same man?'

'No doubt, Steve, definitely him; I got an eye for faces – crap with names.'

'What time would that have been, Harry? It's Sam by the way.'

'Yeah, sorry about that – it was seven fifty-two the first time and eight twenty-nine the second time on the return trip.'

'Impressive – how can you be sure?'

'Never heard of timetables, Shaun? This country runs on them.'

＊

The inside of a police interview room held no fears for Tommy Roddy – he'd seen a few in Ireland. He waited patiently, sipping from a cup of water, but below the surface he was fuming. How could he have been so stupid to let Maurice Stone talk him into using his premises? Of course, Maurice hadn't been completely straight with him about the purpose of using his yard, and he hadn't asked any questions, just accepted the five hundred in cash and taken the dogs home with him for once. Why he'd wanted to dispose of a body in such a way puzzled him; Tommy could've just put it in the boot of a scrapped car and crushed it, leaving no trace.

McNally and Frost entered the room. They were carrying several property bags. Tommy considered casting another flippant remark towards the black DS but thought better of it; she was a tough one. He'd be wasting his time.

Frost opened the interview with introductions, time and location before reminding Roddy he was still under caution, and then McNally's phoned began to vibrate.

'I've got to take this. Only be a moment.'

'What, you forgot to take the kids to school or something?' Roddy asked sarcastically.

Frost stated for the tape that DI McNally had left the room. She sat back and waited, amused at how much Roddy hated the silence.

*

'Hi, Laura, Ryan McNally, we're just about to interview Roddy – you OK?' He could tell something was seriously wrong. 'Hey what's up?'

The surveillance team leader took a breath. 'We lost him, Ryan, towards Reading. He realised he was being followed and took off up the M4. Three of our cars were out of the game immediately due to roadworks. We still managed to get one car and the bike behind him. He cut off the M4 at the very last moment – a miracle apparently that he didn't turn the car over. Our car couldn't make it, but the bike went with him.'

'Hey that's OK. Did you get a registration?'

'Yeah; of course, it's all in the log, but the car registration is cloned from a similar model in Birmingham. I've had some West Mid's officer check it out for us – the owners are both in their late seventies and the car is in their garage.'

'Laura, there's something else you're not telling me.'

'The Mercedes driver stopped in a layby…' She stopped, and all McNally could hear was a stifled cry.

'Laura, what's happened?'

'…As did our bike – he was the only one in pursuit and should've just ridden on – you know, live to fight another day. The driver of the Mercedes pulled a gun and shot the bike's front tyre out and then approached our man, told him to get down on the floor and shot him at point-blank range through his helmet visor. He's dead, Ryan, that bastard executed him.'

*

McNally walked back into the interview room, white-faced, and instructed Frost to end the interview before it had even properly started. She thought of challenging her boss but saw the look on his face and did as he instructed.

'What, you feckers going to let me go already? Good, I'll be home in time for some breakfast.'

McNally looked at Frost and indicated towards the tape machine. 'Off?' he asked. She nodded. McNally lent over the table and grabbed the Irishman by his hair and dragged him to the floor. 'You're going nowhere, you piece of shit. I'm going to make sure I ruin your fucking life and everything you own. You're never going to see the light of day again. You're going to fucking die in prison.' McNally felt Frost's hands firmly on his shoulders, pulling him away. The red mist lifted slightly, and he got to his feet. 'Take this piece of shit back to the cells. We'll deal with him later.'

*

Maurice Stone parked near to the Kennet and Avon Canal near Reading city centre. It was approaching 8am and the city was beginning to stir. A nearby cafe was opening for the day. He looked round carefully, firstly for any CCTV cameras and then for any passers-by; when satisfied he wasn't being observed, he threw the handgun into the canal. He took another set of cloned registration plates from the boot and threw the old ones in the same direction as the gun. He smiled and headed for the cafe – he was starving.

*

'Mr Roddy, we have already asked if you wish to have a solicitor present – one of your own choice or we can provide one for you. You declined earlier. Bearing in mind the seriousness of the charges against you, I would advise that you now reconsider. I'll ask again. Would you like to have some legal representation during this interview and for the rest of the time you'll be in custody at this police station?' Frost waited patiently for an answer.

'I don't need a brief as I've nothing to say to you. Just keep that mad fecker away from me, d' ya hear?'

'Well, just as it is your right to say nothing, we have every right to ask you questions, and I would remind you again that you do not have to say anything, but it may harm your defence if you do not mention, when questioned, something which you later rely on in court. Anything you do say may be given in evidence. Now, bearing in mind the weight of evidence that I'm about to present to you, if I were you, I would consider carefully the repercussions of *not* answering the questions while you have a chance.'

'I'll maintain my rights until I see what you feckers put on the table.'

Frost looked over at McNally, who gave her a reassuring nod. She produced a photocopy of the passport photograph of Frankie Meeres marked SG/1. 'Do you know this man?' Roddy looked at the photograph, sat back in his chair and concentrated on a spot on the wall between his two interviewers – an old Provisional IRA technique. But, unlike a well-trained terrorist, both detectives knew that Roddy wouldn't be able to keep silent for more than a few minutes, let alone days, so they would continue with their questions, revealing more and more of their evidence as they went.

'This is former Detective Sergeant Frankie Meeres. We know that he was murdered sometime in the last week and a half. His body was dismembered and delivered to various parts of London, specifically the railway network. We have evidence to suggest that you were involved in his murder. Did you kill DS Frankie Meeres?' Roddy maintained his stare, managing to control his breathing, but his body released the tension he was feeling by clasping his hands so tightly together his knuckles were turning white; Frost could see that he was desperate to say something. 'I'll ask again, Mr Roddy. Do you know this man?'

Silence.

'Have you ever met him before?'

Silence.

'Were you involved in his death?'

'No comment. Is that all you got?' Frost inwardly smiled; he was cracking – now to up the pressure.

Frost produced a photograph, taken by the CROP officer earlier that morning, marked FG/1. She placed it next to the one of Meeres. 'Do you know this man?'

'No comment.'

'This was taken this morning about five o'clock; the man is leaving the Portakabin situated at your scrap merchant yard in Bunns Lane, Mill Hill. I'll ask again – do you know this man?'

Roddy yawned. It was obviously a sham, to release the pressure he was feeling and give himself a couple more seconds to consider his response. Frost knew she was getting to him. He wasn't as hard as he thought he was, and he was worried. Frost went for the jugular.

'Following his departure from your yard this morning, this man, who we believe is called Maurice, was followed by a surveillance team towards Heathrow Airport.' Roddy sat up in his seat and glanced at both detectives in turn. 'At some stage he realised that he was being followed and took some drastic action on the M4 before leaving the motorway at junction eleven.'

'All very interesting, but what's this all got to do with me?'

'The only surveillance officer to stay with Maurice was a police motorcyclist, a young family man, a father to three children under the age of six. Maurice stopped in a layby, produced a firearm and shot the bike's tyres out.'

'Yeah – and?'

'He then approached the officer and shot him at point-blank range. That officer died before he reached hospital, Mr Roddy, and we believe you supplied the gun that killed him.'

Tommy Roddy's face drained of colour.

'I am further arresting you for conspiracy to murder a police officer,' Frost again cautioned him.

'I think I'd better have a solicitor after all, don't you?'

THIRTY-ONE

WEDNESDAY AFTERNOON

The atmosphere in the incident room was subdued. The team just sat and looked at each other in turn. No words seemed appropriate, even though none of them had ever met the deceased officer, he was one of their own. Each of them non-verbally communicated their feelings to one and another: a half smile, a tear, a look of determination that the bastard would pay. McNally and Plummer entered the room accompanied by a female officer none of the team knew. There was no banter, no wisecracks – even from Graves. They'd lost one of their own for the second time in a week, and it was hurting. Rain lashed at the windows that overlooked Camden Road; the end of the working day saw a logjam of cars and vans jostling for position; the sounding of horns, the odd road rage-based expletive. Life just went on in the outside world as if this were just a normal Wednesday afternoon. The death of a young police officer would do little to change that.

McNally opened the meeting with an introduction. 'This is DS Laura Quinn from Special Ops. Laura is the team leader of the unit that conducted surveillance on our main suspect, Maurice, this morning.' McNally offered a supportive smile and took a seat with his officers.

'Hi, everyone.' Quinn's voice was barely audible – it sounded gravely and sore but still held the attention of everybody in the room; the strain of the day showed clearly on her face. She cleared her throat after taking a mouthful of water; she'd already briefed this information several times this morning, but she was still determined to put as much passion into this update as she had the first of the day. 'As you'll all know by now, this morning's operation ended tragically in the violent death of one of my team. The officer had been part of the surveillance team for only six months. He was married with three children, all under the age of six.' McNally saw that she was gripping the table and just about keeping it together. He didn't want to interrupt but was ready to offer physical support if needed – she looked exhausted. It was important that his team heard what she had to say.

'His family are being looked after by specialist family liaison officers as we speak. I just wanted to come along and brief you personally. He was a very proud, dedicated officer – he loved his job and this force with a passion; he'd told me a few months ago at an annual appraisal that his ambition was one day to be a detective. I know from the look on every face here you will do everything in your power to bring this bastard to justice, and I wish you luck.' Quinn made eye contact with every member of the team, nodding in turn to each one of them, turned quickly and walked out.

McNally got to his feet. 'OK, everyone, we can feel sorry for ourselves and reflect on this tragic loss when we have nailed this bastard.' The feelings of lethargy and tiredness were replaced by one of determination with every person in the room back online. 'DS Frost and I have started to interview Thomas Roddy, identified on the CCTV footage yesterday both at Catford Bridge and Bermondsey stations, following our victim, Frankie Meeres. We've left him with his brief to mull over the fact he's looking at a charge of conspiring to murder both Meeres and our surveillance officer. He seemed genuinely surprised; in fact, it looked like he was going to shit himself when he heard of the shooting. We're going back to the custody suite immediately after this briefing and going in hard. I think he'll turn.' Frost nodded in agreement.

McNally pointed at an intelligence chart fixed to a whiteboard produced by Marie Relish, showing names, vehicles and mobile numbers that connect the various players in the inquiry so far.

'I believe the key to unlocking this investigation is buried in associations: who knows who and how. We know Maurice is associated with Eddie Lee and Thomas Roddy from the boxing picture, but it can't be a coincidence that Lee was in Norfolk chasing after Brian Garvey, whilst Meeres was being murdered in Southeast London. There must be a connection between these three and other people. We have the mobiles of Eddie Lee, killed in the RTA in Norfolk, Jed Jennings and Thomas Roddy. The data – contacts, call history, text and email messages – are being downloaded as we speak. We know that the car driven by Maurice was using cloned registration plates from a similar vehicle up in the West Midlands. This is the registration plate partially identified by the witness who saw Maurice leaving drug dealer Joey Dryden's home address and picked up on the ANPR coming north in the Rotherhithe Tunnel and then crossing back over the Thames on the Dartford Crossing in the early hours of the morning of Dryden's murder. This is also the vehicle followed from Roddy's scrapyard this morning. I think we must assume that, by now, Maurice has either ditched the car or changed the plates again. Linda, can you make sure Thames Valley Police have got all this information? Hopefully they'll be searching ANPR for Mercedes vehicles in and out of Reading; it was early morning – I wouldn't have thought there'd be too much traffic on the roads.

'I want somebody down to York Hall with a copy of the

photograph featuring Roddy, Maurice and Eddie Lee. Speak to anybody who may be able to identify Maurice and anybody else in the picture. Ray, issue that action to Stuart.' Blendell gave his boss the thumbs up.

'Just before you move on, guv,' Blendell said, 'Nottingham and Bedford prisons have come back to me. Jed Jennings visited Eddie Lee at both locations, once in Nottingham and twice a few weeks before his release from Bedford. I've just received an email from Norfolk Police. They've sent me an itemised bill of Lee's mobile, which he purchased the day after his release, probably using the cash he stole from his wife after he beat her up. Jennings' number is on there several times, together with three other mobiles, which we're waiting for subscriber checks on.'

'Jim, Sam, I want to know why Frankie Meeres was at that bus stop for such a long time; we know he was on a missing person's case. It looks like our bus driver may well be the last person to see him alive. Bearing in mind his position at the bus stop, whatever or whomever he was watching must have been in his view. So, get back down to Abbey Street and find me some answers. Linda, when you speak to the Thames Valley Police incident room dealing with the murder in Reading, give them everything we've got, including photographs of Maurice. We need to find him. Unless there is anything urgent that comes out of our interview with Roddy this evening, we'll have another meeting at eight o'clock tomorrow. If you need motivation, which I'm pretty sure none of you will, think of the murdered officer's wife and three kids and what they must be going through at this precise moment. Good luck, everybody.'

*

Maurice Stone was keeping a low profile in the basement of a Victorian three-bedroomed terraced house in Reading. The phone call to the Butcher had been an uncomfortable one. He would lay low for another day or so before carrying out his new instructions.

*

When McNally and Frost walked into the interview room, Tommy Roddy looked composed, even a little cocky. The detectives settled down and introduced themselves again on tape, as did Roddy's legal representative, Mr Purcell-Symons. Frost was again leading the interview.

'Mr Roddy, I'm again going to show you the pictures I asked you to look at earlier today.' Frost laid out the photographs of Meeres and Maurice on the table in front of Roddy. 'I'll ask you again, to look very carefully at each and tell me if you know these people.' Roddy looked at the images and then whispered in the ear of his solicitor, who nodded some sort of agreement.

Roddy pushed the photograph of Maurice back towards Frost. 'I know this man. He's an old friend I used to box with back in the day.'

'When was the last time you saw him?' Frost asked.

'As you well know, I saw him earlier this morning.'

'What is this man's name?'

'Well, that's for me to know and you to find out – I ain't no fecking grass. You lot might stab each other in the back, but where I come from, we don't.'

'Mr Roddy, let me remind you of a few facts. This man, who, as you say, was at your scrapyard this morning, murdered a police officer within an hour of being in your company with a firearm we have reason to believe was supplied by you. If that is the case, you are an accessory to murder.'

'I don't supply firearms to anybody. That's not my game.'

'Then what *is* your game?'

Roddy took a few moments to consider his next comment; he seemed to come to a decision and nodded to himself in confirmation that what he was about to say was the right thing to do. It was now all about self-preservation.

'Look, the guy's name is Maurice Stone – I'm probably not telling you anything you don't already know. We go back a long way, used to go to the same school in Peckham and then the same boxing club. I hadn't seen him in years, when I get a call saying he needs to get abroad for a bit and can I help with a new passport, driving licence and a US visa. That's what I've done in the past – a few documents now and then. I don't produce them myself, not with these fecking hands, but I know a few people who do, as well as somebody in the US Embassy – Irish American, a distant cousin – very handy. But I don't touch guns. If he had a gun, then it was his own.'

'So, was that the reason for the visit in the early hours of the morning?'

'Yeah, he was due to fly out for a couple of weeks this morning. I got another cousin in New York, probably hundreds of them no doubt. He was going to stay with him for a while. I don't know what sort of trouble he was in – he didn't tell me; I didn't ask. So yeah,' Roddy put his hands up as if in surrender, 'guilty of a bit of passport fraud but not supplying weapons. As for murder, you're way off.'

'So, you're telling us that the last time you saw him before early this morning was some time ago?'

'Yes. My life is in North London now – I tend to avoid crossing the river; I got too many enemies down there.'

'Funny that, because we have a witness and some video footage from a security camera that puts our Mr Stone in the vicinity of your place of work, in fact about one hundred metres from your yard, a few nights ago. He dropped in for a visit, didn't he? Don't forget we have your mobile, from which all the data is being downloaded, so think carefully before you answer. Did Maurice Stone come to your scrapyard on Saturday night?' Roddy sighed and looked at his brief, who just gave a shrug.

'I think we need a break, Detective,' Purcell-Symons said.

'Is that right, Mr Roddy, do you need a break? The questions aren't going away; they'll still be here when you come back.'

Roddy shook his head. 'He rang me Friday, I think it was. Said he needed access to the railway line. I didn't know what he was up to. He didn't mention anything a day or so earlier, when he ordered the documents. I wasn't happy. I obviously knew whatever it was wasn't going to be legit, so he suggested cutting the chain on the front gates and keeping the dogs at home with me so I could say somebody had broken in if there was any trouble from you lot, and he gave me a few quid on top of what he owed me for the passport and driving licence. The next thing I know is your lot calling me out early Sunday morning. That's all I know.'

Frost substituted the picture of Maurice Stone with the group of boxers taken from Roddy's office wall. 'That's you in the picture, yes?'

Roddy nodded.

'For the tape, Mr Roddy.'

'Yes.'

'Standing behind you is Maurice Stone, correct?'

'Yes.'

'Do you know who this is, standing on your right?'

'Eddie somebody or other; think he's inside. I ain't seen him in years.'

'Eddie Lee?'

'Yeah, that's him – Eddie Lee, another Peckham lad.'

'Is there anybody else in the photograph you can put a name to?'

'No, not really, it's been a long time.'

'What about this smartly dressed older man and woman? Looks like they're a couple – do you know them?'

'No, he wasn't a boxer. I think he was a local businessman; probably put a bit of money into the club to keep it going, you know, for equipment and transport costs. The picture was taken in York Hall, Bethnal Green. We were there on a fight night – our club was in Peckham – so this geezer and the woman probably come along to support us.'

'So, you don't get over the river much anymore, Mr Roddy?' Frost shuffled a few pieces of paper on purpose to give Roddy some more time to think about what was coming his way next, before she handed him two more CCTV images. 'I asked you a question.'

'No, not really – got no business over there,' Roddy answered, nervously looking at the images from the corner of his eye.

'Do you recognise anybody in these two images?'

Roddy shrugged his big shoulders and looked at his brief, as if he were going to answer for him.

'Come on, Mr Roddy, have another look.'

Purcell-Symons slid the images towards him for a better look; his glance at his client gave it all away.

'Your solicitor seems to recognise somebody – what about you?'

'Yeah, it's me. So what? It's a crime to travel on public transport now, is it? More of a victim nowadays the amount those feckers charge.' Roddy laughed to himself, trying to lighten the mood.

'Mr Roddy, these CCTV images were recorded at Catford Bridge and Bermondsey stations early morning last Wednesday. You just told us that you do not travel south of the river anymore. So why were you in Catford and Bermondsey?'

'Last Wednesday, you say. I can't remember. I mean, Bermondsey is technically south of the river but not really South London, is it?'

'I think you know the answer to that, Mr Roddy. Let's move on.'

McNally could see Frost was enjoying herself – he saw no reason to interrupt her flow of questioning, a mistake even the most experienced interviewers frequently made.

'I want you to look at the picture I showed you earlier in this interview of a man called Frankie Meeres. You said you didn't know him, correct?'

'Not sure I said that, but no, his face doesn't ring any bells,' Roddy answered.

'The man in the photograph is a former detective sergeant with the British Transport Police, who retired a couple of years ago and became a private investigator. He was murdered and his body expertly dismembered sometime later that day, the day that you were in Catford and Bermondsey. Although I appreciate you have already stated to us that you couldn't remember if you were there or not, you agree it is you in the CCTV images, which clearly show the time and date. Have a look at the time on the photograph of you entering Catford Bridge station – maybe you could read out the time for the benefit of the tape?'

Roddy looked at the image. 'My eyes ain't that good.'

'Well, Mr Roddy, maybe Mr Purcell-Symons could help us all out. Sir, if you don't mind.'

'Two minutes past seven,' the solicitor replied.

'Thank you,' Frost said. 'We have a statement from a neighbour of Mr Meeres, who told us she saw him leaving his home address about ten to seven that morning. Do you know where he lives, Mr Roddy?'

'How the feck would I know – I'm sure you're going to tell me.'

'Catford.'

'So, what, thousands of people do – does that prove anything?'

'Bear with me. I want you to have a look at the image from Bermondsey station. Again, sir, if you would oblige for the tape?'

'Seven thirty-three.'

'Thank you. So, there you are, Tommy, leaving Bermondsey station at seven thirty-three. We have another statement from a very helpful bus driver, who tells us that he saw Mr Meeres at a bus stop on Abbey Street a couple of hundred yards from Bermondsey station between seven fifty-two and again later that morning at eight twenty-nine. So, there we have another coincidence, Mr Roddy, our victim a short distance from Bermondsey station less than twenty minutes after you are seen leaving the same station. Can you explain that?'

'Fact is stranger than fiction. It doesn't mean anything. I don't know the guy – never met him before.'

Frost handed two enlarged images of the CCTV footage to Roddy. 'These are the same images but blown up a little to help us all. If you look at both the image from Catford and Bermondsey, do you recognise the man walking several paces in front of you, Mr Roddy?'

Roddy reached out for a plastic cup on the table in front of him and drained the few remaining drops of water. He looked grey; droplets of sweat were forming just below his hairline. He looked at his solicitor and then back at Frost, whose triumphant smile communicated her only thought *I've got you, you bastard.*

'I think I need a break to speak to my solicitor please, Detective.'

THIRTY-TWO

WEDNESDAY EVENING

The hand on her shoulder gave her such a fright she felt her chest tighten.

'Hey, Marie, what the hell's the matter? You're jumpy. I'm just popping out, wanted to know if you'd like a cup of decent coffee bringing back,' Ray Blendell asked her. She took a couple of deep breaths and nodded her thanks. She'd been working hard, updating the data chart as more and more information came in, and hadn't realised the time. She tried to contact Marcia to have a reassuring chat, but her phone was still on silent so assumed they were still interviewing Roddy. She was pleased when Sara Hallam picked up on the second ring and invited her round to stay with her for the night. She knew this couldn't continue, but she calmed down, knowing she would be safe for this evening at least. She heard a phone ring outside the office door; Stuart Graves walked in looking a little red-faced; my God, had he been standing outside listening to her call? It was only a couple of nights ago that she was certain she'd been followed when staying at Marcia's. Suddenly, she didn't feel so safe after all.

*

The fresh air cleared their heads, and they were ready for round three. McNally and Frost returned to the interview room, having checked with the custody officer that Roddy had been given something to eat and drink and that fact had been recorded on his custody record. The time was approaching 7.30pm, both realising they'd been on the go for over fourteen hours. They would have another go at Roddy before calling it a day. Frost knew she had him where she wanted him and cursed when he requested a break to consult his solicitor, but she wasn't going to give him grounds for a complaint of oppressive behaviour by her and McNally or overnight to think of a way out of his predicament. All four settled down and Frost turned on the visual and audible equipment. The tone of the final interview of the day was going to be set with Roddy's answer to her first question.

'Mr Roddy, we ended the last interview asking if you recognised a man just ahead of you in the CCTV images at Catford Bridge and Bermondsey stations – at this point you asked for a break and a chance to speak to Mr Purcell-Symons. The question still stands, Mr Roddy, do you recognise the male in the CCTV images?'

It was Purcell-Symons who broke the silence. 'My client has decided to answer all your questions as truthfully and frankly as he can, on the understanding that you accept that he had nothing to do with the killing of anybody.'

It was McNally who replied, 'Sir, as you know, we will follow the evidence wherever it takes us. We are more likely to believe your client and accept his role in this matter if he *does* answer DS Frost's questions honestly.' Both detectives looked at Roddy, who nodded. 'For the tape, Tommy.'

'Yes, Inspector, I will co-operate, but believe you me, I didn't kill anybody.'

'OK – can you please answer my previous question?' Frost continued.

'Yes, I do recognise the man in the images; it's the same man in the photograph you showed me – the ex-copper – Meeres.'

'Why were you following him?'

'Maurice Stone rang me the week before last, asked if I wanted to earn a few quid. He told me the job was following an ex-copper who'd upset his boss, who'd wanted some revenge. I don't know why and what they had planned. I'd picked him up in Catford on a couple of previous occasions – he always seemed to use the trains. Early last week Maurice told me to buy an untraceable mobile and text Meeres some information about a missing woman he was looking for. It was a set-up – I knew that, but I didn't know he was going to be killed, just thought he'd get a bit of a beating.'

'Do you still have the phone you used to send the message on?' Frost asked.

'No, Maurice told me to ditch it that day.'

'Can you remember the message you sent?'

'It was something like: "You'll find her in Chaplin House, Abbey Street." There was a flat number and something else, but I can't remember. The message also had a photograph of a woman – I've got no idea who she was, probably just a random picture from the internet.'

'We know Meeres was already working on a missing person case because he had an entry in his diary for that day in Bermondsey. Do you know who'd hired him to find this mystery woman in the first place?'

Roddy took his time to consider his answer – it seemed to the detectives that he was genuinely trying to retrieve any information that might be helpful to them – but then shook his head slowly. 'I presume it was Maurice. He was the only one I had contact with, but Maurice isn't the sharpest pencil in the box – you know, probably all that boxing. He was big but not that clever a boxer; took a few shots to the head. I know he works for somebody, but I don't know who – this is all South London based. I'm not really in that loop anymore.'

'So, what were your instructions for that day?'

'Just to send the text message and then follow him and ring

Maurice on that mobile and tell him when Meeres had arrived in the area and keep an eye on him. That's what I did. But instead of going straight to the address, he was a bit cagey and plonked himself down at the bus stop for nearly an hour. I watched him from a distance; I knew he'd pick up on me if I got any nearer – he'd already been doing a bit of checking behind him – so I stayed well back. Eventually, he got up and crossed over Abbey Street and headed for Chaplin House. I rang Maurice and he told me to back off. I didn't hear from him for a few days until he rang me about getting him the documents he wanted, and the rest you know.'

'When you were arrested, Mr Roddy, you said to me,' Frost consulted her arrest notes in her pocketbook and quoted, ' "that piece of shit deserved everything he got and you, you fecking bitch, may well be next." That implies you knew exactly what was going to happen to Mr Meeres and you had the means to implement such actions against me personally. Is that right?'

'I was just angry with you, Stone and more so myself for being so stupid in getting involved. I'm sorry I spoke to you like that, Detective. By then I knew what had happened to Meeres – it was all over the news. I even saw him,' pointing at McNally, 'giving his press conference. I don't like coppers; I make no bones about that, so I said the first thing that came into my mind, but when I was following him and sent that text message and called Stone when he was heading to Chaplin House, I had no idea they were going to kill him. I got a nice legit business, the scrapyard that is, and yes, I do a bit of wheeler-dealing every now and then. I ain't perfect, but I'm no killer.'

'You just said that when you saw Meeres heading towards Chaplin House, you had no idea *they* were going to kill him – who are they?'

'Look, can we turn the tape off for a minute?'

McNally replied, 'Sorry, we have to record everything you say, Mr Roddy.'

Roddy nodded his head. 'OK, well that's all I've got to say then.'

*

McNally and Frost sat in the canteen sipping very hot, black coffee. Both were dead beat. The internal phone rang, and a late turn uniformed officer answered and raised the phone above his head.

'DI McNally?' he called.

McNally put his hand in the air and went and picked the phone up. 'Inspector, Stephen Purcell-Symons. I've just finished talking to my client. He has asked me to pass on a message to you.'

'OK, sir, what is it?'

'You'll have to meet me outside, Inspector. He has given me a piece of paper with some information on it. He has instructed me to pass it on to you and DS Frost. I haven't looked at it; I think it would be best that way.'

'OK, sir, we'll be right down.'

McNally and Frost drank as much of the coffee as they could, transferred the rest to takeaway cups and headed outside, where Purcell-Symons was dutifully waiting. He handed them a piece of paper and, without a goodbye or leave, turned and headed towards the tube station.

McNally and Frost went into the garage and sat in their car. McNally turned the internal light on, unfolded the piece of paper and read the two words written in Roddy's handwriting. He passed it to Frost. She read aloud what she saw, ' "The Butcher".'

THIRTY-THREE

THURSDAY MORNING

'So, who the hell is the Butcher? Sounds like a character from an American horror film, you know with a chainsaw going round killing young girls at will – blood and guts everywhere.' Graves addressed his question in his own inimitable style, not only to McNally but to everybody else in the incident room.

'You don't think he's trying to have you over, guv, do you?' he added.

Frost jumped in. 'He wanted to tell us something off tape but clamped up when we pointed out to him that's not possible. He handed the information to his solicitor to pass on to us. It must have something to do with whoever pulls Maurice Stone's strings.'

'What did Felix Lowther say about the method of dismemberment?' Sally Cook asked.

'Carried out by somebody professionally competent – or words to that effect – he gave us a list: surgeon, vet or even a butcher,' McNally replied. 'Marie, search all the databases – PNC etc – and liaise with Force Intelligence Bureau. Get them to start talking to the Met – see if we can come up with anything relating to the name being used before. You know, has it come up in relation to any investigation in the past etc.'

Relish gave McNally a tired nod – she'd stayed at Sara Hallam's the night before but didn't sleep well; Graves' graphic description of the murder of young girls hadn't helped. Frost could see the events of the last few days were starting to take their toll on her friend. She needed to speak to Sara again about bringing the problem to McNally's attention, although it would probably be the last thing he needed at the moment.

'I want us all to concentrate on finding Maurice Stone. Stuart, how did you get on at York Hall?'

'There was nobody there who recognised anybody in the picture. But I thought the photograph looked professionally taken. Obviously, this was well before cameras on mobiles. To box at York Hall is a big event for any boxer or boxing club…'

'Thomas Roddy told us in interview that all the boxers in the picture boxed for Peckham Boxing Club,' Frost added.

'…Well yes, that was what I was thinking. I figured that the photograph of the group was probably taken by a local news photographer or a freelancer, who may have sold the picture to a local paper. I contacted the *Peckham and Camberwell Gazette* and faxed them a copy of the photograph with a rough date the picture would've been taken. They're going to search their archives for anything on Peckham Boxing Club for that period and get back to me later today.'

'Bearing in mind Stone's car was cloned from a vehicle registration in the West Midlands, have we considered that he's not in the Reading area now but has connections up there and travelled via the A4074 to Oxford and then onto the M40 towards Birmingham and the West Midlands?' Wakefield asked.

'It's a possibility,' Linda Doyle answered, 'but I spoke to the owners of the car yesterday after the West Midlands Police had paid them a visit. They always garage their car and rarely use it about town as the public transport is so good, but they regularly drive down to Orpington in Kent to visit their daughter and grandchildren, not a million miles away from where we think this whole affair centres around, so the car was more than likely cloned during one of these trips to London and Kent.'

'Ray, now we've got his full name, see if we can get a better picture of Stone; at the moment we've only got grainy CCTV images from the doorbell security camera in North London, the photograph from the CROP officer from long range in the middle of the night and a photograph of him as a boxer, which is probably at least twenty years old. I know he's got no police record, but he must have a driving licence, passport, anything that's more up to date that I can give to the media for circulation. Jim, Sam, how're we getting on with the sighting of Meeres in Bermondsey?'

'We know he was sitting there, at the bus stop, for probably up to an hour. We haven't had anybody else come forward who remembers seeing him. The information given by Roddy in your interview, that Meeres was aware, by that time, via Roddy's text message, of the possible location of the missing woman, links in with his unobstructed view of the two entrances to Chaplin House, part of the Bermondsey estate. He must've been waiting for her to come out, and when she didn't, I believe he went in to find her.'

'OK. We need electoral rolls for every flat in Chaplin House. It looks like one of them is possibly our murder scene.'

'What's happening with Roddy, guv?' Doyle asked.

'I've spoken to CPS and asked for authorisation to charge him with supplying false documents, which should keep him in custody for a while; he shouldn't get bail, seeing as he's a flight risk. I tend to believe his version of events. I really don't think he was party to Meeres' murder. I could be wrong, but to be honest, we need to channel all our efforts into finding Stone.

'Linda, I want you to go back and speak to Jasmine Lee. Take the boxing photograph. See if she can shed any light on the identity of the man and woman in the picture and ask if she's ever heard of the Butcher. We know her former husband, Eddie Lee, is associated with Stone and Roddy. Ask her if she knows either of those two. There is somebody in the middle of all this, presumably the Butcher, whom we need to identify. Ray, how're we getting on with past investigations? This whole affair must centre on somebody being really pissed off with Meeres and Garvey.'

'I've got it down to three cases, where Meeres and Garvey were the main investigators. One was the Eddie Lee conviction. He was caught red-handed in a mail break on a train to Sheffield, slashing mailbags open. He went down for theft from the Royal Mail and attempting to wound Meeres with the knife. He admitted the theft charge but fought the attempted wounding at Nottingham Crown Court; his defence was that he never threatened either officer with the knife – their word against his. He got found guilty of the second charge and, with his previous, got ten years. So, Lee had a motive for revenge against both Meeres and Garvey. Obviously, he'd been given the wrong name by his wife and thought it was Garvey who'd been sleeping with her, when we know it was in fact Meeres, but he still hated Meeres enough for, in his eyes, fitting him up with the attempted wounding charge, to go after him when released.

'The second case was a drugs importation case with HMRC; however, the main offender pleaded guilty and then died of a heart attack in his cell three years ago. The last job was a conspiracy to commit armed robbery, going back a bit when stations still had ticket offices and cash was king. Meeres and Garvey were involved in the investigation and were in the arrest car at the rear of a surveillance team following the main suspect and two accomplices – a driver and some muscle. The job was informant led. The DI in charge got a call telling him that it was going down that night, so they put a hard stop in and arrested all three. It was a pretty dirty trial, accusations flying all over the place, in particular against Meeres, who was accused of planting a sawn-off shotgun in the boot of the main suspect's car.

*

It had been nearly thirty-six hours since Maurice Stone had shot and killed the police officer, and he was getting restless. The Butcher had told him to give it two or three days, but he wasn't a patient man. He wanted to get on with the boss's latest instructions and then try to catch a ferry or the Eurostar to France and travel south to Spain or Portugal; he was pissed off with the weather and hiding in a basement. He'd waited until midday, thinking he was less likely to draw attention than leaving early morning. He travelled cross-country in the Mercedes with new false plates and rejoined the M4 south at Maidenhead. By 1pm, he was entering the outskirts of Central London and heading south to Bermondsey.

THIRTY-FOUR

THURSDAY AFTERNOON

Hodge and Wakefield parked their car outside Chaplin House in a position where they had an unobstructed view of the entrance to the premises. The block had nine floors, with ten flats on each level. Blendell and Relish had eliminated several flats from the electoral roll in relation to social circumstances or description of the occupants, age of tenants, family groups and length of occupancy. They'd highlighted the flats with younger couples or single occupancy with a short tenancy. The two detectives would start with the thirty-two flats that remained. They decided to cover each floor together, keeping each other in line of sight as they went to the relevant flats, starting from the first floor and working up. Each detective was in possession of a copy of the passport photograph of Meeres and the best of the CCTV images of Maurice Stone. They were also armed with a questionnaire and explained to residents that they were making enquiries into an incident that had happened in the local area and were trying to trace the men shown to them in the photographs. Of course, they knew that the electoral rolls were only as accurate as information provided by residents or, in several cases, by past residents. Some of the new ones had never bothered. Hodge and Wakefield discovered families with three children living in flats their records indicated were occupied by elderly couples.

The detectives came together on the fourth floor after visiting the identified flats on their list so far. They'd been at it for over an hour with no results. They stood, overlooking the car park, glad to see their car untouched and all four tyres still in place. Hodge glanced skywards to the remaining five floors and the seventeen flats on their list that remained.

Wakefield looked at his list. 'This is bloody hopeless. Most of the occupants of flats I've visited so far have no resemblance to what is on this list. We'll probably need to visit all ninety flats in the end, which is going to take forever.'

Hodge nodded in agreement. 'We should've got some uniform backup, cut the job in half. How many "no answers" did you get?'

'Five, so far. At least two of those flats had somebody in but they chose not to answer. The others, who did open their door, weren't particularly helpful; many didn't even look at the photographs.'

The two detectives were starting to draw the attention of tenants from the adjacent blocks of flats. There were a few insults flying about, and the detectives knew they were on borrowed time. They were just about to turn towards the stairwell when a black Mercedes pulled into the car park below. Hodge grabbed Wakefield's arm and pulled him back to the balcony.

'Jim, a black Merc.' Both detectives waited for the vehicle to park and the driver to emerge.

'Shit!' Hodge whispered. 'That's Maurice Stone.' Both detectives looked at the CCTV image on their clipboards for confirmation. They watched as Stone straightened and stretched his large frame and saw a flash of gold as he yawned out loud. The detectives froze, both considering the conundrum they faced; they were too far away to tell him to stop where he was – by the time they got downstairs, he may well disappear; in the end, their decision was made for them. A shout of 'filth' from an adjacent balcony jolted them from their trance and into action. Stone also heard the call, looked up and saw the two detectives moving away from the balcony. Stone jumped back into the driver's seat and fired the powerful engine.

Hodge and Wakefield took the stairs three at a time, crashing through the communal entrance and out into the car park. They both saw the powerful car manoeuvring towards the entrance, partially blocked by a delivery vehicle entering the estate.

'Get the reg number, Jim. I'll get the car.' Hodge ran to their vehicle, jumped into the driver's seat, started the car and accelerated towards the exit, stopping briefly to allow Wakefield to jump in. Just as the detectives were about to move off in pursuit of the Mercedes, a cement breeze block hit their bonnet – thrown from a significant height above them. It bounced off the bonnet and struck the windscreen, fragmenting the glass into a thousand pieces and showering the occupants; they were lucky it hadn't been a direct hit on the windscreen – one or both would've been killed. The few seconds it took the detectives to overcome the shock, to function and think, the Mercedes had disappeared. The delivery van was heading towards them; they could see the shock on the driver's face. It was at this moment they heard a rumble of sound comparable to a roll of thunder; they looked at each other and realised it was several hundred people standing on the balconies of not only Chaplin House but two adjacent blocks as well. They were banging anything they could get their hands on against the iron balcony railings and brickwork: dustbins lids, frying pans and saucepans – it sounded like a scene from the Battle of Rorke's Drift. Just for one ridiculous split second, Hodge felt like performing a Michael Caine impression. The deafening noise reached a crescendo, accompanied by verbal insults – 'pigs', 'scum' and, the most frightening of all, 'kill' – some of the objects were thrown – raining down on the vehicle – a heavy, glass ashtray struck the metal frame of the shattered windscreen and hit Wakefield full in the face.

'We gotta get out of here, Jim. Hang on, mate, you're bleeding badly!' Hodge accelerated towards the now clear exit to the estate. Two youths ran out in front of the car, one holding a machete. Hodge wasn't stopping; he knew if they did, they were as good as dead. He heard Jim Wakefield on the radio screaming, 'Urgent assistance, urgent assistance.'

Hodge spied another car approaching from the left of the car park at speed; the two occupants in the rear seats were hanging out of the windows, each carrying some sort of weapon, urging the driver to go faster. They were going to try and block them in the estate.

'Hold on, Jim. We're getting out of here.' He stamped on the gas pedal and the car lurched forwards towards the two men on foot. Hodge knew he would hit them intentionally with justification if they didn't move – it was his and his colleague's life or theirs; they jumped out of the way, the machete catching the vehicle, which made a frightening metallic sound, producing several sparks – a sound Hodge and Wakefield would never forget.

Hodge reached the junction with Abbey Street. Maurice Stone was of little concern now. He needed to get Wakefield to hospital. He looked over at his colleague. Wakefield was conscious but a lot of blood was gushing from a gash on his forehead, which he was attempting to stem with a blood-sodden handkerchief. Hodge had never seen so much blood. He headed for the urgent care centre at Guy's Hospital, less than a mile away. The nearest accident and emergency was St Thomas' Hospital, Waterloo, considerably further.

Blue lights were screaming from all directions, heading towards the estate. Hodge was angry; he wanted to go back and dish out a bit of summary justice with his fists and anything else he could use as a weapon. This was bloody war. But he focused all that tension and aggression into driving quickly and safely to get his partner the treatment he needed; by the time he screeched up outside the hospital, Jim Wakefield was unconscious.

*

Maurice Stone drove carefully and well within the speed limit as police car after police car sped past him in the opposite direction. They certainly weren't looking for him. He pulled over when he'd put a few miles between himself and Bermondsey. He unwrapped a pay-as-you-go mobile he'd purchased earlier in the day and contacted the Butcher. Displeased that he hadn't had a chance to carry out the instructions, he'd been told to make his way to Kent. The cutting room would have to wait to be emptied and sterilised. The Butcher watched the carnage being beamed live from a helicopter or drone above the Bermondsey estate on the television, satisfied that it would be a while before police officers would be able to access the estate again.

★

The radio news broadcast was dominated by the public disorder on the Bermondsey estate. Police in full riot gear were attempting to regain control of an angry mob, trying to barricade entrance points to the estate.

Linda Doyle parked her car a couple of streets from Jasmine Lee's road. She'd called to arrange to see her. Jasmine hadn't exactly been keen about the revisit but agreed and asked Doyle to be sensitive to her situation.

It was raining hard. A good thing, she thought; rioters don't like bad weather, hence why most riots were in the summer months. Several police officers had reportedly been injured and taken to hospital. Doyle knew Hodge and Wakefield were conducting enquiries at Chaplin House that very afternoon, and she worried for the safety of the young detectives.

She hunted in the back seat for her umbrella, looked at her watch; she couldn't delay any longer. The rain had set in for the night. She'd taken a longer route to get to Jasmine Lee's house, making sure nobody was paying her or the address any attention. Satisfied, she knocked on the door. Lee opened almost immediately and glanced up and down the street before inviting Doyle in. Doyle took her wet coat off and laid it on the floor.

'Have you 'eard anything from Norfolk yet – about releasing Eddie's body or the inquest?' Jasmine asked, before Doyle's backside had landed on the sofa.

'No, not yet, I'll give them a ring tomorrow, but they won't release the body until the inquest has opened and the coroner agrees to it. Who is taking care of the funeral?'

Jasmine picked at her nail varnish – a rather garish purple, Doyle thought. 'Eddie's family, not 'is mum. She don't know what day it is. His auntie, who's got a few bob, is arranging it. I don't really know her that well. We've met a few times – you know, weddings, funerals and christenings. I know she thought Eddie could've done better for 'imself.' Jasmine rolled her eyes in disgust. 'A fucking mailbag thief, who never worked an 'onest day in his life. It should be the other way round, but you know families. Look after each other, don't they? I've always been treated as a bit of an outsider. I'll probably see them at the funeral and never again after that. I certainly won't see any of their money, that's for sure. Thankfully, they don't know about me having a fling with your colleague. Eddie wouldn't 'ave told 'em. He'd 'ave been too embarrassed. I still 'aven't been asked to go and identify him yet, is that why you're 'ere again? You could've asked me that on the phone.'

Doyle unfastened her briefcase and pulled out a thin folder, which contained several photographs and CCTV images. 'Jasmine, I've got some bad news for you.'

'What, that prick is still alive? You got it wrong.' Doyle could see she wasn't jesting; she was genuinely frightened that Lee had survived and there had been a terrible mistake.

'No. We're sure it was Eddie who was killed – Norfolk Police have confirmed his identity by fingerprints, but they'll still want you to go up and officially identify him before the inquest is opened.' Doyle handed the passport photograph of Frankie Meeres to Jasmine. 'Do you know this man, Jasmine?'

'Well, yeah, of course, it's Frankie; you know the copper I went out with for a time. I thought he retired. 'E alright?'

'Well, no, Jasmine. I didn't tell you this during my first visit because we weren't sure at the time, but we've been investigating a murder for the last week and a half or so – you may have seen it on the television.'

'Yeah, I saw some good-looking DI on telly the other night – I remember him because obviously Frankie was a BTP officer...' This time the purple nail was lodged between her teeth as she started to put the pieces of the puzzle together. '...Oh no. It's not 'im, is it?'

Doyle nodded her head. 'I'm very sorry.'

'We weren't close or nuffink, just 'ad a few good nights out together, that's all, but he was a nice guy, knew how to treat a woman, 'ad manners, opened the door for me. Never had no bloke do that for me before.' Doyle could tell she was upset, certainly more than she had been when told of her husband's demise. She remembered a similar description of Meeres from Holly Harrison, about how kind Meeres had been to her, unconditionally. Doyle considered an arm round her shoulder but thought Jasmine wouldn't be too receptive to such a gesture.

'Jasmine, if you feel up to it, I'd like you to have a look at a couple more images, see if you recognise anybody. This meeting is between us – if you do recognise anybody, I want you to be honest with me. It'll help the investigation into Frankie's death.'

'These people in the pictures, are they responsible for his murder?'

Doyle hesitated.

'Come on, Linda, what did you just say – between us, be honest...'

Doyle nodded. 'Yes, you're right. Have a look first, see if you recognise anybody – if you do, I'll be straight up with you – OK?' Jasmine nodded and took the images, glancing quickly at the boxing group, before placing it next to her on the arm of her chair, then looking at the image of Maurice Stone.

'I have seen him somewhere,' she said, pointing to Stone, 'but I can't remember where.'

'Friend of Eddie's?'

'I don't think so. I've seen him in the past few months but can't remember where; maybe I'm getting 'im mixed up with somebody else.' She picked up the boxing group photo again and studied it more thoroughly this time. 'That's him there, isn't it, the black guy? Looks a lot younger, and that's Eddie, God, I didn't recognise him at first. Sorry, I can hardly bloody see anymore. Let me get me glasses. I don't wear 'em much; they make me look ancient.' She stood up, put her glasses on and went over to a table lamp and studied the photo in more detail. 'They look young as well; this must have been taken twenty years ago.'

'Who're you talking about, Jasmine?'

'The man and the woman; I mean, I ain't seen 'im in years, been banged up in Pentonville since I was in my late teens, right hard nut – Eddie idolised him – but she has aged well, I must say; I wonder if she's got a copy of this.'

'Who are they?' Doyle was getting impatient.

'They are Eddie's Uncle Terry and Aunty Hazel, the one who's going to arrange the funeral.'

*

Doyle got back to her car and shook the rain from her umbrella before throwing it in the boot. She looked at her phone and was about to ring McNally when she saw a group message: 'Jim in hospital suspected concussion, badly cut head, Sam pretty shaken but uninjured – office meeting at 6.30pm sharp – DI Mc'. Doyle glanced at her watch: 5.55pm. She left a lot faster than she'd arrived.

THIRTY-FIVE

THURSDAY EVENING

McNally looked at his watch: 6.45pm. He decided to start the meeting – Linda Doyle had texted him saying she was on her way. He looked round the room at an exhausted group of people. McNally knew they were nearly there; this was the most crucial time of any investigation, when the many pieces of information collated, started to fit together. It was why he did this job.

'Let's get started, everybody. I've just spoken to the hospital. Jim Wakefield is conscious and chatting up the nurses…'

'What, the male or the female ones, guv?' Graves chuckled. There was no malice in his comment. Graves had been as concerned as anybody else in the room, and it had helped break the tension they were all feeling.

'…He's been stitched up and is going to have a cracking bruise. They're keeping him in overnight for observation. Sam is on his way back, I diverted Linda Doyle to pick him up from the hospital, his car is in a bad state, been towed away for forensics to have a look. I spoke to him on the phone ten minutes ago. They saw Maurice Stone drive into the Bermondsey estate, but he was warned and got away; that was when it all kicked off. They were lucky to get out of there alive. Jim managed to get the Merc's registration number – again it's been cloned from a similar car in Denmark Hill this time. The plate has been circulated, but it's probably in some garage now. But him showing up means we are on the right track – I still firmly believe one of those flats in Chaplin House is our murder scene and Stone was going back to clean it out; that's the good news. The bad news is we are unlikely to get anywhere near Chaplin House for the foreseeable future. Anybody got anything else?'

Graves held up a newspaper article emailed over to him minutes before the meeting started. 'I got a breakthrough on the boxing picture from Roddy's scrapyard. The contact at the *Peckham and Camberwell Gazette* has come up trumps. He found the picture in an edition of their paper's archives from twenty-one years ago. Helpfully, there is a list of the names featured in the photo; the ones we know about are: Eddie Lee, Maurice Stone and Thomas Roddy, and a local businessman and his wife—'

'Terence and Hazel Nunn.' Everybody turned as Doyle and Hodge entered the room, accompanied by a cheer for the returning hero. 'Jasmine Lee has confirmed their names from the photograph,' Doyle continued, enjoying taking the wind out of Graves' sail. 'Terry Nunn is no businessman. He is a vicious armed robber, who is currently serving eighteen years for armed robbery in Pentonville Prison. I've got a phone number for the aunty, but Jasmine has only ever been to her house once since she and Lee have been married. But as far as she knows, they have lived in that house for many years, so the address is probably the same as Terry Nunn was living in at the time of his arrest.'

'That's the same prison Daniel Corbell was in. It was Nunn he was going to give to us but never got the chance,' Frost said.

It was Ray Blendell's turn to supply another piece of the puzzle. 'Terry Nunn was the armed robber arrested by Meeres and Garvey and who accused Meeres of planting the sawn-off shotgun in the boot of his car. He was living in a large house in Orpington, Kent, which was searched by Meeres and Garvey after Nunn's arrest. According to other officers present, Hazel Nunn was a right handful.'

⋆

Maurice Stone parked the car in the double garage and walked down the side of the house to a self-contained apartment he'd occupied for the last five years. He didn't appear on any electoral roll, or any records kept by HMRC, DHSS, council tax register or any other local or national government body; he didn't exist, which is the way he, and his employer, liked it.

⋆

Cyril Betts sat in the darkness of his flat on the fourth floor of Chaplin House on the Bermondsey estate, frightened to turn on the lights or even take a peep out of his window. The yellow glow of the estate's streetlights pierced his thin, threadbare curtains, casting terrifying shadows across his living room. He held his breath every time somebody passed his window. There was an eerie quietness to the estate – he could imagine a bloody battlefield being the same after violent conflict. The smell of smoke and burning rubber seeped through the gaps of the ill-fitting front door, and supposedly double-glazed windows, encompassing the interior of the flat in visible toxic smog, making breathing a little difficult for the occupant.

He'd witnessed disorder on the estate on many occasions during the twenty-two years he'd lived here but nothing on this scale. It used to be such a nice place to live: friendly, quiet and tranquil. His late wife had known the names of every tenant in the block. But in the last five years, the estate had taken a turn for the worse; a belligerent mood, fuelled by drugs and antisocial behaviour, dominated the whole estate. Neighbour ignored neighbour; any eye contact with the younger generation was met with hostility and aggressive, abusive confrontation. Graffiti, criminal damage and total lack of respect for one's neighbour and their property had turned the whole estate into a hostile environment for the older generation, especially after dark.

He studied the business card left by one of the detectives who'd visited a few hours earlier. He had, at first, hesitated, before opening his door tentatively as the visitor persisted in ringing his bell; his anxiety grew when he discovered it was the police. He knew, at this very moment, he was being watched by hundreds of pairs of eyes. The young detective had shown him images of two people, a black man and a white man, and asked him if he'd seen either or both on the estate in the last couple of weeks. He almost told them the truth but then considered the repercussions: the detective would want to come in, demand more information, request that Cyril make a statement, maybe escort him to the nearest police station; word would echo round the estate like wildfire that he was helping the police, that he was an informant. He knew any scenario that didn't involve him shaking his head in a negative fashion – for all to see – and closing his door on the officer was suicide. So that was what he did. Now he was regretting his actions.

He couldn't recall the exact day when he had seen the two men, but it had been towards the beginning of last week. He'd followed his usual routine of leaving his flat early – at 8am. He would walk down Abbey Street to a twenty-four-hour mini supermarket and purchase his normal daily paper and essentials, like milk and tea and whatever he was going to eat for the rest of the day. He would then return and sit down on a bench on the edge of a small piece of greenery the council had been ever so thoughtful in supplying the residents and read the first four or five pages and the sports page of his newspaper. This was the only time he felt relatively safe outside his flat. Drug dealers, robbers and the rest of the estate's scum generally didn't get out of bed until at least noon.

On leaving the estate that morning, he'd noticed a white male waiting at the bus stop. He was concentrating on his phone and seemed to pay no attention to an approaching bus. Cyril remembered thinking how people nowadays were glued to their mobiles. He was expecting the man to suddenly look up and jump to his feet and curse loudly as the bus passed by without stopping, but he didn't seem bothered. On the return journey to the estate, some twenty minutes later, the man was still in the same position, but this time looking over to Chaplin House. Cyril had raised a hand and wished him good morning, to which the man repeated a polite greeting. He had recognised him as the white man in the photograph the detective had shown him.

On entering the estate, he'd sat on the bench and begun reading his paper. About half an hour later, he noticed an expensive-looking black car drive into the estate and park. He had no idea about makes and models of cars. A large black man got out from behind the wheel, looked around at the surrounding balconies of the adjacent blocks of flats, with a look on his face that warned anybody who had any intention of touching the car, of the likely consequences. Cyril was sure the black man in the grainy image the detective had shown him, was this man. The man opened the rear of the vehicle as he glanced across to where Cyril was seated. Cyril quickly returned to his paper, without seeing if anybody else got out. The next time he saw him was when he appeared on the balcony of the ninth floor and walked along to the end flat. Cyril knew this flat was no. 91 as his own flat – no. 41 – was directly in line, five floors below. The black male disappeared through the front door, having used a key.

Cyril remembered how cold it was that morning, but even so, how he'd been determined to get his forty-five minutes of fresh air before returning to the confines of his flat for the rest of the day. He remembered folding his paper in half and placing it in his shopping bag when the white male from the bus stop entered the estate. He approached Cyril and asked him which floor flat 91 was on, indicating towards Chaplin House. Cyril had smiled and thought to himself that it was pretty bloody obvious but answered politely and advised the man not to use the lift as, firstly, it stank of urine and, secondly, it would often break down and that the mixture of the two was not a prospect he should relish. The man accepted his advice and Cyril watched as he climbed the stairs, a lot slower than the rather fitter-looking black man had done minutes earlier. When he reached no. 91, the door was answered quickly, and the white man disappeared inside.

Cyril, thinking the morning wouldn't get any more exciting, returned to the fourth floor to settle down for the day and read the rest of the newspaper. He remembered waking up about an hour or so later to some shouting; he must have dozed off. He went out onto his balcony and looked down to the car park and saw the black male closing the rear passenger door of the car he'd arrived in, then shouting up to an adjacent block of flats to a person, whom it would appear he knew, before getting into the car and driving off.

Cyril Betts turned the business card over and over in his hand and thought of what his wife would have done if she were still with him. He picked the receiver of his landline up, steadied his shaking hand, dialled the number on the card and waited patiently.

'DC Sam Hodge – can I help you?'

THIRTY-SIX

FRIDAY MORNING

The Metropolitan Police commander was not happy. McNally stood in her office at Southwark police station, attempting to convince her that it was imperative for his team to enter the Bermondsey estate and search no. 91 Chaplin House. A search warrant had been granted overnight, so it wasn't the legality of such a search that was concerning the commander but the public safety issue. The Met was now in full control of the Bermondsey estate, but it was still a tinder box – ready to ignite with the slightest spark.

'I know your concerns are justified, guv, but it's absolutely imperative that we gain entry into that flat to preserve any evidence before it's destroyed. I believe the murder of a former police officer took place on the premises. We have had a credible witness come forward who puts both Stone and our victim Meeres into that flat at the same time. Stone is also responsible for murdering a young surveillance officer a couple of days ago in Reading. When my officers were here yesterday, they saw the main suspect – Maurice Stone – returning to the estate – I believe he came back to clean out the flat of any remaining evidence. It is quite possible he will return to finish the job, and we'll lose that evidence.'

The commander sat back in her leather-bound office chair and looked through her window into the rear car park of the police station. There was a lot of activity: public order teams on standby, should disorder start again; several forensic teams and detectives preparing to enter the Bermondsey estate, which was now one huge crime scene. She could see black smoke still drifting across the clear morning sky from smouldering cars and barricades, erected by the rioters. The custody suite and cells were full to the brim with prisoners, arrested for various crimes, ranging from public disorder through to arson and serious physical assaults, mainly to the first police responders, who were ill-prepared for what had faced them.

She swivelled her chair back ninety degrees to face McNally. 'OK, Ryan, this is what I propose. The estate is under our control again, with a large presence of uniformed police patrolling inside its perimeters. Local liaison officers have drawn on all their good work over many months and years in conjunction with community leaders, to resume some sort of social equilibrium. I'll get a public order team, who've come to relieve the night staff, to take you in, but I don't want more than two CID officers and a SOCO to enter Chaplin House. For some reason, the troublemakers see detectives as more of a threat than the uniform officers. If at any time the public order inspector tells you to get out, I would ask you to do as they say – agreed?'

'Agreed, guv, thanks.'

*

Jim Wakefield woke up with a huge headache. He'd had a reasonable night's sleep, probably due to a variety of drugs administered the previous evening. He was starving, which was a good sign. His face broke into a big smile when Marie Relish walked in.

'Hi, what you doing here – no work to do?'

'That's a nice welcome from somebody who is laid out in a bed, scratching his balls and no good to anybody. How're you feeling?'

'Don't hold back, Marie, say what you mean, won't you.' Wakefield beamed. 'But don't make me laugh. My head feels like somebody is inside with a hammer trying to get out.'

'The DI asked me to come over and make sure you were doing OK. You and Sam were bloody lucky. Everybody sends their love, even Graves!'

'I know, I honestly thought I was going to die. Luckily, Sam got us out of there. Is he alright?'

'Yeah, he's good, got back for the office meeting last night – I think he's running on adrenaline now. I'm a bit concerned that when he stops, it'll catch up with him. So, what's the prognosis?'

'I'm waiting for a doctor to come round and give me the all-clear, and then I can get back to work.'

'Not sure that's going to happen. The occupational health lot aren't going to let you return until they're sure you're fit for duty, are they? I mean, I know you've got a head made of wood, but you've still got to be careful; concussion is a serious thing, you should know that being a rugby fan.'

'I suppose so. So, what's happening? Has Stone been traced yet?'

'No. He got away. All hell broke loose after you got out of the estate, and he disappeared. But we had a witness ring up last night and speak to Sam. He recognised Meeres and Stone from the photographs you were showing yesterday and remembers seeing both entering a flat on the ninth floor of Chaplin House early last week. The boss, Graves and Sally Cook have got a search warrant and are trying to convince the Met commander to let them into the estate. We've also got an ID on the man and woman in the boxing group photograph. Apparently, the man, Terry Nunn, is a right nasty bastard; he got put away for conspiracy to commit armed robbery a few years ago by Meeres and Garvey. He'd always claimed that he was fitted up by Meeres and threatened him as he was taken down to the cells after being sentenced; looks like we've got a motive at last.

*

McNally decided to take Stuart Graves, as Exhibits Officer, and Sally Cook the SOCO in with him. The estate was eerily quiet; the smell of burnt rubber and old furniture tossed from some of the balconies at police and then used to erect barriers was overpowering. The car park outside Chaplin House was littered with broken glass and masonry. The detectives and SOCO followed two of the public order team into the stairwell; another two covered their backs. They made their way up to the ninth floor; the rear two officers remained by the stairwell; McNally, Graves and Cook walked along the walkway to reach no. 91 with the other two in tow. From this height, the detectives could really appreciate the destruction and damage caused during the serious public disorder that had taken place through the night. McNally felt sad for the law-abiding residents that would have to live with the aftermath and try and build some community spirit again.

No. 91 had suffered some damage to the front window adjacent to the door during the disturbances, and with a deft gloved hand poked through the broken glass, one of the uniformed officers located the door lock and they were inside the flat within seconds of their arrival without attracting too much attention. Whatever McNally and the others expected, this wasn't it: a neat and tidy living room space, reasonably furnished. McNally asked the two uniformed officers to remain outside as the detectives and Cook stepped into forensic suits and pulled on gloves and face masks. The flat was immaculately clean, too clean, McNally thought. He indicated to Graves to take the small bathroom and toilet; Sally Cook opened a door leading to the first of two bedrooms, which had a single neatly made-up bed and a single chair and empty wardrobe. Cook and Graves returned to the living room and shook their heads. There was only one room left.

*

Orpington station hadn't been hard to find, even though Marcia Frost had never been this far south out of London before. She parked up near the taxi rank and waited for the arrival of Linda Doyle's train from London Bridge. The digital clock on the dashboard informed her that it was 8.50am. She was a little frustrated; she wanted to be with McNally and Graves in Bermondsey, but she was experienced enough now to realise most police work was mundane and not all about crashing through doors and arresting bad people. It didn't make her feel any better. She drummed her fingers on the steering wheel and set the route on her satnav to Hazel Nunn's house.

*

Ray Blendell sat back from his desk, looking at the rather large paper file that had been delivered from the archives. The outer cover read 'The Crown v Terence Nunn and Others'. Marie Relish entered the incident room with two coffees. He watched her as she took her coat off and met her eye as she proffered one of the cups of coffee.

'My turn,' she said cheerfully.

'Thanks, Marie – you've perked up – anything to do with visiting a certain young detective? How's he doing?'

Marie was a little taken back. Did she detect a little jealousy? She shuddered and felt a little uneasy in his company for the first time ever. She remonstrated with herself for being so paranoid around any man now. 'Yes. He's doing fine,' she answered. 'The consultant was examining him as I left, and he's just texted me to say he's been discharged and is on his way home. He's got a nasty

274

cut on his forehead and the start of a couple of black eyes. He's going to look like a giant panda by tomorrow. What you got there?'

'The full prosecution file for the Terence Nunn job, the one Meeres and Garvey worked on. From what I've seen and bearing in mind what we now know about the relationship between him and Lee and his connection to Roddy and Stone, the answer to all this must lie within this file. Well, that's my gut instinct anyway. Can you go through the witness statements, and I'll look through the forensics and the transcripts of the interviews with Nunn? Look for anything that may bolster our theory that Nunn, even though he is still serving, is behind Meeres' murder.'

'Have we got anything back on the Butcher yet? I haven't been able to find anything in any of the intelligence databases.'

Blendell shook his head. 'No, nothing yet. Criminal Intelligence at the yard are chasing their informants but zilch so far – their sources either don't know or are too scared to speak.'

'Where is everybody?' Relish asked, looking round the room; they were alone except for a of couple indexers.

'The boss and Graves are in Bermondsey; Sam Hodge is being debriefed by the Met about yesterday; and Marcia and Linda Doyle are in Kent to interview Hazel Nunn.'

'Isn't she supposed to be a bit of a cow?'

'Maybe fifteen years ago. We've done checks with the Met, who cover Orpington. She's apparently a cornerstone of the community now – fundraising for a children's hospice and a campaigner on local issues. People do change you know, Marie.'

*

McNally looked at Cook and Graves; they were all probably thinking the same. If there wasn't anything behind this door, they were going to look stupid. McNally nodded at Graves, who pushed open the bedroom door. The atmosphere inside the room made McNally's balls tighten, as if he were standing on the edge of a cliff with a fifty-fifty chance of falling to his death or surviving. Graves pulled a string normally at home in a bathroom rather than a bedroom, which fired a florescent tube into action above their heads. This was no bedroom. It had a completely different use – one that any of the three present initially struggled to work out.

⋆

The clock's digital display turned to 9am. Frost was about to ring Doyle when a text message came through from her fellow DS: 'Person struck by a train half mile outside Orpington. Train not moving. LD'. Frost mumbled to herself, 'These things happen.' She returned Doyle's text, telling her that she would head over to the address and pick her up when she'd finished on the way back. Frost pressed the start on the satnav and followed the instructions.

⋆

The first thing that stood out was the chest freezer, humming hypnotically away in the corner of the room. A large, laminated table stood against the wall; its legs retracted underneath it. An industrial roll of thick plastic floor covering leant against another wall and two small air conditioning units that were switched off. Apart from those items, the room was empty. McNally, Graves and Cook moved towards the chest freezer. Graves hesitated for a few seconds before lifting the lid of the freezer slowly. All three stared at a single black refuse bag, resting at the bottom of the freezer, covered in fine particles of ice. Cook took out a scalpel from her equipment bag and carefully, as if carrying out a life-saving operation, made a small incision into the plastic and drew the scalpel across from side to side. All three drew in breath as the frozen, lifeless eyes of Frankie Meeres peered out from the darkness.

⋆

The plummy voice of a female actor she couldn't put a name to instructed Frost to join the Sevenoaks Road – A223. On the right she passed a common called Green Street Green before being directed to turn left into Hudson Lane. Frost stopped the car a few metres from the house, looking up the impressive driveway, and watched for any signs of life. She'd decided not to phone ahead but to turn up unannounced, believing that would give her the advantage. She was unsure of the reception she was going to get from an armed robber's wife, but she had questions she wanted answers to in relation to the woman's husband and his nephew and their possible involvement in their investigation.

The house was set back from the road; she decided to walk up the tree-lined, red-bricked approach leading to a mock-Tudor façade, with a substantial solid wooden door dead centre, guarded by two stone lions. She rang a bell that sounded deep inside the house and waited. Frost jumped as a cat entwined itself round her lower legs, purring effortlessly, before sitting itself down on the doormat, waiting to be let in. Frost heard faint footsteps and the sound of a key in the lock. If she'd just glanced to her left instead of stroking the cat, she would have seen, through a small gap in the double garage doors, a black Mercedes.

*

Sally Cook decided to leave the horrific discovery in situ. She returned to her unmarked van, guarded by several public order police officers in full riot gear, except for their helmets, which hung from their belts. She retrieved a body bag, her camera equipment and some additional lighting; one of the officers kindly assisted her with her equipment back up the nine floors of Chaplin House. McNally and Graves knocked on a few neighbouring doors but, unsurprisingly, nobody was willing to talk to them.

McNally had a word with one of the Met officers, a sergeant, and asked for assistance in guarding the flat until a full forensic examination could take place and the remains could be removed. He could do little more so left Graves to act as the exhibit officer and returned to the Camden incident room. He concentrated hard on the road ahead to blur the vivid picture of Meeres' blank expression and lifeless eyes.

*

Ray Blendell was reading the transcripts of the Nunn trial at the Old Bailey, when McNally returned and held a small meeting with those present: Blendell, Hodge and Relish. He updated them on the find at no. 91 Chaplin House.

'Have we had anything back on the movements of Maurice Stone?'

'No, guv, the car was picked up by ANPR on the Old Kent Road about ten minutes after the last sighting leaving the estate, but after that, nothing. This man is a ghost. He has no driving licence or passport under the name of Stone. He doesn't appear on any council tax register or, for that matter, any Inland Revenue database. He has no bank account, credit cards or even a credit rating.' Blendell shuffled some papers on his desk.

'I've also checked with Pentonville Prison. The only person to visit Terence Nunn in the past five years is his wife Hazel, who Frost and Doyle are on their way to interview at Nunn's last known address.'

'What about Thames Valley Police, anything from them? Obviously, we know he's not in Reading anymore.'

'They got a couple of witnesses who spotted the Merc on the outskirts of Reading city centre about twenty minutes after the shooting and Stone entering a cafe near the Kennet and Avon Canal. One witness, a young lad who was out early delivering papers, saw a man, whose description matches Stone, tossing an object in the canal.'

'I don't suppose there's any CCTV?'

'Not so far. They've got officers interviewing the cafe owner. If it was Stone, he must have some bottle, having breakfast in a cafe less than three miles from where he murdered a police officer – or he just doesn't care. They've got a dive team at the site. Fingers crossed they find the gun.'

McNally's mobile started to ring – it was Stuart Graves. 'Stuart, you nearly all done down there. I could do with you back here.'

'Sally said she's going to be another half an hour. She has removed the remains and arranged for them to be taken to the City mortuary, and she has spoken to Felix Lowther. He is operating all day but will be available from late afternoon. Hang on a minute, guv.' McNally could hear Graves talking to somebody in the background. 'Sorry, guv, the Met are getting edgy about us being here. The reason I called was I just got a call from that reporter on the *Camberwell and Peckham Gazette*, the one who gave us that picture of the boxing group published in his paper. He ain't stupid and has pieced together what we're investigating, which of course aroused his interest; he started to do a bit of digging round the wife Hazel and their house in Orpington.'

'Well, at least he has the decency to tell us he's sticking his nose in.'

'It's a bit more than that. He discovered, after talking to some neighbours, who didn't particularly like living next door to the house of an armed robber and a wife who likes the sound of her own voice, that the house was put up for sale about two months ago. It was all done on the quiet through an estate agent in Orpington High Street – no "for sale" boards or anything like that. It just happened that the estate agent plays golf with the next-door neighbour and mentioned it to him, and, in turn, he told our reporter friend.'

'OK, so where is this taking us?' McNally was getting tired and irritable.

'The reporter, sniffing a little story, takes himself off to the estate agent, who was at first reluctant to discuss the transaction but eventually agreed to answer a couple of questions as long as his name was never mentioned. The reporter shows the estate agent the article with the boxing picture and the original proof they used to go to print with. He asked him if the woman in the picture was his client selling the house in Hudson Lane. He confirmed it was Hazel Nunn. Apparently, he dealt with the property when they first bought it donkey's years ago, and he also recognised the man.'

'Well, I suppose he would know Terence Nunn if he dealt with the original purchase of the house, and the Nunns were well known in the area before he got sent down.'

'No, guv, it wasn't Terence Nunn he recognised in the picture – it was Maurice Stone. He remembers Maurice Stone accompanying her to the estate agents a few weeks ago. When the meeting had finished, the estate agent saw them out and watched as Stone opened the rear passenger door of a black Mercedes for her and then drove off.'

McNally had ended the call and was heading towards his office, whilst running through the significance of the information Graves had just reported to him, when Marie Relish interrupted his thoughts.

'Sir, may have something here.'

'Not now, Marie. I need five minutes. My head is spinning.' He suddenly realised the importance of what Graves had told him. If the estate agent was right, then Frost and Doyle were just about to walk into the lion's den. He shouted at Blendell, 'Ray, get Frost and Doyle on the phone. Stop them from going anywhere near Hazel Nunn's house. Tell them to wait for backup; Sam, get a car – now!'

'Sir, it's important. It's about Hazel Nunn,' Relish pleaded. McNally swore under his breath but returned and sat down. 'You all need to hear this before anybody goes near her,' she said to McNally, whilst beckoning Hodge and Blendell over to her desk. 'I've been looking through the witness statements presented at

Nunn's trial. There are several character witness statements in the bundle from friends and relatives of Terence Nunn, all portraying him as a thoroughly nice guy...'

McNally looked at his watch and encouraged Relish to get to the point.

'...In her statement, she mentions how she and Nunn first met. It was through their family businesses – Nunn's father was a second-hand car dealer, and Hazel's dad was a butcher. She took over running the business when he died. Hazel Nunn was a butcher; Hazel Nunn *is* the Butcher.'

THIRTY-SEVEN

FRIDAY AFTERNOON

Doyle's train arrived at Orpington station nearly an hour late. She had tried to ring Frost but was getting no answer. She jumped in a taxi and headed towards Hudson Lane. When her phone rang, she expected it to be Frost, but it was the incident room landline. She could hear Ray Blendell almost shouting at her, but the signal was bad. She asked the taxi driver to pull over and rang the incident room back.

'Linda, you and Frost are not to go anywhere near Hazel Nunn's house – do you understand?'

'Ray, I was late getting here. I'm in a taxi. Marcia would've got to the address over an hour ago. We are turning into Hudson Lane now. She must be inside the address already; I can see her car and she's not in it.'

*

Marcia Frost woke up with a pounding headache and totally disorientated. She remembered stroking a cat on the doorstep before it shot into the house as the door opened. She'd been shown into the hallway by a very pleasant young woman, with a feather duster in her hand. She'd been asked to wait, and the young woman walked away. She couldn't remember anything after that.

Her nose detected a sweet chemical odour; her cheeks and lips tingled. She immediately thought – *chloroform*. It took a few moments for her head to clear and to realise where she was. Frost was strapped to a chair by her arms and legs with silver duct tape, a smaller piece, stretched across her mouth, made it hard to breathe; she forced herself to inhale, slowly, in and out through her nose, to stop herself hyperventilating. Her eyes adjusted to the dim light, emanating from a single bulb that was swinging ever so slightly in a breeze coming from behind her. She could just make out, beyond the circle of light, used tins of paint, hand tools and gardening paraphernalia. The aroma of damp, and smoke from a garden fire, began to dominate her sense of smell. Frost looked down to the floor; the chair on which she was bound sat on a large, thick piece of plastic, maybe three metres square. Suddenly aware of somebody else in the space, she blinked her eyes to clear her vision and saw the massive, threatening shape of Maurice Stone. He grinned at her, his gold teeth glinting intermittently with the swing of the light bulb; he reminded her of a *James Bond* villain. Frost was determined to stay in control of her emotions; forget about being a police officer, she was just a woman, a human being deep in the shit who needed to survive. She knew trying to communicate, to plead for her life, to identify herself as a police officer, would be a total waste of time and energy, so she sat still and returned the eye contact with Stone, which seemed to amuse him.

The cat, that bloody cat, had been a warning. She remembered back to the laughter in the incident room, when Sally Cook had talked about the hair in the sports bag belonging to a domestic animal, and everybody chipping in with examples of the most preposterous animals imaginable, from an alpaca to a parrot.

Stone stepped back into the darkness, as a door opened behind Frost and a figure emerged from her peripheral vision into the arc of light. Frost recognised Hazel Nunn from her photograph; she was a stunning-looking woman for her age, she thought, although most of her beauty probably came from a bottle or a syringe. The atmosphere changed; Stone's eye contact had reflected a certain amount of amusement, but Hazel Nunn's eyes were filled with seething hatred.

✶

The powerful saloon car raced through another red light, its sirens and covert blue lights behind the front grill, warning other road users and pedestrians to get out of the way. Hodge was driving; McNally was shouting down the phone, trying to make himself heard over the sirens. He had first rung Stuart Graves, instructing him to get down to Orpington. He was a good twenty minutes nearer than they were, travelling from Camden. He then spoke to Linda Doyle, telling her to keep an eye on the house for any movement but not to approach until they got there. He requested an armed response team to be in the vicinity; Stone had probably ditched the gun he shot the surveillance officer with, but that was not to say he didn't have access to another firearm, and McNally knew he would use it and wasn't prepared to take a chance with the lives of his officers.

✶

The taxi driver was starting to get edgy. He had heard Linda Doyle's calls to McNally and knew something dangerous was brewing and was no hero, so Doyle paid him off and told him to keep his mouth shut. She bought a paper from a nearby convenience store and found a bench dedicated to some local dignitary on a small patch of grass about one hundred metres from the house. She had a clear view of Frost's car. She sat and waited.

✶

Frost gritted her teeth as Hazel Nunn ripped the duct tape from her mouth. She wasn't going to show her any weakness.

'Tough little bitch, aren't you?' Nunn taunted her as she looked at Frost's warrant card held in her hand. 'Coming here all on your own. Have you come to fit me up like your lot did to my Terry?' Frost remained defiant but silent. 'What's up, gone all shy suddenly? Oh well, if you're not going to talk to me, I'm not going to waste my time.' Nunn replaced the tape on Frost's mouth and called out for Stone. On his return, she looked at Frost. 'You know what to do; don't fuck it up this time.' Stone walked towards Frost; his smile replaced by an evil sneer.

*

On her surveillance course, Linda Doyle had been told to have a reason for being somewhere and a prepared cover story, should anybody get a bit nosey. Doyle looked at her watch; she had been on the bench, pretending to read a newspaper, for nearly twenty minutes. She had noticed a couple of Hudson Lane residents come out of their houses on some pretence, be it to place a bag in a dustbin or retrieve something from a vehicle, and give her a glance, before disappearing back inside; within seconds, several curtains were twitching. She was glad when Stuart Graves' car screeched round the corner; the speed he entered Hudson Lane did nothing for her covertness. She waved at Graves to give the impression to any nosey neighbours that she had been waiting, freezing cold on the bench, for him; she looked at her watch and raised her hands in the air, as if asking where he'd been.

She jumped in the passenger seat. 'Just drive, Stuart. We're getting a lot of attention.' Graves drove more sedately towards Frost's car, both detectives resisting the urge to look at the property it was parked outside. Graves found a spot outside a launderette another hundred metres past Nunn's house and used his rear-view mirror to watch.

McNally came over the radio, informing them they were five minutes away. Doyle gave him a situation report. They were told to stay and maintain observations; the armed response team were minutes behind him. Graves brought Doyle up to date with the fact that Hazel Nunn may well be the Butcher and that an armed Maurice Stone could be inside the property.

'Sod it!' Graves shouted as he looked in the mirror. Doyle looked over her shoulder and saw a supermarket delivery van park in front of Frost's car. 'Linda, you're going to have to get out on foot. I can't see Marcia's car.' He reported the fact to McNally on the radio and asked him to cover Frost's car from the other end of Hudson Lane when they arrived until the van moved on; McNally acknowledged with an ETA of one minute, followed by the armed response vehicle seconds behind him. Doyle took a chance and got out of the car, even though she was exposed; luckily, the van shielded her from direct sight of the house. She heard the slamming of a car door, froze and quickly walked back to the car.

'Stuart. Stone is in the driver's seat of Frost's car. I can't see her.'

'Graves to McNally, you receiving?'

'Go ahead, just turning into Hudson Lane now, over.'

'Guv, Frost's car is moving. Stone is driving. No sign of DS Frost.'

'Stuart, go with the car. The armed response is tuned into our channel. We'll hold here and watch the house; when they catch you up, they'll put a hard stop on Frost's car. You are *not* to intervene – understand?'

'Yes, guv. Standby, the vehicle is pulling out from behind the van and travelling along Hudson Lane in our direction. Confirmation that Stone is driving with no passengers.' Graves pulled away slowly and followed at a distance. Stone pulled up at a red signal. Graves did the same and began a conversation with Doyle to look like a normal couple, should Stone look in his mirrors. A high-powered Audi pulled up behind Graves, who glanced in his rear-view mirror and made eye contact with the driver, who gave a slight nod of his head. The lights turned to green, and Stone turned left, as did Graves and the Audi. At the first opportunity, Graves gave a nearside indication and pulled over – the Audi accelerated past Graves and Doyle and fell in behind Stone. Graves pulled away again and followed. The Audi then suddenly pulled out onto the opposite side of the road and cut in front of Stone. Within seconds, the two rear passengers, sporting police baseball caps, were out and pointing semi-automatic weapons at the car. Graves saw Stone's vehicle reverse lights come on.

'Stuart, he's going to reverse,' Doyle shouted. But Graves had already closed the gap and rammed the car from the rear. The armed officers stood back and were shouting clear instructions at Stone to get out of the car. Their weapons were raised at shoulder height and ready to fire. Stone pushed the driver's door open forcefully. His height and build were, for once, a disability as he struggled to get out of the much smaller car. He swung his legs out first.

'Armed police! Show me your hands – *now!*'

Graves and Doyle watched as Stone reached for something tucked into the rear of his waistband – it was a handgun, which he brought round to the front of him. Before he could raise it and point it at the officers, he was hit three times in the chest by a blast of rapid fire, knocking him violently back against the car before sliding to the floor, losing grip on his weapon, which fell to the ground with a metallic clatter. The next few seconds seemed like hours; time seemed to stand still before anybody else reacted. Several bystanders screamed; traffic at a junction just ahead came to a shuddering halt; car horns blasted with sound. One of the officers kicked away Stone's firearm and checked for signs of life. Linda Doyle whispered, more to herself than anybody else, 'That's for the young surveillance officer, you bastard.'

Graves and Doyle jumped out of their car and approached the armed officers, waving their warrant cards urgently, but were told to fuck off.

'We need to open the boot,' Graves said forcefully. 'One of ours is probably in there.' One of the armed officers kept his firearm pointing directly at the prone figure of Maurice Stone, whilst the second activated the boot from the driver's position. Graves and Doyle stood as the boot automatically opened agonisingly slowly – it was empty.

⋆

Frost's mouth was bone dry, which caused her to cough, forcing the expelled air against the tape and then upwards and through her nose at the same time she was trying to breathe. She started to panic, believing she was going to suffocate to death in this dingy basement – would she ever be found? When Stone had approached her, she believed this was it, until he reached into her jacket pocket and removed her car keys. She thought of her parents, and even her brother, imagining her dad telling everybody who would listen at her funeral that he'd told her not to join the police. Frost realised, if she didn't suffocate first, how she was likely to die. The door from the house into the basement opened and Hazel Nunn walked in.

'Are you ready to talk to me yet?'

Frost looked away; there was movement behind Nunn. It was that bloody cat. Nunn ripped the tape from her mouth and Frost breathed in greedily, filling her lungs to the maximum before exhaling with as much control as she could muster. 'You are some evil bitch.' If she was going to die, she was going down fighting. She received a slap round the face for her insolence.

'I do a job – that's all. I clear up other people's mess. You see I have a skill that's in high demand in the circles me and Terry circulate. I had a call earlier. I believe some of your colleagues found my cutting room. I left them a little surprise. I hope it wasn't too much of a shock. It's a shame really; my parents lived in that flat for many years, and that's where Terry and I used to

288

hang about. He used to live on the estate as well and, thanks to dear old Maggie Thatcher, my parents bought it at a ridiculous price and rented it out for years. My dad had a butcher's shop not too far – that's where I learnt my skills, on pigs and cows initially, of course, human beings came later, hence the name the Butcher; Dad would have been so proud of his little girl.'

'Why Meeres? He was personal, wasn't he? You killed him in that flat; he suffered.'

'Suddenly you want answers. Frankie Meeres set up Terry; the shotgun wasn't his – Meeres planted it in the boot of the car. He got eighteen years for conspiracy to rob. You get less than that nowadays for murder. Terry and I wanted Meeres to suffer; we waited for a few years, then Terry, who'd had a lot of time to think, gave me certain instructions about how he wanted him to die, and I just followed them, like a dutiful wife. Your colleagues will eventually find the middle finger that Meeres so proudly gave Terry, as he was being led down to the cells at the Old Bailey, firmly stuck down his throat – a nice touch, don't you think? Meeres was quite brave; he barely made a sound as I took his left arm, but he wasn't in the best of shape, and his heart gave out. After that, it wasn't so much such fun. The idea about dumping his remains all over London's transport network was Terry's idea; he's got a weird sense of humour and wanted Meeres' old colleagues running round chasing their tails. Mind you, I've been impressed that you put it all together so quickly. It's a shame it wasn't the Met really; we would've been in the clear by now.' Frost watched as Nunn lifted a black holdall onto a table in front of her.

'I supposed it was Maurice who gave it all away. He can get a bit careless, not the brightest, but he is very loyal. We took him off the streets when he was a youngster, looked after him like he was our own. We didn't have kids, problems with Terry's tubes apparently.' Nunn opened the holdall.

'The question is, what am I going to do with you?'

'You could just let me walk out of this place. My colleagues will be here any minute.' Frost tried to sound confident, but it didn't really work.

'If your colleagues were to turn up, they would find that your car is not here – Maurice is taking care of that. They will knock on my door. I will be courteous and polite – I'm very well thought of in the local community now. I'm in the running for the next Mayor of Orpington; can you believe that? I will tell them that you called and that I answered your questions, and you went on your merry way. If they become a little suspicious and succeed in getting a search warrant…' Nunn removed a stainless-steel saw and a cleaver from the holdall, '…by the time they return, there will be nothing left of you to find.'

*

Graves spun the damaged car round whilst Doyle communicated to McNally that, thankfully, Frost was not dead in the boot so must still be in the house. McNally tried to round up some uniformed officers, but the nearest were six to seven minutes away. He saw Graves and Doyle pulling up fifty metres away on the opposite side of the house.

'Sam, we got any stab vests in the car?'

'No, guv, we left in a hurry. I've got some CS spray in my bag, but that's about all.'

McNally lifted the radio transmitter to his mouth. 'Stuart, you and Linda go knock on the front door. From where we are, I can see a side entrance leading to the garden. Sam and I will take that. Let's not get complacent just because Stone is out of the way. This is one dangerous woman. You got anything in the car to put the door in?'

'I borrowed a door ram from the firearms guys. The door looks solid; may be better to go in from the back. I'll know more when we approach.'

'Right, exactly two minutes from when I give the signal, we go in. Marcia is in there. We do whatever is necessary to get her out. I'll take full responsibility.' McNally looked at his watch. 'You ready, Sam?' Hodge was wound up like a rubber band. 'OK, two minutes from... now.'

*

The Butcher expertly sharpened the blade of the cleaver on a well-oiled sharpening stone, more for effect than necessity. Frost's eye followed every movement of the lethal steel blade, gliding rhythmically across the smooth surface. 'These tools were my father's; he gave them to me the day I qualified as a butcher – also the same day he retired and handed the business to me. Terry and I used the business as a front; we opened a couple more shops and laundered drug money through the books. He'd left all that security van stuff behind him. Nobody was paid in cash anymore; the risks weren't worth it, but he wanted to do one more job, loved the buzz of sticking a gun in somebody's face. You know the rest.'

'So, the day he was arrested by Meeres, he *was* in possession of a gun?'

'I think you've just spoken your last words.' Nunn placed the tape over Frost's mouth. Frost pleaded through the tape. She didn't want to die in this shithole. Nunn placed an apron on, followed by gloves and a face mask. She straightened the plastic sheet on the floor. She grabbed Frost's hair in a tight grip and yanked her head backwards in one quick movement, exposing her neck, and raised the cleaver – one forceful strike would be enough to take her head clean off.

*

McNally and Hodge slid down the side of the house at the same time Graves and Doyle approached the front door. Graves tested the solidity of the wood around the lock and decided that he had the strength and determination to put the door in with one hit. All four looked at their watches: ten seconds to go.

⋆

Frost looked at Nunn's eyes pleadingly but saw nothing but pure hate. Frost wondered – as Nunn pulled her hand, holding the weapon, back as far as it would go – if she would feel anything. She recalled reading about the executions of Anne Boleyn and Charles I, how their eyes were still moving after decapitation. How long did the brain remain active, seeing, watching and thinking?

Suddenly, the single light bulb went out. Frost heard a huge crash coming from the front of the house. The pressure on her hair was released. She reacted quickly. She knew this may be her only chance of saving her own life; she used all her strength and will to unbalance the chair, falling to the floor on her side – her head hitting the concrete floor with a bang. Frost felt the air move violently back and forth through the space above – where she had been sitting moments earlier – as Nunn desperately swiped the blade through no man's land several times in an effort to connect with any sort of human flesh. The light came back on again, temporarily disorientating Hazel Nunn; she lashed out indiscriminately.

It was a two-pronged attack. McNally and Hodge entered from the garden and extinguished the light, Graves and Doyle from the stairs leading down from the main house. All four were not prepared for what they saw when the light was switched on. Hazel Nunn was intent on killing anybody in her way. She swung and swiped the cleaver in the direction of any of the officers, who attempted to disarm her. She seemed possessed and was frothing at the mouth. Hodge aimed his CS spray at the aggressor but held off when he realised it was more likely to blind his colleagues and make the situation worse.

McNally could see Frost lying on the floor, looking a little dazed. She was strapped to the chair and gagged. McNally tried to avert Nunn's hateful gaze by indicating to Graves to move around behind her. McNally lunged towards her, grabbing her right wrist – she was buoyed by the will to survive. The cleaver was flying in all different directions as McNally struggled for control. He was being pushed backwards and fell over the prone figure of Frost, surprised at Nunn's strength. Nunn regained her balance and swung the blade around behind her, coming within millimetres of decapitating Doyle. She turned, stood over McNally, raised the cleaver over her head and was about to bring it down with tremendous force, when a violent bang and flash temporarily deafened and blinded them. Nunn's head exploded as the bullet passed through and into the basement wall. McNally looked up and watched as it took almost five seconds for Nunn to lose total control of her legs and fall in a heap, her deadly weapon clanging dangerously to the ground.

'Looks like us Met boys have saved the railway police again,' the firearms officer declared. 'The cavalry has arrived up the road, so we thought we'd come and give our colleagues a hand, just in time, by the looks of it. Everybody OK?'

Doyle helped McNally to his feet; he checked himself over, making sure the blood on him wasn't his own. Graves slowly pulled Frost up into a sitting position and cut away the tape binding her. Doyle removed the tape from her mouth. Frost tried to get to her feet but – what with the after-effects of the chloroform and banging her head as she hit the floor – she felt a little woozy.

Doyle comforted Frost before Graves picked her up in his big arms and carried her towards the fresh air of the garden. 'Let's get you out of here shall we, Sarge?'

Frost genuinely smiled at Stuart Graves, probably for the first time since they'd met. 'I bet this is the first time you've ever picked up a bit of black, Constable. Not too bad, is it?'

THIRTY-EIGHT

ONE WEEK LATER

McNally was powerless to stop the mayhem of the following week; all sorts of inquiries taking place into his and his team's actions, mainly by office-bound non-combatants whose job it was to examine, retrospectively, every action and decision taken by frontline officers doing the job under extreme stress and in real time. The vultures were soon hovering above, waiting to swoop on the tiniest of procedural breaches his team may have contravened: Professional Standards, Health and Safety and counsellors, to name but a few, all wanting a bit of McNally and his team, asking the usual questions of his officers without ever really listening to their answers: why *did* you do that? Why *didn't* you do that? How are you coping? Are you coping? Why *don't* you take some time off? Why *are* you taking time off? You *must* be stressed so you *will* have to have counselling.

Experiences, like the one McNally and his team had gone through, created a bond – a team spirit that is very hard to break. All the paperwork had been completed for now, their accounts recorded for the coroner; it was unlikely there would ever be a criminal trial. Terence Nunn had been interviewed by BTP and

Met Police officers in a joint operation in relation to conspiring with Hazel Nunn and Maurice Stone to murder Frankie Meeres, Joey Dryden and Daniel Corbell. Thames Valley police had carried out a thorough investigation into the murder of the young BTP surveillance officer and submitted the file to the coroner's court, which would undoubtedly return a verdict of unlawful killing; the death of Maurice Stone would see the case closed, resulting in some closure for the murdered officer's wife and young family.

McNally leant back in his chair with a very cold pint of Guinness and surveyed the private area cordoned off at the back of the Lyttleton Arms they had commandeered early afternoon. This was, by far, the best form of counselling available. It was now nearly 7pm, and everybody had relaxed and was enjoying each other's company. It wasn't a celebration – after all, two of their colleagues had been murdered – however, the largest cheer of the afternoon announced the arrival of Jim Wakefield, who, although looking a little battered and bruised, was back to his old self.

Few spoke about the events of a week earlier; they'd all been put through the wringer to justify their actions, McNally in particular. It was good to see every one of his team present but also Nigel Plummer, who, as his boss, had backed him and his team to the hilt, and Sara Hallam, who he realised always made a telling contribution every time he'd asked her for her opinion and often when he'd not. He was particularly pleased to see the two Met firearms officers, one of whom had saved his and Marcia Frost's life, also enjoying a drink. Frost never ceased to amaze him, probably one of the bravest officers he'd ever worked with. Frost caught his eye and gave the slightest of smiles and a nod of the head, an appreciation of the respect they felt for each other and that they had done OK.

McNally was also happy with Linda Doyle, who'd hit the ground running and would be a great addition to the team in the future.

Graves and Hodge were engaged in a discussion about cricket, even though it was January. McNally, although not a cricketing man, was aware the England team were fighting to stay in a test match somewhere on the subcontinent.

The only member of the team who concerned him was Marie Relish – although not a detective, but a civilian analyst, she had proved herself to be an integral part of the last two investigations he had conducted. With Plummer's blessing, she would be posted permanently to his team from now on. She seemed much more relaxed. He was aware there was some underlying problem, be it professional or personal, but was confident Frost and Sara Hallam seemed to be on top of it. Sometimes being a good boss meant knowing when to stay out of a situation and put your trust in others.

Ray Blendell was the first to break ranks and, with a quick wave to everyone, he was out of the door by 7.15pm. Frost looked at her watch and thought it was time to go. She had a quick chat with Sara Hallam, who was going to share a cab home with Relish. They both looked round but couldn't see their friend. Frost checked the ladies' but came back with a shrug of the shoulders. Neither of them saw Graves slip his coat on and leave unnoticed.

THIRTY-NINE

he taxi pulled up halfway along Camden High Street. Relish flopped back into the comfy seat and closed her eyes. She was as relaxed as she'd been for some time, happy in the knowledge that she was to be a permanent member of McNally's team for the foreseeable future – good riddance to fraud investigations. There had been no more phone calls or property going missing over the last week. It even crossed her mind that it had all stopped at the same time the investigation had ended. Could the Nunns or Stone have had something to do with it? Had she been targeted in some way by them? It was a comforting thought in one way, but she realised it was highly unlikely.

She decided to leave the celebrations early – Sara Hallam was having a great time, and Relish didn't want to be babysat anymore, although she'd been extremely grateful to both her and Frost for their friendship and support. She felt positive about the future and, for the first time since leaving home, that she truly belonged somewhere. The cab dropped her outside her block of flats. Making sure she had her new house keys firmly in her grasp she took a cursory glance round the area, this was still London after all. When satisfied there was no danger, she relaxed and touched the fob onto the lobby entrance door. She waited patiently for the lift to arrive, letting out a couple of young people who she didn't recognise before entering, and travelled to the fourteenth floor. She inserted the key in the lock and turned it; suddenly becoming aware of somebody standing behind her.

'Hi, Marie.'

Relish turned, recognising the voice which, just for a split second, strangely comforted her. 'Ray, what're you doing here?' Blendell grabbed Relish round the throat and pushed her backwards through the open front door into hallway clamping his other hand over her mouth before she could scream. Relish struggled and tried to bite his hand and kick his shins, but Blendell was far too strong for her, she started to feel dizzy, due to lack of oxygen, as he throttled her. He forced her towards the bedroom; she knew she didn't have the strength to fight him off as he turned her around grabbing her hair in a tight grip keeping one hand over her mouth. She noticed in the hall mirror that the front door wasn't fully closed – if she could get outside, she could scream and bang on the next-door neighbours' door for help. She wedged both feet against the bedroom door frame and pushed back with all her strength; if he was successful in pinning her to the bed face-down she knew she had little hope of escape. She could feel that he was sexually aroused – he was going to rape her.

'Don't fight me, Marie; you knew it would come to this one day, you and me.' He started to kiss her neck and ear, which revolted her. She again glanced at the wall mirror and saw a second figure looking round the front door behind them; she immediately thought – my God there are two of them. She threw her head backwards striking Blendell's nose and heard the satisfying crack of bone splintering, it made little difference.

'That's better, Marie, fight as much as you like. I know you've always wanted this to happen.'

Blendell felt a strong hand firmly grasp him on the shoulder and pull him backwards. Shocked, he released the grip on Relish's hair as he turned, he was met by Stuart Graves' fist.

*

Blendell sat on Relish's living room floor with blood dripping from his broken nose. He had his hands cuffed behind him. Graves had called the local Met Police as well as McNally, Frost and Hallam. Sara Hallam, who'd been in the back of a taxi half a mile from Relish's flat, was the first to arrive.

Hallam walked through the front door of the flat with two uniformed police officers in tow. Relish explained to the two officers, with encouragement from Hallam and Graves, what had taken place over the last few weeks, culminating in the events of the last twenty minutes. The Met officers arrested and cautioned Blendell, who was in too much pain to reply. He was taken downstairs and transported to Kilburn Police Station. Graves updated McNally by phone and returned to the flat, by which time Marcia Frost had arrived. Relish was surprisingly resolute, even joking with Hallam and Frost, although her voice was shaky; Hallam watched for any signs of shock. It would undoubtedly hit her later, but for now she just seemed pleased it was all over.

Graves saw the three women huddled in the small living room and thought it better to back off and go home; he felt a little out of place.

'Hey, Superman, where d' ya think you're going?' Frost shouted out a little louder than she intended; she'd had more than she realised to drink. 'Sit down and explain yourself. It's the second time in a week you've saved a damsel in distress.'

Graves sat down on the sofa, his cheeks slightly reddening.

'Come on then, tell us what you were doing here! Did Blendell just beat you to it?' Graves screwed his face up in preparation to give Frost a load of abuse, when he saw all three smiling and start laughing. 'Fuck's sake, Stuart, we *are* joking, you prawn.' They all let out a roar of laughter; the evening's alcohol consumption was taking effect.

'A prawn, more like an octopus, you know, hands everywhere,' added Hallam, who stood up and gave Graves a huge hug. 'That's from all of us, especially Marie.' Relish, now fighting back the tears, nodded her approval.

'So come on then, spill the beans, how did you do it, boy wonder?' Frost wasn't letting it go, especially after four large glasses of wine.

Graves explained. 'I knew something was going on with Blendell. I never trusted him. I spoke to a couple of tecs that used to work with him in the Met. They said they were all glad to see the back of him, especially the women; its probably why he transferred to us. I caught him a couple of times sneaking around Marie's desk – he always had an excuse, you know: "I'm looking for an action" or "Marie borrowed my pen, and I can't find it". It was all bollocks, of course. On one occasion, I was outside the incident room just finishing a call and heard Marie talking to you, Sara, about being scared, and I just put two and two together and for once came up with four.

Graves looked a little embarrassed. 'I'm sorry for the way I've spoken to you a couple of times, Marie – it's just my way, you know. My mouth shoots off before my brain engages; I probably won't change. Anyway, I just kept an eye on Blendell and noticed that he was fixated with you. He was clever, never looked at you when you were facing each other. I saw him leave the pub and just thought I'd see where he was going. I thought he might be going back towards Camden, but he headed over towards Mornington Crescent tube, so I went to the toilet and back to the bar. I bought a round of drinks and then saw you leaving on your own, Marie. I didn't see Blendell enter the station, so I got a bit concerned and tried to get your attention but had a tray full of glasses. I didn't say anything to the others but slipped out and saw you get into a cab. I jumped into another cab that was travelling the other way. I said to him – and don't laugh—'

All three women said in unison, 'follow that cab' and went into hysterics.

'All right funny, funny. The cabbie looked at me. I mean, I'd had a few, and I think he thought I was taking the piss until I showed him my warrant card. We followed at a distance, and I saw you enter the lobby of the flats. I paid the cab driver and walked over to the door. I wasn't sure what I was going to do next. I thought if you saw me, it would frighten the life out of you. You got in the lift; a couple came out of the building, and I just walked in. I saw the lift display indicating that you had travelled to the fourteenth floor. So, I got the next lift. I was just going to pop my head out and make sure you were safely inside without you knowing I was there, when I saw your front door partially open. The rest you all know about.'

Frost and Hallam just stared in silence, realising how fortunate their friend had been. Graves got to his feet. 'I'd best be going. Going from zero to hero in one week is tough going.' He ducked as three cushions flew towards him.

When Graves had gone, all three women stood, came together, hugged and cried – for once, words just seemed superfluous.